Texting Fate

LISA-MARIE WILSON

For my Family

Thank you for being patient with me while
I was lost within these pages.

Contents

Chapter One: The Lonely Star

The gates to Charlie Benton's estate parted with a mechanical sigh, iron jaws releasing their grip as he approached. His hands flexed against the steering wheel, knuckles white, then relaxed, white then relaxed, a rhythm he'd maintained since leaving the wrap party three hours ago. The mansion waited at the end of the curved driveway, windows dark and uninviting despite the architect's promises of "welcoming elegance."

Charlie hadn't bothered to leave any lights on that morning—who was there to welcome, after all?

He guided the Mercedes along the smooth pavement, tyres crunching over scattered jacaranda petals that had fallen like purple tears across the driveway. The evening air hung heavy with jasmine and exhaust, that particular Los Angeles perfume that clung to everything. Moonlight spilled across the immaculate lawn, turning the fountain in the centre of the circular drive into a silver sculpture. Charlie cut the engine and sat in the sudden silence, feeling the weight of six months' worth of eighteen-hour days settle into his bones.

The key slid into the front door with a precise click that

echoed through the foyer beyond. Charlie pushed the heavy door open, and darkness spilled out to greet him. He fumbled for the light switch, wincing as chandeliers blazed overhead, their crystal pieces catching and fragmenting the light into too-bright daggers. His footsteps clacked against marble, each step a lonely percussion that bounced off high ceilings and returned to him multiplied.

He dropped his leather weekender bag on the floor, not caring that it cost more than some people's car payments. His shoulder bag followed, scripts and contracts spilling halfway out before he nudged them back with his foot. The studio's car would deliver the rest of his things tomorrow. For now, Charlie was simply a man standing in an oversized foyer, listening to the sound of his own breathing.

"Home sweet home," he muttered, the words absorbed by thick walls and expensive drapery.

He tugged at his tie, loosening the silk noose that had been choking him since the final press junket. The knot surrendered with a soft hiss, and Charlie let the tie slither through his fingers to join his bags on the floor. His fingers moved to his collar, then his cuffs, unfastening, unbuttoning, unravelling the perfect package that stylists had assembled that morning. As he walked deeper into the house, he ran his hand through his hair, destroying the careful architecture that his team had spent forty minutes creating. Dark strands fell across his forehead, and for the first time that day, his scalp didn't itch from product.

The air conditioning hummed with mechanical precision, maintaining a perfect sixty-eight degrees throughout the six-bedroom home. Charlie moved through the great room, trailing his fingers along the back of an Italian leather sofa that had never held the weight of a friendly gathering. The faint scent of lemon polish hung in the air, evidence of the housekeeping service that came twice weekly to dust furniture nobody touched and vacuum floors nobody walked on.

Moonlight filtered through floor-to-ceiling windows, casting long fingers across the hardwood floors. The shadows of carefully place sculptures stretched like strange creatures across the walls. Charlie paused by one window, looking out at the lights of Los Angeles spread below his hillside perch. From here, the city looked like a circuit board of possibility, each light a life in progress. How many of those lights belonged to people sitting with friends, family, lovers? How many were alone as he was?

He exhaled deeply, shoulders dropping as his chest deflated. The sound seemed to ripple through the silence, a stone dropped in still water. Relief flooded through him, relief at the quiet after months of constant direction, constant chatter, constant performance. Yet his eyes kept darting to the empty dining table, the vacant reading nook, the untouched piano. Spaces where people should be.

In the kitchen, Charlie's footsteps transitioned from wood to marble with a subtle change in acoustics. The moonlight caught on the edges of stainless steel appliances, turning them into silver monoliths. He opened the refrigerator, its light spilling across his face, casting harsh shadows under his cheekbones. Inside, everything was arranged with hotel-like precision: pre-made meals in glass containers, each labelled with contents and dates; fresh produce in the correct drawers; beverages aligned with labels facing forward. His assistant had followed his instructions perfectly. It looked like a magazine spread rather than a home.

Charlie let the door swing shut, plunging himself back into half-darkness. His stomach growled, but the thought of eating any of those perfectly arranged meals made him slightly nauseated. He could almost see his nutritionist's disapproving frown, hear his trainer's lecture about maintaining muscle mass now that filming had wrapped. He leaned against the counter, feeling the cool stone through his shirt.

The house creaked, settling into the cooling night. Charlie flinched at the sound, then laughed at himself, a short, sharp sound that died quickly in the cavernous kitchen. He'd spent the last six months surrounded by people—makeup artists, camera operators, sound technicians, fellow actors, directors, producers—a constant stream of human contact that left no room for thought. Now, alone in a house built for entertaining, he felt the silence press against his eardrums like cotton wool.

He pushed away from the counter and wandered back to the foyer, where his discarded tie lay like a dead snake on the marble. His phone buzzed in his pocket, and he pulled it out, squinting at the screen. A text from his brother John: "Survived the wrap up party? Call me tomorrow when you're human again."

A smile tugged at the corner of Charlie's mouth, his first genuine expression since walking through the door. He typed back a quick "Will do" before slipping the phone back into his pocket. His fingers brushed against something else, the house key to his old apartment in New York, the one he kept for 'sentimental reasons' according to his publicist, "emergency escapes" according to John, and 'financial stupidity' according to his business manager.

Charlie moved toward the sweeping staircase, his hand trailing along the banister. Each step took effort, his body suddenly aware of every take, every stunt, every hour standing under hot lights. At the top, he paused, looking down at the expanse of his entryway. From this height, the dropped bags, discarded tie, and jacket he'd shed along the way formed a breadcrumb trail of his passage. Evidence that someone lived here after all.

The house hummed and sighed around him, its expensive

systems working invisibly to maintain perfect comfort. Outside, the wind picked up, sending shadows dancing across the walls as tree branches swayed. Charlie stood still, caught between exhaustion and restlessness, surrounded by everything money could buy and nothing that really mattered.

Charlie moved from the staircase landing into the west wing of the house, where moonlight spilled through skylights onto original artwork he'd purchased on his agent's recommendation. A Rothko hung at the end of the hallway, its bleeding rectangles of colour suggesting depth that Charlie had never quite understood but had paid three hundred thousand dollars to not understand in the privacy of his own home. His fingers drifted to the light switch but stopped short—there was something honest about seeing these spaces in darkness, stripped of their carefully curated glow.

His socked feet whispered against hardwood as he passed door after door: guest room, media room, home gym, another guest room. Each space designed with meticulous attention to both aesthetics and comfort, each one as hollow as a stage set between performances. Charli's shoulders, which had been held at the perfect camera-ready angle all day, gradually curved inward. With each step deeper into his private realm, the invisible audience that followed him everywhere seemed to thin and recede.

He paused at a small side table where a crystal bowl caught moonbeams and scattered them across the wall. Inside lay his house keys, three watches worth more than his father's first house, and a challenge coin given to him by a veteran after his role in a war film. Charlie touched the coin, rubbing his thumb over its raised insignia. "More authentic than most portrayals," the man had said, pressing it into Charlie's palm with calloused fingers. It was the only item on the table Charlie had chosen for himself.

The kitchen gleamed mockingly with stainless steel and

polished stone, a culinary showpiece featured in two separate architectural magazines. Charlie opened the refrigerator again, this time taking inventory of its contents wit ha more critical eye. Prepped protein, portioned vegetables, labelled smoothie ingredients—all arranged with the soulless precision of a personal assistant following a nutritionist's orders. The handwriting on the labels wasn't even his assistant's, but her assistant's Care by proxy, twice removed.

He grabbed a bottle of sparkling water, the glass cold against his palm. The fizz when he twisted the cap echoed slightly in the empty space. Charlie drank, the bubbles sharp against his tongue, and studied the refrigerator's interior. Nothing inside reflected his actual preferences—just the requirements of his current physical training regiment. The last meal he'd truly enjoyed had been four months ago: a greasy burger with his brother, eaten in disguise in a dcorner booth of a diner where the waitress didn't recognise him.

Charlie close the refrigerator and moved through an archway into the living room. A baby grand piano occupied the bay window, its polished surface reflecting the city lights below. He ran his fingers over the keys without pressing them, the cool ivory smooth beneath his touch. The piano had been delivered three years ago after a role required him to learn portions of Chopin. The instructor had come twice weekly for four months, then never again. Sheet music still waited in the bench, creased at the corners where Charlie had once folded them in frustration.

He pressed a single key, the note hanging in the air like a question. Charlie waited until it faded completely before moving on, his reflection fragmenting across various glass surfaces as he passed: windows, framed photographs, the face of an antique clock that kept perfect time for no one's benefit.

The living room opened to a sitting area with couches arranged in a conversational grouping that had never hosted a conversation. End tables held art books selected by his decorator, their spines untracked. A silver tray displayed crystal decanters of spirits—scotch he didn't really drink, bourbon he occassionally did, and cognac that had been opened once when his father visited. Charlie lifted one stopper and inhaled, the peaty aroma triggering memories of promotional events where he nursed the same glass all evening, staying sharp while others grew loose and incautious.

His phone vibrated again. Charlie extracted it from his pocket automatically, a Pavlovian response so ingrained he sometimes reached for phantom vibrations. A notification from his security system confirming his arrival home. No messages, no calls—exactly as expected. The production team would be celebrating at the wrap party, drinks flowing freely now that his 'early exit due to travel commitments' had removed the need for professional restraint. He slipped the phone back into his pocket, then immediately checked it again without thinking.

Charlie's posture straightened as he caught himself in this gesture, shoulders squaring as if someone had just called his name on set. He consciously relaxed again, a deliberate internal direction, and now we see the really Charlie, not the one they paid for. His spine curved slightly, one should dipping lower than the other. He rubbed his jaw where tension had been building all day.

The home theatre waited behind double doors of dark wood. Charlie pushed them open, not bothering with the lights. He could navigate this room blindfolded—had actually done so once during a drinking game with castmates who hadn't called since the premiere. Twelve leather recliners faced a screen larger than those in some independent theatres. A projection booth hummed at the back, ready to display any film from his digital library with the touch of a button on a custom remote.

Along one wall, framed posters documented his career trajectory: the indie darling that caught critics' attention, the romantic comedy that made him bankable, the action franchise that made him a household name. Charlie stood before them, studying his own face through the years. The changes were subtle, a gradual hardening around the eyes, a smile that became more practiced, less spontaneous. His hand moved to his face, fingers tracing the line of his jaw as if comparing the texture of reality to these glossy renditions.

"You look tired, man," he murmured to his two-dimensional self, voice absorbed by acoustic panels designed to optimize sound quality.

He exited through a side door that led to a hallway of guest suites. Charlie pushed open the first door, revealing a room decorated in muted blues and greys. The bed was perfectly made, decorative pillows arranged in a configuration that would require dismantling before anyone could actually sleep there. Hotel corners on the sheets. Fresh flowers on the nightstand, replaced weekly whether visitors were expected or not. The attached bathroom contained toiletries still in their packaging, fluffy towels that had never been used.

Charlie moved to the next room trying to reacquaint himself with his own home, this room was nearly identical but with a green and gold palette. Then the next, with its subtle Asian influence. Each space waited in perpetual readiness for guests who never materialised. Even John used the same room when he visited, leaving the others in pristine abandonment.

In the final guest room, Charlie sat on the edge of the bed, feeling the give of the premium mattress beneath him. His hand smoothed over the duvet, the fabric cool and slick against his palm. A laugh escaped him—small and bitter—as he considered the absurdity of mainting five guest room when he could could on one hand the people who had stayed overnight in the three years he'd owned the place.

His body performed its habitual check: spine straightening, shoulders broadening, chin lifting slightly to eliminate any hint of a double chin—camera-ready adjustments that happened without conscious thought. Then, recognising the empitness around him, Charlie allowed himself to slump. His elbows found his knees, his head bowed, fingers laced behind his neck. In this position, free from observation, his breathing deepenedl The mask of Charlie Benton, bankable star, slid away, leaving behind the exhausted man underneath.

His phone buzzed again. Charlie didn't immediately reach for it this time, letting the vibration run its course against his thigh. When he finally checked the screen, he saw a text from his manager about tomorrow's schedule. Reality intruding already, before he'd had time to remember who he was when nobody was paying for his time.

Charlie's study was the only room in the house that had escaped his decorator's comprehensive vision. Bookshelves lined three walls, filled not with colour-coordinated spines and artistic objects but with dog-eared paperbacks, film theory textbooks, and scripts in various states of annotation. A leather chair, cracked along one arm from actual use, waited beside a reading lamp whose shade tilted at an angle that would have given his interior designer heart palpations. Charlie eased the door shut behind him, feeling the subtle shift in air pressure as this smaller, contained space embraced him with familiar smells: paper, leather, and the faint woody scent of the whiskey he kept in a cabinet behind his desk.

He crossed to this cabinet now, a restored mid-century piece with brass handles that had developed a patina from the oils of his hands. The door opened with a familiar creak. Inside stood an array of bottles—not the showy crystal decanters in the living room, but the actual bottles he drank from, labels worn at the edges from handling. Charlie selected a Macallan, aged eighteen years. The cork came free with a soft pop that broke the silence. Amber liquid caught the lamplight as it spiralled into a heavy bottomed glass, the aroma rising to meet him: honey, oak, and a hint of smoke.

The first sip burned pleasantly, a heat that travelled down his throat and bloomed in his chest. Charlie closed his eyes, savouring the flavour and the quiet. This room contained no awards, no movie posters, no visible evidence of Charlie Benton the brand. Here, surrounded by books chosen for interest rather than appearance, he felt closest to the person he'd been before his name started appearing on marquees.

Glass in hand, Charlie settled into the chair behind his desk. The leather protested softly, conforming to the contours of his body with the ease of long acquaintance. He set the whiskey down and pulled open the bottom drawer, reaching past folders of financial documents to the back corner where a wooden box resided. His fingers found it by touch, the edges smooth from years of handling. Charlie lifted it free and placed it on the desk before him.

The box was unassuming—red cedar with a simple brass clasp, no bigger than a thick hardcover book. Nothing about it suggested its importance. He ran his fingers over the lid, tracing a small dent in one corner from when he'd packed it too hastily during his move to New York for his first significant role. Charlie took another sip of whiskey, letting the warmth settle in his stomach before opening the clasp.

Inside, photographs lay in carefully maintained disorder. No albums, no organisation system, just layers of moments captured on paper, accumulated over years. Charlie's fingers hovered over them briefly before selecting one from near the top. The glossy surface reflected the lamplight as he tilted it to see better.

His own face looked back at him, a decade younger, standing on the red carpet of his first major premiere. The suit was rented, slightly too large in the shoulders, and his tie sat crooked despite his best efforts. But his eyes—Charlie stared at those eyes now, the unguarded excitement visible even in the frozen image. No media training had yet taught him to modulate his expressions, to reveal enough to seem authentic while keeping a protective layer intact. The smile was all teeth and gums, none of the practised restraint that now limited his grin to the perfect proportion of charm to mystery.

"Look at you, you idiot," he murmured, a reluctant affection in his voice. He remembered the night clearly: the overwhelming lights, the disorientation of hearing his name called from multiple directions, the genuine disbelief that he belonged there. His hand had trembled slightly when signing autographs, a detail that had made it into one of the tabloids the next day, described as "endearing nervousness from Hollywood's newest heartthrob."

Charlie set this photo aside and drew another from the box. This one showed him backstage at the Golden Globes five years ago, arm slung around the shoulders of his co-star from the film that had earned them both nominations. They clutched champagne flutes, faces flushed with victory and alcohol. The co-star had sent a congratulatory text when Charlie was cast in his most recent film. Before that, they hadn't spoken in three years.

A soft laugh escaped him as he pulled out another image —a group shot from a wrap party, the entire cast forming a human pyramid on the beach where they'd filmed the final scenes. Half of these people had attended his thirtieth birthday party. None had been at his thirty-third, celebrated quietly two months ago with John and his agent. Charlie's thumb brushed over the faces, remembering names, specific jokes, promises to "definitely keep in touch" that had dissolved like sugar in rain.

His fingers stilled on a particular image, buried deeper in the stack. Charlie extracted it carefully, the paper slightly softened at the corners from frequent handling. This photo predated his career entirely: Charlie at fourteen, seated at a picnic table in his parents' backyard. His mother stood behind him, one hand resting on his shoulder, the other holding a plate of her famous blueberry pancakes. His father sat across from him, mid-laugh at some forgotten joke. John leaned against the table's edge, younger and somehow softer, before the entertainment industry had taught him cynicism.

Charlie's throat tightened. He set the whiskey down, suddenly aware of a tremor in his hand that might send the amber liquid sloshing over the rim. The photo captured the last summer before his first callback, before the guest spot on a crim procedural that led to a recurring role, before the guest spot on a crime procedural that led to a recurring role, before the independent film that caught a famous director's eye. The last summer of normalcy.

His mother still made those pancakes when he visited, but now they were accompanied by sidelong glances at his waistline and comments about his next physical transformation for a role. His father still laughed, but conversations inevitably circled to questions about celebrities he'd met, as if Charlie's proximity to other famous people was his most interesting quality. Only John treated him essentially the same, though even he had developed a habit of filtering information, protecting Charlie from knowledge that might "stress him out" during important projects.

Charlie shuffled through more photographs: studio head-shots from early auditions, candid moments from film sets, publicity stills where his eyes held the careful blend of intensity and approachability his publicist had coached. With each image, he noted the gradual transformation in his expressions—the increasing guardedness, the perfection of a camera-ready smile that revealed nothing of consequence. His physical form changed too, bulking up for action roles, slimming down for dramas, each iteration reflecting someone else's vision rather than his own choices.

A small sound escaped him as he uncovered a particular photo near the bottom of the stack. He lifted it with unexpected gentleness, as if the paper might disintegrate under his touch. The image showed Charlie at perhaps nineteen, standing on a makeshift stage in a college production. The costume was ridiculous—some attempt at Elizabethan doublet and hose made from materials the drama department could afford—but his face was illuminated with pure joy. No audience expectations, no pressure beyond his own desire to embody the character truthfully. Just the simple pleasure of inhabiting a story.

His fingertips brushed the surface of the photo, lingering on this younger self's expression. Charlie felt a warmth in his chest that had nothing to do with the whiskey—a bittersweet recognition of something misplaced rather than truly lost. He rubbed his temple with his free hand, swirled the remaining liquid in his glass, watched his distorted reflection in the whiskey's surface.

The mansion creaked around him, a symphony of settling wood and cooling pipes. Outside, a coyote called, the sound floating through the hills like a lonely question. Charlie reached for the photo of his family at the picnic and the one of himself in the college play. After a moment's contemplation, he propped them against the base of his lamp, positioning them so they would be visible from his chair.

He finished the last of his whiskey in a single swallow and carefully returned the remaining photographs to their box. Each on slid home, memories stacked upon memories, until only the chosen two remained out. Charlie closed the box and returned it to its drawer, movements deliberate and measured.

Standing, he crossed to the window and looked out at the Los Angeles night. His reflection stared back, superimposed over the distant lights—a ghost hovering between worlds. The man in the photographs still existed somewhere beneath the carefully constructed exterior that faced the cameras. Charlie pressed his palm against the cool glass, watching how the heat of his skin created a temporary fog that slowly dissipated.

When he finally turned back to his desk, his eyes found the photographs immediately, drawn to them like a compass finding north. The college actor with his unguarded joy. The family untouched by fame. Charlie Benton before he became "Charlie Benton."

He touched the edge of the family photo one last time before turning off the lamp. In the sudden darkness, the outline of his mansion stretched around him, filled with every-thing money could buy and emptied of almost everything else.

Chapter Two: Bee's Bad Date

The chandelier above Bee Anderson's table caught the light in fractured patterns, casting a warm glow that did nothing to ease the chill of waiting alone. She adjusted the sleeve of her burgundy blouse, fingers tracing the edge of the white tablecloth as she glanced—for the third time in five minutes—at her watch. Eight minutes late. Not enough to qualify as stood up, but enough to add another strike against the man whose carefully filtered profile photos had convinced her to give Tinder one more chance.

The resturant hummed with the particular energy of expensive dining. Conversations floated in carefully modulated tones, just loud enough for intimacy but quiet enough to signal refinement. Servers moved with balletic precision between tables, their black attire blending into shadows while white plates emerged like moons from their hands. Bee's water glass had not been allowed to dip below three-quarters full, a vigilance that made her almost afraid to sip too frequently.

She scrolled through her phone, thumb hovering over the dating app that had brought her here. Her profile photo— candid, unflitered, showing her genuine smile during a hike last summer—seemed almost rebellious among the carefully staged glamour shots that populated the platform. Her friends had insisted she give online dating another try. "You're too amazing to be single," Mia had declared last weekend, wine glass tilted dangerously as she made her point. "The algorithm just needs another chance."

The algorithm, Bee thought now, had a questionable track record. Three dates in the past month: one who spent two hours talking about his ex, one who asked if she'd consider losing fifteen pounds 'for health reasons,' and one who texted her the next morning with a breakdown of split epenses down to the penny.

And now, date number four was running late.

Her finger tapped against the stem of her wine glass, creating tiny ripples in the cabernet. A couple at a nearby table leaned toward each other, their conversation punctuated by soft laughter that seemed to exist in its own bubble of genuine connection. The woman reached across to touch her partner's hand, a casual intimacy that made Bee glance away, suddenly aware of her solitude.

Movement at the restaurant entrance caught her eye. A man in a tailored navy suit scanned the dining room, one hand adjusting an unnecessarily flashy watch. Even from a distance, Bee recognised him from his photos—though the real version was slightly shorter, slightly less broad-shouldered than his carefully angled selfies had suggested. Their eyes met across the room, and his face shifted into a smile that didn't quite reach his eyes but revealed professionally whitened teeth that gleamed under the ambient lighting.

Bee straightened in her chair, arranging her features into a pleasant expression as her date approached. She extended her hand as he reached the table. "Tyler? I'm Bianca."

"Everyone calls me Ty," he replied, his handshake firm and practised, like a move he'd studied in a business seminar. He slid into the seat across from her, immediately signalled a server with a raised finger. "Sorry about the timing. Had to wrap up a call with Singapore—markets wait for no man, right?" He laughed at his own comment.

"No problem," Bee said, though it had been a problem just moments ago. "I was just enjoying the atmosphere."

Tyler—Ty—didn't seem to hear her. He ordered a whiskey neat with a specific brand requirement that made the server nod with practiced deference. Then, without pausing to ask what Bee might want, he launched into conversation.

"So I was telling my client—major player, can't say who, but you'd recognise the name—that the Fed's position is completely unssutainable." His fingers drummed against the table in a rhythm that matched his rapid speech. "I've positioned our portfolios to capitalise on the inevitable correction. My team's analysis suggests a thirty percent upsdie in undervalued energy futures."

Bee's eyebrows rose slightly as she realised this wasn't an introduction but a monologue already in progress. She took a deliberate sip of wine, waiting for the question that would surely follow his opening statement. Something about her work, her interests, perhaps even a comment on the restaurant choice.

The question never came. Ty paused only to accept his whiskey from the returning server, took a swift sip, and continued.

"My approach has always been aggressive growth. Last quarter alone, I moved three clients into positions that yielded eighteen percent returns. Industry average is what, seven? Eight on a good day?" His hand sliced through the air to emphasize his point, nearly toppling the small votive candle between them.

Bee's fingers began a slow, methodical tap against the table's edge. One, two, three, four. One, two, three, four. A rhythm to focus on while her date's voice washed over her, discussing market sectors and investment strategies with the passionate intensity usually reserved for matters of life and death.

She tried to redirect. "That sounds impressive. I've always found—"

"Impressive is just the beginning," Ty interrupted, either not noticing or not caring about her attempt to speak. "My mentor—guy who basically built the firm's international division single-handedly—told me last week I'm on track to make partner before thirty-five. Youngest in the firm's history."

The server returned to take their dinner orders. Bee opened her menu for the first time, scanning it quickly as Ty ordered a steak, rare, with specific instructions about the preparation that made Bee wince in sympathy for the kitchen staff. When the server turned to her, she ordered the first steak dish she saw, barely registering what it was.

"So anyway," Ty continued the moment the server departed, as if there had been no interruption, "I've been renovating my place in West Hollywood. Gutted the entire kitchen. Italian marble countertops, German appliances—the works. I can't help but notice you ordered the steak, do you think it's a good idea at this time of night to eat something so...heavy?" he said looking me up and down. "They have fantastic salmon and salads here." the jerk added, eyes lingering on my waistline.

Bee's smile tightened at the corners. "Wow, that's fascinating. Tell me more about your diversification strategy," she said, her tone flattened with barely concealed sarcasm, choosing to ignore the remark about the food. A couple at the next table exchanged a knowing glance at her words, the woman offering a subtle look of sympathy.

Ty didn't notice the tone. His face brightened as he leaned

forward. "I'm so glad you asked. Most people don't appreciate the nuances of proper asset allocation."

Twenty minutes later, Bee's food remained largely untouched as Ty's detailed explanation of his investment philosophy continued unabated. Her gaze drifted to a couple seated near the windows. The man was listening intently to his companion, nodding occassionally, his expression one of genuine interest. The woman gesticulated as she spoke, her animation suggesting passion for her topic. When she paused, he asked a question. She laughed in response. They shared a moment of eye contact that held meaning.

Bee's attention snapped back to her own table as Ty's voice rose slightly.

"...which is why I told him, if you're not willing to take calculated risks, you'll never see the kind of returns that build real wealth." He punctuated this statement by cutting into his steak.

Bee's fingers had progressed from tapping to gripping the edge of the table, her knuckles whitening slightly. She had managed to insert exactly three comments into the conversation so far. All three had been either ignored or treated as invitations for Ty to elaborate further on his brilliant financial insights.

"And what about you?" Ty asked suddenly, the question so unexpected that Bee blinked in surprise. "Do you follow the markets at all?"

Before she could answer, he continued, "Most women don't which is why they miss out on building real security. I could give you some pointers if you're interested. Set you up with a starter portfolio."

The condescension in his tone made something tighten in Bee's chest. She took a careful breath, then another sip of wine to buy herself a moment. "Actually, I have a fairly diverse investment portfolio. My financial advisor and I meet quarterly to—"

"Financial advisor?" Ty's laugh cut her off. "Those guys take a percentage for basically plugging your info into the same algorithm every other client gets. You're better off learning to manage it yourself. Or finding someone who actually knows what they're doing. Also should we stop by a shop to grab some condoms when I drop you home or do you have that covered?" He tapped his chest with his thumb, smile gleaming.

Ty didn't appear to notice the shocked expression on Bee's face, she could feel her patience that had been stretched thin over the past forty-five minutes, finally begin to tear. She glanced at her watch, then back at Ty, who had already resumed talking about an upcoming conference in New York where he'd been invited to speak on a panel about emerging markets.

As he detailed the expected attendance numbers and his anticipated networking opportunities, Bee made a decision. Her hand reached for her purse, fingers closing around her phone. She needed an exit strategy, and she needed it now.

"Would you excuse me for a minute?" Bee interrupted Tyler mid-sentence, her voice sliding into the briefest pause as he took a breath between market predictions. She didn't wait for permission. Already pushing her chair back, the legs scraping against the hardwood floor with a sound that felt like vindication. Tyler barely broke his rhythm, nodding absently as his monologue continued, now directed at her empty chair. She walked away, each step increasing the distance between her shoulders and her ears as tension began to dissolve.

The path to the restroom took her past couples engaged in actual conversations, past a table where friends laughed with genuine mirth, past a server who gave her a sympathetic smile that suggested she wasn't the first woman to flee from a table tonight. Bee kept her posture straight, her walk deliberate—a habit formed during years of retail management where appearances mattered even when everything was falling apart behind the scenes.

A discreet sign marked the women's restroom, the door heavy enough that pushing it open required intention. The moment it closed behind her, sealing away the restaurant's ambient noise, Bee exhaled so deeply it felt like she'd been holding her breath since Tyler arrived. The bathroom enveloped her in an atmosphere of curated luxury: indirect lighting that flattered rather than exposed, marble countertops in a soft blush tone that reflected warmly against skin, and a subtle floral scent that hovered just at the edge of perception.

Bee caught sight of herself in the ornate mirror—cheeks slightly flushed, eyes bright with suppressed irritation. She touched her hair, tucking a strand behind her ear in a gesture that was more about buying time than fixing her appearance. Another woman emerged from a stall, smiled politely as she washed her hands at the sink, then disappeared back into the restaurant, leaving Bee blissfully alone.

Three stalls stood in a row, their doors gleaming with the same dark wood that featured throughout the restaurant. Bee chose the farthest one, stepped inside, and locked the door with a satisfying click. Only then did she allow her shoulders to drop completely, her spine curving as she leaned against the stall door and closed her eyes.

Her purse yielded her phone, the screen illuminating her face in the dim stall. Her fingers flew across the virtual keyboard, tapping out a message to Mia with the urgency of someone sending a distress signal:

"This guy hasn't asked me a SINGLE question about myself. Just talked abouth is aggressive growth strategy for 45 minutes straight. But did manage to throw in a dig about my choice of food and ask if I had condoms. Kill. Me. Now."

She watched the messaged send, then added:

"He tried to mansplain investing to me. ME. With a finance degree. I mentioned my portfolio and he laughed. LAUGHED."

Bee stared at the screen, waiting. Three dots appeared almost immediately, pulsing as Mia typed her response. The anticipation of sympathetic outrage from her friend was the first pleasant feeling she'd experienced all evening.

The reply arrived: "OMG what a douche! What's his name? I need to visualise him properly when I curse him later"

Bee's lips curved into a genuine smile for the first time that evening. She typed back: "Tyler. But he insists everyone calls him Ty. Because of course he does."

Mia's response was swift: "Bail! Life's too short for finance bros who can't shut up! Fake an emergency. Or just be honest —your time is valuable and he's wasting it talking about his boring ass."

Another message followed quickly: "Also I told you we should've vetted his social media first. Nobody with a watch that expensive in their profile pic is there for genuine connection."

Bee sighed, remembering how she'd waved off Mia's suggestion to do a deep dive on Tyler's instagram before agreeing to the date. "Too time-consuming, I don't do social media" she had argued. "And creepy." Now she wished she'd taken the advice.

"You were right," she typed back. "Next time I'll listen. If there is a next time. I might delete the app tonight."

Outside the stall, the bathroom door opened and closed. Soft footsteps moved across tile, followed by the sound of water running in a sink. Bee waited, not wanting to emerge and risk casual bathroom conversation with a stranger. The water stopped. Hand dryer hummed. Door opened and closed again. Silence returned.

She unlcoked the stall and stepped out, moving to the sink

where she set her phone down on the cool marble surface. The countertop felt smooth beneath her palms as she leaned forward, studying her reflection. The bathroom's strategic lighting softened the lines of frustration around her mouth, but couldn't hide the weariness in her eyes.

The soap dispenser released a pearl of liquid that smelled of lavender and something citrusy—bergamot, perhaps. Bee washed her hands methoidcally, focusing on the sensaiton of water sliding over her skin, the slickness of soap, the ritual of cleansing. It felt symbolic somehow, washing away the residue of a disappointing evening.

She dried her hands on a plush hand towel from a stack arranged in a perfect pyramid. Her phone vibrated with another message from Mia: "Want me to call with an emergency? I can be very convincing. My cat is sick. My apartment is flooding. I've been arrested for punching a finance bro who wouldn't stop talking about himself."

Bee smiled again, typing back: "Thanks, but I think I'll handle this one directly. If I'm not home in an hour, assume I've been arrested for the same offense."

She slipped the phone back into her purse and turned to face the mirror again. The woman who stared back at her looked perfectly put together—dark hair falling in soft waves past her shoulders, blue eyes bright with determination rather than defeat, lipstick still intact despite the wine she'd been drinking to cope with Tyler's monologue.

The faint sounds of the restarurant filtered through the door—clinking glasses, indistinct conversation, the subtle notes of the background music selected to enhance the dining experience without drawing attention to itself. Somewhere out there, Tyler was probably still talking, perhaps not even having noticed how long she'd been gone.

Bee straightened her blouse, adjusted her posture, and took a deep breath. The scent of expensive hand soap clung to her skin as she reached for her purse, the soft leather familiar under her fingers. She thought about all the evenings she'd spent like this—making excuses to escape terrible dates, hiding in bathrooms while texting friends for moral support, trying to decide whether honesty or politeness would serve her better in extracting herself from uncomfortable situations.

She was tired of it. Tired of men who viewed dates as opportunities. To deliver presentations about themselves. Tired of swiping through photos trying to determine which smiles were genuine and which hid narcissists. Tired of sitting across tables from strangers who remained strangers even after sharing a meal.

Her mother's voice echoed in her head: "You're too picky, Bianca." Maybe she was. Or maybe she simply refused to settle for someone who couldn't be bothered to ask a single question about her life, her work, her thoughts.

Bee squared her shoulders and lifted her chin, meeting her own gaze in the mirror. Decision made, resolution formed. She would end this date cleanly and efficiently. No drama, no extended explanations—just a firm exit that valued her time as much as she wished Tyler had.

The marble felt cool against her fingertips as she pushed away from the counter. The bathroom door swung open under hand, releasing her back into the restaurant's atmosphere with renewed purpose. Each step back toward the table felt more confident than the ones that had brought her to the bathroom. The weight of obligation had lifted, replaced by the lightness of imminent escape.

Tyler's voice reached her before she fully returned to the table—a continuous stream of financial jargon that hadn't paused during her absence. His fork gesticulated in the air, punctuating some point about market corrections while his half-eaten steak congealed on the plate. Bee slid into her chair with the careful movements of someone who had already mentally left the building. She placed her napkin in her lap, more from ingrained politeness than any intention to continue the meal, and waited for the briefest natural pause in his monologue.

"—which is why you should never trust analysts who haven't worked on the trading floor. The just don't understand the psychological components of—"

"Tyler," Bee interjected, her voice firm but not unkind. "I'm sorry to interrupt, but I'm going to have to cut our evening short."

He blinked, fork suspended in mid-air as if someone had pressed pause on a financial advising infomercial. For a moment, confusion crossed his features—the first genuine emotion she'd seen all evening.

"I've got an early morning meeting tomorrow," she continued, the lie sliding easily from her lips. "Quarterly review with our biggest client. I should have mentioned it earlier."

Tyler lowered his fork, his expression recalibrating. "Oh, sure. No problem." He glanced at his watch—the third time he'd checked it since sitting down, though the first time he'd done so in response to something she'd said. "I've got some emails to send tonight anyway. The Asian markets open soon."

Bee nodded, relieved at how easily he accepted her excuse. "It was nice meeting you," she said, another social nicety that bore little resemblance to truth. Her hand reached for her purse, fingers curling around the strap like a lifeline.

"Likewise," Tyler replied, already pulling out his phone, thumb scrolling through notifications that had accumulated during dinner. "We should do this again sometime. Next week I'm—"

"I'll be in touch," Bee interrupted, unwilling to endure

even a preview of future plans that would never materialise. She signalled a nearby server. "Could I get the check, please?"

"I've got it," Tyler said, the automatic response of a man accustomed to picking up tabs. He pulled a credit card from his wallet without looking up from his phone. "Business expense."

Under different circumstances, the casual dismissal might have irritated her further. Tonight, it simply smoothed her exit. Bee gathered her jacket from the back of her chair, sliding her arms into the sleeves with efficient movements.

"Thanks for dinner," she said, standing beside the table. "Good luck with those Asian markets."

Tyler glanced up, offered a distracted smile that didn't reach his eyes, and nodded. "I'll walk you out," he said, though he made no move to stand.

"No need," Bee replied quickly. "Finish your meal. I can see myself out."

She turned before he could respond, though she doubted he would. Three steps away from the table, she heard his voice resume—not calling after her, but continuing his financial monologue, now directed into his phone. She didn't look back to confirm her suspicion that he'd immediately called someone else to continue the conversation she'd escaped.

The hostess nodded as Bee passed the front desk, the woman's professional smile containing a hint of understanding. Outside, the restaurant's doors swung shut behind her with a soft whoosh, sealing away the ambient music and muted conversations. The night air enveloped her immediately —cooler than inside, carrying the complex scent of the city: exhaust fumes, distant restaurant kitchens, the subtle perfume of night-blooming jasmine from planters that lined the sidewalk.

Bee inhaled deeply, her lungs expanding with teh first genuinely satisfying breath she'd taken since Tyler sat down across from her. The tension in her shoulders began to dissolve as she moved away from the restaurant's warm glow. Street lamps cast pools of light at regular intervals, her shadow stretching and contracting as she passed through them. Nearby, a valet whistled for a car, the sound piercing the urban soundtrack of distant traffic and mumured conversations from restaurant patios.

Bee pulled her phone from her purse, the screen iluminating her face with a blue glow that momentarily made her look ghostly in a darkened storefront window she passed. Her thumb hovered over the Tinder icon, the familiar flame symbol that had promised connection but delivered mostly disappointment. She tapped it with more force than necessary, as if punishing the app for its false advertising.

Tyler's profile appeared at the top of her matches, his carefully curated photos showing him on a yacht, at a charity gala, posing beside an expensive car. The same practiced smile in each one, the same careful angle to emphasize his jawline. Bee's thumb hovered over his profile for only a moment before swiping left with such vehemence that she nearly dropped her phone. The screen flickered, replacing his face with another potential match—a bearded man holding a fish in his profile picture.

Left swipe.

The next profile showed a shirtless gym selfie.

Left swipe.

A group photo where she couldn't determine which man was the actual profile owner.

Left swipe.

With each rejection, her pace quickened, heels striking the pavement with increasing force. A couple stepped apart to let her pass, the woman's eyes following her with curiosity. Bee barely noticed, focused on the parade of disappointing options scrolling beneath her thumb. How had she let Mia convince her to try this again? Every conversation began the same way—superficial compliments leading to superficial conversations. The rare connections that progressed to actual dates inevitably disappointed, the men either nothing like their profiles or exactly like them in all the worst ways.

She stopped abruptly, causing a man walking behind her to sidestep awkwardly. Bee murmured an apology without looking up, then moved to the edge of the sidewalk where a jewellery store's recessed doorway offered a momentary haven from the flow of pedestrians. She leaned against the cool glass of the display window, her reflection ghostly against the backdrop of glittering diamonds and platinum settings.

Her phone vibrated with a notification—a text message from a number she vaguely recognised. She opened it automatically, scanning the brief message: Had a great time last week. Dinner again soon?"

Bee stared at the text, trying to place it. The name, Mark, triggered a vague memory: her date from last week, the one who had texted her the next morning with an itemized list of shared expenses down to a 50/50 split of the Uber. She'd politely declined a second date, but apparently the message hadn't registered.

Irritation flared, hotter and more intense than the situation warranted—but it wasn't just about Mark. It was about Tyler and his financial monologue. About the gym selfies and fish photos. About every date that felt like a job interview or, worse, an audience for someone else's one-man show. About the accumulation of disappointments that had led her to this moment, standing alone on a sidewalk while around her, couples walked hand-in-hand through the evening.

Her thumbs flew across the screen, tapping out words fuelled by the evening's frustration:

"You know what buddy you were a complete ass tonight... I wish Tinder had a review feature! Talks only about himself, interrupts constantly, mansplains finance to a woman with a finance degree, and checks his watch while pretending to listen. One star, would not recommend."

She pressed send with a decisive tap, a tiny release of the tension that had accumulated throughout the evening. That would show him! She glanced back over her shoulder, suddenly realising that she may have remembered the number wrong in her haste.

"Shit," she whispered, staring at the screen as the message showed delivered. Her finger hovered over the delete option, but she knew it was too late—the damage was done. For a moment she considered sending an apology, explaining the mistake, but what would be the point? Some random person had just received her dating rant. They'd probably ignore it or block her number, no need to make it more awkward.

A car horn blared nearby, startling her out of her momentary panic. Bee took a deep breath, locked her phone, and slipped it back into her purse. The night air suddenly felt cooler against her skin, a breeze carrying the promise of the ocean miles away. Around her, the city continued its evening rhythm—traffic lights changing, pedestrians flowing around her still form, distant laughter spilling from a rooftop bar half a block away.

She pushed away from the storefront window, adjusting her jacket and squaring her shoulders. The misdirected text was embarrassing but ultimately meaningless—a small ripple in the vast ocean of digital miscommunications happening every second. By tomorrow, she'd have forgotten all about it. The unknown recipient certainly would.

Bee rejoined the flow of pedestrians, her pace more measured now, the sharp edge of her frustration dulled by the small catharsis of having expressed it, however misdirected. She would delete the app when she got home, take a break from the exhausting cycle of hope and disappointment.

Maybe Mia was right about meeting people the old-fashioned way—though in Los Angeles, Bee wasn't sure what that even meant anymore.

The traffic light ahead turned from red to green, and she stepped off the curb with the surge of crossing pedestrians, unaware that her impulsive text had just landed in the phone of a man who was, at that very moment, feeling as disconnected from the world as she was.

Chapter Three: A Fortuituous Mistake

Charlie drifted from his study back toward the kitchen, trailing his fingers along the wall as he moved through the darkened hallway. The photos he'd been examining had stirred something in him—a restlessness, a hunger for connection that seemed both pathetic and desperately human. His socked feet whispered against the hardwood floors, the sound swallowed by the vastness of his empty home. Three years in this place, and it still felt more like an elaborate hotel suite than anywhere he belonged.

The kitchen waited for him, its sleek surfaces gleaming in the half-light. Charlie opened the refrigerator again, the cool air washing over his face as he stared at the precisely arranged contents. Nothing appealed. He closed it, turned, and leaned against the counter. Outside, a distant coyote called again, the sound floating through the hills like a question he couldn't answer.

His hand moved to his pocket automatically, retrieving his phone. The screen illuminated his face with its artificial glow, harsh in the dim kitchen. Another pointless check, another habitual motion performed without thought or purpose.

Emails from his manager, texts from his publicity team about tomorrow's schedule, social media notifications he never read but couldn't bring himself to disable.

The phone vibrated in his hand.

Charlie blinked, momentarily confused by the unfamiliar sensation. Not many people texted him directly anymore—most communication came through his team, filtered and processed before reaching him. His thumb swiped across the screen, opening a message from a number he didn't recognise.

"You know what buddy you were a complete ass tonight... I wish Tinder had a review feature! Talks only about himself, interrupts constantly, mansplains finance to a woman with a finance degree, and checks his watch while pretending to listen. One star, would not recommend."

He read it twice, then a third time, his brain slowly processing the realization that this wasn't meant for him. A wrong number. Some stranger venting about a bad date, accidentally sending their frustration into his carefully guarded digital space. The words carried an undiluted emotion that felt startlingly real after a day of crafted statements and camera-ready expressions.

Charlie found himself smiling, a small, private curve of his lips that had nothing to do with the practiced grin he deployed for public consumption. He could picture it clearly—some finance bro holding court across a restaurant table, checking his watch while his date silently plotted her escape. The scenario was so far removed from his own reality that it felt almost exotic in its ordinariness.

His thumb hovered over the screen. The sensible response would be no response. Delete the message, block the number if necessary. That's what his publicist would advise, minimal digital footprint, no unnecessary interactions, nothing that could be misconstrued or exploited later.

But something in the raw frustration of the messaged

called to him. When was the last time someone had spoken to him—even accidentally—without an agenda? Without knowing who he was or what they might gain from the interaction? The thought was intoxicating in its simplicity.

Before his better judgement could intervene, Charlie's fingers began tapping out a response. If this person was going to mistakenly berate him for being an awful date, he might as well play along. He could be anyone in this exchange—just a normal guy responding to a wrong number text with self-deprecating humour. Not Charlie Benton the actor, not the carefully constructed public persona, just ...a guy.

"I'm sorry! Was it when I talked about my action figure collection or when I asked if you'd be willing to meet my mother on the second date?"

He reread his message, adding a winky face emoji, then deleting it. Too flirtatious. This was just a friendly response to a wrong number, not an attempt at connection. He settled on ending the message with a simple question mark, letting the self-deprecating joke stand on its own.

His finger hovered over the send button. A voice in the back of his mind, one that sounded suspiciously like his publicist, whispered cautions about engaging with unknown numbers, about digital footprints and security concerns. But a stronger impulse pushed against these warnings, one born of the evening's melancholy reflections and the photos he'd been examining in his study. The hunger to interact, just once, as himself. Or at least, as someone who wasn't Charlie Benton, star of...

The kitchen felt suddenly too quiet, the silence pressing against his eardrums. Outside, the lights of L.A twinkled like distant stars, each one representing lives in progress, connections being made and broken. The coyote called again, its howl seemingly closer now.

Charlie hit send.

The message whooshed away, disappearing into the digital ether. Immediately, a nervous energy fluttered in his stomach —an unfamiliar sensation he eventually identified as anticipation. When was the last time he'd felt genuinely uncertain about someone's response to him? His interactions were so carefully choreographed now, each party knowing their role in the dance. But this ...this was unscripted.

He set the phone down on the counter, face up where he could see it if a response came through. Then he deliberately turned away, opening a cabinet to retrieve a glass. Water from the filtered tap poured crystal clear, but Charlie barely noticed the taste as he drank. His attention remained fixed on the silent phone, willing it to vibrate again.

The muscles in his shoulders had tensed, he realised with mild surprise. As if this response from a stranger actually mattered. As if this fleeting, accidental connection carried weight. Perhaps it did, in a house full of empty rooms and carefully curated possessions. Perhaps any genuine human interaction would feel this significant after months of performing humanity rather than experiencing it.

Charlie's reflection watch him from the stainless steel refrigerator door, distorted but recognisable. The man looking back at him seemed younger somehow, more vulnerable than the confident persona he projected to the world. His hair fell across his forehead in a way his stylist would never allow, his expression open in a way that would never make it to a promotional photo.

The phone remained silent, its screen darkening to save battery. Charlie resisted the urge to check it, to see if his message had been delivered or read. Instead, he moved to the window overlooking the back garden, where landscape lighting illuminated sculptural plants and the geometric lines of the swimming pool. His own reflection superimposed over the view, a ghost hovering between worlds.

A soft buzz broke the silence. Charlie turned so quickly he nearly spilled his water. The phone's screen had illuminated with a notification—a response from the unknown number. His heart rate quickened as he set down his glass and reached for the device, a physical reaction that seemed disproportionate to the situation but felt entirely natural in the moment.

His finger hesitated for the briefest second before unlocking the screen. Whatever this stranger said, whether they apologised for the wrong number, played along with his joke, or simply told him to get lost, their response would be genuine. Unfiltered by knowledge of who he was. Uncoloured by what they might want from him.

In that moment, Charlie realised how desperately he had been craving exactly that.

Bee kicked her apartment door shut behind her, the deadbolt sliding home with a satisfying chunk that felt like punctuation to her evening. She dropped her keys into the ceramic bowl on the entryway table, a handmade piece from a craft fair that clashed cheerfully with the sleek, mass-produced furniture surrounding it. The silence of her apartment wrapped around her, a welcome contrast to the practiced ambience of Lucent and Tyler's unrelenting monologue. She slipped off her heels, feeling the immediate relief of bare feet against the cool hardwood, and padded toward her living room, already unzipping the side of her dress.

Her apartment occupied the second floor of a converted 1920s building in Los Feliz—smaller than she'd like but with character that compensated for square footage: crown moulding, hardwood floors, and windows that actually opened. The living room welcomed her with familiar disorder: books stacked on the coffee table, a half-empty mug from that morning, a throw blanket bunched at one end of her sofa. Unlike the pristine surfaces of Lucent, her space showed evidence of actual habitation.

Bee peeled off her dress, letting it pool on the floor with a whispered promise to hang it up later. She pulled on the oversized USC sweatshirt that lived on the back of her bedroom door, cotton soft from a hundred washes. The transformation from Restaurant Bee to Home Bee complete, she collapsed onto her sofa, legs stretched across cushions that remembered the shape of her body.

"Another one bites the dust," she murmured to the empty room, fishing her phone from her purse. She navigated to the Tinder app, thumb hovering over the icon with grim determination. One more swipe through the deck of disappointment before she deleted the whole thing. Her mother's voice echoed in her head—"You'll never meet anyone if you're so picky, Bianca"—but tonight, the accusation felt like a promise rather than a warning.

The first profile featured a man in sunglasses holding a surfboard, his bio a collection of emojis that communicated nothing of substance. Left swipe. The next showed someone with an artfully trimmed beard staring moodily into middle distance. His profile mentioned loving "adventures" without specifying what qualified. Left swipe. Another featured a group shot where she couldn't determine which man owned the profile. Left swipe, left swipe, left swipe—a mindless rhythm that matched the bitter cadence of her thoughts.

Her phone vibrated, interrupting the parade of disappointment. A text notification slid across the top of her screen. Bee tapped it automatically, expecting Mia checking in for post-date details.

Instead, an unfamiliar number appeared, with a message that made her eyebrows lift toward her hairline: "I'm sorry! Was it when I talked about my action figure collection or when I asked if you'd be willing to meet my mother on the second date?"

Bee sat up straighter, confusion furrowing her brow as she tried to place the number. Recognition dawned slowly—this was a response to her misdirected rant, the one she'd accidentally sent to a stranger instead of Tyler. But instead of ignoring her or responding with confusion or hostility, this person had...played along?

A surprised laugh escaped her, the sound bouncing off the walls of her apartment—the first genuine laugh she'd experienced all evening. She read the message again, noting the self-deprecating humour, the complete lack of defensiveness that would have characterised Tyler's response had the message actually reached him.

Bee's posture shifted unconsciously. She tucked her legs underneath her, leaning forward toward the blue glow of her phone screen. Her thumb hovered over the keyboard as she considered her response. The decent thing would be to apologise for the misdirected message, of course. But something about this stranger's willingness to joke rather than take offense made her want to respond in kind.

Her fingers moved across the screen, deleting and retyping phrases as she crafted her reply. She found herself biting her lower lip in concentration, aware of a flutter of anticipation that seemed wholly disproportionate to the situation. Finally, she settled on: "Oh god, wrong number! Though your response makes me think your date went about as well as mine. For the record, I'd be more concerned about the mother comment than the action figures. At least collecting shows commitment."

Bee reread her message, surprised by the playful tone that had emerged naturally. She added a laughing emoji, then deleted it—too casual for a stranger? Then added it again.

With a small shrug, she hit send before she could overthink further.

The message disappeared with a soft whoosh, and Bee immediately set her phone face-up on the coffee table, within easy view. She reached for the TV remote, clicking through streaming services without really seeing the options. Her attention remained fixed on the silent phone, waiting for the screen to illuminate with a response.

Why did she care what this wrong number person thought of her message? Why was she suddenly perched on the edge of her sofa, one foot tapping an impatient rhythm against the floor? The evening had left her raw, she rationalised. Tyler's self-absorption followed by the embarrassment of sending a rant to a stranger—perhaps she simply wanted to end the night on a less mortifying note.

Her phone buzzed, the screen lighting up. Bee's hand darted toward it with an eagerness that would have embarrassed her had anyone been there to witness it.

"My evening consisted of heated arguments with my reflection and the constant judgmental stare of my empty refrigerator. So probably better than yours, but not by much. And you're right about the action figures—I've maintained a consistent relationship with my Boba Fett longer than with any actual person."

Another laugh escaped her, this one warmer and less surprised than the first. Bee curled deeper into the corner of her sofa, her feet tucking underneath her as she typed a response. The words flowed easily, her fingers moving across the screen with a speed and confidence that reflected genuine engagement rather than social obligation.

"At least your refrigerator was there for you. My date spent 90 minutes explaining investment strategies to me WITHOUT ONCE asking what I do for a living. Plot twist: I have a finance degree. I could've corrected at least three of his 'expert' opinions."

She hit send, then immediately followed with another message: "And don't sell yourself short—I'm sure Boba Fett appreciates your loyalty. Most bounty hunters have commitment issues."

Bee realized she was smiling at her phone, the tension that had coiled in her shoulders during dinner finally unravelling. The bitter taste of the evening began to fade, replaced by the unexpected pleasure of this strange connection. A wrong number, of all things, had somehow salvaged a night she'd written off as a complete waste.

She glanced around her apartment, seeing it with fresh eyes after the evening's disappointments. The books stacked haphazardly on end tables, the mismatched furniture collected from thrift stores and family hand-me-downs, the framed concert posters that had never made it into proper alignment on the wall—all of it suddenly seemed less like evidence of her failure to achieve adult perfection and more like proof of a life actually lived. Unlike Tyler with his clinical descriptions of marble countertops and German appliances, her space told stories.

Her phone buzzed again. Bee found herself reaching for it before the sound had fully registered, her body responding with an eagerness that bypassed conscious thought. Whatever this stranger said next, it would almost certainly be more interesting than anything Tyler had offered over an expensive steak.

The realisation should have depressed her. Instead, Bee felt a flicker of something that felt surprisingly like hope.

Charlie found himself pacing the length of his living room, phone clutched in his hand like a talisman. Each vibration announcing a new message sent a ridiculous thrill through him, as if he were a teenager rather than a man in his thirties with a shelf full of industry awards. Outside his floor-to-ceiling windows, L.A sprawled in a glittering expanse of lights, millions of people, thousands of stories unfolding in real time, yet this single conversation with an unknown woman felt more substantial than any interaction he'd had in months.

His thumb moved across the screen with increasing confidence as their exchange continued, the initial awkwardness of a wrong number giving way to something that felt strangely like connection.

"So what was his field of expertise that he felt compelled to mansplain to you?" Charlie typed, a smile playing at the corners of his mouth. "Let me guess, crypto? Startup culture? The subtle art of checking one's watch while pretending to listen?"

He paused by the window, his reflection a darker shadow against the night beyond. While waiting for her response, he found himself straightening his posture, then deliberately relaxing it again—a physical manifestation of the strange tension between his public and private selves. Even alone in his home, texting a stranger who had no idea who he was, old habits emerged unbidden.

The reply came swiftly: "Investment banking. The kind where you say aggressive growth strategy every third sentence and refer to yourself as a disruptor without irony. He ordered a $75 steak, talked about his Italian marble countertops, then implied I shouldn't order steak because it was 'heavy'. Sir, you don't get to have opinions about my digestive system when we've known each other for 7 minutes."

While reading that text another followed "AAAANNNNDDDD he managed to throw in do I already have condoms covered or should he stop and pick some up on the way to my house, the presumptuous jerk!"

Charlie laughed out loud, the sound startling in the quiet house. Not the careful chuckle he deployed during interviews —genuine laugh that came from somewhere unguarded. He could picture this woman so clearly—sharp, observant, unwilling to suffer fools. Her words carried an authenticity that felt almost exotic after years of carefully curated interactions.

"Wait has that ever worked? Maybe I've been doing it wrong all this time! My last date asked for my zodiac sign, then spent 20 minutes explaining why Taurens and Geminis are fundamentally incompatible," he typed back, drawing on a story from his early dating life before stardom. "When the check came, she announced she doesn't believe in societal constructs like financial transactions and vanished to the bathroom. Never returned."

He hit send, then immediately followed with: "I'm the Tauren, by the way. In case you were concerned about our astrological compatibility as wrong-number texting partners."

Charlie resumed his pacing, moving from the living room through the archway into the kitchen, trailing his fingers along cold marble countertops that suddenly reminded him of her date's boasting. His phone vibrated against his palm.

"Oh god, she GHOSTED before the bill? That's simultaneously terrible and impressive. My zodiac knowledge extends to Capricorns are supposedly stubborn and nothing else, so our text compatibility remains uncharted astrological territory. But if you start explaining investment strategies to me, all bets are off."

Across the city, Bee's apartment filled with the sound of her laughter, a warm contrast to the silence that had greeted her return home. She'd migrated from the sofa to her bed, propped against pillows with a mug of chamomile tea on her nightstand. The conversation had flowed so naturally that she'd barely noticed an hour passing, the bitterness of her evening with Tyler fading with each exchange.

"So what do you do when you're not defending yourself against zodiac compatibility assessments?" she typed, curiosity growing about the person behind these witty responses. "I'm picturing you as either a stand-up comedian or someone who writes those snarky greeting cards that make people uncomfortable at drugstores."

She bit her lower lip, waiting for his response, fingers absently twisting a strand of hair. The anticipation she felt was disproportionate to the situation—this was just a wrong number conversation, a strange cosmic accident—yet something about his responses had hooked her interest more effectively than any dating app match had managed.

In his mansion on the hill, Charlie stared at her question, fingers hovering over the keyboard. Here it was—the inevitable inquiry about his life, his identity. His usual defences rose automatically, media training kicking in with practiced deflections and vague answers that revealed nothing of consequence.

He started typing, then deleted the words. Started again, deleted again. What could he say? "I'm an actor" would lead to questions he couldn't answer without revealing too much. "I'm famous" would sound both arrogant and paranoid. The truth was impossible but outright lies felt wrong given the unexpected authenticity of their exchange.

Finally, he settled on: "I work in entertainment. Behind the scenes mostly, nothing glamourous. Mainly I observe people pretending to be what they're not, which is probably why I've developed an appreciation for authenticity. What about you? Besides having a finance degree that you're not allowed to mention on dates?"

Charlie hit send, then moved to the couch, sinking into its leather embrace as he awaited her response. The house creaked around him, settling into the night but for once the sound didn't emphasize his solitude. Instead, the phone in his hand provided a tether to the outside world—one unmediated by publicists, managers, or the expectations of fame.

Bee read his message with a slight narrowing of her eyes. "Behind the scenes in entertainment" could mean anything in L.A—production assistant, talent manager, the guy who made sure craft services had the right brand of sparkling water. There was a vagueness to it that might have raised flags in another context, but after Tyler's exhausting specificity about his career, she found the mystery refreshing.

"Retail management," she replied. " I manage a boutique in Silver Lake that sells clothes that us mere mortals couldn't possibly afford. Less glamourous than entertainment, but I get to observe humanity in its natural state—trying on pants that don't fit while insisting they're just a bit snug. Speaking of observations on human nature—favourite movie? This is a test of character. Choose wisely."

Charlie smiled at her directness, the way she moved confidently from topic to topic. The question about movies made him laugh, how many interviews had he done where he'd been asked this exact thing? But those answers had been calculated: indie films to establish credibility, blockbusters to show mainstream appeal, classics to demonstrate depth. Never his actual favourites.

"Tough one," he typed, suddenly wanting to be honest. "The Apartment, Wilder at his best, cynicism with a beating heart underneath. Lost in Translation for capturing loneliness in a crowded room. And—don't judge—The Princess Bride, which I've seen approximately 47 times and still find perfect. Your turn, and I'm judging harshly."

Their conversation flowed from movies to books to travel

disasters, each exchange revealing small fragments of themselves while maintaining the strange, liberating anonymity of their connection. Charlie found himself sharing stories he'd never tell in interviews—his fear of heights, his childhood obsession with maps, the fact that he sometimes drank milk straight from the carton despite having been raised better.

Bee told him about her collection of vintage postcards, her disastrous attempt at making sourdough during quarantine, her firm belief that cilantro tasted like soap despite all scientific evidence suggesting this was genetic and not a moral failing.

As they talked, Charlie moved from room to room in his vast, empty house, the phone in his hand creating an invisible companion that made the space feel less hollow. At one point, he found himself in the theatre room, sitting in the dark, laughing at her description of a catastrophic blind date that ended with spilled wine and a small kitchen fire.

Across the city, Bee curled deeper into her blankets, the warmth of her tea matched by the unexpected pleasure of this strange connection. At some point, she realised that two hours had passed, the clock on her nightstand showing nearly midnight. A weeknight, with an early meeting tomorrow. Responsibility tugged at her, even as she found herself reluctant to end the conversation, on the chance it would be the end of the connection.

"I should probably sleep," she finally typed, fingers hesitating over the screen. "Early meeting with suppliers who don't understand why I won't stock clothes that only fit people shaped like celery stalks."

Charlie stared at her message, feeling an irrational disappointment. Of course she needed to sleep. Normal people with normal jobs didn't stay up until dawn texting strangers. He had nowhere to be tomorrow, a rare gap in his schedule before promotion for his next film began, but she couldn't know that.

"Sleep is apparently necessary for human functioning," he replied, aiming for lightness despite his reluctance. "Though I have my doubts. Thanks for the conversation, it's been the highlight of an otherwise exceptionally mundane evening of arguing with my reflection."

Bee smiled at his response, appreciating the acknowledgement of their strange connection without making it weighted or awkward. "Thank you for not being offended by my misdirected rant. And for restoring my faith in text conversations. At least I know there's one person in LA who doesn't want to explain investment banking to me."

Charlie's reply came quickly: "Sweet dreams. May your suppliers see reason, may your customers appreciate normal human proportions, and may your next date ask at least one question about your life."

"Goodnight, wrong number," Bee typed back. "May your reflection lose the next argument, and may your Boba Fett appreciate your ongoing loyalty."

With that final exchange, Charlie set his phone down on the nightstand beside his bed. He lay back against the pillows, staring at the ceiling with a strange lightness in his chest. The mansion still sprawled around him, rooms empty and echoing, but the silence felt different somehow—charged with possibility rather than emptiness.

A genuine smile lingered on his face, the first in months that hadn't been calculated for effect or practiced in a mirror. His last thought before sleep claimed him was a quiet amazement at how the misdirected frustration of a stranger had somehow pierced the carefully constructed isolation of his life.

Across the city, Bee's eyes grew heavy as she reread their conversation, scrolling through the messages with a sense of wonder at how quickly they'd established a rhythm, a rapport that had been entirely absent during her dinner with Tyler. Her phone slipped from loosening fingers as sleep approached, the device coming to rest on the blanket beside her.

She fell asleep with the ghost of a smile on her lips, her phone still clutched in her hand like a promise.

Chapter Four: The Morning After

Morning crept into Charlie's bedroom through blinds he'd forgotten to close, casting thin stripes of gold across his face. His eyes opened slowly, consciousness returning in gentle waves rather than the usual jolt of alarm. For a moment, he lay perfectly still, savouring the unfamiliar sensation that had followed him from his dreams—a lightness in his chest, a warmth he couldn't immediately place. Then he remembered: the wrong number text, the conversation that had stretched into the night, the strange intimacy of exchanging thoughts with someone who had no idea who he was.

His hand moved before his mind fully formed the intention, reaching for his phone on the nightstand. The screen illuminated his face as he pulled up their conversation, scrolling back through messages that now seemed impossibly intimate for strangers. His lips curved into a smile at her final text: "May your reflection lose the next argument, and may your Boba Fett appreciate your ongoing loyalty."

The clock in the corner of his screen showed 8:42 AM—later than he usually slept, evidence of how long he'd lain awake thinking about their exchange. Charlie sat up, sheets pooling around his waist as he reread portions of their conversation, fingertips tracing over her words as if they might reveal more about her through touch. Retail management in Silver Lake. A finance degree. Vintage postcards and strong opinions about cilantro. Small fragments that constructed a partial image, like looking at someone through frosted glass—the outline clear but the details blurred.

His thumb hovered over the keyboard. Should he text her again? The thought sent an unexpected thrill through him, followed immediately by doubt. What was the protocol for continuing a conversation that had begun by accident? Would she find it strange, intrusive? Or would she welcome it, as he would welcome hearing from her?

Charlie swung his legs over the edge of the bed, toes curling against cold hardwood. His bedroom—like every room in this house—was designed to suggest both luxury and restraint: muted colours, custom furniture, art chosen more for investment value than personal connection. He padded toward the bathroom, phone still in hand, as if distance from it might server this tenuous connection.

The marble floor of his ensuite bathroom sent a chill up through his feet. Charlie set his phone carefully on the counter, where he could see it while he brushed his teeth, while he showered, while he shaved with practiced precision. The screen remained dark. Of course it did—she was at work by now, managing her boutique, dealing with customers who didn't appreciate normal human proportions. The thought made him smile again, toothpaste foam threatening to escape the corner of his mouth.

Water pounded against his skin, hot enough to redden but not quite burn. Charlie closed his eyes, letting it sluice over his head, plastering his hair to his skull. The shower was designed for two, with multiple heads and a bench built into one wall.

Like everything else in this house, it was an aspiration rather than a reality—space for a life he wasn't actually living.

Wrapped in a towel, hair still damp, Charlie returned to his bedroom. The house stretched around him, silent except for the distant hum of air conditioning. No roommates making breakfast, no partner complaining about his wet footprints on the floor, no neighbours' music filtering through shared walls. Just Charlie and the echo of his own movements.

He dressed with the efficiency of someone accustomed to having others watch the process: dark jeans, a simple t-shirt that cost more than it looked like it should, bare feet against the floor. Casual but camera-ready, a habit he couldn't seem to break even on days without appointments. The closet door swung shut with a soft click that seemed to reverberate through the empty room.

In the kitchen, Charlie moved through the ritual of coffee preparation. The machine—imported from Italy, professional grade, capable of producing coffee that would make baristas weep with envy—responded to his touch with mechanical obedience. Beans ground with a whir that momentarily filled the silence. Water heated to the precise temperature. Espresso dripped into a cup that had been warmed on the machine's dedicated cup warmer.

The scent filled the kitchen, rich and complex. Charlie inhaled deeply, letting the aroma centre him. His phone sat on the counter beside the machine, screen still dark. No new messages. He picked it up, opened their conversation again, and began to type: "Good morning. I was thinking about what you said about—"

He deleted it immediately. Too eager. Too presumptuous to assume she wanted to continue their conversation.

He tried again: "Hey, just wanted to say thanks again for the accidental—"

Delete too awkward. Too obviously fishing for response.

Charlie set the phone down, picked up his coffee, and moved to the wall of windows overlooking LA. Morning light gilded the hills, transforming the city into something that looked almost magical from the distance. Down there, she was moving through her day, unaware that he was standing here, thinking about her words, wondering if she was thinking about his.

His phone buzzed. Charlie turned so quickly that coffee sloshed over the rim of his cup, burning his fingers. He set the cup down with more force than necessary, reaching for the device with a surge of anticipation that would have embarrassed him had anyone been there to witness it.

The notification wasn't from her. Just his email, pinging with a message from his agent about scheduling conflicts for an upcoming press tour. Charlie's shoulders dropped slightly as he opened the email, forcing himself to focus on the words. Dates, cities, talk show appearances, photoshoots. The machinery of his career grinding forward, demanding his attention.

He tried to concentrate, he really did. But his gaze kept drifting back to their conversation, thumb scrolling to reread exchanges that now felt like artifacts from another life—one where he was just a man texting a woman, no expectations beyond the pleasure of connection.

"Just text her," he said aloud, voice startling in the quiet kitchen. "What's the worst that could happen?"

Rejection, his mind supplied immediately. Disinterest. The realisation that their connection had been a momentary aberration rather than the beginning of something. Or worse —what if she googled his phone number, discovered who he was, and the entire dynamic shifted? What if genuine conversation morphed into the familiar pattern of people wanting something from him?

Charlie set the phone down and moved to the refrigerator,

pulling it open with more force than necessary. The contents stared back at him, still perfectly arranged by his assistant's assistant, still entirely unappealing. He closed it without taking anything, returning to his coffee, now cooling in the cup.

His footsteps echoed against marble and hardwood as he carried both coffee and phone to his study, the only room where he felt truly comfortable. Here, surrounded by books chosen for content rather than appearance, he might find distraction from the strange pull of a wrong number text that had somehow become the most honest conversation he'd had in years.

The computer screen illuminated as he woke it, displaying a desktop crowded with scripts his agent wanted him to consider. Charlie opened the first one, trying to lose himself in the story, to focus on whether the character was one he could inhabit convincingly. The words blurred before his eyes. He picked up his phone again, opened their conversation, and began to type once more: "I hope your meeting with the celery-shaped clothing suppliers goes well today. My reflection and I have declared a temporary truce, but I suspect hostilities may resume by evening."

His thumb hovered over the send button, doubt and hope warring in his chest. Then, with a decisive motion that belied his uncertainty, he pressed send and set the phone face-down on the desk, turning resolutely back to the script before him.

The message disappeared into the digital ether, carrying with it a question he wasn't quite ready to articulate, even to himself: what would it mean if she responded?

Harrington's occupied the corner of a renovated Art Deco building in Silver Lake, its windows displaying mannequins draped in clothing that suggested both exclusivity and approachability—the perfect balance to attract customers who wanted luxury without ostentation. Inside, track lighting cast a flattering glow over carefully arranged merchandise, the minimalist displays creating negative space that made each garment seem more precious for its isolation. Bee adjusted the sleeve of a silk blouse, aligning it precisely with the edges of the display table. Three years of management had taught her that retail was theatre, and she was both director and leading actress in a production where the wealthiest customers always received the best reviews.

The boutique hummed with quiet activity—two women browsing a rack of summer dresses, a college student hovering near the sales section, a man sitting patiently in one of the velvet chairs positioned strategically for bored companions. Soft music flowed from hidden speakers, the kind of independent artists whose obscurity was their primary appeal. Bee moved through the space with practiced grace, straightening a stack of cashmere sweaters, her burgundy dress and low heels marking her as staff without requiring a name tag. The bell above the door chimed with delicate precision. Bee's spine straightened automatically, shoulders squaring as she turned toward the entrance. Victoria Harrington crossed the threshold with the assured steps of someone who had been born into spaces where others dared not tread. Her ash blonde hair—freshly highlighted, Bee noted— caught the light in a way that suggested both significant expense and regular maintenance. The Hermes bag dangling from her forearm cost more than Bee's monthly rent.

"Bianca," Victoria said, not quite a greeting but an acknowledgement of presence. She prounounced it "Be-ahhn-ca," stretching the syllables into something that felt like a different name entirely. "I need something for the Children's Hospital gala next Saturday. Something appropriate."

"Good morning, Mrs. Harrington," Bee replied, her voice

calibrated to the perfect pitch of deference without obsequiousness. "We just received several pieces that would be perfect for the gala. Let me show you what we have."

Victoria followed her to a rack near the dressing rooms, her gaze sweeping the store with the calculated assessment of a general surveying disputed territory. Bee selected a midnight blue gown with a delicate beading along the neckline, holding it up for inspection.

"Too severe," Victoria declared before Bee had fully extended her arm. "I'm supporting children with cancer, not preparing for their funerals."

Bee's smile remained fixed in place, though something tightened in her jaw, a small muscle flexing beneath smooth skin. "Of course. Perhaps something with colour." She replaced the blue gown and selected a deep emerald dress with a subtle A-line silhouette. "This shade would complement your colouring beautifully."

Victoria's fingers brushed the fabric, her French-manicured nails scraping lightly against the silk. "The cut is matronly. I'm not trying to look like someone's grandmother."

A college-aged girl browsing nearby glanced up at this comment, her eyes meeting Bee's for a fraction of a second—a flash of silent sympathy that Bee acknowledged with the slightest tilt of her head. The girl returned to the rack, but her posture suggested continued eavesdropping.

"We have something more contemporary," Bee offered, moving to another section where newer arrivals hung in careful colour progression. She selected a raspberry gown with an asymmetrical neckline, modern without being too avant-garde. "This designer is very well-received at charity events. Senator Mitchell's wife wore one of his pieces to the gubernatorial dinner last month."

Victoria's lips thinned slightly. "Senator Mitchell's wife

could wear a paper bag and still look desperate for attention. Besides, I wore raspberry to the symphony gala in February. I can't be seen in the same colour palette twice in one season."

Bee nodded as if this were the most reasonable concern imaginable, while ijside her head, a less professional voice wondered how Victoria remembered what she wore to every event but couldn't recall her grandchildren's birthdays—a fact Bee knew from the panicked last-minute gift purchases Victoria often delegated to her or her assistant.

"Let me show you something truly special," Bee said, moving toward the back of the store where the most exclusive piece were displayed. She lifted a champagne-coloured gown from its padded hanger, the fabric catching the light as it moved. "This just arrived yesterday. Only three were made in this could, and we received one specifically with you in mind."

The last part was a carefully crafted fiction—the dress had been ordered for inventory like everything else—but Victoria's expression softened slightly at the suggestion of exclusivity. Even though her last husband gifted this store to her she was still just a shopper. She reached for the gown, fingers exploring the intricate beadwork along the bodice.

"It's...interesting," she admitted, which from Victoria constitued high praise. "But this neckline—I'm not convinced it's appropriate for a children's charity event."

"The designer specifically created this as eveningwear for philanthropic events," Bee countered smoothly. "The less than conservative neckline balances the more dramatic back, allowing you to appear elegant yet conservative enough to not distract from the cause." She turned the dress to reveal the back, which featured a tasteful cutout that suggested sensuality without crossing into impropriety.

Victoria considered this, head tilted in deliberation. A woman in her early thirties approached the counter with a cashmere sweater, clearly ready to purchase. Bee caught the eye of her assistant, who moved to help the customer while Bee remained focused on Victoria.

"This simply won't do for the charity gala," Victoria said, dismissively pushing the dress aside. "I need something that makes a statement without looking desperate, unlike that awful thing the mayor's wife wore last year." She shuddered delicately at the memory. "Sequins before seven PM. As if the rules of decent society no longer apply."

Bee maintained her pleasant expression through sheer force of will. "I completely understand. Perhaps we could look at our designer cookbooks? Several collections are arriving next week, and we could expedite a piece specifically for you."

Victoria checked her watch—a Cartier that gleamed against her tanned wrist. "I suppose that's our only option, given the limited selection here." She gestured vageuly around the boutique, which contained over two hundred carefully curated items. "Though I had hoped to resolve this today. The gala committee meets for lunch tomorrow, and I wanted to casually mention what I'd be wearing."

"Let me bring the lookbooks to the private sitting area," Bee suggested, directing Victoria the cordoned section with plush seating and a small table where champagne often appeared for the most valued customers. "I'll have Meredith bring you something to drink while you browse. Still sparkling water with a twist of lime?"

"A twist of lemon today," Victoria corrected, as if Bee had committed a grave error. "Lime disagrees with my new supplement regimen."

Bee nodded, gesturing for her assistant to fetch the water while she collected several heavy lookbooks from behind the counter. Her shoulders remained perfectly straight, her smile fixed in place, but a small vein pulsed at her temple—the only external sign of the tension building inside her.

For the next forty-five minutes, Bee turned pages, noted

preferences, made suggestions, and absorbed criticisms that ranged grom the reasonable ("That shade of yellow makes everyone look jaundiced") to the absurd ("I can't wear anything with buttons—they photograph poorly from my right side"). Throughout it all, she maintained the pleasant, slightly deferential demeanour that had made her successful in luxury retail despite her private disdain for it excesses.

Other customers came and went. Some cast sympathetic glances toward the private sitting area, where Victoria's voice occasionally rose as she rejected another option. Bee's assistant handled the regular transactions while Bee remained trapped in Victoria's orbit, a satellite unable to break free of gravitational pull.

"This one," Victoria finally declared, pointing to a custom gown that would require rush production and alterations that would cost more than most people's monthly mortgage payment. "But in a cooler shade of ivory—this sample looks too yellow. And the beading should be silver, not gold. Gold washes me out."

"An excellent choice," Bee confirmed, making careful notes on the order form. "I'll contact the designer personally to ensure they understand exactly what you need. We'll arrange fittings as soon as the sample arrives."

Victoria nodded, satisfied at last. "See that they understand the timeline. I won't accept delays." She gathered her bag, already moving mentally to her next appointment. "And Bianca? Make sure they don't send a junior seamstress for the fittings this time. The last one kept pricking me with pins. I'm certain it was intentional."

"Of course, Mrs. Harrington. I'll oversee everything personally."

As Victoria swept toward the door, the bell chiming her exit, Bee felt her facial muscles ache from maintaining her professional expression. The door closed, and she allowed herself exactly three seconds of closed eyes and deep breathing before turning back to the sales floor, where real life—and her phone—awaited.

The bell's gentle chime faded as the door swung shut behind Victoria, taking with it the cloud of expensive perfume and exacting standards that had dominated the boutique for the past hour. Bee's practiced smile dissolved the moment Victoria turned her back, replaced by the brief, unguarded expression of someone who has just removed too-tight shoes after a long day. She rolled her shoulders subtly, releasing tension that had accumulated like sediment, layer upon layer of small irritations compressed into physical discomfort. Her assistant caught her eye from across the store and mimed drinking, her thumb and pinky extended in the universal symbol for "we need alcohol after that." Bee responded with a tiny nod that acknowledged both the sentiment and the impossibility of acting on it during business hours.

"I'll handle the order form," her assistant offered, voice low enough that the single remaining customer—an older woman browsing scarves—couldn't hear. "You look like you need a minute."

"Thanks, Meredith," Bee murmured, gratitude softening her features. "Just going to check inventory in the back."

The small fiction granted her permission to retreat, if only briefly. Bee moved through the boutique with unhurried steps that belied her internal eagerness to escape. The store had entered its mid-morning lull—that quiet period between the early shoppers and the lunch crowd, when sunlight streamed through the front windows, illuminating dust motes that danced in the still air. Music flowed from hidden speakers, a female vocalist whose melancholy lyrics about lost connection seemed suddenly, uncomfortably relevant.

Bee slipped behind a tall display of cashmere sweaters, each folded with mathematical precision to create a gradient of blues from palest sky to deepest navy. Here, partially hidden from both the entrance and the register, she allowed her professional posture to relax. Her shoulders dropped. Her spine curved slightly. The muscles in her face softened into an expression that belonged to Bianca Anderson rather than the retail manager persona she wore like a uniform.

Her phone nestled in the pocket of her dress, its weight suddenly more noticeable as she became aware of it. Bee's fingers dipped into the pocket, extracting the device with quiet reverence of someone handling a secret. The screen illuminated at her touch, displaying the time (11:27 AM) and a notification from her banking app, but nothing from the unknown number that had dominated her thoughts since the previous evening.

She opened their conversation, scrolling back to the beginning—her misdirected rant about Tyler, his unexpected humorous response, the easy flow of their exchange that had stretched into the night. Her thumb traced over the words on the screen, a small smile playing at the corners of her mouth as she reread his description of arguing with his reflection, his defence of his loyalty to Boba Fett, his surprisingly thoughtful movie preferences.

"The Apartment," she whispered, recalling his first choice. Not the response she'd expected from a wrong number text, yet somehow perfect in its unexpectedness. She'd watched it years ago in a film appreciation class, remembered the bittersweet ending, the complex emotions beneath the comedy. It said something about him, that choice—something that intrigued her more than any dating profile ever had.

Would he text again? The question had hovered at the edges of her consciousness all morning, surfacing during quiet moments between customers. She'd caught herself checking her phone more frequently than usual, the gesture becoming almost compulsive. Was it ridiculous to feel this connection to a stranger whose name she didn't even know? A wrong number that had somehow more meaningful than months of carefully curated dating app conversations?

The bell above the door chimed, startling Bee from her reverie. She slipped her phone back into her pocket, shoulders straightening automatically as she stepped out from behind the display. A group of three women entered, chatting among themselves, shopping bags from nearby boutiques suggesting a day of retail therapy in progress. Bee's professional smile reappeared, her voice modulating to the perfect pitch of helpful without hovering as she greeted them.

"Welcome to Harrington's. Please let me know if I can help you find anything specific today."

The next hour dissolved into the familiar rhythm of retail —offering suggestions, retrieving different sizes, providing honest (but tactful) feedback about fit and style. Bee moved through these interactions with practiced ease, her mind partially present while a corner of her thoughts remained wrapped around the text conversation and the stranger behind it. Each time the door opened, she felt the weight of her phone in her pocket, a silent reminder of connection in the midst of transaction.

When the store emptied again, Bee seized the opportunity to refresh the front window display. The task required both creativity and precision—positioning mannequins, adjusting lighting, creating a scene that would entice passerby without looking overtly commercial. She lost herself in the work, hands moving with practiced confidence as she draped a silk scarf just so, angled a mannequin's arm to suggest motion rather than rigidity, adjusted a display of leather bags to catch the light from the street.

Her phone buzzed against her thigh.

Bee's hands stilled, the vibration sending a jolt through her that seemed disproportionate to the small physical sensation. She remained frozen for a moment, mannequin arm still in her grip, heartbeat accelerating in a way that would have embarrassed her if anyone could hear it. It could be anything—a reminder about her dentist appointment, a promotional text from her cell provider, her mother checking in.

It could be him.

She forced herself to complete the adjustment, to step back and assess the composition of the display, to make one final tweak to the lighting. Only when she was satisfied with the arrangement did she allow her hand to drift toward her pocket, fingers brushing against the phone without removing it. Not yet. Not while standing in the front window like a display herself, visible to anyone passing by.

Bee retreated to the counter, checking that Victoria had indeed left the vicinity—the woman had been known to circle back with additional demands if she spotted Bee through the window. The street outside remained free of ash blonde highlights and Hermes bags. Only then did Bee withdraw her phone, illuminating the screen with a touch that felt more significant than it should.

A notification banner displayed a message preview from the unknown number: "I hope your meeting with the celery-shaped clothing suppliers goes well today. My reflection and I have declared a temporary truce, but I suspect hostilities may resume by evening."

Heat bloomed in Bee's chest, a warmth that radiated outward until she felt it in her cheeks. A laugh escaped her, soft but genuine, drawing a curious glance from Meredith who was organising receipts at the other end of the counter. Bee turned slightly away, creating a bubble of privacy around herself and the message.

He had texted again. Had thought about their conversation, remembered details she'd shared, crafted a message that continued their peculiar connection with the same humour and warmth that had marked their exchange. The realisation carried a pleasure that seemed almost illicit in its intensity—this small, private joy in the midst of a workday defined by Victoria Harrington's demands and the performance of professional deference.

Bee's fingers hovered over the keyboard, possibilities unfolding in her mind. She could be casual, friendly but not too eager. Could match his humour with her own. Could acknowledge the strangeness of their connection while nurturing its continuation. The cursor blinked expectantly, awaiting her response.

A small smile played at the corners of her mouth as she began to type, the words flowing naturally, as if continuing a conversation with an old friend rather than a stranger who had entered her life through digital happenstance. In this moment, with Victoria's criticism still echoing in her ears and the weight of professional politeness still heavy on her shoulders, the simple act of responding honestly felt like the most authentic thing she'd done all day.

Chapter Five: Brotherly Advice

Charlie arranged ingredients across the marble island with the precision of a surgeon preparing for an operation—olive oil, garlic, fresh herbs, a selection of vegetables in graduated sizes. The knife in his hand moved with practiced efficiency, but every thirty seconds his eyes darted to his phone, positioned carefully beside the cutting board like a talisman. Its screen remained stubbornly dark, offering no relief from the strange anticipation that had followed him since morning, when he'd sent that text to the wrong-number woman whose words had somehow pierced the carefully constructed isolation of his life.

He checked the time again—five forty-three. No response to his message about the truce with his reflection. Had he overstepped? Been too familiar? Maybe she'd shown the message to friends who pointed out how bizarre it was to continue texting a wrong number. Or perhaps she was simply busy with those celery-shaped clothing suppliers she'd mentioned. The knife's rhythm faltered as Charlie caught himself smiling at the memory of her description.

The kitchen gleamed around him, pendant lights

suspended from the vaulted ceiling casting warm pools across stainless steel and polished stone. Through floor-to-ceiling windows, evening settled over L.A, the sky painted in gradients of amber and lavender. The view had cost millions, but tonight Charlie barely noticed it, his attention fixed on the small rectangle of glass and metal that hadn't lit up in hours.

His phone vibrated suddenly, the sound almost violent against the marble. Charlie's hand jerked, nearly slicing through his fingertip instead of the basil. He wiped his hands hastily on a kitchen towel, reaching for the device with fingers that betrayed an uncharacteristic tremor.

The notification wasn't from her. Just an email from his assistant confirming tomorrow's schedule. Charlie's shoulders dropped as he set the phone down, annoyed at his own disappointment. What was wrong with him? He was behaving like a teenager, not a grown man with a shelf of industry awards and a carefully curated public image.

The security system chimed, announcing an arrival at the gate. Charlie glanced at the panel on the wall, recognising his brother's car. He buzzed John in without checking the from windows, returning to his methodical chopping with renewed focus. By the time the front door opened and familiar footsteps echoed through the foyer, Charlie had composed himself into something resembling normalcy.

"Something smells promising," John called, his voice carrying through the house. "Please tell me it's not one of your sad protein bowls. I cancelled dinner with a very attractive dermatologist for this."

Charlie smiled despite himself. "You're in luck. It's actual food tonight. Homemade pasta."

John appeared in the kitchen doorway, eyebrows lifting in exaggerated surprise. He looked rumpled in the way of someone who cultivated an appearance of not caring about appearances—chambray shirt with sleeves rolled unevenly, dark jeans worn at the knees, hair that suggested either artistic dishevelment or a recent nap. He carried a bottle of wine in each hand.

"Homemade pasta? Who are you and what have you done with my nutritionally regimented brother?" John set the bottles on the counter with a gentle clink. " I brought options. Red for celebration, white for consolation. Your text was cryptic."

Charlie glanced up from his chopping. "What text?"

"Come for dinner. Need to talk." John mimicked Charlie's serious tone, then gestured around the kitchen. "Hence my confusion at this domestic scene. I was expecting career crisis, not...whatever this is." He waved vaguely at Charlie's arrangement of ingredients.

"I can have a conversation without a crisis," Charlie protested, returning to his basil. The leaves released their scent as the knife moved through them, filling the air with the promise of summer.

John made a noncommittal sound, moving around the island to peer at Charlie's work. "You're doing that thing with your face."

"What thing?"

"That thing where you're trying not to smile but failing miserably." John leaned against the counter, studying his brother with the uncomfortable perceptiveness that had always been his gift. "It's disturbing. You look happy."

Charlie's phone vibrated again. His eyes snapped to it instantly, knife pausing mid-chop. The screen illuminated with a notification, and this time the number was hers. Charlie set the knife down with deliberate care, but his hand moved toward the phone with unconscious urgency.

"Wow," John said slowly, watching this display with growing interest. "This is...new."

Charlie barely heard him, already absorbed in reading her

message: "Meeting successfully survived! One supplier actually brought a measuring tape to demonstrate why 'real women' shouldn't wear their jeans. I may have accidentally broken it. My reflection sends her regards to yours—she suggests counselling might help resolve your ongoing conflicts."

A laugh escaped him—not the careful chuckle he deployed during interviews, but something unguarded and genuine. His thumbs moved across the screen immediately, composing a response with the focus of someone defusing a bomb.

"Are you...giggling?" John asked, incredulity colouring his voice. "Who is texting you? Your publicist finally develop a sense of humour?"

Charlie held up one finger in the universal sign for "wait," still typing: "Breaking a measuring tape seems like appropriate response to fashion fascism. My reflection appreciates the suggestion but remains sceptical of therapy—trust issues, apparently. Though we've found common ground in our mutual appreciation of pasta."

He hit send, then looked up to find John staring at him with the expression of someone witnessing a rare astronomical event.

"Okay, Hollywood. Spill it. Who's got you checking your phone like it might explode if you don't answer within three seconds?"

Charlie set the phone down, turning back to his neglected basil with feigned nonchalance. "It's nothing. Just a...a person I've been texting with."

"A person," John repeated, his voice flat with disbelief. "The last time I saw you smile like that at a text, it was your agent telling you Scorsese wanted to meet."

"It's complicated," Charlie said, gathering the chopped basil and transferring it to a small bowl. He reached for the garlic, his movements precise but charged with an energy that belied his attempt at casual dismissal.

John opened the refrigerator, extracting a bottle of sparkling water. "Complicated is your middle name. But this —" he gestured at Charlie with the bottle, "—this is different. You're practically vibrating."

"I got a wrong-number text from a woman ripping on her terrible date," he said, excitement creeping into his voice. "So, I—uh—responded. Pretended to be the bad date." He gestured wildly. "I joked about my action-figure collection and whether asking to meet my mother was too much."

John nearly snorted out his drink. "Professional smooth talker, huh? Hollywood's finest."

"But she wrote back!" Charlie pressed on. "She realised it was a wrong number, but we just kept texting—movies, books, travel disasters..." His words tumbled faster as his smile grew slack-jawed.

John leaned on the counter. "You just kept texting? That's not stalkerish at all."

"Shh!" Charlie wagged a finger, back at the herbs. "It was hilarious. And then..."

He trailed off, noticing John's suddenly calculating look. "What?"

John moved to the stove where tomato sauce was threatening to bubble over. He lowered the flame. "Last time I saw you this worked up was when you thought your co-star was a secret agent."

Charlie's fingers twitched toward his phone, then back to the cutting board. He cleared his throat. "Her name's Bee—Bianca, actually. She works in retail in Silver Lake, has a finance degree, but ended up selling vintage postcards. Thinks cilantro tastes like soap."

John whistled. "I mean, you knew where to find her in a few texts? Impressive, still leaning towards stalkerish." Charlie jabbed him lightly with the knife handle. "Stop. I'm not obsessed—well, maybe a little."

"Does Bee know she's texting People magazine's Sexiest Man Alive 2021?"

Charlie's smile faltered. "No. And that's the magic. She's talking to me, not Charlie Benton." His voice went quiet. "It feels...normal."

John ducked a mock dodge under the knife's arc. "Watch it, Emeril. Some of us don't have stunt doubles."

Charlie laughed, shaking his head. He glanced at his phone. "Her texts have been about her life too, about supplier meetings and twelve-year-old-gymnast sample sizes."

John howled. "She's perfect." He grinned, studying Charlie: the way his shoulders were no longer locked against the world, the genuine lift at the corners of his mouth. "You do know this will get complicated once you drop the fame bomb."

Charlie's face sobered. "I know. But for now..." He looked at his phone, the screen casting a hopeful glow on his features. "For now, it's just me talking to a girl."

John nodded. "You deserve that. And now—more bruschetta prep." They fell into the easy rhythm they'd had long before stardom, companions in cooking and life.

"Managing the boutique in Silver Lake," Charlie said, a smile playing at his lips. "She deals with entitled customers all day. I love the fact that she thinks cilantro tastes like soap."

"That's...specific," John said, studying his brother with growing interest. "How long have you been texting with her?"

"Since last night," Charlie admitted, looking up from the pot with a slightly sheepish expression.

"Last night," John repeated, a grin spreading across his face. "You've been texting for less than twenty-four hours, and you're already cooking homemade pasta and grinning like an idiot every time your phone buzzes. This is gold, Hollywood. Pure gold."

Charlie's cheeks warmed slightly. "It's not—I'm not—"

"Oh, you absolutely are," John laughed, reaching for a cherry tomato from the pile Charlie had meticulously arranged. He popped it into his mouth, grinning around it. "Charlie Benton, serial monogamist and master of the amicable three-month relationship, has a schoolboy crush on a wrong number."

"It's not a crush," Charlie protested, snatching the bowl of tomatoes away from his brother's marauding fingers. "It's just...refreshing to talk to someone without all the baggage."

"Your face suggests otherwise," John said, reaching around Charlie to adjust the flame that had climbed too high while Charlie was distracted. "I haven't seen you this animated about a woman since...actually, I'm not sure I've ever seen you this animated about a woman."

Charlie's phone vibrated again. His head snapped toward it with such speed that John burst into laughter.

"Not a crush at all," John said, shaking his head as Charlie practically lunged for the device. "Totally casual, just refreshing. Got it."

Charlie picked up the phone, unable to suppress the smile that spread across his face as he read her latest message. John watched him, his teasing expression softening into something more thoughtful.

"What's her name again?" he asked, his tone gentler now.

Charlie looked up, his eyes bright with an emotion John hadn't seen in years. "Bianca," he said. "But everyone calls her Bee."

Steam rose from the plates of handmade pappardelle tossed with olive oil, garlic and fresh herbs—simple but executed with the precision that characterised everything in Charlie's life except, apparently, his current emotional state. They had migrated to the kitchen table, a custom piece of burnished walnut positioned to capture the sunset view that Charlie typically admired alone. Wine glasses caught the fading light, casting ruby shadows across the polished surface as John watched his brother over the rim of his glass, his earlier teasing giving way to quiet observation.

"This is actually good," John said, twirling pasta around his fork. "When did you learn to cook like this?"

Charlie shrugged, his attention divided between his plate and his phone, which he'd placed face-up beside his water glass. "Had some time between projects last year. Took a few classes."

"A few classes," John repeated, amused. "Most people binge Netflix between jobs. You master artisanal pasta making."

The kitchen had settled into the gentle hush of evening—the bubbling of the sauce reduced to the occasional pop, the hum of the refrigerator a barely perceptible note beneath their conversation. Outside, Los Angeles transformed into a constellation of lights, each one representing lives in progress, connections being made and broken. Charlie's gaze drifted to the window, then back to his silent phone.

John set down his fork, studying his brother with newfound intensity. The teasing had served its purpose—breaking through Charlie's initial reserve—but now he saw something that demanded a different approach. Charlie's face in repose held an expression John hadn't witnessed in years, perhaps not since before the fame had calcified around his brother like an exoskeleton.

"You look different," John said finally, the observation quieter than his previous needling.

Charlie glanced up, his fork suspended halfway to his mouth. "Different how?"

"I can't quite place it." John tilted his head, squinting slightly as if adjusting focus. "Happy, but not your usual happy. Not the smile you dust off for talk shows or premieres."

Charlie's hand moved unconsciously toward his face, fingers touching the corner of his mouth as if he might feel the difference John observed. "I smile all the time."

"No," John corrected gently. "You perform happiness all the time. This is...something else."

The observation hung between them, more profound than the casual dinner conversation warranted. Charlie looked away, uncomfortable with his brother's scrutiny yet unable to deny the truth in his words. His phone remained stubbornly dark beside his plate, a silent participant in their exchange.

"Tell me about her," John said, reaching for his wine glass again. "Not the resume—boutique manager, finance degree, postcard collector. Tell me what you know about her."

Charlie's expression shifted, wariness giving way to something softer. "She's direct. Says what she thinks without that...filter everyone in our world seems to have. Gets frustrated with customers who expect clothes to magically transform them but aren't willing to accept their actual bodies." He twirled pasta around his fork, gathering his thoughts. "She has this dry sense of humour, particularly about terrible dates. Appreciates old movies but won't pretend to like something just because it's supposed to be a classic."

John nodded, his earlier teasing entirely absent. "And she has no idea who you are."

It wasn't a question, but Charlie answered anyway. "No. She thinks I work behind the scenes in entertainment. I was vague about specifics."

"And you didn't correct her," John observed, watching his brother's face carefully. "Why not?"

Charlie set down his fork, appetite temporarily forgotten. "I was going to, at first. But then the conversation just... flowed. And I realised if I told her who I was, everything would change. It always does."

"It would," John agreed, his tone neutral. "That's reality, Charlie.

"I know." Charlie ran a hand through his hair, the carefully styled strands falling across his forehead. "But for a few hours, I got to be just...a guy. Not Charlie Benton, not a commodity or a photo opportunity or a career advancement strategy. Just someone she found interesting enough to keep texting."

The admission hung in the air between them, more revealing than Charlie had intended. He reached for his wine glass, needing the momentary distraction of a sip, the brief shield it provided against his brother's perceptive gaze.

"So what happens now?" John asked, gentler than before. "You keep texting anonymously? Meet her as some fictional version of yourself? How does that work, exactly?"

Charlie's expression clouded, the joy John had observed earlier now complicated by uncertainty. "I don't know. I haven't thought that far ahead."

"Yes, you have," John countered, knowing his brother too well to accept the evasion. "You've played it out in your head a dozen different ways since last night. I can see it in your face."

Charlie stared down at his plate, the perfectly prepared pasta suddenly less appealing. "If I tell her now, she'll think I was playing some weird game. If I wait longer, it gets worse. If I meet her without telling her, I'm lying by omission. If I never meet her..." He looked up, meeting John's eyes with rare vulnerability. "Then I miss out on whatever this could be."

John nodded, understanding the impossible calculus his

brother faced daily—the careful weighing of privacy against connection, authenticity against protection. "You like her," he said simply. "Not just the idea of her or the anonymity she represents. Her."

"Yes," Charlie admitted, the single syllable carrying unexpected weight. "I do."

His phone vibrated suddenly, screen illuminating with her name. Charlie's eyes darted to it automatically, but he made no move to check the message, his attention remaining fixed on his brother. The moment felt too important to interrupt, even for her.

John noticed the restraint, another sign of how seriously Charlie was taking this conversation. He reached for the bottle, refilling both their glasses with deliberate movements that gave him time to frame his thoughts.

"I've watched you navigate this circus for years." John said finally, setting the bottle down. "Seen you date women who wanted the idea of you, not the reality. Women who were so intimidated by the whole Charlie Benton machine that they never really got to know my brother." He swirled the wine in his glass, the liquid catching the light. "I've also seen how careful you've become. How you hold yourself back even when the cameras aren't rolling, like you're afraid to be genuine with anyone."

Charlie didn't deny it. Couldn't. The observation was too accurate, too close to the bone. "It's easier that way."

"Easier, sure," John agreed. "Also lonely as hell. Which is why seeing you like this—" he gestured at Charlie's entire being, "—actually excited about someone, is kind of a big deal."

Outside, a coyote called, the sound floating through the hills like a question. Charlie's gaze moved to his phone, then back to his brother, his expression caught between hope and hesitation.

"You think I should pursue this," he said, not quite a question.

John leaned forward, elbows on the table, his expression serious despite the casual posture. "I think genuine connections are rare for anyone, famous or not. I think you've spent years building walls to protect yourself, and somehow this woman's texts went right through them."

He reached across the table, hand settling on Charlie's shoulder with firm pressure. "Be careful, Charli. Not just for your sake, but for hers. Fame complicates everything it touches. But don't let fear stop you from something real. You deserve that much."

The advice settled between them, simple yet profound. Charlie nodded, accepting both the encouragement and the warning it contained. His hand moved to his phone, fingers curling around it like something precious yet dangerous—much like the connection it represented.

"I'm going to tell her," he decided, his voice quiet but certain. "Not everything, not yet. But enough that when we meet—if we meet—it won't be built entirely on omission."

John's expression softened with approval. "That's my actual brother talking, not Hollywood Charlie."

Charlie smiled—a real smile, unguarded and slightly lopsided in a way that would never make it to a publicity photo. "Hollywood Charlie wouldn't be this nervous about texting a woman he's never met."

"No," John agreed, raising his glass in a small toast. "But I like the guy who is."

Chapter Six: The Spark Ignites

Three hours after John's departure, Charlie paced the empty hallways of his mansion, his socked feet making no sound against the hardwood floors. The house had returned to its usual silence, but something had shifted in the atmosphere—a subtle change, like air pressure before a storm. His phone remained clutched in his right hand, screen occasionally illuminating his face in the dimming light as he checked it, then darkened again when he found no new messages.

He wandered from his study to the living room, then to the kitchen, a restless circuit that had become familiar over the past hours. John's advice echoed in his mind. "Be careful, Charlie. Not just for your sake, but for hers." The words carried weight, laden with years of watching Charlie navigate the treacherous waters of fame and connection.

In the kitchen, Charlie stopped, placing his phone on the island. The marble felt cool beneath his fingertips as he leaned forward, staring at Bee's contact information—just a number, no photo, no last name. An anonymous connection that somehow felt more real than anything in his carefully curated life.

His hand moved to his hair, fingers raking through the dark strands until they stood in disarray, nothing like the carefully styled look his team created for public appearances. The gesture betrayed his nervousness as he picked up his phone again, opened their conversation thread, and began typing.

"Just saw the trailer for that new superhero movie. Thoughts on whether a man who can control traffic lights is really superhero material?"

His thumb hovered over the send button before he deleted the entire message with a frustrated sigh. Too forced, too obviously fishing for conversation.

He tried again: "Is your reflection still being cooperative? Mine's looking increasingly judgmental about my pasta consumption."

Delete. Too referential to their earlier jokes, maybe pushing the intimacy too quickly.

Charlie's fingers tapped against the marble countertop, a nervous rhythm that matched his quickening thoughts. Why was this so difficult? He'd performed intimate scenes with Oscar-winning actresses, delivered lines crafted by the industry's best writers, yet crafting a simple text to this woman tied his stomach in knots.

He tried once more, typing slowly: "Have you seen that new superhero film? The one where the guy can talk to buildings? My friend dragged me to it last weekend. I'm still trying to understand the plot twist involving the sentient skyscraper."

He read it over twice, then hit send before he could overthink it again. The message disappeared with a soft whoosh, and Charlie set the phone down as if it might burn him. He moved to the refrigerator, opened it without seeing its contents, then closed it again without taking anything. His eyes returned to the phone, still silent on the counter.

Was the message too random? Too presumptuous? Too—

The screen lit up. Charlie moved so quickly he nearly stumbled, grabbing the phone with an eagerness he was glad his brother was no longer there to tease him about.

Bee kicked her apartment door shut behind her, wincing as her shoulder protested the motion. Eight hours of reshuffling the store's summer collection to accommodate fall arrivals had left her body aching in places she hadn't known could ache. She dropped her keys into the ceramic bowl by the door, the metal clinking against its sides with a familiar sound that signalled the blessed end of her workday.

Her shoes came off next, kicked into the corner where they joined a small collection of discarded footwear—a retail manager's graveyard of once-comfortable options that had betrayed her during long shifts. Bee padded in stockinged feet to her kitchen, extracting a bottle of wine from the refrigerator with movements made efficient by routine.

The first sip of Pinot Grigio washed away the remnants of a particularly difficult customer who had insisted that a size 8 should fit her despite all evidence to the contrary. Bee carried her glass to the living room, settling onto her couch with a sigh of relief that seemed to emanate from her very soul.

Her phone buzzed in her pocket. Probably Mia checking in about their weekend plans, or her mother with another not-so-subtle inquiry about her dating life. Bee extracted it with the wariness of someone who'd had enough human interaction for one day.

The number that appeared made her sit up straighter, wine glass paused halfway to her lips. Her wrong number man —as she'd come to think of him—had texted again. Warmth spread through her chest that had nothing to do with the alcohol.

"Have you seen that new superhero film? The one where the guy can talk to buildings? My friend dragged me to it last weekend. I'm still trying to understand the plot twist involving the sentient skyscraper."

A laugh escaped her, surprising in its genuine delight after a day of professional courtesy smiles. She curled her legs beneath her, suddenly energized despite her earlier exhaustion.

"I haven't seen it yet, but now I'm intrigued. A sentient skyscraper sounds more interesting than most of the men on dating apps. At least it has a solid foundation."

She hit send, then immediately followed with another message: "Though I'm not sure I trust the judgement of someone who argues with his reflection. What if the building has reflective surfaces? Will it start arguing back?"

Charlie's response came faster than she expected: "Fair point. Though my reflection and I have established boundaries now. The buildings might need more time to develop healthy communication skills."

Bee's smile widened as she typed: "Speaking of questionable superhero premises, my brother once convinced me that controlling puddles was a legitimate superpower. I spent an entire summer staring intensely at rainwater."

"Did it work?" Charlie replied immediately.

"If by 'IT' you mean making the neighbourhood kids think I was possessed then yes, but sadly my puddle commanding abilities remain dormant to this day."

Their messages flowed back and forth, the conversation shifting effortlessly from superhero critiques to childhood memories of movie theatres with sticky floors and overpriced popcorn.

"I once snuck into an R-rated film at 15," Charlie wrote. "Felt like a master criminal until I realised it was a terrible art house movie where nothing happened for three hours. Karma, I suppose."

"The universe has a sense of humour," Bee replied. "I paid full price to see a film where the main character was a silent sock. Not a puppet—just a sock with googly eyes. My standards were questionable."

Charlie's fingers moved across his screen with increasing confidence, the initial awkwardness fading as their rhythm established itself again. "In my line of work, I've seen some truly terrible productions. The kind where everyone on set knows it's going to bomb but we all pretend it's the next breakthrough hit."

"What exactly do you do in entertainment?" Bee asked. "Director? Producer? The person who makes sure the star's coffee has exactly seven ice cubes?"

Charlie hesitated, then chose his words carefully: "I work with actors mostly. Behind the scenes stuff. Less glamourous than it sounds—a lot of waiting around while people more important than me make decisions."

The partial truth felt uncomfortable, but not as uncomfortable as the full revelation would be. Not yet, at least.

"Sounds more interesting than measuring inseams for people who insist they're two sizes smaller than reality." Bee responded. "Though I did once have to explain to a customer that no, we cannot 'just cut out the size tag' to make her feel better about the number."

Charlie laughed, the sound echoing in his empty kitchen. "Retail therapy indeed."

"Speaking of embarrassing moments," Bee wrote, "has your entertainment work ever rivalled my third-grade talent show disaster? I attempted a magic act where I was supposed to pull a rabbit out of a hat. Instead, I pulled out my mother's underwear that had somehow gotten mixed up with my props. Twenty-five years later, and my family still calls me 'The Magnificent Underwear Girl.'"

Charlie's smile grew wider as he pictured this younger version of Bee, mortified but perhaps already showing the directness and humour he'd come to appreciate in their brief acquaintance.

"That's actually impressive," he typed back. "The most embarrassing thing I've done is show up to an important meeting with my shirt inside out. No one told me until after a two-hour presentation where I kept wondering why people were smirking."

In her apartment, Bee laughed, loud and uninhibited, nearly spilling her wine. She couldn't remember the last time a text conversation had felt this easy, this genuine. She typed quickly: "Please tell me it was a shirt with an obvious front-to-back difference. Like a band logo or 'Professional' written across it."

"Worse," Charlie replied. "It had care instructions and a size label clearly visible at my collar. Nothing says 'take me seriously' like 'Machine Wash Cold' hovering beneath your chin."

Charlie settled against his kitchen counter, a genuine smile softening his features for the first time in weeks. Outside, Los Angles continued its evening rhythm—cars navigating winding roads, lights flickering on in distant windows, lives unfolding in parallel to his own. But for once, the mansion didn't feel quite so empty, the silence not quite so absolute. Somewhere across the city, Bee was laughing at his jokes, sharing her stories, creating a connection that defied the usual barriers of his existence.

His phone buzzed again, and Charlie felt something he hadn't experienced in longer than he cared to admit—the simple, uncomplicated joy of looking forward to someone's next words.

As their conversation flowed, Charlie abandoned the kitchen's harsh overhead lighting for the softer ambiance of his living room. He sank into the leather couch facing the wall of windows, Los Angeles spreading below him like a sea of stars—countless lives contained in each pinpoint of light. His mansion hummed with its usual emptiness, but the constant vibration of his phone created the illusion of company, of connection reaching across the city's sprawl to wherever Bee was at this moment.

He wondered which of those distant lights might be hers. Was she in an apartment with roommates? A small house? Did she have plants she forgot to water, books stacked by her bedside, mismatched furniture collected over years rather than ordered in a single delivery like his own?

His phone buzzed again, pulling him from his reverie: "My retail horror stories could fill volumes. The woman today insisted she was a summer when she was clearly an autumn. I've never seen someone so offended by colour theory."

Charlie smiled, thumb moving across the screen: "In my world, people regularly throw tantrums about the shade of blue in a scene. Ocean blue, not sky blue! As if the camera can tell the difference."

Across the city, Bee moved from her living room to her bedroom, bringing her wine glass and phone with her. The day's fatigue lingered in her shoulders, but her mind felt more alert than it had all day. She set her wine on the nightstand and reached for the lavender candle that had been a self-care purchase after a particular difficult week at the boutique. The match struck with a soft hiss, flame catching the wick and casting a warm glow across her space.

She settled against her pillows, the scent of lavender slowly filling the room as she returned to their conversation. His response about blue shades made her laugh—another glimpse into his world of entertainment production that seemed both foreign and somehow familiar in its absurdity.

"The customer is always right, even when they're objectively, scientifically wrong about what season they are," she typed back. "Though I suppose your blue-tantrum people sign bigger checks than my colour theory deniers."

Charlie's response came quickly: "Bigger check, bigger egos. Ever notice how the most insecure people are often the loudest about their preferences?"

Bee bit her lip, considering this. The conversation had shifted, moving from anecdotes toward something more reflective. She typed carefully: "All the time. The woman with the most vocal opinions about our dress sizes is always the one most uncomfortable with her own body. The loudest dates are the ones with the least to say."

In his mansion, Charlie's fingers hovered over the screen, sensing the opening toward more personal territory. The blue light illuminated his face in the darkened room, the city lights a distant backdrop to his solitude.

"It's strange," he wrote, "how hard it is to find people who are just...real. Especially in my industry. Everyone's performing all the time, even when the cameras aren't rolling." He paused, then added: "I've gotten so used to it that sometimes I forget what genuine connection feels like."

He hit send, then immediately regretted the vulnerability of the admission. Would it seem strange, too intense for what was still essentially a conversation between strangers? Charlie set the phone beside him on the couch, rubbing his palms against his thighs as he waited, a nervous gesture left over from childhood auditions.

Bee stared at his message, something in his words

resonating with an unexpected depth. The candle flame flickered as she shifted, casting dancing shadows across her walls. There was an honesty in his admission that felt rare—the kind she hadn't encountered in years of dating profiles and first-date performances.

"I understand that more than you might think," she wrote back. "Retail is its own kind of performance. I smile through rudeness, pretend wealthy clients are fascinating when they're tedious, nod sympathetically about fashion emergencies that are really just entitlement in disguise." She paused, then added: "Dating feels the same lately. Everyone trying to present their most marketable version instead of their actual selves. It's exhausting."

Charlie read her response, his heartbeat quickening at the resonance between their experiences. He leaned forward, elbows on knees, suddenly more engaged in this text exchange than he had been in conversations with people physically present in his life for months.

"Exactly," he typed, fingers moving with urgency. "It's like everyone's trying to sell something—themselves, their image, their personal brand. I keep meeting people who want something from me, not actual connection." The admission skirted dangerously close to revealing his fame, but contained enough universal truth to pass as normal frustration.

Bee's response appeared moment later: "The number of dates I've endured where the guy spent two hours giving me his resume instead of having a conversation...I've started to think genuine interest is extinct in the wild."

Charlie laughed, the sound warm in his otherwise silent house. "Exhibit A: Your finance bro from the original wrong number text. I'm still not over him mansplaining investment strategies to someone with a finance degree."

"He represents a specific subspecies of L.A male." Bee replied, a smile playing at her lips as she typed. "Wears watches worth more than my car, orders expensive wine but doesn't know how to taste it, thinks dropping names is a personality trait."

Their conversation shifted again, flowing into preferences and opinions that revealed the contours of their personalities. Charlie confessed his love for classic novels that most people only pretended to have read, while Bee admitted her collection of true crime books that sometimes gave her nightmares but she couldn't stop reading.

"Pet peeve: people who stand on the wrong side of escalators," Charlie wrote

"People who talk during movies." Bee countered

"Loud chewing," from Charlie

"Men who call women Missy," from Bee

"Reality TV presenters who say literally when they mean figuratively," Charlie added.

"People who bring fourteen items to the ten items or less checkout," Bee responded.

Each exchange revealed another facet of their personalities, another point of connection that seemed to bridge the digital distance between them. Charlie found himself laughing more frequently than he had in months, genuinely amused by her observations rather than performing the careful chuckle he deployed during interviews.

In her bedroom, Bee caught herself biting her lip as she waited for his responses, her wine forgotten on the nightstand as the conversation consumed her attention. She laughed aloud at his description of being trapped in a car with a driver who played only pan flute covers of 80s power ballads—"A very specific circle of hell Dante somehow overlooked."

The candle burned lower, shadows lengthening across her walls, but she barely noticed the passing time. There was something freeing about this conversation—no pressure to impress, no careful self-editing to appear more dateable, just the easy flow of thoughts between two people who seemed to understand each other's frequency.

"I can't remember the last time I connected with someone this easily," Charlie wrote, the admission slipping out before his usual caution could intervene. "It's usually like pulling teeth to get past the small talk."

Bee stared at his words, feeling a flutter of something warm and terrifying in her chest. "I'm usually much more guarded," she admitted. "Ask my friends—they'll tell you I have trust issues the size of small countries. But this is... different somehow."

Charlie read her message, his breathing catching slightly. He ran a hand through his hair, a smile spreading across his face that no one was there to witness—genuine, unguarded, reaching his eyes in a way that would have startled his publicist with its authenticity.

"Different is good," he typed back. "Different is refreshing."

In her bedroom, Bee hugged a pillow to her chest with her free arm, the candle's glow illuminating her smile. "Different is terrifying," she replied, then immediately followed with: "But in a good way. Like standing at the edge of something exciting rather than dangerous."

Charlie's heart raced as he read her words. This connection with Bee felt like finding something he hadn't realised he was missing—authenticity in a world of careful performance, genuine interest in a landscape of transaction. It terrified him, yes, but also exhilarated him in equal measure.

The night deepened around them both—Charlie in his mansion overlooking the city, Bee in her apartment with its flickering candlelight. Separated by distance and circumstance, yet somehow creating a space between them that felt more real than the physical rooms they occupied. Their conversation continued to flow, each message a step further into unfamiliar yet welcoming territory, guided only by the strange certainty that this accidental connection was something worth exploring, despite—or perhaps because of—the uncertainty that surrounded it.

The clock on Charlie's phone showed 1:17 AM when he finally noticed the time. Their conversation had flowed so naturally that hours had slipped by unacknowledged, the outside world fading to irrelevance compared to the words appearing on his screen. He had migrated from the living room to his bedroom without any conscious decision, drawn by habit rather than fatigue. Now he stood before the floor-to-ceiling windows, city lights spread below him like fallen constellations, his reflection a ghostly presence against the glass. Sleep seemed an intrusion, an unwelcome reminder that this connection, however compelling, existed in limited hours stolen from the edges of their separate lives.

"I just realised it's past midnight," he typed, fingers moving more slowly now, reluctant to acknowledge the hour. "Time apparently ceases to exist during good conversations."

Across the city, Bee lay in her bed, the lavender candle long since extinguished, only her bedside lamp casting a warm circle of light around her. She'd changed into sleep shorts and an oversized t-shirt at some point, the day's work clothes discarded on a chair, but sleep remained far from her mind. Her phone buzzed with his message, illuminating her face in the dimness.

"My alarm clock is judging me harshly," she replied. "Apparently, I have to be a functioning human in six hours. Though I am not convinced that is actually necessary."

Charlie smiled at her response, turning from the window to sit on the edge of his bed. His bedroom—designed by a celebrated interior decorator who had insisted on a palette of soothing neutrals—felt strangely impersonal compared to the vibrant presence he sensed behind Bee's messages. He wondered what her space looked like. Colourful, he guessed. Lived-in. Actually personal rather than professionally "personalised".

"What would you do if functioning wasn't required?" he asked. "If retail management wasn't the necessity it is?"

The question hung between them, more intimate somehow than their earlier exchanges. It asked not about past experiences or present circumstances, but future desires—the dreams people often kept guarded, protected from casual scrutiny.

Bee stared at his message, lips pursed in consideration. No one had asked her this in a long time. Dates wanted to know her job, her hobbies, her taste in music—surface details that required little vulnerability. Even friends tended to accept her current path without questioning whether it aligned with deeper aspirations.

"I'd open my own place," she finally typed, the admission coming easier than expected. "Not just retail—a community space. Part boutique, part gallery for local artists, part work-shop where people could learn to make or mend their clothes. A place that celebrates creativity and sustainability rather than just consumption."

She paused, then added: "I have a business plan drafted. Been saving for three years. Probably need another two before it's realistic."

In his bedroom, Charlie read her words with growing warmth. He could see it clearly—Bee in a sunlit space, arranging displays with the same care she likely brought to her current job, but with the freedom to follow her own vision rather than someone else's. The image felt right, aligned with the person he was coming to know through these digital exchanges.

"That sounds incredible," he wrote back. "A space that

reflects your values instead of just making someone else money. I'd visit on opening day."

"Bold promise for someone who doesn't know where it would be located," Bee teased, but the message carried a pleased undertone he could almost hear despite the digital medium.

"I'd make the trip," Charlie replied simply. Then, curious: "What would you call it?"

"ThreadBare," Bee answered immediately. "One word. Capital B in the middle. It's a play on words—threads as in clothing, bare as in honest and stripped down to essentials."

"Perfect," Charlie typed, smiling at how clearly she had thought this through. "I can already see the logo."

"What about you?" Bee countered. "If the entertainment industry didn't have its hooks in you, what would you be doing?"

Charlie's hands stilled over the screen. The question should have been simple, but in his reality, it carried complications she couldn't understand. What would he do without fame, without the constant performance his life had become? He barely remembered the person he'd been before that first big role, before his name became a brand rather than just an identity.

"Something quieter," he finally wrote. "Maybe teaching. Drama, probably. Helping people find their voice instead of always using mine." The admission felt more revealing than he'd intended, hovering dangerously close to truths he wasn't ready to share.

Bee sensed something vulnerable in his response, though she couldn't quite identify its source. She rolled onto her side, cradling the phone closer as if proximity might bridge the digital gap between them.

"You'd be good at that," she replied. "You listen. That's rarer than it should be."

A comfortable silence settled between them, both aware of the hour but neither willing to be the first to suggest ending the conversation. Charlie moved fully onto his bed, back against the headboard, legs stretched out across the custom mattress.

"Important question," he typed suddenly. "One that reveals true character. Is cereal a soup?"

Bee's laugh echoed in her bedroom, unexpected and genuine. "Absolutely not," she replied immediately. "Soup is cooked. Cereal is cold. Non-negotiable distinction."

"Gazpacho is cold," Charlie countered. "Still soup. Cereal sits in liquid with floating components. Textbook soup behaviour."

"By that definition, my bath is soup if I drop a loofah in it," Bee argued. "Temperature aside, soup requires intentional flavour development. Cereal is just victim to milk."

Charlie grinned at her response. "Victim to milk? That's the most poetic cereal description I've ever heard. But what about oatmeal? Hot cereal that's suspiciously soup adjacent."

"Oatmeal is porridge," Bee stated definitively. "Entirely different food category with its own rich taxonomical history. I won't be taking questions."

Their debate shifted seamlessly to whether a hot dog qualified as a sandwich, "It's clearly a taco," Bee insisted, while Charlie maintained it was "a sandwich that failed to commit fully to the bit", whether pineapple belonged on pizza, both agreed it did, though Charlie confessed this opinion had once caused a near-riot on a film set he refused to name, and whether coffee counted as a soup or a tea, both agreed this question was too philosophically complex for the late hour.

As their playful arguments wound down, Charlie felt the weight of time pressing against him. His eyes burned slightly from staring at the screen, but the thought of ending their conversation left him cold. His thumb hovered over the keyboard, uncertain how to navigate this transition without seeming either too eager or too dismissive.

He typed: "I should probably let you get some sleep. Early morning retail emergencies await."

Then deleted it immediately. Too presumptuous, assuming she needed his permission to end the conversation.

He tried again: "It's getting late, but I've really enjoyed talking with you."

Deleted again. Too obvious, too needy somehow.

Finally, he settled on: "I've really enjoyed talking with you tonight. Haven't connected with someone like this in a long time."

His thumb hovered over the send button, doubt and hope warring in his chest. The message felt too revealing, too honest —and yet anything less would be disingenuous after the hours they'd spent in conversation. With a small breath, he hit send, watching the message disappear with a mixture of relief and trepidation.

In her bedroom, Bee stared at his words, something warm unfurling in her chest. Her fingers hovered over the screen, uncertainty momentarily freezing her response. The sincerity in his message deserved equal honesty, but expressing it felt like stepping onto uncertain ground—acknowledging that this wrong number exchange had become something meaningful, something she wasn't quite ready to name.

"I feel the same way," she finally typed. "This conversation has been the highlight of my week. Maybe longer."

Charlie read her response, his breath catching slightly. He hadn't realised how much he'd been bracing for rejection until relief flooded through him at her words.

"We should do it again sometime," he wrote, the casualness of the phrase belying the significance he felt. "Though maybe starting earlier so we're not both zombies the next day."

"Definitely," Bee replied, her smile evident even in the

single word. "Though I make a very fashionable zombie. The boutique customers might not even notice the difference."

Charlie laughed softly: "Goodnight, Bee. Sweet dreams."

"Goodnight, wrong number," she responded. "May your reflection be kinder to you in the morning light."

With the final exchange, silence settled over both their spaces. Charlie remained sitting against his headboard, phone still in hand, unwilling to set it aside just yet. He scrolled back through their conversation, reading passages at random, her story about the talent show disaster, his confession about inside-out shirts, their debate about movie endings and soup definitions. Each exchange revealed another facet of connection, another thread binding them across the digital void.

Across the city, Bee hugged her phone to her chest for a moment, eyes closed, a smile playing at her lips. The simple gesture felt both childish and necessary—a physical acknowledgement of something that existed only in digital space but had somehow pierced the careful barriers she maintained against disappointment. Finally, she placed the phone on her nightstand, switched off her lamp, and settled into the darkness of her bedroom.

Neither fell asleep immediately. Charlie stared at the ceiling, replaying moments from their conversation, analysing his own responses, wondering if he'd revealed too much or too little. The weight of his unshared identity pressed against him, a complication he'd eventually have to address. But for now, in the quiet darkness of his bedroom, he allowed himself to simply appreciate the unexpected gift of genuine connection.

In her apartment, Bee curled onto her side, eyes open in the darkness, mind still buzzing with their exchanges. She'd shared things with this stranger that she rarely discussed with friends—her dreams for ThreadBare, her frustrations with frustrations with superficial connections, her childhood embarrassments. The ease of it all should have frightened her, but instead it felt like rediscovering something long missed, something worth protecting and nurturing despite the uncertainty.

Both eventually drifted toward sleep, carried by the gentle current of possibility that flowed between them—unspoken but undeniably present, fragile but persistent, complicated but worth exploring. Their last conscious thoughts mirrored each other across the city: wondering what tomorrow's messages might bring, and hoping they wouldn't have to wait too long to find out.

Chapter Seven: Digital Dance

Charlie woke with a jolt, his hand already reaching for his phone before his eyes fully opened. The screen illuminated his face in the pre-dawn darkness, casting sharp shadows across features still soft with sleep. No new messages. He exhaled, a sound that seemed to echo in the vastness of his bedroom, and set the phone down with deliberate care. Too eager. The sheets rustled as he pushed them aside, bare feet meeting the cool hardwood with a shock that didn't quite dispel the lingering disappointment.

Outside his windows, Los Angeles still slumbered, the city lights dimming as the first hints of dawn crept above the eastern hills. Charlie moved to the glass, pressing his palm against its cool surface as if reaching for the invisible connection stretching across those miles of concrete and asphalt. Somewhere out there, Bee slept, perhaps with her phone nearby as his was, perhaps thinking of their conversation as he had been before sleep finally claimed him.

"Ridiculous," he murmured to his reflection, the word forming a small cloud on the glass. He was Charlie Benton—

sought after by directors, pursued by admirers, never lacking for attention. Yet here he stood, anxious about texting a woman who didn't even know his full name.

His phone remained where he'd left it, a dark rectangle against the pale sheets. Charlie turned away from it, padding through the doorway into the hallway beyond. The house stretched around him, cavernous and quiet. His footsteps echoed against marble and hardwood as he moved from his bedroom to the kitchen, trailing his fingers along the wall as if to confirm his own solidity.

The coffee machine hummed to life under his touch, its familiar ritual offering none of the comfort it usually provided. Charlie's gaze drifted back toward the bedroom, toward the phone waiting there. He drummed his fingers against the counter, a nervous rhythm that matched the coffee's slow drip.

"She's busy," he told the empty kitchen. "She's sleeping. She's not thinking about some wrong number."

But the conversation had felt like more than that, a connection that transcended its accidental beginnings. He remembered her words from the night before: "This conversation has been the highlight of my week. Maybe longer." The memory sent a current of warmth through him that no coffee could match.

Charlie abandoned the half-filled cup, returning to the bedroom with steps that grew more purposeful with each stride. The phone sat untouched, exactly as he'd left it. He grabbed it, thumb moving to unlock the screen with practised motion. Their conversation history appeared, messages stretching back to her initial misdirected rant.

His thumb hovered over the keyboard. What to say? Something casual, friendly but not presumptuous. Charlie began to type: "Good morning, Just wondering if—"

He deleted it immediately. Too formal.

He tried again: "Hey, hope your day starts better than—"

Delete. Too generic, too much like a line he'd delivered in a romantic comedy.

The minutes ticked by as Charlie paced the length of his bedroom, phone clutched in his hand like a lifeline. Each step carried him past another artifact of his carefully curated existence—the awards shelf he never looked at, the closet full of designer clothes selected by stylists, the art chosen for investment value rather than personal connection.

The sun breached the horizon fully now, flooding the room with golden light that would have looked stunning in a photograph but merely emphasised the emptiness to Charlie's eyes. He stopped by the window again, watching as L.A stirred to life below—cars crawling along distant highways, early joggers traversing palm-lined streets, the city shaking off sleep and assuming its daytime persona.

Just as Charlie did before every public appearance.

The realisation struck him with unexpected force. With Bee, there had been no performance, no carefully constructed responses designed to maintain his image. Just conversation, flowing with an ease he'd forgotten was possible.

His fingers moved across the screen before doubt could intervene again: "My reflection and I reached an agreement this morning. He gets the good side of the mirror if I get the first cup of coffee. I think I was swindled. How's the retail front today? Any customers insisting their colour season has magically changed overnight?"

Charlie read it over once, the corner of his mouth lifting in a smile that reached his eyes. Without allowing himself another moment of hesitation, he hits send. The message disappeared with a soft whoosh, carried across the city to wherever Bee began her day.

The weight of anticipation settled in his chest as he set the phone down. Not expectation—he'd had enough of that in his career—but something lighter, more buoyant. Possibility. Charlie returned to the kitchen, retrieved his abandoned coffee, and moved through the rest of his morning routine with his phone always within reach, always within sight.

Across the city, fluorescent lights buzzed overhead as Bee arranged a display of summer dresses, her hands moving with practised precision despite her sleep-deprived state. The boutique wouldn't open for another hour, but Victoria Harrington insisted on fresh displays each week, positioned just so to catch the morning light through the front windows. Bee stifled a yawn, blinking against the harsh overhead lighting that made everything look slightly washed out, slightly less than real.

"The blue one needs to be centred," called her assistant from the register, where she counted the previous day's receipts with meticulous attention. "Victoria mentioned it specifically yesterday."

Bee nodded, shifting the dress on its mannequin with a small sigh. Victoria's micromanagement extended to every aspect of the boutique, from display arrangements to the precise temperature of the water offered to customers. Some days, Bee found it harder than others to maintain her professional demeanour in the face of such exacting standards. Today, with only five hours of sleep cushioning her from yesterday's frustrations, the challenge felt particularly acute.

Her phone buzzed in the pocket of her dress, the vibration startling against her thigh. Bee glanced toward her assistant, who remained absorbed in her counting, then slipped the device from her pocket with practised discretion. The screen illuminated with a notification, and Bee's heartbeat quickened as she recognised the number—her wrong number man, texting again.

The fluorescent lights suddenly seemed less harsh, the

boutique's clinical perfection less oppressive. Bee ducked behind a tall rack of designer coats, using their bulk to shield her from view as she opened his message. A smile bloomed across her face as she read his words, warmth spreading through her chest and into her fingertips as they hovered over the screen.

"Tell your reflection he's been scammed," she typed back, her thumbs moving with eager precision. "Coffee negotiations require at least three witness signatures and a notary. Retail chaos already in full swing—had a woman try to return a dress she clearly wore to an event, complete with wine stain that she insisted was a manufacturing defect in the dye. When I pointed out the stain smelled like Cabernet, she asked to speak to my manager. Plot twist: I am the manager. Her face achieved a shade of red that precisely matched the wine."

Bee sent the message, then immediately tucked the phone back into her pocket as her assistant rounded the corner with a clipboard in hand. "Inventory sheets," the younger woman said, holding them out. "And Victoria called. She'll be stopping by this afternoon to check the new display."

Nodding, Bee accepted the clipboard, her professional mask sliding back into place even as the warmth of the text exchange lingered inside her. The boutique's precise lighting, designed to flatter both merchandise and customers, created pools of brightness that never quite reached the corners where shadows collected like secrets. Bee moved through these contrasting zones as she returned to work, straightening dresses and arranging accessories with renewed energy.

Her phone remained a warm weight against her hip, a tangible connection to the man whose morning unfolded in ways she could only imagine—perhaps in a small apartment with morning sun streaming through blinds, or in a crowded house with roommates shuffling through shared spaces. Whatever his reality, it had intersected with hers through an accident of digits, creating a connection that now felt like the most genuine part of her carefully managed days.

Outside, L.A continued its morning transformation—the same sun illuminating both Charlie's hillside sanctuary and Bee's carefully curated retail stage, the same air carrying messages between their devices, the same city holding them in separate orbits that had, against all odds, begun to converge.

Later in the morning found Charlie in his home theatre, sprawled across a leather recliner designed for optimal movie viewing but now serving as his texting headquarters. The massive screen before him remained dark, the film he'd intended to watch forgotten as him attention fixed on the much smaller screen in his hands. His thumbs hovered over the keyboard, a smile playing at his lips as he composed his morning message to Bee. Three days into their accidental connection, and already it had developed its own rituals, its own rhythms—the good morning text had become his favourite part of waking up.

"My reflection sends his regards," he typed, continuing their ongoing joke. "He's still bitter about the coffee negotiation but has moved on to complaining about my choice in breakfast cereal. Apparently, adults shouldn't eat anything with marshmallows. How's the boutique this morning? Any fashion emergencies requiring your expertise?"

Across town, Bee flipped the boutique's sign to "Open," her phone buzzing in her pocket as she did. She glanced over her shoulder, confirming her assistant was occupied with the register, then slipped behind a tall display rack. His message made her smile, the brightness of it catching her by surprise in the still-quiet store.

"Your reflection sounds like my mother," she replied quickly. "Next he'll be asking when you're getting a real job and settling down. Store just opening, but I've already had a call from someone asking if we can hold a dress in a size we don't carry because she's planning to lose fifteen pounds before Saturday, I admire her optimism if not her planning skills."

She tucked her phone away as the first customer pushed through the door, the familiar bell chiming her return to professional reality. But the warmth of their exchange lingered, carrying her through the morning's tasks with an energy that hadn't been present in weeks.

By midday the next day, their exchanges had developed a comfortable rhythm. Charlie's phone chimed as he sat in a production meeting, the vibration drawing his gaze even as the director outlined changes to the upcoming schedule. He angled the screen discreetly under the table, a smile threatening to break his carefully neutral expression as he read Bee's message.

"SOS. Customer just asked if we have a dress like the one in that movie with the blonde actress who dated that famous guy. When I asked for more details, she said, You know the one. She wore it to that event. I've offered to show her our entire inventory but she insists I should know exactly which dress she means. Send help."

Charlie bit his lip to suppress a laugh, earning a curious glance from his agent across the table. He waited until attention had shifted back to the production notes before typing a response.

"Clearly it's the blue dress. Or possibly the red one. The one with the fabric. From the scene where she walked and possibly also talked. How are you not getting this? So unprofessional."

Bee read his response while hiding in the stockroom, her hand pressed against her mouth to stifle her laughter. The text exchange had become a lifeline during her workday, small moments of connection that made the hours of customer service more bearable.

"What exactly do you do in entertainment?" she asked later, curiousity finally overcoming her reluctance to seem too inquisitive. "You have mentioned sets and directors before. Are you a producer? Writer? Make-up?"

Charlie stared at her question, tension creeping into his shoulders. The truth hovered at his fingertips—"I'm an actor, actually. One you've probably seen in theatres or streaming"—but he couldn't bring himself to type those words. Not yet. Not when this connection felt so refreshingly free of the expectations that accompanied his name.

"Like I said I work mostly behind the scenes," he wrote back, choosing each word with care. "Production stuff. Making sure things run smoothly. A lot of problem-solving and managing egos. Hollywood magic is mostly just people with clipboards making sure everything happens on schedule."

The partial truth sat uncomfortably in his chest, but the conversation flowed on, shifting to safer topics—their shared hatred of people who talked during movies, their mutual addiction to a specific bran of mint chocolate ice cream, their agreement that morning people and night owls could never truly understand each other's experience of the world.

On the third morning, Charlie woke to a longer message from Bee, sent late the previous night after they'd said their virtual goodnights.

"I keep thinking about what you asked the other day, about what I would do if money weren't an issue. I have never really told anyone about what I told you, the dream of opening up my own place. My desire for it not to just be another boutique, but something different, something more. I thought people would find it weird and a waste of time. Some days at work, when Victoria is being particularly demanding, I close my eyes and imagine the layout of my own store, the artists I'd feature, the community we'd build. Anyway, just wanted to share with you that...well, I haven't shared that with anyone until you. Sweet dreams."

Charlie read the message twice, then a third time, something warm unfolding in his chest at her willingness to share this dream with him. He sat up in bed, propped against pillows that rivalled a luxury hotels' and composed a response that matched her vulnerability with his own.

"I don't think it is weird at all, I think it's an incredible idea. I'm truly honoured that you chose to share that with me. Perhaps it's the anonymity that makes it easier to confide in a stranger, much like patrons opening up to a bartender. For what it's worth, I'd invest in ThreadBare without hesitation."

By the fourth day, their exchanges had developed layers of meaning, inside jokes building upon shared references that required no explanation between them. Morning greetings evolved to include updates from their respective reflections. Midday messages carried them through work frustrations. Evening exchanges stretched longer, deeper, more personal as they retreated to their separate homes but shared a growing digital intimacy.

"The customer who wanted the movie dress returned today," Bee typed one afternoon while hiding behind a display of cashmere sweaters. "She's decided it was pink, not blue, or red, and worn by a brunette actress who dated a musician, not a blonde who dated an actor. Progress! Though she still thinks I should instinctively know which dress. I almost sent her to your department to look for the mysterious film in question."

Charlie received her message during a costume fitting, the tailor pinning his sleeve as he checked his phone. The smile that spread across his face caught the attention of the wardrobe supervisor, who exchanged a knowing glance with the makeup artist. Charlie Benton, known for his professional focus during preparation, now seemed perpetually distracted by his phone.

"My department would only confuse her further," he replied. "We'd start asking which filter was used in the scene and whether the dress moved from stage left or stage right. Film people are the worst. You've been warned."

When his phone chimed with her response, Charlie felt a physical reaction that startled him with its intensity—a quickening heartbeat, a warmth that spread from his chest to his fingertips, a smile he couldn't suppress even when his publicist gave him a curious look across the room. The anticipation of her words had become a physical sensation, a Pavlovian response to the simple electronic tone.

Meanwhile, Bee folded sweaters with mechanical precision, her hands knowing the motions without requiring her full attention. Her mind drifted to their conversation from the previous evening—his description of a sunset viewed from his window, her account of a childhood memory involving a failed attempt at baking that resulted in a kitchen evacuation. The intimacy of these exchanges, the gradual revealing of selves through carefully chosen anecdotes and observations, had begun to colour her days with anticipation.

"You're smiling at that sweater like it just told you a secret," her assistant commented, eyebrows raised in curious amusement. "Same one as yesterday, and the day before. Something you want to share with class?"

Bee arranged the final sweater on the display, her cheeks warming slightly under her colleague's knowing gaze. "Just remembering something funny," she deflected, though the explanation felt hollow even to her own ears.

That evening, their exchange ventured into territory that

acknowledged the strangeness of their connection, the unexpected depth it had developed in less than a week.

"Do you ever think about how random this all is?" Charlie typed from his balcony, the city lights spread below him like fallen stars. "If you hadn't misdirected that rant about your terrible date, if I hadn't decided to joke back instead of ignoring it, if either of us had been too busy to continue the conversation...so many points where this connection might never have formed."

Bee read his message in her bathtub, bubbles gradually dissolving around her as the water cooled. Her fingers hovered over the screen, droplets falling onto the glass as she composed her reply.

"I think about that a lot, actually. How the most significant connections often come from the most unexpected sources. I've been on dozens of carefully arranged dates that led nowhere, but accidentally texted a wrong number and found someone who actually gets me. Maybe there's something to be said for randomness over algorithms. For what it's worth, I'm glad your number was one digit off from Finance Bro. The universe has a strange way of getting things right sometimes."

Charlie read her words with a sensation that felt dangerously close to falling—that moment of suspended breath before gravity claims you completely. Five days of text exchanges, of morning greetings and midday confessions and evening revelations, had somehow created a connection more genuine than relationships he'd spent months cultivating in person. Her words existed in a space untouched by his fame, uncoloured by expectations or agendas, and in that space, something fragile and essential had begun to take root.

"Me too," he typed back, the simple response carrying more weight than its brevity suggested. "More than I can properly express in a text."

. . .

The week ended as it had begun—with Charlie on his balcony, phone in hand, the vast sprawl of L.A transforming below him as sunset painted the sky in strokes of amber and rose. Six days since Bee's misdirected text had breached the carefully constructed walls of his existence. Six days of conversations that had quickly become the axis around which his hours revolved. The evening air carried the scent of jasmine from the gardens below, but Charlie barely noticed, his attention fixed on the screen where he was attempting to frame thoughts that felt too significant for the medium that contained them.

His fingers moved across the keyboard with uncharacteristic hesitation, composing and deleting words that seemed simultaneously too revealing and not revealing enough. The truth hovered at the edges of their exchanges—not just about his identity, but about the effect these conversations had on him, the way they had illuminated the emptiness that success had carved into his life.

"Can I tell you something strange?" he finally typed, the simple question carrying more weight than its words suggested. "I'm surrounded by people all day—colleagues, assistants, industry contacts. Constant interaction, constant conversation. But this past week, talking with you has made me realise how isolated I've actually been. How rarely those conversations touch anything real. It's like being in a crowded room where everyone's speaking a language that sounds like English but isn't quite—all the words are familiar but the meaning never quite connects."

He read the message over twice, thumb hovering above the send button. Too much? Too soon? Six days of text exchanges hardly warranted such confessions. Yet the digital distance between them had somehow created a space where honesty felt safer than it did in his physical reality. Charlie pressed send before doubt could intervene, watching the message disappear with a mixture of relief and trepidation.

Across the city, Bee curled into the corner of her sofa, wineglass balanced on the armrest beside her. Her apartment settled around her in comfortable disarray—books stacked on the coffee table, a half-folded basket of laundry by the wall, the miscellany of a life actually lived rather than merely displayed. Outside her window, the same sunset that Charlie observed from his hillside mansion filtered through power lines and apartment buildings, casting long shadows across her small living room.

Her phone chimed with his message. The sound sent a current of anticipation through her that seemed disproportionate to the simple electronic tone, yet had become a Pavlovian trigger for the warmth that followed their exchanges. Bee set aside the book she'd been pretending to read, her attention immediately and completely redirected.

As she read his words, something shifted in her chest—a recognition that moved beyond the casual banter and shared jokes that had characterised their earlier conversations. His confession touched a loneliness she recognised in herself, one she rarely acknowledged even in her own thoughts.

"I understand that more than you might think," she typed back, her wineglass forgotten as she curled more tightly into the sofa's embrace. "Dating has felt like that for years now— everyone performing versions of themselves, speaking a language that sounds like connection but isn't real. I was beginning to give up thinking that it might just be me, I might just be expecting more than what regular people offer." She paused, then added, "These conversations with you have been the most honest exchanges I've had in longer than I care to admit. No agenda, no perpformance, just...talking. It's refreshing in a way that probably says something sad about modern connection, but there it is."

In his mansion, Charlie read her response with a sensation that bordered on physical relief, as if tension he hadn't realised he was carrying had suddenly released. He moved from the balcony into the house, phone clutched in his hand like something precious as he wandered from room to room. The space felt different somehow—still too large, still too carefully curated, but no longer quite so empty. Her words travelled with him, a presence that softened the hard edges of his solitude.

"Maybe that's why wrong number connections should be a dating app feature," he wrote back, a smile playing at his lips. "All the algorithms in the world can't create what randomness sometimes delivers by accident."

He settled onto his bed, back against the headboard, legs stretched out across the custom mattress. Another message began to form in his mind—one that acknowledged the strange attraction developing between them, the way her words had begun to colour his thoughts even when they weren't actively texting. His fingers moved to express this, then stilled, erasing the half-formed confession. Too soon. Too complicated, given the truths still unshared between them.

In her apartment, Bee faced a similar struggle. She took a sip of her wine, then set it down with more force than necessary, wine sloshing dangerously close to the rim. Six days of text exchanges shouldn't feel this significant. Six days shouldn't be enough to create this peculiar intimacy, this sense that she knew him in ways that transcended the digital medium of their connection.

She began to type a response that hinted at these feelings, then deleted it, starting again with something more measured, less revealing. The cycle repeated three times before she set the phone down entirely, pressing her palms against her eyes as if the pressure might clear her thoughts.

Earlier that day, her distraction had become noticeable

enough that her assistant had commented on it directly. They'd been unpacking a new shipment, Bee's hands moving mechanically through the familiar routine of checking items against the invoice while her mind replayed their conversation from the previous evening.

"That's the third time you've checked the same blouse," her assistant had observed, head tilted in curiosity. "And you've been smiling at your phone all week like it's telling you secrets. Is there something—or someone—I should know about?"

Bee had deflected with a vague comment about a funny text thread with friends, but the knowing look in her colleague's eyes suggested the explanation hadn't been entirely convincing. The truth—that she'd developed an intense connection with a wrong number—seemed too bizarre to share, too fragile to expose to outside scrutiny.

Now, alone in her apartment with only her thoughts and his messages for company, Bee picked up her phone again, returning to their conversation with renewed resolve to keep things light, manageable. But his response had already arrived, shifting the tone once more.

"I keep thinking about your ThreadBare idea." Charlie had written. "About creating a space that reflects your values instead of someone else's. Most of us spend our lives building other people's dreams because it feels safer than risking our own. The fact that you're actually working toward something that matters to you...it makes me question what I'm actually building with all these hours I spend doing the things I do."

"You don't seem like someone who would shy away from pursuing their passion," Bee replied. Charlie's heart raced, a storm of emotions swirling inside him. He needed to meet her —he was certain of it, and he desperately hoped she felt the same. His fingers trembled over the keyboard, hovering in hesitation, before he finally mustered the courage to type, "I want to meet you." He hit send with a pounding heart, before doubt could creep in and stop him. Each second stretched into an eternity as he awaited her reply, his mind a tumult of anticipation and anxiety. Finally, her response flashed on the screen, "I would love that."

"

Chapter Eight: The Setup

The Airbnb in Silver Lake looked nothing like Charlie's hillside mansion, which was precisely the point. He shifted the paper grocery bags in his arms as he fumbled with the unfamiliar key, the door finally swinging open to reveal a modestly furnished apartment that could have belonged to anyone—a teacher, perhaps, or a graphic designer with minimalist tastes.

Nothing about the space suggested wealth or celebrity, nothing that would trigger recognition or expectations in Bee's eyes when she arrived for dinner. Charlie stepped inside, the door clicking shut behind him with a finality that made his pulse quicken. Tonight, for the first time in years, he would be meeting someone who knew him only as himself, not as Charlie Benton, and the thought terrified him almost as much as it thrilled him.

He set the groceries on the kitchen counter and surveyed his surroundings. The living room flowed into an open kitchen with serviceable appliances—not the professional-grade equipment he'd grown accustomed to, but adequate for the meal he'd planned. Afternoon light filtered through blinds that needed dusting, casting striped shadows across a coffee table adorned with generic art books. Charlie moved to the windows, adjusting the blinds to create a softer illumination, one that would transition well into evening ambience. His fingers lingered on the plastic slats, meticulously arranging them until the light fell just so across the modest dining table.

His phone vibrated in his pocket—his agent, no doubt, still fuming about the week of meetings he'd rescheduled. Charlie ignored it, focusing instead on the space that would frame his first meeting with Bee. He shifted a chair slightly, moved a questionable ceramic sculpture from the centre of the coffee table to a less prominent position on a bookshelf. The artwork throughout the apartment had clearly been selected to offend no one—muted landscapes, abstract splashes of complementary colours, a black and white photograph of the Hollywood sign shrouded in fog. Anonymous art for an anonymous encounter.

Charlie unpacked the groceries methodically—fresh herbs, butter, garlic, potatoes, green beans, and the steaks, thick cut and marbled with fat, wrapped in butcher paper rather than sterile plastic. He'd visited three different markets, paying cash at each, wearing a baseball cap pulled low over his eyes. The last thing he needed was a fan encounter, a photo circulating online of him shopping for a dinner that carried more emotional significance than any press junket or premiere.

His phone buzzed again. Charlie pulled it from his pocket, glancing at the screen—Marissa, his agent, with a third call in as many hours. He declined it without hesitation, opening instead his message thread with Bee. Their last exchange had ended with her saying she was looking forward to tonight, followed by an emoji of a steak that had made him laugh out loud in the middle of the grocery store.

Bee's Los Feliz apartment looked like it had been hit by a category-two clothing hurricane. Dresses, blouses, and jeans lay scattered across her bed in abandoned combinations, casualties of her indecision. She stood before the full-length mirror attached to her closet door, critically eyeing a burgundy sweater held against her chest, then tossing it onto the growing pile of rejects with a frustrated sigh. Dressing for work was easy—professional but approachable, stylish enough to represent the boutique without intimidating customers. First dates usually warranted her standard uniform: dark jeans, a nice top, boots with a sensible heel. But this wasn't a standard first date. Nothing about meeting the wrong-number man who had somehow become the brightest part of her days felt standard at all.

The apartment around her reflected her actual life rather than the curated perfection she maintained at Harrington's. Vintage concert posters hung slightly askew on walls painted a warm terra cotta. Bookshelves overflowed with paperbacks arranged by colour rather than author, creating a rainbow effect that pleased her eye if not any conventional organisational system. Plants thrived on every available surface—resilient varieties she'd chosen for their ability to forgive occasional neglect during her busiest retail weeks.

Bee turned back to her closet, pushing hangers aside with increasing urgency. The black dress seemed too formal, too much like she was trying to impress. The floral jumpsuit she'd worn to her cousin's graduation felt too statement-making for a first meeting. Everything either screamed "I tried too hard" or "I didn't try at all," with no comfortable middle ground.

Her phone chimed from somewhere within the clothing debris field on her bed. Bee dug through layers of rejected outfits until she found it, her heart doing a small, familiar leap when she saw his name on the screen.

Charlie composed a new message, deleting and rewriting it three times before settling on: "Just confirming we're still on for 7? I promise not to explain investment strategies or ask about meeting my mother until at least the second course."

The callback to their first exchange—her misdirected rant about a terrible date, his joking response that had started it all—felt like the right note to strike. Light, referential to their shared history, acknowledging the strangeness of their situation without dwelling on it. His thumb hovered over the send button for a moment before pressing it, a flutter of nervousness in his stomach that seemed absurdly teenage for a man in his thirties.

While waiting for her response, Charlie surveyed the kitchen, opening drawers and cabinets to familiarise himself with their contents. The knives were disappointingly dull, but he'd anticipated this and brought his own, wrapped in a kitchen towel and tucked into a side pocket of one grocery bag. He extracted it now, the weight familiar in his hand, and began to prep the ingredients with the focus that had once helped him prepare for difficult scenes.

Garlic minced into precise, identical pieces. Potatoes scrubbed and quartered with mechanical precision. Herbs stripped from their stems and chopped with practised efficiency. The familiar rhythm of food preparation centred him, each completed task a small victory against the anxiety threatening to overwhelm his carefully maintained composure.

A laugh escaped her, genuine and unguarded in the privacy of her bedroom. The reference to their first exchange, it sent a wave of warmth through her chest. How strange that a wrong number had led to this, to clothing strewn across her bed and butterflies in her stomach and plans to meet a man whose face she'd never seen but whose thoughts had become intimately familiar.

Bee sat on the edge of her bed, pushing aside a silk blouse

to make room. "Absolutely still on," she typed. Though I'm disappointed about the investment strategies—I was so looking forward to explaining how actually, the market fluctuates based on lunar cycles and horoscope compatibility."

A smile spread across Charlie's face, tension momentarily forgotten. He typed back immediately: "I stand corrected. Please bring your investment zodiac charts. I'll supply the steak, medium rare as previously discussed, unless you've reconsidered your position on the objectively correct way to cook beef."

This had been another running joke between them—his insistence that medium rare was the only was the only acceptable steak preparation, her devil's advocate position that perhaps different people might enjoy different levels of doneness. The debate had evolved over several days, becoming increasingly elaborate and absurd, until Bee had declared him a "beef elitist" and herself the "champion of steak democracy."

Charlie set his phone down and returned to his preparations, retrieving the steaks from their paper wrapping. His hands trembled slightly as he laid them on a cutting board, a physical betrayal of the nerves he was trying to suppress. He took a deep breath, steadying himself as he reached for the salt, applying it with deliberate care to the meat, watching as it began to draw moisture to the surface. The pepper grinder came next, the sharp aroma rising as he cracked fresh peppercorns over the seasoned beef.

His phone buzzed again—not Bee this. Time, but a text from Marissa: "Harrison's people called again. The contract needs your signature by EOD. Not optional, Charlie Call me."

He dismissed the notification, tonight wasn't about contracts or Harrison or his agent's increasing frustration. Tonight was about meeting the woman whose texts had somehow become the most honest conversation in his carefully curated life.

Charlie moved to the living room, surveying the space with a critical eye. The couch looked comfortable but uninspired, its neutral tone chosen to complement any décor. He adjusted a throw pillow, then readjusted it, then moved it to another section of the couch entirely. The coffee table needed something—flowers would have been too corny, so he arranged a few of the art books in a casual fan, as if they had been casually perused rather than deliberately positioned.

Back in the kitchen, he selected a bottle of red wine from the paper bag, a vintage impressive enough to show consideration but not so rare as to suggest wealth beyond what his fictional behind-the-scenes entertainment job might provide, part of him still clung to the hope that maybe she had lived under a rock and wouldn't recognise who he was immediately.

He set it on the counter to breathe, positioning two wine glasses beside it, then repositioning them, then moving them again. Each adjustment felt necessary, vital to the success of the evening, though Charlie recognised the absurdity of his growing obsession with details.

The bathroom required attention next. Charlie wiped down the already clean counter, straightened the hand towels, and removed a scented candle that smelled artificially floral. In the bedroom, he closed the door firmly—the space beyond was irrelevant to tonight's dinner, and leaving it open felt presumptuous in ways he didn't want to consider.

As seven o'clock approached, Charlie completed his final preparations. The table was set with the apartment's mismatched but serviceable dishes. Candles waited to be lit. Music played at a carefully calibrated volume—loud enough to fill silences but soft enough to talk over. The steaks rested at room temperature, ready to be cooked at precisely the right moment.

. . .

She set her phone aside and pulled a dark green blouse from it hanger. The colour brought out the blue in her eyes, and the cut was flattering without being obvious about it. She paired it with black jeans that hit at just the right point on her ankle, turning before the mirror to check the effect. Still missing something. Bee rummaged through her jewellery box, selecting silver earrings—small enough to be subtle, unusual enough to be interesting. The outfit was taking shape, striking the elusive balance between effort and authenticity.

As she slipped the blouse over her head, Bee's thoughts drifted to the man she was preparing to meet. Their conversations had revealed someone thoughtful, funny, occasionally vulnerable in ways that resonated with her own carefully guarded soft spots. He worked in entertainment, behind the scenes as he'd put it, making sure productions ran smoothly. She'd pictured him as someone observant, the kind of person who noticed details others missed. Medium height, perhaps, with expressive hands and eyes that crinkled at the corners when he laughed.

But what if the reality didn't match her imagination? What if the easy flow of their text exchanges didn't translate to in-person conversation? What if the chemistry that seemed so obvious through messages dissipated in physical proximity?

Bee shook her head, dismissing the spiral of doubt. The connection they'd formed felt genuine in a way that transcended medium. Whatever he looked like, whatever awkwardness might accompany their first face-to-face meeting, the person behind those texts was someone worth knowing. Someone who had seen her more clearly through digital messages than men she'd dated for months had ever managed in person.

She stepped into low heeled boots—comfortable enough

for walking but polished enough for a dinner date—and surveyed her reflection with critical eyes. The outfit struck the right note: put-together without looking like she'd agonised over it (despite the evidence strewn across her bed), attractive without seeming like she was trying too hard. Bee nodded once at her reflection, a small gesture of approval, before moving to her bathroom to address makeup.

Her approach to cosmetics had always been minimal—enough to enhance but not enough to mask. Bee applied tinted moisturiser rather than foundation, defined her eyes with a subtle sweep of brown liner, added mascara and a touch of blush. Her lips she left for last, selecting a shade that looked like her natural colour but slightly amplified. The routine was familiar, grounding in its simplicity, and she found her hands steadying as she completed each step.

Through the bathroom door, she could see the clock on her nightstand—6:20. She had to leave in ten minutes to arrive by seven, accounting for traffic and the time it would take to find parking in Silver Lake. Bee applied a final touch of lip colour, then stepped back to assess the complete picture. The woman in the mirror looked like herself, but slightly enhanced —the version of Bianca Anderson who felt confident enough to meet a stranger who somehow wasn't a stranger at all.

Back in her bedroom, Bee gathered essentials into a small crossbody bag—wallet, keys, lip colour for touch-ups, a pack of mints. Her hand hesitated over a small bottle of perfume, a scent she rarely wore but enjoyed. After a moment's consideration, she applied it lightly to her wrists and neck—not enough to announce her presence from across a room, just enough to be noticed in closer proximity.

Her phone chimed once more as she slipped it into her bag. "Just leaving now," she typed. "Should be there in about 20 minutes. Slightly nervous but in a good way. Is that weird to admit?"

Charlie stared at her words, relief washing through him. "Not weird at all," he typed back. "I've reorganized the throw pillows four times, so I think I've got you beat on the nervousness scale."

The admission felt good—a small truth offered before the larger ones that would inevitably follow. Charlie set his phone down and moved to the stove, turning on a burner under the cast iron pan he'd found in a cabinet. As the pan heated, he looked around the ordinary apartment with its ordinary furnishings, the mundane setting for what felt like the most extraordinary risk he'd taken in years.

For a moment, doubt crept in. What was he doing, meeting a woman who had no idea who he really was? How could this possibly end well? But then he remembered their conversations, the ease with which they shared thoughts and jokes and small vulnerabilities. The connection that had formed so unexpectedly from a misdirected text.

The pan began to smoke slightly, ready for the steaks. Charlie picked up his phone, checking the time—6:47. Thirteen minutes until she was scheduled to arrive. Possibly less, possibly more, depending on traffic and her punctuality and a dozen other factors outside his control.

For a man who had spent years carefully controlling every aspect of his public persona, the uncertainty should have been terrifying. Instead, Charlie found himself smiling as he placed the steaks in the hot pan, the sizzle and aroma filling the borrowed apartment. Whatever happened next would be real in a way that much of his life had not been for a very long time, and that reality—unpredictable, unscripted, unmediated by publicists or cameras—felt like the most valuable thing he could offer her, and himself.

The message made her smile, easing some of the tension that had gathered between her shoulder blades. There was something wonderfully human about the image of him fussing with throw pillows, something that aligned perfectly with the thoughtful, slightly overthinking person she'd come to know through their exchanges.

Bee took a final look around her apartment—at the clothing scattered across her bed, the half-empty mug of tea on her nightstand, the small chaos of her authentic life so different from the precision of Harrington's displays. She'd have to deal with the mess later, but for now, it waited as evidence of decisions made and unmade, of the care she'd taken in preparing for this meeting.

At her door, Bee paused with keys in hand, drawing a deep breath that expanded her ribs against the soft fabric of her chosen blouse. The nervousness remained, but it had transformed into something lighter, more akin to anticipation than anxiety. She was about to meet the man whose thoughts had coloured her days, whose humour had brightened her nights, whose understanding had touched places she'd kept carefully guarded from recent disappointments.

Whatever happened next—awkwardness or ease, connection or distance—at least it would be real. After years of dating profiles designed to sell a product rather than reveal a person, after countless first dates that felt like job interviews with cocktails, the simple authenticity of their accidental connection felt worth pursuing, worth the vulnerability of stepping into the unknown.

Bee locked her apartment door behind her, the familiar click grounding her in the moment. As she walked toward her car, each step carried her closer to the evening ahead, to the man who had begun as a wrong number and become something she wasn't quite ready to name but wasn't willing to let it slip away.

The cast iron pan sizzled as Charlie laid the steaks onto its scorching surface, the sound sharp and satisfying in the quiet apartment. A perfect sear required heat and patience—too much movement would prevent the crust from forming, too little attention would lead to overcooking. He watched the edges of the meat begin to caramelise, the aroma of beef and butter filling the space with a richness that transformed the anonymous rental into something more intimate, more intentional. The timer on his phone counted down the precise moment to flip them—not by predetermined time, but by the visual cues he'd learned through practice, the slight curl of the meat's edge that signalled readiness. Every detail within his control had been considered, measured, executed with care. Charlie took a deep breath, steadying his hand on the spatula. Perfect steaks wouldn't guarantee a perfect evening, but they were one variable he could manage in an equation with too many unknowns.

Across the city, Bee slid into the driver's seat of her practical sedan, tossing her small crossbody bag onto the passenger seat beside her. The familiar scent of the vanilla air freshener hanging from her rearview mirror mingled with the faint new perfume on her wrists as she adjusted her mirrors and buckled her seatbelt. These habitual movements anchored her, a counterbalance to the fluttering sensation that had taken up residence beneath her ribs. Through the windshield, her Los Feliz street looked the same as always—the Ethiopian restaurant on the corner with its string lights already illuminated against the deepening evening, the bodega where she bought emergency coffee when she ran out at home, the row of jacaranda trees now past their purple bloom but still offering dappled shade. The ordinariness of the scene stood in stark contrast to the extraordinary circumstances propelling her toward Silver Lake and a dinner with a man who had become something she couldn't quite define.

Charlie flipped the steaks with practised precision, the second side meeting the hot pan with another satisfying hiss. In the smaller saucepan, green beans simmered with slivers of garlic and a squeeze of lemon. The roasted potatoes waited in the oven, their edges crisping to a golden brown. He moved between these elements with the focus of a conductor coordinating different sections of an orchestra, each component requiring its own attention while contributing to the harmonious whole. The apartment filled with layered aromas—the mineral richness of searing beef, the earthiness of roasting potatoes, the bright citrus note cutting through it all. Charlie checked the meat with a gentle press of his finger, feeling for the slight resistance that indicated medium-rare perfection. Not quite there—another minute perhaps. He glanced at his watch, then at the door, then back to the steaks. Timing was everything, in cooking as in life.

Bee turned onto Sunset Boulevard, immediately confronted by a line of brake lights stretching ahead of her. A delivery truck had double-parked, reducing the flow to a single constricted lane. She drummed her fingers against the steering wheel, eyes flicking to the clock on her dashboard—6:42. Still enough time to make it by seven if traffic cleared quickly, but L.A rarely offered such mercies. As her car inched forward, Bee rehearsed potential conversation starters in her mind, then immediately criticised herself for treating this like any other first date. Their digital connection had already moved beyond small talk about jobs and hometowns, beyond the careful script of initial meetings. They had built something more authentic through their messages, something that shouldn't require the safety net of practised lines. Still, she found herself rehearsing topics—questions about his work in entertainment that wouldn't sound too probing, observations about Silver Lake that wouldn't seem too obvious. The traffic ahead shifted, opening slightly, and Bee pressed the gas with perhaps more eagerness than the situation warranted.

Charlie transferred the steaks to a wooden cutting board, covering them with foil to rest while he plated the sides. Each movement was deliberate, almost ritualistic in its precision. Potatoes arranged in a small stack rather than scattered haphazardly. Green beans aligned in a neat row, their vibrant colour contrasting with the white of the plates he'd found in the Airbnb's cabinets. He opened the drawer for cutlery, selecting the least worn pieces, polishing each with a clean kitchen towel before placing them on the table. The candles came next—nothing scented that might compete with the food, just simple tapers in glass holders that cast a warm, flickering light across the setting. Charlie adjusted their position three times before being satisfied with the effect. The playlist he'd created specifically for the evening—acoustic covers of familiar songs, nothing too obvious or distracting.

The GPS on Bee's phone recalculated as she detoured around the traffic congestion, taking her through residential streets where jacarandas gave way to palm trees and craftsman bungalows nestled alongside modern architectural experiments. The familiar landmarks of her daily life receded in her rearview mirror as she navigated toward the address he'd provided. The neighbourhood grew less familiar with each turn, not threatening but simply unknown, like the man she was about to meet. Bee checked the address again—a street she'd passed but never explored, in a section of Silver Lake that existed adjacent to her usual paths. The apartment number gave no clues about the building or its character. Would it reflect something about him? Would it be sleek and modern, traditional and comfortable, or simply convenient? She found herself studying the homes she passed with new interest, wondering which architectural style might align with the thoughtful, slightly self-deprecating voice that had become so familiar through text.

Charlie uncorked the wine, pouring a small amount into each glass to allow it to breathe. The deep ruby liquid caught the candlelight, casting small red reflections on the white tablecloth he'd found in a drawer and shaken free of wrinkles as best he could. He plated the steaks last, slicing them against the grain into thick, perfect pieces that revealed the gradient from caramelised exterior to rosy centre. A small dish of flaky sea salt stood ready for final seasoning. The table complete, Charlie stepped back to assess the effect—intimate without being overtly romantic, thoughtful without appearing overly calculated. He glanced at himself in the hallway mirror, running a hand through his hair which immediately fell back into its usual style. His reflection looked back at him with an expression that mixed excitement with trepidation—the face of a man about to step off a cliff, uncertain whether he would fly or fall.

Bee finally found parking half a block from the address, the minor victory lifting her spirits after the frustrating traffic delay. She checked the time—6:58, technically on time but without the cushion she'd hoped for. The evening air felt cooler than it had in Los Feliz, carrying the faint scent of someone's backyard grill, of blooming jasmine from a nearby fence, of the particular Los Angeles alchemy of exhaust and flora that defined the city. Bee locked her car and began walking toward the address, each step carrying her closer to the moment when digital connection would transform into physical presence. The neighbourhood unfolded around her—modest apartment buildings interspersed with renovated homes, strings of lights crisscrossing a small parklet, a cat watching from a windowsill with amber eyes that caught the streetlight. The ordinary tableau of urban life continued unaffected by the significance of her journey through it. A dog barked. A car door slammed. A couple passed her on the sidewalk, hand intertwined, laughing at a private joke. And still she walked, the address numbers climbing toward her destination.

Charlie heard it—the distinct sound of a car door closing on the quiet street below, followed by footsteps too measured to be a casual passerby. He froze in place, wine bottle still in hand, ears straining to track the progress of those steps. They paused briefly, then continued with purpose. His heart rate accelerated despite his attempts to remain calm. Weeks of text exchanges, days of planning, hours of preparation, all converging on this moment when Bee would cross the threshold from digital presence to physical reality. Charlie set down the wine bottle with deliberate care, straightened the already straight cutlery, adjusted a napkin that needed no adjustment. These small movements anchored him as the footsteps grew louder, closer, until they stopped altogether outside his door.

Bee stood before apartment 3B, her fingertips trailing over the embossed numbers as if confirming their reality. The building was neither impressive nor disappointing—a well-maintained 1960s structure with clean lines and recently painted trim, the kind of place that housed young professionals and small families. From inside, she could detect the faint notes of music, could smell something delicious that made her suddenly aware of her hunger. For a moment, she simply breathed, gathering herself for the transition from anticipation to actuality. All week, this man had existed as words on a screen, as thoughts and jokes and observations that had woven themselves into the fabric of her days. Now, on the other side of this door, he waited as a physical being—with a face she'd never seen, a voice she'd never heard, a presence she'd never occupied space with. Bee raised her hand, hesitated for the briefest moment, then pressed the doorbell. The chime echoed inside, marking the point of no return.

Inside, Charlie moved toward the door with measured steps, wiping his palms against his jeans. The distance between kitchen and entryway had never felt so significant, each step carrying him closer to the moment when he would be seen— not as Charlie Benton, not as the carefully constructed public persona that graced magazine covers, but simply as the man behind the texts that had created this unexpected connection. His hand closed around the doorknob, cool metal against his warm palm. On the other side, separated by mere inches of wood and air, stood Bee—no longer just words on a screen but a woman who had somehow pierced the carefully constructed isolation of his life without even knowing who he truly was. The doorbell's echo faded, leaving a silence charged with possibility. Charlie took one final breath, turned the handle, and opened the door to whatever waited on the other side.

Chapter Nine: The Big Reveal

The door swung open, and time suspended itself. Bee's prepared smile froze, then crumbled as recognition hit her like a physical blow. Standing before her was not some unknown entertainment industry worker but Charlie Benton—the Charlie Benton whose face had gazed from billboards and movie posters, whose interviews she'd absently watched while folding laundry, whose celebrity dating history had scrolled past her on magazine covers in checkout lines. The man from her texts, her wrong number, her increasingly important daily connection, was on of the most famous actors in Hollywood. Bee felt the blood drain from her face as her lungs seemed to forget their purpose.

"Fuck off," she whispered in disbelief, the words escaping before she could catch them, hanging in the air between them like visible breath on a cold day.

Charlie's practised smile—the one that had launched a thousand promotional campaigns—faltered at the edges, revealing something raw and uncertain beneath. His hand still gripped the doorknob as if it might provide stability in this suddenly tilting world. Behind him, the apartment smelled of seared meat and garlic, the domestic normalcy a bizarre counterpoint to the surreality of the moment.

"I can explain," he said, his voice lower than she'd imagined it, rougher around the edge than the polished tones from talk show appearances.

Silence stretched between them, elastic and taut. Bee stood motionless on the threshold, her bag clutched against her side like a shield. Charlie Benton. The man whose split from actress Claire Vanderholt had fuelled tabloid speculation for months. The man whose new action franchise had broken box office records last summer. The man who had texted her about arguing with his reflection and the proper cooking temperature for steak.

"Soooo...I am guessing works in entertainment was a bit of an understatement? Bee finally said, sarcasm providing thin cover for the tremor in her voice.

Charlie's laugh sounded nothing like the confident chuckle he deployed on red carpets—it was higher, nervous, almost fragile. His hand released the doorknob and moved to his hair, fingers raking through the dark strands in a gesture she now recognised from interviews. The familiar movement in this unfamiliar context made the reality of his identity even more disorienting.

'Yeah, you could say that." His eyes—green, she noted, actually green and not just photoshopped that way for movie posters—darted from her face to the floor and back again. "I wanted to tell you, but then we started talking, and it was so... normal. So real. I was afraid that would change if you knew who I was."

From deeper within the apartment the sound of the music changing and the distinct aroma of the dinner he had already plated wafted through the door. Charlie's head jerked toward the kitchen, his expression shifting from nervous to dismayed.

"The steaks," he muttered, then turned back to Bee with a

look of such genuine conflict that it cut through some of her shock. "Please, come in? Let me at least explain while I try to salvage dinner?"

Bee remained frozen for a moment longer, her mind replaying every text exchange, every confession, every joke they'd shared, now colored by this new context. Had she said anything embarrassing? Had she ever mentioned seeing his movies? The thought made her stomach twist with a strange, inverted embarrassment—not for being unimpressive to him, but for possibly having unknowingly complimented or criticized his work.

The apartment beyond him was nothing like what she'd expected from a movie star—modest, rental-plain, with furniture that looked borrowed rather than chosen. A small dining table had been carefully set with mismatched dishes and flickering candles. The effort was evident in every detail, from the folded napkins to the wine glasses waiting to be filled. This was not the home of Charlie Benton, film star. This was a space created specifically for their meeting, neutral ground where he could be just Charlie.

The realisation softened something in her chest even as her mind continued to reel.

"It smells delicious, it would be tragic for it to go to waste." She said, taking a small step forward, crossing the threshold into this new, complicated reality.

Relief washed across Charlie's face, his shoulders dropping slightly from their tense position near his ears. He stepped back to allow her entry, closing the door behind her with a soft click that seemed to seal them into this shared moment of revelation.

"Thank you," he said, the simple words carrying a weight that suggested he was thanking her for more than just coming inside. His posture shifted as he moved toward the kitchen—shoulders slightly hunched despite his height, hands fidgeting at his sides, eyes still avoiding direct contact for more than a second or two.

Bee followed, her legs moving automatically while her mind continued to process.

"So," she said, leaning against the doorframe between kitchen and living room, maintaining a careful distance, "this explains why you were so vague about your job in entertainment.".

Charlie's laugh was more genuine this time as he took the plates to the table, "I've gotten pretty good at being vague about a lot of things." He glanced up at her and motioned for her to sit. "Occupational hazard when everyone you meet already thinks they know everything about you."

The scent of rosemary and garlic filled the space between them, oddly comforting in its ordinariness. Bee watched his hands as he worked organising the dishes—the same hands that had typed all those messages that had gradually become the brightest part of her days. Famous hands that had probably signed countless autographs, held countless props in blockbuster films, but were now simply turning steaks and adjusting heat with careful attention.

"I think," she said slowly, stepping into the kitchen proper, her decision made even as she spoke the words, "you have a lot of explaining to do."

Charlie looked up, meeting her eyes fully for the first time since opening the door. The vulnerability there was unmistakable—hope warring with preparation for rejection, sincerity edged with fear. "I do," he agreed quietly. "And I will. If you'll stay for dinner?"

He gestured toward the table again, candles still flickering, wine still waiting to be poured. A normal dinner setting for what had become the least normal evening of Bee's life. She nodded once, decision crystallising into certainty. Whatever game or deception had brought them to this point, the connection they'd formed through those texts had been real. That, at least, deserved a chance to be heard.

"I'll stay," she said. "But I have questions. A lot of questions."

The relief that transformed Charlie's face was nothing like any expression she'd seen in his films or interviews—it was too raw, too genuine, too unguarded for public consumption. This, she realized, was the man behind the text messages, finally visible beneath the famous facade. And despite everything, she still wanted to know him.

The candles flickered between them, casting shadows that danced across the carefully arranged table. Bee watched his hands as they moved, still reconciling them with the image of Charlie Benton she'd carried in her peripheral awareness for years. The wine poured with a gentle gurgle, breaking the silence that had settled since they'd moved from kitchen to table. Neither seemed to know how to begin now that the script they'd been following for days had been so thoroughly rewritten.

"I hope it's still edible," Charlie said, nodding toward the steak on her plate. "They were perfect before I... before you..."

"Before I showed up and recognized you as an A-list celebrity?" Bee supplied, her tone dry but without the sharp edge of earlier shock.

Charlie's smile was small but genuine. "That."

Bee cut into her steak, the knife sliding through with satisfying ease despite the slightly darkened exterior. The first bite melted on her tongue—perfectly seasoned, still pink in the center, rich with butter and herbs. Whatever else Charlie Benton might be, he knew his way around a kitchen.

"It's good," she said after swallowing. "Better than good, actually." A small concession, but his expression brightened as if she'd offered far more.

"Thanks. I took some classes last year between projects.

Needed something..." He trailed off, searching for the right word.

"Normal?" Bee suggested.

Charlie looked up, meeting her eyes with a startled recognition. "Yes. Exactly."

They ate in silence for a moment, the clink of silverware against plates the only conversation. Bee felt the weight of unsaid words building between them, questions piling up behind her teeth. She took a sip of wine—rich and full-bodied, clearly chosen with care—and decided to dive in.

"So," she said, setting down her glass with deliberate precision. "You're Charlie Benton."

He nodded, his fork pausing halfway to his mouth. "I am."

"And you let me ramble about bad dates and retail nightmares for a week without mentioning that small detail."

Charlie set his fork down, his shoulders tensing slightly. "I know how it sounds. At first, I just didn't think it mattered— it was a wrong number, a one-time exchange." His fingers tapped a nervous rhythm against his wine glass. "But then we kept talking, and it was so... refreshing. You weren't performing for me. You weren't trying to impress me or get something from me."

"Because I didn't know there was anything to get," Bee pointed out, though her tone had softened.

"Exactly." Charlie ran a hand through his hair, the gesture so familiar from their texts that it created a strange sense of déjà vu. "Do you know how rare that is? To have someone talk to me like I'm just a person? Not a connection or a photo opportunity or a status symbol?"

The naked honesty in his voice cut through some of Bee's lingering defensiveness. She studied him across the table—not Charlie Benton the movie star, but the man who had texted her about cereal being soup, who had shared his dreams of teaching drama instead of performing it, who had become an unexpected bright spot in her days.

"I'm guessing it doesn't happen often," she said.

Charlie's laugh held little humor. "The last time someone looked at me without seeing the celebrity was probably my brother, and even he can't help bringing up industry stuff sometimes." He took a drink of wine, his eyes distant. "Most people see the character, not the person." His fingers resumed their nervous tapping on the wine glass. "After a while, you start to wonder which is which."

Bee considered this as she took another bite of steak. The man across from her bore little resemblance to the confident, slightly cocky persona she'd seen in interviews. This Charlie was quieter, more thoughtful, his movements betraying an uncertainty that never showed on screen.

"So who am I having dinner with?" she asked. "Charlie Benton the actor, or Charlie the guy who argues with his reflection?"

A genuine smile broke across his face, reaching his eyes in a way that transformed his features. "Definitely the reflection-arguer. Though they're not entirely separate people."

"Just different versions of the same person," Bee nodded, understanding. "Like how I'm different at Harrington's than I am with friends."

"Yes, but imagine if millions of people only knew your Harrington's persona and thought that was the whole you." Charlie leaned forward slightly, animated by her understanding. "Imagine if you could never drop that persona in public because people are always watching, always documenting."

Bee shuddered slightly. "That sounds exhausting."

"It is." Charlie's posture relaxed marginally, as if her simple acknowledgment had loosened something tightly wound inside him. "That's why these texts with you have been so...

important. You weren't talking to Charlie Benton. You were just talking to me."

The admission hung between them, weighted with vulnerability. Bee felt her earlier anger at his deception softening further, though wariness still lingered at the edges. She speared a roasted potato, considering her next words carefully.

"I don't do social media," she said finally, glancing up to find Charlie watching her with curious intensity. "No Instagram, no Twitter. I deleted Facebook years ago. I probably couldn't name half the movies you've been in."

Charlie's expression transformed from curiosity to disbelief, then to something that looked remarkably like relief. "Seriously? None of it?"

"None." Bee shrugged. "It always seemed like more performance than connection. More stress than it was worth." She took another sip of wine, finding it easier to meet his eyes now. "I prefer actual conversations with actual people."

"Like arguing about whether cereal is soup?" Charlie's smile had a boyish quality now, the tension in his shoulders visibly dissipating.

"Exactly like that." Bee found herself smiling back. "Though you're still wrong about that, by the way."

Charlie's laugh—his real laugh, she realized, not the polished chuckle from interviews—filled the space between them, breaking through the last layer of formality. "I maintain my position. Anything in liquid with solid components is soup-adjacent at minimum."

"Soup-adjacent? That's not even a real category!" Bee protested, the familiar rhythm of their text debates translating seamlessly to spoken words.

The conversation flowed more easily after that, their bodies gradually relaxing into the chairs. Charlie's gestures became more animated, less contained, as Bee asked pointed questions about his work that focused on craft rather than celebrity. She noted how he leaned forward when particularly engaged, how his eyes crinkled at the corners when genuinely amused, how different his real expressions were from the ones she'd seen on screens.

Bee found herself laughing at his impression of a director who insisted every scene be shot from seventeen different angles, her earlier shock receding as the person from their texts emerged more clearly from behind the famous facade. The candles burned lower, casting warmer light across their faces as the distance between them—both physical and emotional— seemed to shrink with each exchange.

"Wait," Charlie said, setting down his empty wine glass, "so you've really never seen 'The Harbinger'? It was everywhere last year."

"I think I saw a poster," Bee admitted, enjoying the look of mock outrage that crossed his face. "I'm more of a book person, honestly. Movies are fine, but I can never fully shut off the part of my brain that knows it's all just people pretending."

"That's..." Charlie paused, considering. "That's actually refreshing to hear." He reached for the wine bottle, refilling their glasses with a comfortable ease that would have seemed impossible an hour earlier. "Most people I meet either pretend to have seen everything I've done or actually have and want to discuss every scene in excruciating detail."

"Sorry to disappoint," Bee said, not sounding sorry at all.

"You're not," Charlie replied, his gaze holding hers for a beat longer than casual conversation warranted. "Disappointing, I mean."

The simple statement carried a weight that settled in the air between them, neither awkward nor unwelcome. Bee felt a warmth that had nothing to do with the wine, a connection that had survived the shock of revelation and was now cautiously reestablishing itself on new, more honest ground.

The chocolate mousse caught the light like silk, its surface a perfect dark pool in the small glass dishes Charlie had arranged on the coffee table. They had migrated to the living room by unspoken mutual agreement, the formality of the dinner table giving way to the softer intimacy of the couch. Outside, Los Angeles unfurled beneath them, a sea of lights glimmering against the darkened sky. Inside, the candles Charlie had placed strategically around the room cast their faces in gentle amber, softening the edges of this newly complicated reality they now shared.

Bee sank into the couch, conscious of Charlie settling beside her—close enough that the cushion dipped slightly toward him, not so close as to suggest presumption. The distance between them measured perhaps a foot, yet it felt charged with a current that had nothing to do with celebrity and everything to do with the connection that had developed through their messages.

"I'm not usually this accomplished with desserts," Charlie admitted, handing her a small spoon. "But my brother assured me it's impossible to mess up this recipe."

Bee took a taste, the chocolate rich and bitter-sweet against her tongue. "Your brother was right. It's perfect."

Charlie smiled, relief visible in the softening around his eyes. They ate in companionable silence for a moment, the clink of spoons against glass the only sound besides the faint music still playing from hidden speakers. Through the windows, the city lights twinkled like earthbound stars, cars moving along distant streets like luminous insects.

"I need to apologise properly," Charlie said finally, setting his empty dish on the coffee table. His hands—those famous hands that had probably held a dozen actresses in carefully choreographed embraces—twisted together in his lap, betraying his nervousness. "For not telling you who I was. For letting you walk into this without warning."

Bee watched him over the rim of her dessert dish, noting

how different he looked in this soft light—less the polished icon from billboards, more the uncertain man whose texts had gradually become essential to her days. His profile against the window, backlit by city lights, seemed strangely vulnerable.

"I kept telling myself I would tell you before we met," he continued, his voice lower now, weighted with what sounded like regret. "But each time I started typing it out, I... I couldn't. These conversations with you became the most honest part of my life, and I was afraid..." He trailed off, eyes fixed on the distant lights.

"Afraid I'd turn into a fawning fan? Or sell your texts to the tabloids?" Bee asked, her tone gentle despite the direct questions.

Charlie's laugh held little humor. "Both. Either. Or that the whole dynamic would change—that suddenly you'd be talking to Charlie Benton instead of just Charlie." He turned to face her fully, and the rawness in his expression caught her off guard. "My life is full of people who think they know me because they've seen my movies or read interviews. But with you... you actually got to know me. The real me. Not the public version."

Bee set her dessert dish beside his, considering his words. The deception still troubled her, but she couldn't deny the truth in what he was saying. Their conversations had carried a genuineness that felt rare in her experience—a connection built on shared humor and gradual revelation rather than the careful performance of typical first dates.

"I understand why you did it," she said finally, measuring her words. "I'm not saying it was right, but I understand."

She studied him for a moment longer, this strange collision of the man from her texts and the celebrity she'd absently registered for years. The same person, yet fundamentally different from what she'd imagined—both more and less than the construction she'd built in her mind.

"Famous or not, you're still the same guy who spent an hour debating the merits of pineapple on pizza with me," she continued, a small smile playing at the corners of her mouth. "Still the same person who thinks cereal is soup and that reflections have independent consciousness."

The tension visibly drained from Charlie's shoulders, as if her words had released a valve holding back tremendous pressure. His exhale was audible in the quiet room, his body seeming to settle more naturally into the couch cushions.

"Thank you," he said, the simple words carrying a weight of gratitude that seemed to fill the space between them. "For giving me a chance to explain. For staying."

"I almost didn't," Bee admitted. "When I first saw you, I thought this whole thing had been some kind of joke or game."

Charlie's expression clouded. "It wasn't. None of it was."

"I know that now." She shifted slightly, turning toward him so that the distance between them decreased by inches. "The question is, where do we go from here? Because this—" she gestured between them, "—is obviously more complicated than wrong-number texts between strangers."

The candlelight caught in Charlie's eyes, reflecting like twin flames as he considered her question. Outside, a helicopter moved across the darkened sky, its searchlight sweeping over distant neighborhoods before disappearing behind the hills.

"I'd like to keep talking to you," he said finally. "In person, not just texts. If you want that too."

The simplicity of the request belied the complexity behind it—the challenges of his public life, the scrutiny that would inevitably follow if they were seen together, the fundamental imbalance of a relationship between an ordinary person and someone whose face appeared on billboards.

"It won't be simple," Bee said, voicing the concerns neither had explicitly acknowledged. "Your life is...different from mine."

Charlie nodded, the movement casting shifting shadows across his features. "It is. But the person living that life is the same one you've been texting. The one who wants simple conversations more than red carpet events. The one who values your honesty more than you can probably understand."

His hand moved cautiously across the cushion between them, not quite touching hers but close enough that she could feel the warmth radiating from his skin. An invitation, not a demand.

"I'm not asking for promises," he added, voice dropping lower. "Just... a chance to see if what we started in those texts can be something real, despite everything else."

Bee looked down at his hand, then back to his face—open, vulnerable, so different from the confident persona he projected in public. She thought of the texts that had brightened her days, the laughter his messages had brought her, the genuine connection that had developed despite the unlikeliest of beginnings.

"I should go," she said softly, glancing at the time displayed on her phone. "It's getting late."

Charlie nodded, disappointment flickering across his features before being carefully masked. They rose together, the moment suspended between resolution and uncertainty as they moved toward the door. Bee collected her bag from where she'd left it on an entryway table, suddenly aware of the strangeness of the evening—dinner with Charlie Benton in an anonymous apartment, the entire experience existing in a bubble separate from both their normal lives.

At the door, she turned to face him one last time. "I don't care about Charlie Benton the movie star," she said, her voice steady despite the emotions swirling beneath her composed exterior. "I just like talking to Charlie. The one who listens.

The one who gets excited about pasta and old movies and thinks deeply about things most people ignore."

The smile that transformed his face seemed to come from somewhere deep inside him, genuine in a way that made his public smiles seem like pale imitations. Relief and hope mingled in his expression, his posture relaxing into something more natural than the careful stance he'd maintained much of the evening.

"So... can I text you tomorrow?" he asked, the question hovering between them like a tangible thing.

Bee nodded, her own smile small but sincere. "I'd be disappointed if you didn't."

Their goodbye was neither a kiss nor a formal handshake, but something in between—his hand briefly touching her arm, a moment of connection that acknowledged what had passed between them while leaving space for whatever might follow. As Bee stepped into the night air, the door remained open behind her, Charlie's silhouette framed in the warm light from within.

She felt his gaze following her as she walked to her car, his presence a physical sensation against her back. At the curb, she turned once more to see him still watching from the doorway, his expression a mixture of hope and uncertainty that matched the tumult in her own chest. Bee raised her hand in a small wave, receiving one in return before she slipped into her car.

As she drove away, the apartment building receded in her rearview mirror, growing smaller until it disappeared altogether. But the evening's revelations remained, reshaping her understanding of the connection they'd formed and the possibilities it held—complicated, unexpected, but undeniably real.

Charlie remained in the doorway long after her taillights had disappeared around a corner, the night air cool against his face. Inside, the remains of their dinner waited to be cleared, the candles burned low, the evidence of their evening together still tangible in the space he'd created for this meeting. He closed the door finally, turning back to the apartment that had briefly held something precious—a genuine connection in a life too often defined by performance and perception.

Tomorrow he would text her. Tomorrow they would begin navigating this new, complicated reality they'd created together. But tonight, in the quiet aftermath of revelation and acceptance, Charlie allowed himself to feel something he hadn't experienced in longer than he could remember: the simple, terrifying hope that comes with being seen—truly seen—by another person.

Chapter Ten: Paparazzi Problems

Morning light filtered through Charlie's bedroom windows, casting long shadows across the rumpled sheets. He'd barely slept, his mind replaying every moment of dinner with Bee—her shock at discovering his identity, her initial anger, and then, miraculously, her willingness to listen, to understand. He reached for his phone, the screen illuminating his face in the half-darkness. His thumb hovered over their message thread, uncertainty gnawing at his confidence. What exactly did you say to a woman who had discovered you were famous in perhaps the most awkward way possible, yet had still left with a promise that she wanted to hear from you again?

Charlie typed, deleted, and retyped a dozen variations before settling on: "Good morning. My reflection says I should apologise again for last night, but I'm hoping we can start fresh today instead. Coffee later? My treat.

He hit send before he could overthink it further, then tossed the phone onto the bed beside him as if it had suddenly grown hot in his palm. The ceiling above him offered no reassurance as he waited, his heartbeat marking time with maddening slowness.

Across town, Bee woke to the gentle vibration of her phone against her nightstand. She blinked against the morning light, remnants of dreams still clinging to the edges of her consciousness—dreams where Charlie Benton had been simply Charlie, the wrong number who had somehow become right. The memories of the previous night crashed over her with renewed force as she reached for her phone, expecting a message from her assistant about the day's shipments.

Instead, Charlie's name filled the screen. Not Charlie Benton, just Charlie—she hadn't changed his contact information yet, unsure how to reconcile the two versions of the same man. She read his message, a smile tugging at her lips despite the storm of emotions still swirling beneath her ribs. The joke about his reflection, the self-deprecating mention of the steaks—this was the Charlie she'd come to know through their texts, not the polished celebrity whose face adorned billboards.

She sat up, hair falling in tangled waves around her shoulders as she considered her response. Last night, lying awake in the darkness of her bedroom, she'd cataloged all the reasons this connection was doomed: his fame, the inevitable scrutiny, the fundamental imbalance between their worlds. Yet something in her resisted the neat, practical conclusion that they should end things before they properly began.

"Your reflection gives terrible advice," she typed back. Coffee sounds perfect, though I reserve the right to order something with an embarrassing amount of sugar and whipped cream."

Her finger hovered over the send button, a moment of doubt freezing her in place. Was she making a mistake? Stepping willingly into a complication that could only end in disappointment? But the thought of never hearing from him again, never discovering if this strange, unexpected connection could become something real—that felt like the greater risk.

She pressed send.

Charlie was out of the shower when her reply came through, a towel wrapped around his waist, water droplets tracing paths down his shoulders. He reached for his phone with still-damp hands, heart lurching at the sight of her name on the screen. The tension that had coiled between his shoulder blades since waking began to dissolve as he read her words, a laugh escaping him that echoed off the bathroom tiles.

"Thank god," he murmured to his reflection, which looked back at him with the same relief written across its features.

They settled on a small cafe in Los Feliz—not too far from her apartment, but removed enough from Hollywood haunts that Charlie might pass unrecognized. He suggested noon, she countered with eleven, and they agreed on eleven-thirty with an ease that belied the complications surrounding them.

Charlie arrived twenty minutes early, choosing a table in the back corner that faced away from the entrance. He'd dressed carefully—casual enough not to draw attention, nice enough to show he cared. His leg bounced beneath the table as he waited, eyes flicking to the door every time it opened, the espresso before him cooling untouched.

She appeared exactly on time, sunlight catching in her dark hair as she stepped through the doorway. Charlie's breath caught in his throat. Last night, she'd been a shock against the backdrop of his carefully planned evening—today, seeing her scan the room with quiet confidence, he was struck by how perfectly she fit into the ordinary setting. She wore a deep blue dress that caught the light as she moved, her steps purposeful as she navigated between tables.

Their eyes met across the room, and the smallest smile

touched her lips—tentative but real. Charlie stood as she approached, unsure of the protocol for greeting someone who had discovered your celebrity identity over dinner the night before. A handshake seemed too formal, a hug too presumptuous.

Bee solved the dilemma by setting her bag on the empty chair and offering a simple, "Hi."

"Hi," Charlie echoed, suddenly tongue-tied despite years of delivering lines in front of cameras and crews.

They sat, a beat of awkward silence stretching between them before Bee gestured to his untouched espresso. "Is it that bad?"

Charlie glanced down, as if surprised to find the cup still before him. "Oh—no, I just... got distracted."

"By what?" Her head tilted slightly, a gesture he recognized from their dinner, a tell that she was genuinely curious rather than making polite conversation.

"Trying to figure out what to say to you that doesn't sound like a line from a script," he admitted, the honesty easier than he'd expected.

Bee's smile widened, reaching her eyes in a way that transformed her face. "How about 'what ridiculously sweet coffee concoction are you going to order?'"

The tension between them fractured, dissolving into something warmer as Charlie laughed. "Perfect. What ridiculously sweet coffee concoction are you going to order?"

"I was thinking a caramel macchiato with extra caramel and whipped cream. The kind that barely qualifies as coffee," she replied, her expression daring him to judge.

"Dessert masquerading as breakfast. I respect the commitment."

Their conversation flowed more easily after that, finding its rhythm as Bee returned from the counter with her elaborate drink. Charlie watched, fascinated, as she peeled back the plastic lid to reveal a mountain of whipped cream dusted with cinnamon.

"That's... impressive," he said, eyebrows raised.

"Life's too short for boring coffee." She took a sip, leaving a small dot of whipped cream on her upper lip that she quickly wiped away. "So. Here we are."

"Here we are," Charlie agreed, his expression sobering slightly. "Thank you for coming. After last night, I wouldn't have blamed you if you'd blocked my number."

Bee's fingers traced patterns in the condensation on her cup, her eyes following the movement. "I thought about it," she admitted. "Not because I was angry, but because it would be the sensible thing to do."

"And yet, here you are."

She looked up, meeting his gaze directly. "I'm not always sensible. And I think... I think I'd regret it if I didn't at least see where this might go."

Something warm unfurled in Charlie's chest, a feeling so foreign he almost didn't recognize it as hope. "I would too," he said quietly. "Regret it, I mean."

Their fingers rested inches apart on the table between them, neither quite brave enough to bridge the gap. Around them, the cafe hummed with ordinary life—students hunched over laptops, friends catching up over pastries, a barista calling out orders with cheerful efficiency. For once, Charlie felt like part of this mundane tapestry rather than an anomaly within it.

"It won't be easy," he said finally, voicing the concern that had kept him awake. "Being... connected to me. There are complications I can't control."

"I gathered that much," Bee replied, her tone dry but not unkind. "I'm not naive, Charlie. I know what I'm potentially getting into. The question is whether what's between us is worth navigating those complications."

"And what do you think?" he asked, unable to keep the vulnerability from his voice.

Bee studied him for a long moment, her expression thoughtful. Then, with deliberate care, she moved her hand across the table until her fingers rested lightly atop his. "I think we owe it to ourselves to find out."

The simple touch sent electricity racing up his arm, more powerful than any staged kiss or choreographed embrace he'd performed for cameras. Charlie turned his hand beneath hers, their palms meeting, fingers interlacing with tentative precision.

Their conversation shifted then, moving from the weight of potential futures to lighter topics—her morning shipment at the boutique, his brother's reaction to their dinner, the book she'd started reading the night before to distract herself from overthinking. Laughter came more easily, their bodies gradually leaning closer across the table, the space between them charged with possibility.

Charlie was explaining his brother's terrible cooking advice when he noticed Bee's attention drift past his shoulder, her expression brightening.

"Is that a farmers market?" she asked, nodding toward the window where canopies and stalls were visible in a nearby park.

Charlie turned, following her gaze. "Looks like it. Sunday market, I think."

"Want to check it out? I'm a sucker for fresh bread and overpriced jam."

The invitation hung between them, simple yet significant —an extension of their time together, a step beyond the controlled environment of the cafe into the unpredictable public space beyond. Charlie considered the risks—being recognized, photographed, interrupting this fragile new beginning with the intrusion of his public identity.

Then he looked at Bee, at the warmth in her eyes and the slight upward tilt of her chin that suggested she understood exactly what she was asking, and found himself nodding.

"I'd love to," he said, meaning it entirely.

"I think you're overestimating how effective those are," Bee said, gesturing to the sunglasses Charlie had slipped on as they left the cafe. The late morning sun caught in her hair, turning the dark strands almost blue in the light. Charlie adjusted the brim of his baseball cap, pulled low over his eyes in what she clearly considered a laughable attempt at anonymity. Her teasing smile made something warm unfurl in his chest, despite the nervous flutter that accompanied any public outing.

"It's worked before," he defended, though his tone betrayed his lack of conviction. "You'd be surprised how much people see what they expect to see. Charlie Benton doesn't shop at farmers markets on Sunday mornings."

"And what does Charlie Benton do on Sunday mornings?" Bee asked, falling into step beside him as they crossed the street toward the canopies visible in the park beyond.

Charlie considered this, realizing how rarely he spent Sunday mornings doing anything that wasn't scheduled by his team. "Usually? Boxing with a trainer, or script readings, or..." He trailed off, embarrassed by how structured his supposedly free time had become.

"Well, today Charlie Benton is buying overpriced organic produce with me," Bee declared, her fingers finding his with surprising ease. The simple contact sent electricity racing up his arm, more powerful than any choreographed romantic scene he'd ever filmed.

The farmers market spread before them in neat rows of white canopies, a patchwork of colors and textures beneath. People milled between stalls, canvas bags filled with fresh purchases, children darting between adults' legs with sticky fingers and wide eyes. The normalcy of it struck Charlie with unexpected force—how long had it been since he'd done something so ordinary, so unplanned?

"Where do we start?" he asked, acutely aware of Bee's hand in his, of how right it felt despite the strangeness of their situation.

"Bread first," she replied without hesitation. "Always bread. I can smell the sourdough from here."

She tugged him toward a stall where loaves were arranged in rustic baskets, their crusts golden and cracked, promising tangy interiors and the perfect balance of chew and tenderness. The baker, a woman with flour dusting her forearms and a gray braid wrapped around her head, offered them samples without a second glance at Charlie's half-hearted disguise.

"Try the olive loaf," she suggested, pushing a small piece toward them. "Made it this morning."

Charlie watched as Bee closed her eyes to taste, her expression shifting to one of simple pleasure. The baker nodded approvingly, recognizing a kindred spirit in appreciation. When Charlie tried his piece, the salt of the olives burst against his tongue, the bread's subtle sourness a perfect complement.

"We'll take one," Bee decided, reaching for her wallet.

Charlie gently intercepted her hand. "Let me." When she began to protest, he added, "Please. Consider it payment for showing me what normal people do on Sundays."

The baker wrapped their selection in brown paper, the rustle and crinkle joining the ambient symphony of the market—vendors calling out specials, children laughing, the low hum of conversations, a guitarist playing somewhere in the distance. Charlie felt his shoulders relaxing incrementally as they moved between stalls, no one giving him a second look beyond the occasional appreciative glance that he suspected had more to do with Bee than any recognition.

They stopped at a honey vendor next, rows of amber jars

catching the sunlight like liquid gold. The beekeeper, a man with weathered skin and gentle hands, explained the differences between varieties—clover, wildflower, orange blossom—his passion evident in the careful way he handled each jar.

"This one," he said, offering a small wooden stick drizzled with a dark amber liquid, "is blackberry honey. My favourite."

Bee tasted first, then held a second stick to Charlie's lips. The gesture was intimate, almost domestic, and Charlie felt heat rise to his cheeks as he accepted it from her fingers. The honey was complex—floral and sweet with a hint of tartness that lingered pleasantly.

"That's incredible," he murmured, the taste mingling with the warmth of Bee's fingers against his lips.

They left with two jars, Charlie insisting on carrying the growing collection of purchases in a paper bag tucked against his side. His free hand remained entwined with Bee's, their fingers fitting together with an ease that belied how recently they'd met.

The morning stretched around them, golden and unhurried. They sampled fresh cheese from a local dairy, debated the merits of different apple varieties, and lingered over a display of handmade ceramics. Bee held up a mug glazed in deep blue, turning it to catch the light.

"This reminds me of your eyes," Charlie said without thinking, the words escaping before he could filter them.

Her smile in response made his heart stutter. "Smooth, Benton. Very smooth."

He bought her the mug.

The scent of fresh flowers drew them next—buckets filled with dahlias, sunflowers, and late summer blooms arranged in a riot of colour. Charlie watched as Bee leaned close to inhale the fragrance of a particularly vibrant bunch, her profile outlined against the flowers. The image struck him with unexpected force—her simple joy, untainted by performance or expectation, existing purely in the moment.

"What?" she asked, catching his gaze.

"Nothing," he replied, then corrected himself. "No, not nothing. I just... I like seeing you like this."

"Like what?" Her head tilted, curious rather than defensive.

"Happy. Unguarded." He gestured around them at the market, at the ordinary Sunday unfolding in all its mundane glory. "This is the most normal I've felt in years."

Something softened in her expression. "That's sad, in a way."

"Maybe," he acknowledged. "Or maybe I just needed the right person to do normal things with."

The moment hung between them, weighted with possibility, neither quite ready to name what was developing but both acutely aware of its presence. Around them, the market continued its steady rhythm—a woman haggled over the price of tomatoes, a child dropped an ice cream cone and wailed in despair, a dog strained at its leash to investigate a fallen crumb.

Bee's fingers tightened around his. "Come on, there's a jam stall on the other side that supposedly makes the best strawberry preserves in the city."

They were halfway across the central aisle, passing a stall selling fresh pasta, when Charlie heard it—the sharp intake of breath that he'd learned to recognize over years of public appearances. His body tensed instinctively, eyes scanning for the source behind his sunglasses.

"Oh my god," came the whispered exclamation, too loud in its attempt at discretion. "That's Charlie Benton."

The voice belonged to a teenage girl, perhaps fifteen or sixteen, standing with a friend beside a display of honey sticks. Her eyes were wide, phone already halfway out of her pocket, expression wavering between excitement and disbelief.

"Are you sure?" her friend asked, squinting in their direction.

"I'm positive," the first girl insisted, her voice rising with certainty. "I've seen all his movies. That's definitely him."

Charlie felt the shift in the air around them, subtle at first —a few heads turning, curious glances becoming more focused, the ambient conversation dipping momentarily before resuming with a different quality. Beside him, Bee stiffened slightly, her hand tightening in his.

"I think your disguise just failed its saving throw," she murmured, her attempt at humor not quite masking the tension in her voice.

"We should go," Charlie replied, keeping his voice low. "Once it starts, it spreads fast."

But it was already happening. The teenage girl had nudged her friend, who was now openly staring. A man at the cheese stall had paused mid-purchase, phone raised in what he probably thought was a subtle attempt at a photo. A woman whispered to her partner, both turning to look with undisguised interest.

Then came the phones—emerging from pockets and purses, raised with varying degrees of pretense. Some didn't bother with subtlety at all, cameras pointed directly at them, flashes occasionally firing despite the bright daylight. The murmurs grew, spreading through the market like ripples in water:

"Is that really him?"

"Who's the girl?"

"Charlie Benton, I swear it's him..."

"Get a picture before he leaves..."

Charlie's arm moved instinctively around Bee's shoulders, drawing her closer to his side in a protective gesture he'd performed a hundred times with co-stars on red carpets but never with such genuine intent. He felt her body tense against his, her breath catching as she registered the rapidly changing atmosphere.

"Charlie," she whispered, her voice small against the growing swell of attention surrounding them.

"It's okay," he said, though they both knew it wasn't. "Just stay close to me."

The market, which moments before had been a haven of ordinary pleasure, had transformed into a gauntlet. Each stall they passed now held people with phones raised, whispers trailing in their wake like disturbed water. The teenage girl who had first recognized him was now openly following them, her phone held high as she narrated to what was likely a social media livestream.

"Oh my god, guys, it's really him, Charlie Benton is at the Los Feliz farmers market and he's with some girl I don't recognize..."

Charlie kept his face carefully neutral, the expression he'd perfected over years of unwanted attention—not friendly enough to encourage approach, not cold enough to generate negative press. His hand pressed gently against Bee's back, guiding her toward the market's edge, toward escape.

But with each step, the crowd seemed to thicken, more people turning to look, more phones appearing, more whispers crescendoing into a low roar of curiosity. A path that had taken them ten leisurely minutes to walk now stretched before them like an impossible distance, each foot of progress an exercise in navigating increasingly pointed attention.

"Just a little further," Charlie murmured, feeling Bee trembling slightly against him. Whether from anxiety or anger, he couldn't tell, but the protective instinct that surged through him was primal and fierce. This was exactly what he'd feared— her first real taste of the fishbowl he lived in, thrust upon her without warning or preparation.

The sunlight that had seemed so golden and gentle earlier

now felt harsh and exposing, leaving nowhere to hide from the dozens of eyes tracking their movement, the dozens of cameras capturing every expression, every gesture, every moment of what should have been a private connection. The simple pleasure of their morning had shattered, replaced by the all-too-familiar sensation of being observed rather than experienced.

Charlie pulled Bee closer still, his body curved around hers as if he could somehow shield her from the growing intrusion, knowing even as he did that it was already too late. Their first steps into the public world had been documented, dissected, and would soon be distributed across platforms he couldn't control, to audiences he couldn't address, with narratives he couldn't correct.

The bread, the honey, the blue mug—treasures from a moment of normalcy now burdens in his hand as they quickened their pace toward the market's edge, toward the uncertain safety beyond.

Charlie's hand pressed against the small of Bee's back, firm but gentle as he guided her through the thickening crowd. Bodies seemed to materialize around them, faces alight with recognition and curiosity, phones raised like periscopes above the sea of heads. He kept his expression neutral, years of practice preventing him from revealing the anxiety coursing through his veins. Bee moved beside him in rigid silence, her earlier ease replaced by a tension he could feel beneath his palm as they navigated the final stretch toward the parking lot.

"Just a few more steps," he murmured, close to her ear. "Car's right there."

A woman stepped directly into their path, phone already recording. "Charlie! Who's your new girlfriend? Can we get a statement about—"

Charlie sidestepped smoothly, angling his body to create a barrier between the woman and Bee. "Not today, thanks." The words were polite, his tone final—a dismissal wrapped in courtesy that his PR team had drilled into him years ago.

More voices called his name as they reached the lot, questions flying like arrows:

"Charlie, over here!"

"Are you dating?"

"What happened with Claire?"

"Just one photo, Charlie!"

He unlocked the car with trembling fingers, opening the passenger door for Bee before anyone could intercept them. She slid inside without a word, her face carefully composed, though he caught the slight tremble in her hands as she clutched her bag against her chest. Charlie closed the door firmly, then rounded the hood with quick, practiced movements, ignoring the phones tracking his progress.

The driver's seat enveloped him in familiar leather as he shut the door, the sound of it closing like a seal breaking—separating them from the growing crowd with blessed finality. Charlie started the engine, the purr of the expensive motor vibrating beneath them as he navigated out of the lot, conscious of the faces still watching, the phones still recording.

Neither spoke as he turned onto the main road, putting distance between them and the market. The paper bag of their purchases sat between them on the console, the blue mug and honey jars and bread a surreal reminder of the normal morning they'd briefly enjoyed. Charlie's hands gripped the steering wheel too tightly, his eyes flicking constantly to the rearview mirror, checking for cars that might be following.

"I'm sorry," he finally said, breaking the silence as they stopped at a red light. "That was... not how I wanted your first public outing with me to go."

Bee stared straight ahead, her profile etched with an emotion he couldn't quite read. "Is it always like that?"

"Not always," he answered honestly. "Sometimes it's worse."

A humorless laugh escaped her, sharp and brief. "Great."

Her phone chimed from inside her bag, then again, and again—a cascade of notifications that didn't stop. Bee pulled it out, staring at the screen with widening eyes.

"That was fast," she murmured, unlocking the phone with a swipe.

Charlie watched from the corner of his eye as her expression shifted from confusion to disbelief. Her thumb scrolled through what appeared to be a series of text messages, each one seemingly accompanied by images that made her cheeks flush.

"My roommate from college," she said, her voice strangely distant. "She sent a screenshot from Instagram. Someone captioned it 'Charlie Benton's mystery woman' with about twenty question marks." She continued scrolling. "And here's one from my cousin... and my high school friend... and my mother. My mother, Charlie."

He swallowed hard, guilt sitting like a stone in his stomach. "What does your mother say?"

"'Call me immediately. Is this you? What's going on?'" Bee read, her voice gaining a slight tremor. "There's three missed calls from her already."

Charlie navigated onto the freeway, choosing the route that would take them toward his home rather than back to her apartment. The city slipped past their windows, oblivious to the small crisis unfolding inside the car.

"It moves fast," he said quietly. "Social media, the gossip sites. They'll have your name by the end of the day, probably. Your workplace too."

Bee's phone continued to buzz relentlessly in her hand. She stared at it as if it had transformed into something alien and threatening. "I have thirty-seven notifications. I never get notifications. I post about twice a year."

Before Charlie could respond, his own phone rang through the car's Bluetooth system, the name "Toby Chalmers" appearing on the dashboard display. Charlie's jaw tightened, tension radiating from his shoulders.

"I need to take this," he said apologetically. "It's my agent."

Bee nodded, still staring at her own phone's endless stream of alerts.

Charlie pressed the button on his steering wheel. "Toby."

"What the actual hell, Charlie?" The voice filled the car immediately, sharp with alarm and irritation. "I'm looking at photos of you and some woman all over Twitter right now. Who is she? Why am I finding out about this from fucking TMZ alerts?"

Charlie's knuckles whitened on the steering wheel. "Good morning to you too, Toby."

"Don't good morning me. I've got Harrison calling from the studio asking if this is going to affect promotion for the Miller project, I've got Claire's publicist wanting to know if we need to coordinate statements, and I've got seventeen journalists asking for confirmation on your 'new relationship status.' All before my first coffee, Charlie."

Bee stiffened beside him, her eyes now fixed on the dashboard as if she could see the man behind the voice. Charlie shot her an apologetic glance before responding.

"Toby, I'm not alone right now."

A beat of silence. "She's with you? Jesus, Charlie, put me on your phone. This isn't a conversation for an audience."

"No," Charlie said firmly. "Whatever you need to say, you can say it now or wait until later."

Toby's sigh crackled through the speakers. "Fine. Who is she? At least give me that much so I can prepare a statement."

Charlie glanced at Bee, a silent question in his eyes. She nodded once, a small gesture of permission.

"Her name is Bianca Anderson. She goes by Bee. She manages a boutique in Silver Lake. We've been seeing each other..." He hesitated, unsure how to categorize what they'd been doing. "We're getting to know each other."

"Getting to know each other," Toby repeated flatly. "Well, now the whole world is getting to know her too. Does she understand what she's in for? The scrutiny? The gossip? The paparazzi camped outside her apartment? Because that's what happens, Charlie. You know this. What were you thinking, taking her to a public market without any security?"

Charlie's face hardened, a muscle jumping in his jaw. "I was thinking I'd like to have a normal Sunday morning for once."

"You don't get normal Sunday mornings," Toby shot back. "Not anymore. Not for years. Christ, Charlie, we've been through this. After that disaster with Claire—"

"Don't," Charlie interrupted, his voice low with warning. "That was different."

Another sigh from Toby, this one heavier. "Look, I need to get ahead of this. The photos are everywhere already. You're trending. 'Charlie Benton's mystery woman' is trending. I need to know what you want me to say."

Charlie stared straight ahead at the road unfolding before them, acutely aware of Bee beside him, of her phone still buzzing with notifications, of the surreal speed with which their private connection had become public spectacle.

"Say that I'm seeing someone, and that I'd appreciate privacy during this time," he said finally. "Nothing more."

"Privacy," Toby echoed with grim amusement. "That ship has sailed, my friend. I'll do what I can, but you know how this works. They'll be at your gates within the hour. Probably already there."

The call ended with a click that seemed to echo in the suddenly silent car. Charlie exhaled slowly, fingers flexing on the steering wheel as he tried to release some of the tension coiling through his body.

"So that's Toby," he said finally, attempting a lightness he didn't feel.

"He sounds... intense," Bee replied, her voice carefully neutral.

"He's good at his job. Which is managing situations exactly like this." Charlie glanced at her, trying to gauge her state of mind. "Are you okay?"

Bee's laugh held no humor. "My phone won't stop buzzing with people I haven't talked to in years suddenly very interested in my life. My mother thinks I've been hiding a secret relationship. And apparently there will be paparazzi at my apartment." She turned to face him fully. "So no, I'm not particularly okay right now."

The guilt that had been building in Charlie's chest expanded, threatening to crush his ribs from the inside. He'd known this would happen—had warned her it might—but the reality was so much more immediate, more invasive than any explanation could have conveyed.

"I'm so sorry," he said, the words feeling wholly inadequate. "This is exactly what I was afraid would happen."

Traffic slowed ahead of them, forcing Charlie to brake. In the momentary stillness, he turned to look at Bee directly, taking in the tightness around her eyes, the slight pallor beneath her usual complexion, the rigid set of her shoulders.

"We can turn around," he offered quietly. "I can take you home, have Toby issue a statement saying we're just friends, hire security to keep photographers away from your building for a few days until it dies down. This doesn't have to—" He swallowed hard. "You don't have to do this."

Bee held his gaze, something complicated moving behind her eyes. "Is that what you want?"

"What I want," Charlie said carefully, "is for you not to regret meeting me. What I want is impossible—to be with you without all of... this." He gestured vaguely at their phones, at the invisible but palpable presence of public attention now surrounding them. "But since I can't have that, what I want is whatever causes you the least pain."

The traffic inched forward again. Charlie returned his attention to the road, giving Bee space to consider his words. Her phone continued its persistent buzzing, each notification another thread in the web of scrutiny rapidly spinning around them.

"Where are we going?" she asked finally, noticing they had passed the exit that would have taken them toward her neighborhood.

"My place," Charlie admitted. "I thought... I don't know what I thought. That it might be safer, more private. But I can take you home if you prefer."

Bee was silent for a long moment, staring out at the city sliding past their windows. When she spoke again, her voice was quieter but steadier than before.

"No, let's go to your place. I think... I think I need to understand what I'm getting into. Really understand, not just theoretically."

Charlie nodded, relief and anxiety mingling in his chest as he navigated toward the canyons, toward the isolated sanctuary that had never felt particularly like home until now, when he had someone to bring into it.

"I'm so sorry," he said again, the words heavy with genuine regret. "This is exactly what I was afraid would happen."

Charlie's mansion sprawled across the hillside like a modernist's dream, all clean lines and vast windows that seemed to capture pieces of sky. Bee stood in the great room, feeling strangely diminished by the soaring ceilings and carefully curated art that probably cost more than she'd earn in a decade. The space was beautiful in the way expensive things often were—perfect, polished, but somehow untouched by the messy warmth of actual living. She wandered toward the wall of windows, arms wrapped around herself as if for protection, her reflection a small, uncertain figure against the panoramic view of Los Angeles spread below.

Charlie had disappeared into his home office immediately upon arrival, the tense set of his shoulders telegraphing stress as he went to call Toby back. "Make yourself comfortable," he'd said, the phrase sounding hollow in a space that seemed designed for appearance rather than comfort. Now, left alone, Bee paced the length of the room, her footsteps silent against the expensive hardwood.

Her phone had finally stopped its incessant buzzing, silenced and buried deep in her bag where she didn't have to watch the notifications accumulate. Thirty-seven messages had become over a hundred in the span of their drive. Friends she hadn't spoken to in years, distant relatives, even her high school English teacher—all suddenly intensely interested in her life, all sharing screenshots of her face alongside Charlie's, all asking variations of the same questions: Is this real? How did you meet him? How long has this been going on?

The mug from the farmers market sat on the kitchen counter where she'd placed it, its deep blue glaze catching the light. Such a simple object, purchased in a moment that already felt like it belonged to another lifetime—before the cameras, before the whispers, before her private life had become public property.

Bee traced her fingers along the edge of a pristine sofa that looked like it had never known the imprint of a human body. Everything in the room spoke of careful selection rather than organic accumulation—the art chosen for investment value, the furniture arranged for maximum aesthetic impact, the technology discreetly hidden behind custom panels. This was Charlie's world, she realized. Not the Airbnb where they'd had dinner, not the cozy cafe where they'd shared coffee, but this rarefied space separated from ordinary life by wealth, fame, and the long, winding driveway that kept the public at a distance.

Except that distance was rapidly collapsing. Through the vast windows, Bee noticed movement at the property's main gate far below—one car, then another, parking along the road. Even from this height, the long camera lenses were visible, pointed toward the house like accusing fingers. The photographers had found them, just as Toby had predicted.

Bee pressed her palm against the cool glass, watching as more vehicles arrived. How had they known to come here? How had they found Charlie's home so quickly? The speed of it all left her dizzy, her quiet life suddenly accelerated into something unrecognizable. Less than a week ago, she'd been just another anonymous person in a city of millions. Now her face would be on websites, in tabloids, subject to scrutiny and speculation from people who knew nothing about her.

From somewhere deeper in the house, she heard Charlie's voice rise momentarily—not the words, just the tone, tense and frustrated—before falling back to an indistinct murmur. What was he telling Toby? What strategies were they planning to "manage" this situation? To manage her?

The thought sent a chill through her that had nothing to do with the perfectly regulated temperature of the house. She wasn't prepared for this—for becoming a character in someone else's narrative, for having her words twisted, her intentions questioned, her history excavated for anything that might generate clicks or sell magazines.

Movement at the gate caught her attention again. The cluster of photographers had grown, joined now by what appeared to be a news van. Bee felt her throat tighten, tears threatening for the first time since the market. This wasn't just an inconvenience or a temporary embarrassment. This was her new reality if she chose to pursue whatever was developing between her and Charlie.

The soft sound of footsteps behind her announced Charlie's return. Bee didn't turn, keeping her eyes fixed on the gathering crowd below, willing the tears not to fall.

"They're already here," she said, her voice steadier than she felt.

Charlie moved to stand beside her, close but not touching, his reflection appearing next to hers in the window. He looked exhausted, the carefully maintained public persona stripped away to reveal something raw and vulnerable beneath.

"I'm sorry," he said, the words weighted with genuine regret. "Toby's arranging for security, but it'll be a day or two before they disperse. They're like—"

"Vultures?" Bee suggested, finally turning to face him.

"I was going to say 'particularly persistent mosquitoes,' but vultures works too." His attempt at humor fell flat, his expression too strained to support it. "Are you okay?"

The question hung between them, simple yet impossibly complex. Was she okay? How could she possibly answer that? Bee turned back to the window, watching another car join the growing collection outside the gate.

"I don't know," she answered honestly. "This morning I was just Bee Anderson, retail manager with an unexpected text friend. Now I'm..." She gestured toward the photographers. "Whoever they decide I am."

Charlie moved closer, his reflection overlapping with hers in the glass. "You're still you," he said quietly. "They don't get to change that."

A bitter laugh escaped her. "Easy for you to say. You've had years to adjust to this. I've had minutes."

"You're right." He ran a hand through his hair, the familiar gesture somehow more poignant here in his home than it had been in the Airbnb or cafe. "And no one would blame you if you wanted to walk away from this. From me."

There it was—the out she'd been half-expecting, half-dreading. Bee turned to face him fully, taking in the tension in his shoulders, the careful distance he maintained, the way his eyes held hers with an intensity that belied his casual tone. He was preparing himself for rejection, she realized. Had perhaps been preparing for it since the moment she recognized him at his door.

"Is that what you want?" she asked, echoing her question from the car.

"What I want hasn't changed," Charlie replied, his voice low and strained. "But what I want doesn't matter if it makes your life impossible."

Bee felt the tears she'd been fighting finally spill over, tracing warm paths down her cheeks. Charlie moved as if to comfort her, then stopped himself, uncertain of his welcome.

"It's all happening so fast," she said, wiping at her face with the back of her hand. "We were just getting to know each other, and now there are photographers at your gate and my mother thinks I've been hiding a secret relationship and my co-workers are probably being hounded for information about me. It's..." She took a shuddering breath. "It's a lot."

Charlie nodded, guilt evident in every line of his body. "I know. And it doesn't get easier, Bee. This is the reality of being connected to me. The scrutiny, the invasion of privacy, the constant speculation. People will make up stories about you, about us. They'll dig into your past, analyze your clothes, your expressions, your words. They'll decide they know you based on nothing but photographs and rumors."

The stark honesty of his words hit her with physical force.

This wasn't a temporary inconvenience that would fade in a few days. This was potentially her new normal.

"How do you live with it?" she asked, genuinely curious. "How do you go to a farmers market or have coffee or just... exist... knowing someone might be watching, recording, judging?"

"You build walls," Charlie said simply. "You create a public version of yourself that they can pick apart while protecting what's real. You learn to recognize the places and times where you can be yourself, and the ones where you have to perform." He hesitated, then added, "It's lonely."

The admission hung in the air between them, vulnerable and raw. Bee looked at him—really looked at him, beyond the handsome face that had graced movie posters, beyond the celebrity she'd recognized at his door. She saw the man who argued with his reflection, who cooked steaks with nervous precision, who had reached through a wrong number text to connect with her in a way that felt more genuine than relationships she'd spent months cultivating.

"I knew what I was getting into," she said finally, wiping away the last of her tears. "Mostly. I just didn't expect it to happen so fast."

Hope flickered across Charlie's face, quickly tempered with caution. "What are you saying?"

Bee took a deep breath, gathering her courage. "I'm saying that walking away now, before we even have a chance to see what this could be... I'd regret that. And I try not to make decisions based on fear."

She stepped closer to him, the distance between them shrinking both physically and emotionally. "I can't promise I won't get overwhelmed sometimes. I can't promise I'll always handle the attention gracefully. But I want to try. If you do."

Charlie's expression transformed, relief and joy breaking through the careful restraint he'd maintained. "I do," he said, the words carrying a weight that seemed to fill the space between them. "I really do."

Bee reached for his hand, her fingers finding his with the same ease they had at the farmers market, before everything had changed. His palm was warm against hers, solid and real amidst the surreal circumstances surrounding them.

"So we try," she said, looking up at him with determination replacing the uncertainty that had clouded her eyes moments before. "We figure it out together."

Charlie's other hand rose to brush a strand of hair from her face gently, the touch so tender it made her breath catch. "Together," he agreed, his voice rough with emotion. Their eyes locked, and in that charged moment, they leaned in, sharing a first tender kiss. Her lips were soft against his, sending a tingling warmth through them both. Charlie's arms wrapped around her, pulling her close, their hearts beating in a synchronised rhythm. But as the embrace tightened and the kiss deepened, they slowly pulled apart, breathless and yearning. Charlie murmured an apology, admitting he got carried away. Bee softly reassured him, "No apologies are necessary, I was 100% in that, but..." she moved back a small measure to allow some inches between them, but took his hand in hers, "we should just take a minute before letting ourselves get carried away, I need to feel my feet on the ground first."

Outside, the photographers continued to gather, their lenses pointed toward windows that revealed nothing from this distance. Inside, Bee and Charlie stood with their hands entwined, the vast space around them no longer feeling quite so empty, quite so perfect, quite so untouched by life. He pulled her in for a hug, and they stood embracing, taking a moment to let their new reality sink in.

The blue mug from the farmers market caught the light on the counter, a small, ordinary treasure amid the carefully curated luxury. Like their connection—unexpected, imperfect, but somehow more valuable than all the calculated acquisitions surrounding them.

"What happens now?" Bee asked, her voice steady despite the uncertainty ahead.

Charlie's smile reached his eyes, crinkling the corners in a way no camera had ever quite captured. "Now," he said, "we write our own story. Not theirs."

Outside the gates, the world waited to define them, to categorise and analyse and judge. But here, in this moment, they defined themselves—two people choosing to walk forward together despite the complications, despite the scrutiny, despite the fear. Not because it would be easy, but because some connections were worth fighting for, worth protecting, worth the risk of pain and exposure and misunderstanding.

Worth trying for.

Chapter Eleven: Standing Strong

The boutique's glass door felt unusually heavy as Bee pushed it open the next morning, as if the building itself resisted her entry. Fluorescent lights cast their merciless glow across the polished floor, illuminating racks of designer clothing that had once represented her professional pride but now felt like costumes in someone else's performance. She had barely stepped inside when the hushed conversation near the register abruptly ceased, three faces turning toward her with expressions that poorly masked their eager curiosity. Between their fingers, phone screens glowed with images she didn't need to see to recognise—her face alongside Charlie's captured in the farmers market ambush, now circulating through celebrity gossip channels like blood cells through veins.

"Good morning," Bee offered, her voice steadier than she felt. The artificial floral scent that Victoria insisted on pumping through the ventilation system suddenly seemed cloying, choking, mingling with the metallic taste of anxiety coating her tongue.

Her assistant, Meredith, broke first. "Oh my god, Bee! You

didn't tell us you were dating Charlie Benton!" The words tumbled out in a rush of excitement, phone clutched to her chest like a precious artifact. "These photos are everywhere! Is it serious? How long has it been going on?"

Bee forced her lips into what she hoped resembled a smile rather than a grimace. "I'd rather not discuss my personal life at work," she said, moving toward the back room to deposit her bag. The weight of their stares followed her, pressing against her shoulder blades with almost physical force.

She had barely set down her things when the boutique manager, Sandra, appeared in the doorway, her carefully contoured face arranged in an expression of concerned interest that didn't reach her eyes.

"Bee, darling," Sandra's voice dripped with feigned sweetness. "Can we chat for a moment? Privately?"

The small office felt airless as Sandra closed the door behind them, immediately dropping any pretence of professional distance. "So it's true? You and Charlie Benton? How did that even happen? Did you meet him here? Was he shopping for someone?" Her eyes narrowed slightly. "You should have told me if he came into the store."

"It's complicated," Bee replied, maintaining eye contact despite the urge to look away. "And honestly, not relevant to my work here."

Sandra's laugh held no humour. "Not relevant? Darling, you're dating one of the biggest stars in Hollywood. That's extremely relevant." She leaned forward, voice dropping to a conspiratorial whisper. "What's his place like? Those hillside mansions much have incredible views. Is it as gorgeous as they say?"

Bee felt her jaw tighten. "I need to get the new shipment unpacked before we open," she said, standing abruptly. "Shall

I focus on that, or would you prefer a detailed floor plan of a house that is not mine, nor mine to give detail on?"

Sandra's smile thinned but remained in place. "Of course, the shipment. We'll talk more later." The unspoken promise hung in the air like the artificial floral scent—this conversation wasn't over, merely postponed.

Out on the floor, Bee threw herself into the methodical task of organising a rack of designer dresses, her hands moving with practised efficiency even as they trembled slightly. She could hear the whispers from the register, the occasional laugh, the way conversation suspended whenever she moved within earshot. The familiar routine of checking inventory, adjusting displays, and preparing for opening offered little of its usual comfort.

The shop bell chimed precisely at 10 AM, heralding Victoria Harrington's arrival like a royal announcement. She swept in on a cloud of expensive perfume—something French and exclusive that probably cost more than Bee's monthly rent. Her ash-blonde hair was freshly highlighted, her casual day outfit likely also worth more than most people's formal wear. Two shopping bags from competing boutiques dangled from her wrist, a silent reminder that Harrington's wasn't her only option.

"Good morning, Victoria," Sandra gushed, materialising from wherever, over paid ass kissers usually hide when actual work needs doing. "Lovely to see you. Can I show you our new arrivals?"

Victoria's eyes scanned the store with practised indifference until they landed on Bee. Something shifted in her expression—a predatory interest replacing the boredom. "Actually," she said, voice carrying easily across the quiet space, "I'd like Bianca to assist me today."

Bee maintained a neutral expression as Victoria approached, the scent of her perfume growing stronger, almost suffocating. "Good morning, Ms Harrington. What can I help you with today?"

Victoria fingered a silk blouse, rubbing the fabric between manicured fingers with unnecessary force. "I saw the most interesting photos this morning," she said, voice pitched to carry without seeming intentional. "Someone who looked remarkably like you, with Charlie Benton." Her diamond bracelet caught the light as she gestured dismissively. "Though I'm sure it was just someone similar. Celebrities rarely waste time with...ordinary people."

Bee's face burned, but she kept her voice level. "The Valentino collection just arrived. Would you like to see the pieces you pre-ordered?"

"Not just yet." Victoria moved to a rack of evening dresses, pulling one out with casual disregard for the careful arrangement. "I've always found it fascinating how some people will do anything to elevate their status." She glanced at Bee over the dress. "Social climbers are so transparent, don't you think? Especially these temporary celebrity flings. They never last."

Bee's knuckles whitened around the hanger she held, but she maintained her professional smile. "This particular style is very popular this season. The cut is universally flattering."

Victoria replaced the dress, deliberately misaligning it with others. "Tell me, dear," she said, her voice dripping with mock innocence, "does he introduce you to his important friends, or do you wait in the car?"

The boutique seemed to still, conversations pausing, even the background music momentarily less audible. Bee felt something shift inside her chest— a final thread of tolerance stretched beyond its capacity, snapping with an almost audible sound.

"Actually, Victoria," she said, the formality of the address dropped like an unnecessary accessory, "I believe that question would be better directed to your third ex-husband's twenty-three-year-old girlfriend. She might have more experience waiting in cars than I do." Bee delivered bluntly, reminding Victoria of her ex-husband's face in headlines caught with his now girlfriend in a compromising position in his Porsche.

A shocked gasp escaped from somewhere near the register. Victoria's face froze, lines deepening around her mouth as colour flooded her cheeks. A customer browsing nearby suddenly became intensely interested in a handbag display, shoulders shaking with poorly suppressed laughter.

"How dare you," Victoria hissed, her composure fracturing. She pulled an evening gown from the rack—one of the most expensive pieces in the store—and deliberately let it slip from her fingers to the floor. "Pick that up."

Bee looked at the crumpled silk on the floor, then back to Victoria's challenging stare. Years of retail submission, of swallowing pride for a pay check, of smiling through insults thinly veiled as feedback—all of it crystalised in this moment.

"No," she said, the single syllable ringing with finality.

Victoria's eyes widened. "Excuse me?"

"I said no." Bee's voice gained strength with each word. "I won't pick it up. In fact, I won't be picking up anything else in this store, ever again. I quit."

The silence that followed was absolute, as if everyone in the boutique had collectively held their breath.

"You can't quit," Victoria sputtered, her perfect composure now thoroughly shattered. "You're fired!"

"Too late." Bee smiled, genuine for the first time that morning. "And while we're being honest, Victoria your taste has always been as overpriced as your personality. You don't buy clothes; you buy the validation that comes with the price tag. It's transparent, desperate, and honestly, a little said, and also exactly the reason all men of standing side step you at parties, you are the over priced hooker who is known for her gold digging desires, and face it honey, you are old enough to be a grandma."

She unclipped her employee badge and place it on the counter with deliberate care. The weight that had pressed against her chest all morning lifted, replaced by a buoyant sensation that felt dangerously close to freedom.

"Sandra, I'll email you my formal resignation." Bee said calmly. "Victoria, I suggest the green dress instead of the blue —it'll better hide the cosmetic work you had done last month."

With that, she retrieved her bag from the back room, walked through the silent store, and pushed open the heavy glass door. Outside, the morning sun felt warmer, more genuine than the artificial lighting she was leaving behind. Bee took a deep breath of unscented air and pulled out her phone to text Charlie about what had just happened. For the first time since their photos had surfaced, she felt not like a woman caught in a celebrity's orbit, but like herself—perhaps braver and more outspoken than before, but authentically, unapologetically Bee.

The director's chair creaked slightly as Charlie shifted his weight, the script pages in his hands blurring into meaningless symbols as his mind drifted elsewhere. Around him, the studio lot hummed with controlled chaos—lighting technicians adjusted equipment, makeup artists hovered near their stations, production assistants scurried between tasks with the desperate energy of people whose careers depended on anticipating needs before they were voiced. None of it reached him fully, the familiar rhythm of pre-interview preparation reduced to background noise against the louder concerns occupying his thoughts. His phone sat heavy in his pocket, a connection to the world beyond this artificial environment, to Bee and whatever aftermath she might be facing from their public outing.

The device vibrated against his thigh. Charlie set aside the script pages and retrieved his phone, tension easing from his shoulders when he saw Bee's name on the screen. The message loaded—a paragraph-length text that began with "I just quit my job" and continued with a detailed account of her confrontation with Victoria Harrington. Despite the stress of his upcoming interview, Charlie felt his lips curve into a genuine smile as he read Bee's description of telling Victoria that her taste has always been as overpriced as her personality."

His thumbs moved quickly across the screen: "I'm sorry you had to deal with that, but I am also incredibly impressed. Victoria sounds like she deserved every word. Are you okay? Do you need anything? I'm in the middle of press, but I can call as soon as I'm done."

He was still looking at his phone, waiting for her response, when a throat cleared pointedly beside him.

"Mr. Benton? We need to start makeup if we're going to stay on schedule."

Charlie nodded, slipping his phone back into his pocket with reluctance. "Of course, sorry about that."

The makeup chair offered no escape from the day's recurring theme. The artist—a woman in her thirties with purple-tipped hair and an impressive collection of vintage band pins on her denim jacket—began applying foundation with practiced strokes while launching immediately into the conversation he'd been dreading.

"So," she said, her eyes bright with barely contained curiosity, "I saw the photos this morning. Your new girlfriend is gorgeous in a real-person way. Refreshing to see you with someone who hasn't had all the work done."

Charlie maintained his professional smile with effort. "I'd rather not discuss my personal life, if that's alright."

"Oh, of course, of course," she agreed, though her next words contradicted this entirely. "It's just, you know, everyone's talking about it. How did you two meet? She works in retail, right? That's what TMZ said this morning."

"Powder's a bit heavy on the right side," Charlie deflected, internally counting to ten.

The makeup artist adjusted her approach, apparently interpreting his redirection as an invitation to continue from a different angle. "Sorry about that. My sister works in retail too —brutal industry. All those rich customers thinking they own you because they're spending money." She paused, brush hovering near his cheekbone. "Did you meet her while shopping? Was it like Pretty Woman but reverse? Not that she's anything like—I just meant the whole different worlds thing."

Charlie's jaw tightened almost imperceptibly. "Could we keep the conversation professional? I'm trying to get into the right headspace for this interview."

"Right, right, sorry." She applied powder to his forehead with quick, light strokes. "It's just exciting, you know? After Claire Vanderholt—she was so...Hollywood. Your new girlfriend seems real, I really wish you guys luck shes a mere mortal it is going to be tough."

The distinction between "Hollywood" and "real" scraped against Charlie's already frayed nerves, the implicatin that his previous relationship had been somehow less authentic, that his world was inherently fake, that Bee existed in a separate category of genuine humanity. He breathed through the irritation, maintaining the pleasant expression that had become as much a part of his professional equipmet as his ability to memorise lines, because deep down he knew her assessment was accurate.

"All set," the makeup artist said finally, stepping back to inspect her work. "You look perfect."

Perfect. The word echoed hollowly as Charlie stood, thanking her with automatic courtesy before making his way toward the interview area. Perfect meant camera-ready, meant marketable, meant the version of Charlie Benton that existed for public consumption. Perfect had nothing to do with the man who texted Bee about cereal being soup, who rearranged pillows because he was nervous about dinner, who longed for ordinary Sunday mornings at farmers markets.

He had nearly reached the interview set when a commotion erupted near one of the building entrances. A group of women—five or six, it was hard to tell in the sudden chaos—had somehow gotten past the first security checkpoint and were moving toward him with the focused determination of heat-seeking missiles.

"Charlie! Oh my god, Charlie!"

"We love you!"

"Can we get a picture?"

Security was moving too slowly, the women reaching him before guards could intervene. They surrounded him in a cloud of competing perfumes and excited voices, phones raised at various angles to capture his image. Charlie stepped back, maintaining his public smile while trying to create distance, his body automatically shifting into the practised posture of celebrity accessibility that contained clear boundaries.

"Ladies, I'm sorry, but I'm heading to an interview. Security will help you—"

A woman in a low-cut top pressed against him before he could finish, her arm sliding around his waist as she angled her phone for a selfie. "Just one picture," she insisted, her body uncomfortably close, her free hand slipping something into his pocket with practiced subtlety. "Call me later," she whispered, her lips nearly brushing his ear. "I'll show you a better time than a retail girl."

Charlie's practised smile faltered, his hand moving to remove whatever she'd placed in his pocket—a folded slip of paper with a phone number, he discovered as he pulled it out.

The invasiveness of the gesture, the entitlement behind it, the dismissive reference to Bee—it all struck him with unexpected force, cracking the veneer of professional tolerance he typically maintained.

Another woman called out from the edge of the group, her voice carrying clearly: "Dump the plain Jane and call me! I'll make it worth your while!"

Security finally arrived, creating a barrier between Charlie and the women, but the damage was already done. He looked directly at the woman who had pressed against him, holding out the paper with her number.

"I think you dropped this," he said, his voice calm but firm. "And I'd appreciate it if you'd all respect that I'm in a committed relationship."

He turned to the second woman, meeting her gaze directly. "There's nothing plain about my girlfriend. And comments like that say far more about you than they do about her."

The security team escorted the women toward the exit, their expressions oscillating between embarrassment and indignation. Charlie straightened his jacket, the momentary satisfaction of standing up for Bee and himself already fading as he registered the dozens of phones that had captured the exchange. By evening, his words would be dissected across social media, analysed for hidden meanings, presented as either chivalrous defence or celebrity arrogance, depending on who was framing the narrative.

"So, Charlie, there' been quite a buzz about your new relationship," she said, leaning forward slightly as if they were friends sharing confidences rather than performers executing a transaction of personal information for publicity.

"It's an unexpected choice for someone in your position. What drew you to someone so...outside the industry?"

Charlie's smile remained in place, though it no longer reached his eyes. "I'm here to discuss the film, which I think audiences will find both entertaining and thought-provoking."

"Of course, of course," she agreed smoothly, "but your fans are naturally curious about your personal happiness. After your relationship with Clair ended so publicly, many were surprised to see you with someone so...different."

Different. Outside the industry. Unexpected choice. The careful euphemisms grated against his patience, each one a thinly veiled reference to the fundamental question they were all asking: why would someone like him choose someone like Bee?

The interviewer's expression suggested she recognised she'd hit a wall but wasn't ready to abandon the line of questioning entirely. "That's beautiful, Charlie. And how does she handle the spotlight? It must be quite the adjustment for someone used to a more...ordinary life."

Charlie's answers grew increasingly clipped as the interview progressed, his customary charm giving way to a more guarded professionalism. By the time the cameras stopped rolling, his shoulders ached with tension, his face stiff from maintaining a pleasant expression through increasingly intrusive questions. The artifice of it all—the practised curiosity, the boundary-pushing disguised as friendly interest, the relentless focus on Bee as an anomaly rather than a person—left a bitter taste in his mouth.

As soon as he was clear of the set, Charlie pulled out his phone, needing to hear Bee's voice, to reconnect with something genuine amidst the performance his day had become. Whatever challenges they faced in navigating their public relationship, moments like today reinforced that they would face them together, two real people against an industry that traded in carefully crafted illusions.

The café existed in that perfect state of obscurity—known enough to locals to stay in business, unknown enough to tourists to maintain character. Tucked away on a side street where the urban sprawl of L.A momentarily forgot itself, its exterior offered no hint of the warm wood and brass interior, the mismatched chairs, the pendant lights that hung low over each table creating pools of amber intimacy. Bee arrived first, slipping through the door with a quick glance over her shoulder—a habit she'd developed over the past forty-eight hours. She chose the corner booth where shadows gathered thick enough to blur features, where the ambient music would cover quiet conversation, where she could see the door without being immediately visible from it.

Charlie arrived seventeen minutes later, baseball cap pulled low, shoulders hunched slightly in the posture of someone hoping to go unnoticed. He paused just inside the door, eyes adjusting to the dimness, scanning until he found her waiting in the corner. The smile that transformed his face then belonged to Charlie her wrong-number friend, not Charlie Benton the actor—unguarded, slightly crooked, reaching his eyes in a way that publicity shots never captured.

He slid into the booth across from her, his hands immediately finding hers across the worn wooden table. His fingers were warm against her skin, the contact sending a current of comfort up her arms and into her chest where tension had made its home since the farmers market incident.

"Hi," he said simply, the single syllable carrying more weight than elaborate greetings could have managed.

"Hi yourself," Bee replied, the tightness in her shoulders easing for the first time since she'd walked into Harrington's that morning. "Quite a day."

Charlie's thumb traced small circles against her wrist. "I

was surprised at your text. I still can't believe you actually quit."

"You should have seen Victoria's face." Bee straightened her posture, rearranging her features into an exaggerated mask of shock, nostrils flaring slightly, eyes widening to comic proportions. "It was like someone had told her money couldn't actually buy happiness. Complete existential crisis."

Charlie's laugh rumbled low in his chest, genuine and unfiltered. "What about the comment on her cosmetic work? What that true?"

"Absolutely." Bee leaned forward, lowering her voice conspiratorially. "She thinks no one notices, but she comes back from spa weekend with mysteriously tighter skin every few months." She affected Victoria's clipped, aristocratic tone: "One simply must maintain standards, darling. Aging is for the middle class."

Charlie shook his head, still holding her hands, his shoulders relaxing as he absorbed her story. "Well, your spectacular exit gave me the courage to stand up to some invasive fans today." His expression sobered slightly. "One actually slipped her number into my pocket while pressing herself against me for a selfie."

Bee's eyebrows rose. "Bold. What did you do?"

"Gave it back to her and made it clear I'm in a committed relationship." His thumb continued its gentle movement against her pulse point, a physical anchor as he recounted the uncomfortable encounter. "Another one called suggesting I should dump the plain Jane, that's when I really got irritated."

Bee's chest tightened, no from jealousy but from a more complicated emotion—the strange vertigo of having strangers form opinions about you without knowing you exist as a full person. "What did you say?"

"That there's nothing plain about you. And that her comment said more about her than about you." His eyes held hers across the table, intent and sincere. "The interview afterward was worse though. So many questions about why I'd choose someone outside the industry, as if that's some kind of inexplicable deviation from proper behaviour."

Their conversation paused as a waiter approached, a young man with carefully curated stubble and an assessing gaze that sharpened with recognition as it landed on Charlie. Bee watched the familiar transformation—the initial widening of eyes, the quick recalibration to professional nonchalance, the slightly higher pitch to his voice as he greeted them.

"Good evening. Can I get you started with some drinks?" His eyes kept darting to Charlie despite his obvious efforts to treat them like any other customers.

They ordered—a craft beer for Charlie, a glass of red wine for Bee—and selected meals with minimal deliberation. As the waiter departed, Charlie leaned closer across the table.

"Ten bucks says he's texting someone about us before he reaches the kitchen." He said, running a finger down her cheek, his voice husky.

"No bet," Bee replied with a small smile and a peck on the lips. "His hands were already twitching towards his pocket as he walked away."

Their drinks arrived with suspicious promptness, followed by their food—a burger for Charlie, pasta for Bee. The conversation flowed easily between them, discussing everything except the most obvious topic: what their relationship meant now that it existed under public scrutiny. They had nearly finished their meals when Charlie's posture suddenly stiffened, his eyes focusing on something beyond Bee's shoulder.

"Don't look now," he said quietly, "but the couple at the two-top by the window has been taking photos of us for the last five minutes."

Bee resisted the urge to turn, instead watching Charlie's face as it settled into the careful neutral expression she was learning to recognise as his public mask. The muscles around his jaw tightened, his eyes lost some of their warmth, his entire body seeming to brace against intrusion.

Without hesitation, Bee reached across the table and stole a fry from his plate, popping it into her mouth with exaggerated satisfaction. Charlie blinked, momentarily startled out of his tension.

"I'm sorry, did you need that?" she asked innocently.

A reluctant smile tugged at his lips. "I was saving it for later."

"Too bad. I'm starting to understand why celebrities are so entitled. Dating you clearly gives me special privileges." She leaned forward, voice dropping to a dramatic whisper, while edgeing him closer in what looked like an intimate encounter to everyone else. "What should we tell the tabloids next? I'm thinking we need to create some really outrageous fake stories just to mess with them."

Charlie's smile widened, real amusement replacing the tension in his eyes. "What did you have in mind?" he whispered huskily, brushing a hair away from her eyes.

"Well..." she gulped. "First, I am going to back up or it will be scandalous alright, but not safe for work," she said, sitting back slightly, "Tell them I'm an undercover agent investigating Hollywood corruption," she suggested, stealing another fry. "Deep cover operation. Years in the making. My retail job was just a front."

Charlie leaned in, playing along. "No, no. You're my alien bride from Planet Zircon. We met when your spacecraft crashed in my pool. It was love at first abduction."

Their laughter mingled in the space between them, creating a bubble of shared humour that temporarily pushed back the awareness of being observed. Bee felt something warm unfurl in her chest as she watched Charlie's face transform with genuine mirth, the public mask completely abandoned in this moment of connection.

"Maybe," she continued, warming to their game, "we're actually conducting secret experiments on celebrity culture. Your fame is just an elaborate social experiment, and I'm your academic research partner, and I chose you because you're so pretty." She said, emphasising the word pretty in a playful tone and batting her eyes.

"Perfect," Charlie agreed, his eyes crinkling at the corners. "Or we could say we're time travellers here to prevent the robot uprising of 2027. Very serious mission. The fate of humanity depends on our relationship," he paused, "wait that was done, Terminator."

The couple by the window had grown bolder, their phone now held up without pretence of subtlety. But within the Amber pool of light surrounding their corner booth, Bee and Charlie had created something that couldn't be captured in those stolen images—a private language of jokes and references, a shared resilience against public intrusion, a connection that existed beyond the narratives being constructed around them.

When they finally paid their bill and prepared to leave, Charlie moved with deliberate care, positioning himself between Bee and the still-watching couple. His hand found the small of her back, a gentle protective pressure guiding her toward the door. Outside, the evening air carried the particular L.A mixture of jasmine and car exhaust, the street quieter than it had been when they arrived.

"I'm sorry about that," Charlie said softly as they walked toward his car. "The photos, the staring. It doesn't stop."

Bee glanced up at him, noting the way his body remained angled slightly, a physical barrier between her and potential intrusion even here on a nearly empty sidewalk. The gesture touched her—not because she needed protection, but because it revealed how deeply he cared about shielding her from the harsh edges of his world.

"We'll figure it out," she replied, slipping her arm through his. "Bedsides, they completely missed the real story."

"Which is?"

"That I stole your last fry, and you let me. That's true love right there."

Charlie's laugh echoed against the buildings, genuine and unguarded in the darkness. His arm tightened around hers as they walked, two people navigating not just the physical path to his car but the more complex journey of building something real under the distorting spotlight of public attention.

Evening draped itself over L.A like expensive silk, soft and indulgent. Through the vast windows of Charlie's hillside mansion, the city transformed into a carpet of lights that stretched to the horizon, each pinprick representing lives being lived in anonymity—a luxury Charlie and Bee no longer shared. Inside, lamps cast pools of warm light across the living room, softening the clean architectural lines and reflecting off the leather couch where they had settled, shoes discarded, bodies turned toward each other in the familiar choreography of conversation. The day's tensions had begun to dissolve in the second glass of cabernet, in the quiet that existed between them, in the absence of watching eyes that had marked their public encounters.

Charlie refilled Bee's glass, the wine catching the light as it arced from the bottle to the glass. The distant hum of traffic filtered through the windows, a reminder of the world continuing beyond their temporary sanctuary. Bee curled her legs beneath her, the leather couch creaking slightly as she shifted, her shoulders relaxing further with each sip of wine.

"I still can't believe you actually quit, " Charlie said, shaking his head with admiration. "Most people fantasize about telling off their boss. You actually did it."

"I can't quite believe it either." Bee ran a finger around the rim of her glass, creating a faint musical note. "Six years at that boutique. Victoria's been making passive-aggressive comments the entire time, and I just...took it. Until today."

"What pushed you over the edge?"

"When she deliberately dropped that dress—a twenty-thousand-dollar Valentino, by the way—and ordered me to pick it up." Bee straightened, mimicking Victoria's rigid posture and imperious expression. "Pick that up," she intoned, capturing the precise mixture of entitlement and disdain that characterised the boutique owner. "Like I was a disobedient dog who needed to be reminded of the hierarchy."

Charlie's expression darkened momentarily. "I almost wish I'd been there to see her face when you refused."

"It was magnificent," Bee confirmed, settling back against the cushions. "Pure shock, like she'd suddenly discovered gravity works differently for her. But the best part was telling her she was basically a hooker." A laugh escaped her, genuine and unrestrained. "I've been thinking that for years but never imagined I'd actually say it to her face."

Charlie's fingers found their way to her hair, gently playing with the dark strands as he listened. The casual intimacy of the gesture sent warmth spreading through Bee's chest—this connection that had begun through text messages now expressed in physical touch, in shared space, in the comfortable silence that existed between stories.

"So," he said finally, "what happens next? Job-wise, I mean."

Bee sighed, leaning slightly into his touch. "I have some savings. Not enough to live on indefinitely, but enough to figure things out. I've always wanted to open my own place eventually—something focused on sustainable fashion, local designers. Maybe this is the universe's not-so-gentle nudge in that direction."

"I could invest," Charlie offered, then immediately held up his free hand when Bee's expression shifted. "Not charity. A legitimate business investment. I've been looking to diversify anyway."

"We'll talk about that later," Bee said, neither accepting nor rejecting. "First, we need to figure out how to navigate... this." She gestured between them, then toward the windows where, far below, a small cluster of paparazzi still maintained their vigil at the property's gate. "The public version of us."

Charlie nodded, his expression growing more serious. "Toby's arranged for additional security. Both here and at your apartment, at least for the next few weeks. And I know it sounds ridiculous, but disguises actually work sometimes— the right hat, sunglasses, change in posture. People see what they expect to see."

"So I should expect a closet full of fake moustaches and wigs?" Bee teased, though there was a genuine question beneath the humour.

"Only if you want them." Charlie's smile faded slightly, his eyes growing more intent. "Actually, I've been thinking. This house...it's pretty exposed. Great for views, terrible for privacy. I have a place up the coast—smaller, more secluded. Much harder for photographers to access. We could...I mean if you wanted, we could spend some time there. Get away from the immediate pressure."

Bee studied him, noting the careful way he presented the suggestion, the slight tension in his shoulders as he waited for her response. The implication extended beyond a simple getaway—it suggested a deeper commitment, a shared space, a deliberate choice to face their circumstances together rather than separately.

"Are you willing to upend your life for me?" she asked, the question emerging more vulnerable than she'd intended. "We've known each other for what—two weeks? Most of that through text messages. And now you're talking about relocating, about investing in a business, about security teams and disguises. That's...that's a lot of change very quickly."

Charlie's hand stilled in her hair, then moved to cup her cheek, his palm warm against her skin. "My life before you was just going through the motions," he said, his voice low and intent. "Scripts and premieres and publicity tours. Moving between carefully scheduled appointments that looked like a full life from the outside but felt hollow from within. This—us—is the first real thing I've felt in years, maybe ever."

The simple honesty of his words struck her with unexpected force, resonating with something in her own experience —the difference between existing and living, between performing the expected roles and discovering authentic connection.

"I'm scared," Bee admitted, setting her wine glass on the coffee table to free her hands, which twisted together in her lap. "Not of the photographers or the gossip. I'm scare of not fitting into your world. Of being the awkward retail manager who doesn't know which fork to use at industry dinners or what to say to directors at parties. Of embarrassing you."

"Embarrassing me?" Charlie looked genuinely bewildered. "Bee, you're the most authentic person I've met in years. Do you know how rare that is in my world? How valuable? Besides," he added, his voice lightening, "I've seen you handle Victoria Harrington. Hollywood power players should be terrified of you, not the other way around."

A reluctant smile tugged at her lips. "I did put her in her place rather effectively."

"Exactly." Charlie pulled her closer, until her head rested against his chest, his heartbeat steady beneath her ear. "We'll figure it out together. The security, the public stuff, all of it. I'm not saying it will be easy, but..." His arms tightened around her, secure and grounding. "We're a team now. Partners against the circus."

"Partners against the circus," Bee repeated softly, feeling the tension that had coiled in her shoulders since the farmers market finally begin to unwind completely. "I like that."

The television played an old movie neither of them was watching, the black-and-white images flickering across the screen like shadows from another era. Outside, the city continued its eternal dance of light and movement, indifferent to the small dramas played out within its boundaries. The wine bottle stood half-empty on the coffee table, glasses abandoned as conversation gave way to comfortable silence, then to the deeper quiet of shared rest.

Bee felt herself drifting, lulled by the steady rhythm of Charlie's breathing, by the warmth of his body against hers, by the sense of safety that existed within the circle of his arms. The leather couch that had seemed so pristine, so unlived-in when she first entered his home now cradled them both, bearing witness to this moment of vulnerability and connection that no paparazzi lens could capture.

Charlie's hand moved slowly up and down her back, a soothing rhythm that matched the cadence of his heartbeat beneath her ear. "Stay," he murmured, the word vibrating through his chest as sleep began to claim them both. "Stay tonight."

"Okay," Bee whispered back, her eyes already closed, her body already surrendering to exhaustion.

They fell asleep like that, intertwined on the couch, the city lights bearing witness through the vast windows, the world with all its complications temporarily held at bay by the simple fact of their bodies forming a united front against whatever waited outside. The movie played on unwatched, the wine remained unfinished, and somewhere far below, photographers waited for a story they couldn't possibly understand from their distance—the story of two people who had found each other through a wrong number and were now navigating a world that insisted on turning their private connection into public property.

In sleep, Charlie's arms remained protectively around Bee, even as his features relaxed into an expression rarely captured by cameras—unguarded, peaceful, genuine. And Bee, whose life had transformed so completely in the span of a few days, slept more soundly than she had since the farmers market, anchored by the certainty that whatever challenges awaited them in the morning, they would face them not as Charlie Benton the celebrity and Bee Anderson the retail manager, but as partners, together.

Chapter Twelve: Home Sweet Home

The evening light filtered through Charlie's floor-to-ceiling windows, painting elongated shadows across the living room where they sat in a secluded corner. Three days had passed since Bee had first stayed the night—unplanned, both of them falling asleep on the couch during a movie—and the paparazzi situation had only intensified. Charlie's fingers tapped an anxious rhythm against his knee as he studied Bee's profile, her attention momentarily captured by the last crimson streaks of sunset bleeding into the darkening sky beyond the glass.

"They were outside your apartment building again today," he said finally, breaking the comfortable silence that had settled between them. "My security team counted seven photographers this morning. That's more than yesterday."

Bee turned from the window, her expression carefully neutral though Charlie could see the tension gathering in the corners of her eyes. "Nine by the time I left for my interview. One of them followed me to the coffee shop afterward."

The interview had been for a management position at a small boutique in Silver Lake—a temporary solution while she developed plans for her own business. Charlie had offered to drive her, but she'd insisted on going alone. Independence, he was learning, was something Bee guarded fiercely.

"I'm sorry," he said, the words inadequate against the reality they were facing. "This isn't what you signed up for."

She offered him a small smile that didn't quite reach her eyes. "I knew what I was getting into." Her fingers curled around the stem of her wine glass. "My neighbor Mrs. Levinson called today. Apparently someone offered her five hundred dollars for 'insights into my daily routine.' She told them to go to hell, thankfully."

Charlie's jaw tightened. The invasion had moved beyond simple photography into something more intrusive, more disturbing. He'd seen it before—the way public interest could transform into entitlement, the way privacy became a commodity to be bought and sold. His fingers resumed their nervous tapping against his knee as he gathered his courage.

"I've been thinking," he began, then paused, searching for the right words. "Your apartment... it doesn't have proper security. No gate, no cameras, not even a doorman."

Bee raised an eyebrow. "Most normal people don't have fortresses for homes, Charlie."

"I know. I know that." He ran a hand through his hair, a gesture she'd come to recognize as a sign of his nervousness. "It's just—they're not going to stop. Not anytime soon. And I'm worried about what happens when they get bored with just taking pictures. When they start trying to get reactions, provoke you, follow you more aggressively."

The concern in his voice was genuine, and Bee felt some of her defensiveness soften. She set her wine glass on the side table and turned more fully toward him. "What are you suggesting?"

Charlie's eyes met hers, then darted away, focusing instead on his hands. "Maybe you could stay here for a while? Just until things settle down." The words came out in a rush, followed immediately by clarifications. "I have plenty of space. The security system is top-of-the-line. There's a private entrance you could use to avoid the main gate where they've been camping out."

His fingers had moved from tapping his knee to fidgeting with the seam of his jeans, betraying the casualness he was attempting to project. Bee watched the movement, struck by how this man—whose face appeared on billboards across the city, who commanded millions per film—could appear so vulnerable in the simple act of inviting her into his space.

The suggestion hung between them, weighted with implications beyond the practical. Moving in, even temporarily, meant crossing a line in their still-new relationship, accelerating its natural progression under the pressure of external circumstances rather than personal choice.

Bee looked around the vast living room, taking in the soaring ceilings, the carefully curated art pieces, the seamless blend of luxury and comfort that characterized Charlie's home. Could she imagine herself here? Waking up in this space, moving through these rooms, returning to this address at the end of each day? It was a far cry from her modest apartment with its mismatched furniture and crowded bookshelves.

"I don't want to lose my independence," she said finally, giving voice to her primary concern. "I've worked hard to build my life on my terms. Living here, in your world..." She gestured at the expansive space around them. "It would be easy to get lost in all this."

Charlie nodded, understanding visible in his expression. "I wouldn't want that either. Your independence, your perspective—they're part of what makes you..." He paused, a slight flush colouring his cheeks. "What makes you you."

He leaned forward, his posture earnest. "You'd have your own suite. Complete privacy. Come and go as you please. His voice softened, revealing the vulnerability beneath the practical reasoning. "I just want you to be safe, Bee. I hate that this part of my life is affecting you this way."

The guilt in his expression tugged at something in her chest. This wasn't about control or rushing their relationship. It was about protection—clumsy perhaps, colored by his privilege and resources, but genuine in its intention.

"I could pay rent," she suggested, testing the idea aloud. "Make it a proper arrangement rather than just staying as your guest."

Charlie's expression shifted to one of mild horror. "Absolutely not. That's not—I wouldn't want—" He stopped, taking a breath. "This isn't about money, Bee. It's about keeping you safe from a situation I inadvertently created by being who I am."

Bee felt the last of her resistance soften at the raw honesty in his voice. The practical reality was undeniable—her apartment had become a target, her neighbors collateral damage in the media's fascination with their relationship. And beyond practicality, there was the simple truth that she wanted to be near him, to explore what was developing between them without the constant pressure of public intrusion.

"Okay," she said finally. "But it's temporary. Just until things calm down." She sat straighter, establishing the boundary clearly. "And I maintain my own life—my job search, my business planning, my friends. This can't become some gilded cage, Charlie."

The relief that washed across his face was immediate and profound, his shoulders visibly relaxing as he reached for her hand. "Of course. Absolutely. I wouldn't want anything else." His thumb traced gentle circles against her palm. "I can have security help bring whatever you need from your apartment. Tomorrow, if that works?"

Bee nodded, a strange mixture of anxiety and anticipation

swirling in her chest. She was about to step even further into Charlie's world, with all its complications and privileges. Yet as she looked at him—his expression open and grateful, his hand warm around hers—she couldn't bring herself to regret the decision.

"Tomorrow," she agreed, squeezing his hand in return. "But fair warning—I have a lot of books."

Charlie's smile bloomed slow and genuine, transforming his entire face. "I think we can handle that."

Outside, the last light of day surrendered to darkness, the city beyond the windows transforming into a constellation of distant lights. Inside, something shifted between them—not just the practical arrangement they'd agreed upon, but a deeper commitment to navigating this strange new territory together, whatever it might bring.

The following morning, Charlie led Bee through the grand entryway of his mansion with the slightly awkward air of someone unused to giving tours. Sunlight streamed through skylights overhead, illuminating marble floors that gleamed like still water. The space opened vertically as well as horizontally, ceilings soaring to heights that made Bee's modest apartment seem like a dollhouse by comparison. Their footsteps echoed against stone and glass, announcing their presence to empty rooms that branched off the main hall like tributaries from a river.

"So, this is... the entrance," Charlie said unnecessarily, his hand making a vague gesture that encompassed the vast foyer. "The decorator wanted to put a fountain here, but I managed to talk her out of it. Seemed a bit much."

Bee tilted her head back to take in the full sweep of the space, momentarily speechless. A curved staircase of pale wood and glass rose like a sculpture to her right, leading to a gallery that overlooked the entryway. To her left, a sitting area with furniture that probably cost more than her car nestled beneath a chandelier that caught the morning light and scattered it like diamonds across the walls.

"This is where normal people say 'honey, I'm home,' right?" she quipped, her voice sounding small in the cavernous space.

Charlie's laugh held a note of relief, as if he'd been holding his breath waiting for her reaction. "Usually I just dump my keys on that table and head straight for the kitchen. The rest is..." He shrugged. "Window dressing."

He guided her forward, past arrangements of fresh flowers that must be replaced weekly and artwork that made Bee itch to check the signatures for recognizable names. Her fingertips trailed along a hand-carved banister as they moved deeper into the house, the cool, smooth wood grounding her as the scale of Charlie's life unfolded before her.

"Living room," Charlie announced as they entered a space Bee had already seen, though now she noticed details she'd missed before—the subtle recessed lighting designed to high-light art pieces, the way the furniture was arranged to maxi-mize both the view and conversation potential, the hidden speakers that allowed music to seem ambient rather than sourced. "The decorator went a bit overboard in here. I told her I wanted comfortable, she heard 'showcase worthy.'"

His self-deprecating tone couldn't quite mask the slight discomfort that straightened his posture as he watched Bee absorb his surroundings. He moved quickly through the space, as if eager to get the formal areas behind them, pointing out features with dismissive comments: "Never use that fire-place," and "Those chairs look nice but feel like sitting on concrete."

Bee paused beside a side table where a worn paperback lay splayed open, face-down to hold someone's place. She tilted her head to read the spine—a dog-eared copy of Ray Bradbury's "The Martian Chronicles" with a cracked spine and pages soft from repeated readings.

"This doesn't look like part of the decorator's vision," she observed, smiling slightly.

Charlie's expression softened. "No, that's all me. I've had that copy since college. It travels from room to room, depending on where I last had time to read."

The simple admission—that this immaculate space contained a wandering, well-loved book—humanized the room in a way all the expensive furnishings couldn't. Bee found herself looking more closely at her surroundings, searching for other traces of the actual Charlie amid the curated luxury.

She found them as they continued through interconnected spaces: a throw blanket bunched at one end of a pristine sofa, indented by someone who'd actually sat there; a coffee mug with dried remnants in its bottom, forgotten on a windowsill; a pair of reading glasses perched atop a stack of scripts on an otherwise immaculate desk.

"Formal dining room," Charlie said, gesturing toward a space centered around a table that could comfortably seat sixteen. "I barely use half these rooms. The last time this table saw action was when my brother John visited with some friends for my birthday."

As if summoned by the mention, Bee noticed photographs displayed on a credenza against the far wall. Unlike the carefully composed portraits she'd half-expected, these showed Charlie in unguarded moments—laughing with a man who shared his nose and jawline but carried himself with less careful precision, the two of them on what appeared to be a fishing boat, another of them as teenagers with arms slung around each other's shoulders.

"That's John?" she asked, moving closer to examine the images.

Charlie nodded, his expression warming visibly. "Yeah. Those are from last summer when we took a trip up the coast. He's the only one who still treats me exactly the same as before all this." He gestured vaguely at their surroundings. "He's completely unimpressed by... everything."

Bee studied the photographs, struck by the unguarded joy in Charlie's expression—so different from the careful smiles he offered in public settings. "You look happy there. Relaxed."

"I was." A simple admission that carried unexpected weight.

They continued through corridors lined with subtle lighting, past rooms designed for specific purposes—a morning room bathed in eastern light, a study paneled in dark wood, a conservatory where plants thrived in carefully maintained humidity. Each space was immaculate, beautiful, and strangely impersonal—until Bee spotted something that didn't align with the designer's vision.

In a hallway leading toward what Charlie called "the east wing" (a phrase that made Bee stifle a smile), a series of framed posters caught her attention. Unlike the museum-quality art displayed elsewhere, these were movie posters—but not the glossy blockbusters that had made Charlie famous. Instead, they were from smaller productions, including what appeared to be his first film—a coming-of-age drama she'd never heard of, the poster showing a much younger Charlie looking earnestly into the camera.

"'The Edge of Summer,'" Charlie said, noticing her interest. "My first real role. Tiny independent film that played at exactly three festivals before disappearing into obscurity." His voice held no bitterness, only a nostalgic fondness. "I was so proud of that part. Lived on ramen for months afterward, but I thought I'd made it."

Bee looked from the eager young face in the poster to the man standing beside her, seeing both the distance he'd traveled and the thread of continuity between them. "You keep these displayed rather than the big hits."

It wasn't a question, but Charlie nodded anyway. "They remind me where I started. Why I wanted to act in the first place, before it became about box office numbers and franchise potential." He ran a hand through his hair, a gesture she now recognized signaled either nervousness or deep feeling. "Probably sounds pretentious."

"No," Bee said softly. "It sounds human."

Their eyes met, and something shifted in Charlie's expression—a guardedness falling away, replaced by a vulnerability that transformed his features. For a moment, the mansion with its opulence and enormity receded, and they were simply two people connecting across the space between them.

The moment broke when Charlie cleared his throat, gesturing down the hallway. "Let me show you where you'll be staying. It's the best guest suite—private bathroom, sitting area, good morning light."

As they continued their tour, Bee found herself looking less at the architectural details or expensive furnishings and more at Charlie himself—the way his shoulders gradually relaxed as they moved into spaces he actually used, the way his descriptions became more animated when sharing something he genuinely cared about, the small reveals of personality scattered like breadcrumbs through the impersonal grandeur of his home.

This massive house, she realized, was both a fortress and a façade—a space created to project an image rather than nurture a life. Yet within it, Charlie had carved out pockets of authenticity, small rebellions against the artifice in the form of dog-eared books, meaningful photographs, and mementos from the journey that had brought him here.

The realization made her look at him with new understanding. Behind the movie star who owned a mansion with marble floors and soaring ceilings was a man who valued connection over perfection, who felt the need to apologize for his success while simultaneously trying to share it. As they turned down another corridor, Bee found herself wondering not about the rooms they'd yet to see, but about the other pieces of himself Charlie might be waiting to reveal.

"The security system extends throughout the property," Charlie explained as they continued down a hallway where recessed lighting cast a warm glow against pale walls. He pointed toward a nearly invisible camera tucked into the corner where wall met ceiling. "They're designed to blend in with the architecture. Same with the motion sensors." Bee followed his gesture, noting how the security features were integrated so seamlessly that she would never have spotted them without guidance. There was something comforting yet vaguely unsettling about the invisible web of protection surrounding them—a constant reminder of why she was here in the first place.

"All the windows are reinforced," Charlie continued, tapping lightly on a pane that looked out over the hillside. "Not bulletproof, exactly, but highly resistant to both breakage and long-range photography." His mouth quirked in a half-smile that didn't quite reach his eyes. "The paranoia comes with the territory, I'm afraid."

They passed a discreet panel embedded in the wall, its surface glowing with a soft blue light. Charlie paused, gesturing toward it. "Main security interface. The system recognizes authorized residents by facial recognition and movement patterns." At Bee's raised eyebrow, he added quickly, "I'll have you added to the primary access list. Otherwise, it might get annoying having the house questioning your right to open the refrigerator."

"The house talks?" Bee asked, only half-joking.

"Only when necessary," Charlie assured her, though his

expression suggested this definition might differ from hers. "It's mostly passive monitoring unless there's a breach or unusual activity. The security team handles the actual surveillance from a remote location."

There was a practiced quality to his explanation that spoke of having given this tour before—though perhaps not often, and not with such attention to detail. Bee wondered briefly who else had received this orientation to Charlie's fortified world, then pushed the thought aside as they turned down a sun-filled corridor.

"This is the guest wing," he said, his posture relaxing slightly as they moved away from the security discussion. "Your suite is at the end—best views and most privacy."

The door he opened revealed not merely a bedroom but a comprehensive living space that made Bee's breath catch. Sunlight poured through floor-to-ceiling windows that offered an unobstructed view of the canyon beyond. A king-sized bed anchored one end of the room, draped in linens that looked soft enough to dissolve at a touch. A sitting area with a small sofa and armchairs created a conversation space near the windows, while a desk with clean lines occupied a corner beneath a piece of abstract art in cool blues and greens.

"The bathroom's through there," Charlie indicated a doorway of frosted glass. "And there's a walk-in closet beside it."

Bee stepped into the space, feeling the plush carpet beneath her feet. The room was larger than her entire apartment, decorated in soothing neutrals with occasional bursts of color from artwork and textiles. It was beautiful, comfortable, and entirely impersonal—a high-end hotel suite rather than someone's bedroom.

"This is... a lot," she said finally, turning to face Charlie who hovered in the doorway as if uncertain whether to enter. "My entire apartment would fit in here with room to spare."

"Too much?" he asked, concern crossing his features. "There are smaller rooms if you'd prefer something less—"

"No," Bee interrupted, finding herself smiling at his earnestness. "It's perfect. Just... different from what I'm used to." She ran her fingers along the back of a chair upholstered in soft linen. "I've never had a sitting area in my bedroom before. Usually I just throw clothes on any available surface."

Charlie's expression relaxed into a genuine smile. "I do the same thing. Drives my housekeeper crazy. She's always finding my socks in unexpected places."

The casual admission—that even in this palatial space, he still engaged in the ordinary human habit of scattering clothes—made the room suddenly feel more accessible, less intimidating.

"The rest of the tour?" she prompted, and Charlie nodded, leading her back into the hallway.

They continued through corridors lined with subtle lighting, Charlie pointing out features and occasionally dropping personal details that humanized the sprawling mansion. A kitchen "where I actually learned to cook properly after years of takeout," a small morning room "where I have coffee when I need to think," a gym "that started as my brother's idea but I've grown to appreciate." With each revelation, Bee filed away another piece of the puzzle that was Charlie Benton—not the celebrity whose face appeared on billboards, but the man who lived behind that image.

As they approached a heavy wooden door at the end of a quiet hallway, Charlie's pace slowed, his hand hesitating on the polished handle. "This is my study," he said, his voice taking on a different quality—something almost vulnerable. "I don't bring many people in here."

The significance of the statement wasn't lost on Bee. After rooms designed to impress and security systems designed to protect, he was offering something more personal: a space that existed solely for himself.

The door swung open to reveal a room unlike any they'd passed through before. Where the rest of the house maintained a curated elegance, this space felt organically accumulated—bookshelves climbing the walls, filled not with color-coordinated spines selected for visual appeal but with actual reading material, some volumes standing upright, others stacked horizontally where space allowed. A leather chair showed the imprint of regular use, a throw blanket draped carelessly over one arm. A desk faced the window rather than the door, its surface bearing the productive clutter of someone mid-project: open notebooks, stacked reference materials, a laptop surrounded by handwritten notes.

"It's nothing special," Charlie said, though his body language—shoulders relaxing, stance widening—suggested the opposite. "Just where I go when I need space to think."

Bee moved into the room slowly, absorbing details that revealed more about Charlie than any interview ever had. The books ranged from classic literature to contemporary fiction, with significant sections devoted to theatrical theory, film history, and biographies of directors and actors from cinema's golden age. Framed playbills from theater productions—not Hollywood blockbusters—held places of honor on one wall. A collection of vintage cameras occupied a shelf, alongside what appeared to be actual film reels in metal canisters.

"You're a collector," she observed, running her fingers lightly over the spines of books organized not by appearance but by some personal system meaningful only to their owner.

"Not deliberately," Charlie replied, moving further into the room with the ease of someone in their natural habitat. "These are just things that matter to me. Pieces of projects or periods that shaped me somehow."

Bee noticed how different he seemed in this space—more

fluid in his movements, more animated in his expressions, as if the careful composure he maintained elsewhere could finally relax. Here, surrounded by the physical manifestations of his actual interests rather than the trappings of his public persona, Charlie appeared more fully himself.

They gravitated toward one of the bookshelves, Charlie explaining the significance of certain volumes—a collection of plays annotated during his theater days, first editions found in obscure bookshops during location shoots, dog-eared paperbacks read so many times their covers had separated from their bindings. His passion for these objects was evident in how he handled them, how his voice warmed when describing their origins.

"This one's a favourite," he said, reaching for a well-worn volume of poetry at the same moment Bee's hand extended toward it, their fingers brushing in the narrow space between.

The contact was brief, incidental, ordinary—and yet it wasn't. Something electric passed between them in that momentary touch, an awareness that transcended the casual. Charlie's words faltered mid-sentence, his eyes meeting hers with an intensity that made the spacious room suddenly feel much smaller. Bee felt heat rise to her cheeks, her fingertips tingling where they had connected with his.

For a suspended moment, they remained frozen in that configuration—hands still extended, bodies angled toward each other, the book forgotten between them. The carefully maintained distance they'd preserved throughout the tour collapsed into something more immediate, more visceral. Bee could see the fine lines at the corners of Charlie's eyes, the slight unevenness of his stubble where he'd missed a spot shaving that morning, the subtle shift in his pupils as they dilated slightly.

Charlie cleared his throat, breaking the spell. His hand withdrew, running through his hair in that now-familiar gesture of uncertainty. "We should probably continue," he said, his voice rougher than it had been moments before. "There's still the home theater to see. I think you'll like it."

Bee nodded, her own voice temporarily unreliable. As Charlie moved toward the door, she cast one more glance around the study, understanding now why he had hesitated before showing it to her. This wasn't just another room in his mansion—it was a window into who he was beneath the celebrity, a physical space that represented his internal land-scape. That he had shared it with her spoke volumes about the trust developing between them, a trust that made the lingering warmth of their accidental touch feel like both a beginning and a promise.

Charlie led Bee down a short flight of carpeted stairs, the lighting gradually dimming with each step as if they were descending into a different world entirely. The air changed too —cooler, with a subtle shift in acoustics that muffled the sounds of the house above them. "The theater's my favorite room in the house," Charlie admitted, his voice taking on the subtle animation that Bee was learning to recognize as genuine enthusiasm rather than polite tour-guide patter. "After a life-time of watching films in actual theaters, having this space feels like the most indulgent thing I've ever done for myself."

At the bottom of the stairs, he paused before a set of double doors upholstered in deep burgundy fabric. "Ready?" he asked, a boyish excitement replacing his earlier tour-guide formality. Without waiting for her answer, he pushed the doors open and flipped a switch just inside the threshold.

Soft ambient lighting illuminated the space gradually, revealing a room that managed to be both technologically advanced and surprisingly intimate. Tiered seating rose in gentle steps—not the rigid rows of commercial theaters but curved arrangements of oversized chairs and love seats uphol-stered in plush midnight-blue velvet. The walls were covered in acoustic panels designed to look like abstract art pieces in complementary tones of blue and gray. At the front of the room, a massive screen descended silently from a recessed compartment in the ceiling, its surface so pristine it seemed to glow even before any image appeared on it.

"This is incredible," Bee murmured, stepping into the space and feeling thick carpet absorb the sound of her footsteps. The room wasn't cavernous like commercial theaters—instead, it felt cocoon-like, designed for perhaps a dozen people at most.

"The acoustics are calibrated for this exact space," Charlie explained, moving toward a control panel discreetly built into the arm of what was clearly the prime viewing seat in the center of the middle tier. "The sound system is completely hidden behind the panels, but it's set up for true spatial audio —you can hear a pin drop in the background of a scene and know exactly where it fell in the fictional space."

Bee ran her hand along the velvet upholstery of the nearest seat, feeling its plushness give slightly beneath her fingers. "No stale popcorn or sticky floors," she observed with a small smile. "Though that does add to the authentic experience."

Charlie laughed, the sound richer and more uninhibited in this acoustically perfect room. "I can provide both if you're feeling nostalgic. Though I draw the line at mysterious unidentified liquids on the armrests."

He moved toward a wall panel that slid open at his touch, revealing an elaborate system of digital equipment that Bee couldn't begin to identify. "The projection system is completely digital now, though I kept the original film projector too." He nodded toward a vintage machine displayed like a sculpture in a glass case near the entrance. "Sometimes there's nothing like the authentic experience of film running through sprockets, little imperfections and all."

As he spoke about aspect ratios and light calibration, Bee

watched his body language transform. The slight stiffness that had accompanied their tour of the mansion's more formal spaces had completely vanished, replaced by animated gestures and an expressiveness that made him appear younger, less guarded. This was Charlie in his element—not the careful celebrity navigating public spaces, but a man genuinely passionate about the art form that had shaped his life.

"What kind of films do you watch here?" Bee asked, settling experimentally into one of the plush seats, which seemed to embrace her in cushioned comfort.

"Everything," Charlie replied, his face lighting up at the question. "New releases I need to screen for work, classics I've seen a hundred times, obscure foreign films that never got proper distribution. I probably spend more time in this room than anywhere else in the house."

"Do you have 'Casablanca'?" Bee asked, naming the film that had been her introduction to classic cinema as a teenager. "I watch it at least once a year. There's something about the dialogue, the atmosphere—it never gets old."

Charlie's expression transformed from general enthusiasm to specific delight. "You're a 'Casablanca' fan?" He moved immediately toward a hidden cabinet, sliding open another panel to reveal an extensive collection of films organized in some personal system comprehensible only to him. "It's one of my desert island movies. The economy of the storytelling, the perfect balance of cynicism and romance..." He glanced over his shoulder at her, a new warmth in his eyes. "Most people know it from film classes or best-of lists, but don't actually love it."

"My grandfather introduced me to it," Bee said, watching as Charlie's fingers moved deftly through his collection. "He had this ancient VHS copy that we'd watch on holidays. I think I could recite most of Rick and Ilsa's lines from memory."

Charlie pulled out a case with reverence. "This is a restored 4K transfer from the original negatives. The detail is incredible —you can see textures in the fabrics, the grain of the wood in Rick's bar." His enthusiasm was infectious, technical details delivered not with showoff precision but with the genuine passion of someone sharing a beloved experience. "Want to watch it? I mean, not the whole thing necessarily, but I could show you how it looks on this system."

The question carried an undercurrent of vulnerability, as if he feared she might find the suggestion childish or excessive. Bee found herself charmed by this version of Charlie—eager rather than smooth, genuine rather than calculated.

"I'd love to," she said, settling deeper into the comfortable seat. "Though I warn you, I have strong opinions about the airport scene that might be controversial."

Charlie's smile widened, relief and pleasure mingling in his expression. "Let me guess—you think Rick made the wrong choice letting Ilsa go?"

"Not at all," Bee countered, enjoying the surprise that flickered across his face. "I think it was the only choice that honoured who they both were. Nobility isn't about grand gestures—it's about recognizing hard truths."

Charlie paused in the act of preparing the film, looking at her with an intensity that made the spacious room suddenly feel much smaller. "That's... exactly what I've always thought," he said quietly. "Though most people prefer the romantic fantasy of them running away together."

"Most people prefer easy answers," Bee replied with a shrug. "Art isn't about easy answers."

Something shifted in Charlie's expression—a deepening of interest, a recognition of unexpected common ground. Without further comment, he turned to the control panel, fingers moving with practiced ease across buttons and dials. The ambient lighting dimmed further, plunging the room into darkness broken only by the soft blue glow of the control interfaces and small guide lights along the floor.

When the screen illuminated with the Warner Brothers logo, the sound that filled the space was so pristine that Bee felt as if she were inside the music rather than merely hearing it. The black and white images that followed possessed a clarity and depth she'd never experienced before, each frame revealing details lost in standard presentations.

"This is extraordinary," she breathed, genuinely impressed by how the familiar film had been transformed into something new while remaining true to its original vision.

Charlie settled into the seat beside her, his earlier tour-guide formality completely abandoned as he leaned forward slightly, eyes fixed on the screen with the appreciation of someone who could never tire of this particular magic. "Wait until you see the scene in The Blue Parrot," he said, voice low with anticipation. "The shadows in the background tell a whole separate story that most viewers never notice."

As the familiar story began to unfold before them, Bee found herself watching Charlie almost as much as the screen —the way his lips moved slightly with particularly beloved lines, the subtle changes in his expression that reflected his deep engagement with the material. This was Charlie Benton stripped of celebrity pretense, sharing not his wealth or status but something far more personal: his genuine passion for the art form that had shaped his life.

The formality that had characterized much of their tour had dissolved completely, replaced by a shared enthusiasm that felt more authentic than any carefully designed space or expensive feature. Here in this darkened room, surrounded by perfect sound and vision, they were no longer a famous actor and a retail manager navigating an unusual arrangement, but simply two people connecting through a shared appreciation for something that mattered to them both.

When Rick delivered his first sardonic line, they both smiled in unison, and Bee felt something settle into place between them—a recognition, a resonance, a possibility that extended beyond their unusual circumstances into something that might have found them regardless of who they were or how they had met. The thought was both comforting and slightly terrifying, like standing at the edge of something vast and unexplored, uncertain of its depths but irresistibly drawn to discover them.

Hours had passed in a blur of black and white classics and colour-saturated modern films, the outside world forgotten as Charlie and Bee lost themselves in their impromptu movie marathon. Empty popcorn bowls and discarded candy wrappers surrounded them, evidence of Charlie's mid-afternoon dash to the kitchen between films to gather provisions. The formal distance that had characterized their tour earlier in the day had vanished completely. Now Bee's feet were tucked beneath her on the oversized seat, her shoes abandoned somewhere on the floor, while Charlie had shed his careful posture along with his jacket, his body angled toward hers as they debated the merits of the film they'd just finished.

"You can't possibly defend that ending," Bee insisted, reaching for the last Red Vine in the package between them. "It completely undermines everything the character stood for during the first two hours."

Charlie shook his head, the gesture looser and more animated than anything he'd displayed during their house tour. "That's exactly why it works! The ambiguity forces you to question everything you thought you understood about his motivations." He ran a hand through his hair, which had long since lost its styled precision and now fell across his forehead in a way that made him look younger, more approachable. "The director is deliberately frustrating your expectations."

"There's a difference between subverting expectations and

betraying your narrative contract with the audience," Bee countered, biting into the Red Vine with emphatic punctuation. "You can't spend two hours establishing a character's moral compass and then have them abandon it without proper groundwork."

Their debate about "The Conversation"—the third film in their unplanned marathon after "Casablanca" and "The Third Man"—continued with the comfortable rhythm of people who genuinely enjoyed the exchange of ideas. There was none of the careful politeness that often characterized discussions with someone famous; Bee challenged Charlie's opinions without hesitation, and he responded with delighted engagement rather than the practiced charm he deployed in interviews.

Charlie found himself watching Bee more than the screen during their viewing, captivated by the play of emotions across her face—the slight furrow between her brows during intense scenes, the unconscious smile that appeared at particularly clever dialogue, the occasional surprised laugh that escaped her at unexpected moments. Her reactions were unfiltered, unselfconscious in a way he rarely experienced from people who knew his identity. She watched films not as an industry professional analyzing technique, but as someone who genuinely loved the medium and engaged with it emotionally as well as intellectually.

"What time is it, anyway?" Bee asked suddenly, stretching her arms above her head in a gesture that spoke of complete comfort in the space.

Charlie glanced at his watch, surprised by what he saw. "Almost one in the morning," he admitted, equally surprised by how quickly the hours had evaporated. What had begun as a quick showcase of his theater's capabilities had somehow evolved into nearly eight hours of continuous viewing, their conversation flowing seamlessly between films.

"One in the morning?" Bee repeated, eyes widening. "We completely lost track of time. I didn't even notice it getting dark outside."

"There are no windows down here," Charlie pointed out, gesturing to the cocoon-like space designed specifically to eliminate external distractions. "It's a temporal black hole. I once watched an entire trilogy without realizing I'd missed two meals and a scheduled phone call."

Bee laughed, the sound unreserved and genuine in a way that seemed to fill the space more completely than the perfect acoustics could explain. "I should probably be responsible and suggest we call it a night," she said, though her tone carried a reluctance that made Charlie's chest warm with something that felt dangerously like happiness.

"Probably," he agreed, making no move to end their session. Instead, his fingers hovered over the control panel, ready to queue up another film at the slightest encouragement.

Their eyes met in the dim light, and Charlie felt something shift in the atmosphere—not the electric tension from their accidental touch in his study, but a different kind of intimacy. This was the comfort of genuine connection, of shared enthusiasm and easy conversation that required no performance, no careful self-editing.

"One more?" Bee suggested, her expression hopeful in the blue glow of the control lights. "Something completely different from what we've been watching?"

"Absolutely," Charlie agreed without hesitation, relief and pleasure mingling in his voice. "What are you in the mood for?"

"Something with colour and movement after all that noir," she decided. "Something joyful."

Charlie scrolled through his collection, the familiar ritual of film selection now transformed by the presence of someone who approached it with matching enthusiasm. "How about 'The Red Shoes'? Powell and Pressburger at their most visually lush, and the ballet sequences are still breathtaking seventy years later."

"Perfect," Bee agreed, settling deeper into her seat with the air of someone exactly where they wanted to be. "I haven't seen it since college, but I remember being stunned by the use of colour."

As Charlie prepared the film, he found himself marveling at the transformation that had occurred in his home over the course of a single day. This theater had always been his favorite room, but it had still maintained the slightly sterile quality that characterized most of the mansion—a perfect space designed for optimal experience rather than lived-in comfort. Now, with Bee curled comfortably in the seat beside him, with the detritus of shared snacks scattered around them, with the animated conversation still hanging in the air between them, it felt different. Warmer. More genuine.

The realization expanded to encompass the entire house. For years, the mansion had functioned as both showcase and fortress—a space that reflected his success while protecting him from its consequences. He had never disliked it, exactly, but he had never felt that indefinable sense of rightness that people associated with the word "home." It had been a place to sleep, to store his possessions, to entertain when necessary— but not a space that held meaning beyond its functional purpose.

Yet somehow, in the span of hours, Bee's presence had begun to transform it. Her genuine reactions to both its grandeur and its more personal corners had allowed him to see it through new eyes. Her footsteps had echoed alongside his on marble floors that usually knew only his solitary tread. Her laughter had filled spaces designed for acoustic perfection but rarely hosting actual joy.

The film began, its famous opening credits appearing on the massive screen. But Charlie found his attention repeatedly drawn to Bee rather than the masterpiece unfolding before them. She watched with the unselfconscious absorption of someone completely present in the moment, occasionally murmuring appreciation for particularly beautiful shots or clever transitions. Without planning to, Charlie had shifted closer during their marathon, their shoulders now nearly touching in the dim light.

"The colour saturation is incredible," Bee observed as the ballet sequence began, her face illuminated by the reds and golds from the screen. "You can almost feel the texture of the costumes."

Charlie nodded, though his appreciation was now divided between the film's artistry and the way Bee's eyes reflected its vivid palette. "They hand-painted some of the frames to enhance the effect," he explained. "Completely groundbreaking for the time."

Their commentary continued in comfortable exchanges, observations flowing naturally between them without the self-consciousness that often characterized Charlie's conversations with new acquaintances. There was no calculation here, no mental filtering to determine which thoughts were safe to express, which opinions might be misconstrued, which references might seem pretentious. Just the genuine pleasure of sharing something beloved with someone who approached it with equal enthusiasm.

As the ballet reached its climax on screen, Charlie realized with startling clarity that this was what he had been missing—not just in his home, but in his life. This unguarded exchange, this shared appreciation, this freedom to be completely present without performance or pretense. For years, his existence had been compartmentalized: public appearances where every word was calculated, private spaces where solitude provided safety but not connection, professional relationships defined by the industry's complex power dynamics.

Bee had somehow bypassed all those carefully constructed boundaries, creating a space where he could simply be Charlie —not Benton the celebrity, not the carefully managed public figure, but the man who argued about film endings and got overly excited about restoration techniques and fell asleep on couches during movies.

When she enthusiastically pointed out a particularly innovative camera move, her hand briefly touching his arm for emphasis, Charlie felt the last of his habitual guardedness dissolve. Whatever complicated circumstances had brought them together—wrong number texts, paparazzi invasions, security concerns—he couldn't regret any of it if it had led to this moment, to this feeling of his cavernous mansion finally transforming into something that felt, improbably but undeniably, like home.

Chapter Thriteen: A Night to Remember

The credits of "The Red Shoes" scrolled across the massive screen, the music swelling to its final crescendo as Bee leaned forward, captivated until the very last note faded into silence. Charlie, however, found himself watching her rather than the film—the way the shifting light played across her features, how her eyes remained fixed on the screen even as the names of long-dead performers drifted upward into darkness. When she finally turned to him, her face still luminous with the pleasure of artistic appreciation, something caught in his chest, a strange tightness that wasn't entirely uncomfortable.

"That was even better than I remembered," Bee said, reaching for her wine glass and finding only a few drops remaining. "The restoration is incredible. It's like seeing it for the first time."

Charlie nodded, reluctant to break the spell of the moment with words. The theater felt smaller somehow, more intimate than its actual dimensions, the space between them charged with something that hadn't been there eight hours ago when they'd started their impromptu marathon.

"What time is it now?" she asked, stretching her arms above her head in a gesture that exposed a sliver of skin where her shirt rode up.

Charlie checked his watch and winced. "Almost two-thirty."

"Seriously?" Bee laughed, the sound warm and unrestricted in the perfect acoustics of the room. "We've been down here for over five hours. That has to be some kind of record."

"For most people, maybe." Charlie smiled, reaching for the control panel. "My personal record is twenty-two hours. I fell asleep somewhere in the middle of film four and woke up during film six."

"Let me guess—you were watching Lord of the Rings? Extended editions?"

"Star Wars, actually. Original trilogy, then prequels, then I passed out before the sequels. Probably for the best."

Bee's laughter bubbled up again, her body shifting closer to his on the oversized seat they'd been sharing since halfway through "The Third Man." The casual intimacy of their positions—her feet tucked beneath her, his arm stretched along the back of the seat behind her shoulders—felt both new and strangely familiar, as if they'd been finding their way to this configuration for years rather than hours.

"We should probably call it a night," Charlie suggested without conviction, his fingers still hovering over the controls.

"Probably," Bee agreed, making no move to rise. Instead, she reached for the remote that lay between them. "Or we could watch one more. Something completely different."

"Like what?" Charlie asked, suddenly very aware of her proximity, of the faint scent of her shampoo mingling with the buttery remnants of popcorn.

"Something mindless. Something that doesn't require emotional investment or intellectual analysis." She scrolled through his digital collection, her nose crinkling slightly as she concentrated. "My brain is too tired for anything else profound."

"I do own some films without artistic merit," Charlie admitted with mock defensiveness. "Though I try to keep them hidden from serious cinephiles."

"Show me your guilty pleasures, Benton." Bee's voice took on a teasing lilt. "I bet there's a whole secret folder of cheesy action movies and romantic comedies too formulaic to admit enjoying."

Charlie reached for the remote, but Bee pulled it away, holding it just beyond his grasp. "Ah-ah. Let me discover your shameful secrets myself."

"Some of those are contractual obligations," he protested, leaning toward her to reclaim the remote. "I had to keep copies. Industry courtesy."

"Sure, blame it on contracts." Bee extended her arm further, laughing as Charlie made another grab for the device. "Oh my god, you have the entire 'Fast and Furious' franchise? All nine of them?"

"Research for a role I was considering," Charlie insisted, though his ears reddened slightly at the exposure of his less sophisticated tastes.

"And what about 'The Holiday'? Research too?" Her eyebrows rose in mock judgment. "Twice in one year, according to your viewing history."

Charlie lunged more decisively this time, his body half-covering hers as he reached for the remote. "That's private information!"

Bee twisted beneath him, laughing as she held the remote high above her head. "Cameron Diaz or Kate Winslet? Which one's your type?"

"Give me that," Charlie growled playfully, his fingers

closing around her wrist as he tried to pry the remote from her grip.

They struggled, both laughing too hard to be truly effective, bodies pressing against each other in ways that were rapidly transforming the nature of their contact from playful to something else entirely. Bee's free hand pushed against his chest without any real intention of creating distance. Charlie's legs tangled with hers as they wrestled across the plush cushions, the remote forgotten even as they contained their mock battle for it.

Then suddenly, like a scene transitioning from comedy to drama without warning, they froze. Charlie found himself suspended above her, his body bracketing hers, their faces separated by mere inches of charged air. Bee's laughter faded, her eyes widening slightly as she registered their position, the pressure of his weight against her, the synchronisation of their accelerated breathing.

Time stretched between them, elastic and uncertain. Charlie could feel his heart hammering against his ribs, could see the pulse fluttering at the base of Bee's throat, could sense the subtle shift as her body softened beneath his. The remote slipped from her fingers, landing with a muffled thud on the carpeted floor beside them.

Charlie swallowed, suddenly terrified of misreading the moment, of shattering the delicate understanding that had been building between them throughout the day. Bee's eyes met his, questioning but not retreating, her lips slightly parted as if on the verge of speaking.

"Bee," he whispered, her name carrying all the questions he couldn't articulate.

Her hand, no longer pushing against his chest, curled into the fabric of his shirt. The smallest of tugs, barely perceptible but unmistakable in its intent.

Charlie lowered his head, hesitating one final moment

before crossing this threshold. Bee's eyes fluttered closed, her chin tilting upward in silent permission. The space between them disappeared as his lips finally met hers.

The kiss began softly, tentatively—a question rather than a statement. But as Bee responded, her mouth moving against his with increasing certainty, the hesitation dissolved. Charlie's hand trembled slightly as he cupped her face, his fingers threading into her hair with a gentleness that belied the intensity building between them. Bee's grip on his shirt tightened, pulling him closer as the kiss deepened, became hungrier, more urgent.

Years of Charlie's careful isolation, of holding himself separate from genuine connection, seemed to melt away with each passing second. Bee's wariness, her protective independence, dissolved beneath the undeniable rightness of this contact. The kiss transformed, evolved from exploration to affirmation, their bodies communicating what words had circled around for days.

When they finally separated, both slightly breathless, Charlie remained close enough that their foreheads touched, his eyes searching hers for confirmation that he hadn't imagined the significance of what had just passed between them.

Bee's hand moved from his shirt to his face, her fingers tracing the line of his jaw with a tenderness that answered his unspoken question. The projector's soft glow illuminated them in gentle, shifting light, the abandoned remote and scattered snack bowls silent witnesses to a threshold crossed, a new chapter beginning in the dark cocoon of the theater where time had already proven itself malleable, hours compressing into moments and moments expanding into lifetimes.

The lingering sweetness of wine mingled with the taste of each other as their kiss deepened, any remaining hesitation dissolving beneath waves of increasing desire. Charlie's hand slid from Bee's face to the curve of her neck, his thumb tracing the accelerated rhythm of her pulse as her fingers threaded through his hair, drawing him closer still. Their bodies, previously held in the artificial restraint of playfulness, now pressed together with deliberate intent, each point of contact generating heat that seemed to burn through layers of clothing.

Bee arched against him, a soft sound escaping her throat that vibrated against Charlie's lips. His response was immediate and visceral, his arm tightening around her waist, eliminating what little space remained between them. The plush cushions of the theater seat molded around them as Charlie shifted, aligning their bodies more perfectly, his weight supported on one elbow while his free hand explored the contours of her side, her hip, the exposed skin where her shirt had ridden up.

The cool air of the theater against that small patch of revealed flesh made Bee shiver, a reaction Charlie misinterpreted as uncertainty. He pulled back slightly, his breathing uneven, eyes searching her face in the soft glow from the now-dormant screen.

"Is this okay?" he asked, his voice rough with restraint. "We can stop if—"

Bee's answer came not in words but in the upward lift of her body, her mouth reclaiming his with a certainty that eliminated any doubt. Her hands moved to the buttons of his shirt, fingers working with deliberate intent as she maintained the kiss, her message clear: far from wanting to stop, she wanted more.

Charlie's hesitation evaporated, replaced by a focused intensity as he helped her with the buttons, then shrugged the shirt from his shoulders without breaking contact. The thin t-shirt beneath followed quickly, revealing skin that gleamed in the dim light, warm beneath Bee's exploring hands.

"Your turn," Charlie murmured against her lips, his fingers

finding the hem of her sweater, seeking permission with a questioning pause.

Bee nodded, lifting her arms to allow him to pull the garment over her head. The simple black bra beneath presented both barrier and invitation, lace-edged shadows against skin that flushed with awareness of his gaze. Charlie's hand trembled slightly as he traced the line where fabric met flesh, the restraint evident in the careful control of his touch.

"You're beautiful," he whispered, the words carrying none of the practiced smoothness of lines delivered for cameras, instead rough with genuine feeling.

Bee's fingers found the clasp of her bra, releasing it with a practiced motion, the garment falling away to reveal herself fully to him. The heat in Charlie's eyes as he looked at her—not with the assessment of a critic but with the reverence of a worshipper—sent a current of pleasure through her that had nothing to do with physical contact.

Their remaining clothes fell away piece by piece, each new revelation met with appreciative touches and kisses. Charlie's mouth traced the curve of Bee's shoulder, the hollow at the base of her throat, the sensitive skin beneath her ear. Her hands mapped the contours of his chest, his back, the muscles that shifted beneath her touch as he moved above her.

The theater seat, while luxurious, soon proved too confining for the exploration they both craved. Charlie drew back slightly, his eyes meeting hers with a question that was both practical and laden with significance.

"My bedroom?" he asked, the simple phrase carrying the weight of threshold-crossing.

Bee nodded, reaching up to trace the line of his jaw. "Yes."

In a motion that combined strength and tenderness, Charlie gathered her into his arms, lifting her against his chest as he rose. Bee's arms circled his neck, her body instinctively curving toward his warmth as the cool air of the theater raised goosebumps on exposed skin. Their eyes held as he carried her from the darkened room, up the stairs and through corridors now lit only by the ambient glow of recessed night lights.

His bedroom—a space Bee hadn't yet seen during their house tour—reflected the same blend of luxury and personal touches she'd observed elsewhere, though she registered only impressions: expansive windows revealing star-scattered sky, the massive bed with its inviting expanse of dark sheets, the absence of the formal perfection that characterized more public areas of the house.

Charlie laid her gently on the bed, the cool silk of the sheets a shocking contrast to the heat of their skin as he followed her down, their bodies reconnecting with new intensity. The taste of wine still lingered on their lips as they kissed again, deeper now, unhurried despite the urgency building between them.

"I want this," Bee whispered against his mouth, her directness unchanged by vulnerability. "I want you."

The simple declaration broke something loose in Charlie—not control, but restraint. His kisses grew more purposeful, trailing down her neck, across her collarbone, finding sensitive places that made her breath catch and her fingers tighten in his hair. The sounds she made—soft sighs, occasional murmurs of encouragement—filled the otherwise silent house, mingling with his own deeper responses as they learned each other's bodies.

As Charlie's lips traveled down Bee's body, he unbuttoned her jeans and slid them down her legs, leaving her in just a pair of black lace panties. His fingers traced the edges of the delicate fabric, teasing her before slipping his hand beneath the waistband. The way she gasped and arched her back told him he'd found the right spot.

With gentle yet firm pressure, he massaged her clit, watching as Bee's eyes fluttered closed and her breathing grew ragged. After a few moments, she reached for him, pushing his boxers down to free his erection. He groaned as she wrapped her fingers around it, stroking him slowly at first but increasing in pace as their mutual arousal built.

As they continued to pleasure one another with their hands, their mouths met again in a passionate kiss. Their hips began grinding together instinctively, seeking friction and intimacy in equal measure.

Charlie broke away from their heated kiss and trailed kisses down Bee's neck, chest, and stomach until he reached the edge of her panties. He looked up at her for approval before tugging them off to reveal her wetness. He took a moment to savor the sight before burying his face between her thighs.

Bee couldn't help but moan as Charlie's tongue explored her, licking and sucking at her swollen clit while his free hand massaged one of her breasts. Her fingers tangled into his hair, urging him on. As waves of pleasure washed over her, Bee felt an urge to reciprocate the intense sensations Charlie was giving her.

Reluctantly breaking away from Charlie's mouth, Bee guided him back up to face level and then pushed him onto his back. She straddled him and bent down to kiss him deeply on the lips before working her way down his body with soft bites and licks.

When she reached his throbbing cock, she licked a long stripe along the underside before taking him into her mouth. She swirled her tongue around the head, savoring the taste of him as she bobbed her head up and down his length. Charlie's hands gripped the sheets tightly as he moaned Bee's name.

Bee's lips and tongue continued their dance until she could feel Charlie nearing his breaking point. She stopped and moved back up his body, positioning herself above him. They shared a lingering kiss before she reached between them to guide him inside her.

As their bodies joined, they both gasped at the sensation, overwhelmed by the intensity of their connection. Bee began to move slowly, grinding her hips against Charlie's as he thrust upwards into her. They moved in unison, their pleasure building with each stroke.

Charlie caressed Bee's body as they made love, running his hands over her breasts, hips, and thighs. At one point, he flipped them both over so he was on top, driving into her with newfound urgency while she wrapped her legs around his waist to pull him deeper.

Their moans and sighs filled the quiet room as they moved together, completely in sync. As they neared their climax, Charlie captured Bee's lips in one final desperate kiss.

The wave of pleasure that crashed over them was like nothing either had ever experienced before – a powerful combination of physical satisfaction and emotional connection that left them both breathless and trembling as they came down from their high.

In the aftermath, they remained connected, neither willing to break the physical bond that seemed to symbolize something larger. Charlie's weight rested partially on Bee, his breathing gradually slowing to match hers, his hand gently stroking her hair back from her face. The silence between them held no awkwardness, no uncertainty—only the peaceful understanding of having crossed a threshold together into something new, something that defied the convenient labels of physical attraction or emotional convenience.

The star-scattered sky beyond the windows bore witness to their stillness, the universe spinning on while they existed momentarily outside time, cocooned in the warmth they'd generated between them, more intimately connected than either had imagined possible when they'd settled into the theater seats hours earlier to watch a film about love and art and sacrifice.

Time melted into meaninglessness as they lay tangled in the sheets, sweat cooling on their skin, bodies still touching as if neither could bear even momentary separation. Moonlight spilled through the uncurtained windows, painting silver-blue patterns across their intertwined forms and casting gentle shadows in the valleys created by limbs and rumpled bedding. Charlie's fingers traced idle patterns along Bee's shoulder, following the path of light and darkness with reverent attention. The silence between them felt complete, perfect in its wordlessness—until it wasn't, the weight of unspoken thoughts gradually transforming comfort into a different kind of intimacy: the courage to speak truth.

"What are you thinking?" Charlie asked, his voice barely above a whisper, as if normal volume might shatter the delicate atmosphere surrounding them.

Bee turned her head slightly, her cheek pressing against his chest where she could feel the steady rhythm of his heart. "That I can't remember the last time I felt this... present. Not worried about tomorrow or replaying yesterday. Just... here."

Charlie's hand stilled momentarily on her skin before resuming its gentle exploration. "I know exactly what you mean."

Another stretch of silence, comfortable yet charged with unspoken significance. Outside, a night bird called, the sound distant and mournful through the perfect insulation of Charlie's windows. Inside, the almost imperceptible hum of the security system provided a constant, subtle reminder of the barriers between their private world and the public one waiting beyond.

"I'm afraid," Charlie admitted suddenly, the words seeming to surprise even him as they escaped. His fingers tensed against Bee's skin before deliberately relaxing. "Not of this—of what comes after this. Of what being with me will do to your life."

Bee shifted, propping herself up on one elbow to look at him directly. The moonlight carved his features into stark relief—vulnerability written in the tension around his eyes, the slight furrow between his brows. "What do you think it will do?"

"Change it. Irrevocably." His eyes held hers, unflinching despite the fear evident in them. "The photographers at the farmers market? That's just the beginning. They'll follow you, dig into your past, create narratives about you that have nothing to do with reality. Friends will treat you differently. Strangers will feel entitled to opinions about your life." His hand moved to cup her face, thumb brushing her cheekbone with heartbreaking gentleness. "And eventually, that pressure drives people away. It always has."

The raw honesty in his voice touched something in Bee's chest, a recognition of the loneliness that had shaped him just as her own wariness had shaped her. She turned her face slightly, pressing a kiss into his palm.

"I have my own fears," she admitted, matching his honesty with her own. "I've worked hard to build my life on my terms. I'm afraid of losing that—my independence, my privacy, my ability to just... be ordinary when I want to be." She laid her hand over his heart, feeling its beat accelerate slightly beneath her touch. "I'm afraid of becoming an accessory to someone else's story instead of the protagonist of my own."

Charlie nodded, understanding visible in his expression. "That's fair. More than fair."

"But," Bee continued, her voice strengthening, "I'm more afraid of walking away from this—from you—because I'm too cautious to take a risk." Her fingers spread across his chest, claiming the territory beneath them. "I've spent years building walls to keep myself safe. Maybe it's time to see what happens when I let someone inside them."

Moonlight shifted as clouds moved across the night sky,

briefly dimming before brightening again, the patterns on their skin changing with the celestial dance outside. Charlie's arm tightened around Bee, drawing her closer against him, his face turning to press into her hair.

"I've never felt this way about anyone," he confessed, the words muffled against her dark strands. "Never. Not even close." His voice roughened with emotion. "And I'm terrified of screwing this up. Of not knowing how to be with someone when cameras aren't rolling, when there's no script to follow."

Bee pulled back slightly, enough to meet his eyes again. "Then don't," she said simply, her characteristic directness undiminished by vulnerability. "I'm not going anywhere unless you give me reason to."

The simplicity of her statement—neither a promise of blind devotion nor a conditional acceptance—seemed to reach something essential in Charlie. His expression softened, the tension in his shoulders easing visibly.

"The practical reality won't be easy," he said after a moment. "The paparazzi won't lose interest anytime soon. Your friends, your family—they'll be approached for information. Social media will explode with speculation every time we're seen together." His fingers traced the line of her collarbone, as if memorizing its contours. "Even with security, with publicists managing the narrative, there will be intrusions we can't control."

"I know," Bee acknowledged, her gaze steady. "I've had a crash course in fame-by-association these past few days." Her lips curved in a small smile that held both humor and determination. "But I'm adaptable. And stubborn. And remarkably good at telling pushy people to go to hell when necessary."

Charlie's laugh was quiet but genuine, vibrating through both their bodies where they pressed together. "You are that," he agreed, some of the heaviness lifting from his expression.

"Victoria Harrington can testify to your skill in that department."

"Exactly." Bee's fingers found his, intertwining with deliberate intent. "I won't pretend it doesn't scare me—all of it. The loss of anonymity, the scrutiny, the weird power dynamics that come with dating someone famous." Her thumb brushed across his knuckles. "But I think what we've found here is worth fighting for. Worth figuring out how to navigate together."

"Together," Charlie repeated, the word carrying weight beyond its simple syllables. "I like the sound of that."

"So do I." Bee shifted closer, her body aligning with his in a way that felt both new and familiar, as if they'd been designed to fit together. "So what do we call this? What are we to each other now?"

The question hung between them, simple yet profound. Charlie's free hand moved to trace the curve of her cheek, his touch reverent in its gentleness.

"Partners," he suggested, echoing their earlier conversation. "Against the circus and everything else."

"Partners," Bee agreed, the term feeling right in its balanced implication of equality, of mutual support, of chosen connection. "And more," she added, her eyes holding his with meaningful intent.

"And more," Charlie agreed, his voice deepening. "My girlfriend sounds inadequate for what you are to me, but—"

"It's accurate, if incomplete," Bee finished for him, her directness once again a perfect complement to his more careful phrasing. "I am your girlfriend. You are my boyfriend. The rest... we'll define as we go."

The simplicity of the labels belied the complexity of what lay beneath them—the rare connection they'd found, the unique challenges they faced, the choice they were making with open eyes and willing hearts. Charlie's arms tightened around Bee, drawing her fully against him, their bodies remembering the contours discovered earlier.

"So we're official," he murmured, his breath warm against her temple. "Exclusive. Together."

"Together," Bee confirmed, tilting her face up to his. "Despite the paparazzi, the gossip, the invasion of privacy. Despite all of it."

"Because of all of it, in a way," Charlie amended softly. "If not for that wrong number text, if not for the restaurant recognition..."

"We might never have found each other," Bee completed the thought, understanding perfectly. "Everything that complicates this also created it."

Their lips met in a kiss that sealed their decision, gentle yet certain, a promise exchanged without words. Outside, the security system hummed its quiet, constant vigilance, protecting them from the world that would soon enough intrude upon their newly-defined relationship. For now, though, in the silver-blue darkness of Charlie's bedroom, they existed in a bubble of their own creation—not naive about the challenges ahead, but determined to face them side by side.

As the kiss deepened, a subtle electronic tone sounded from somewhere in the house—the security system acknowledging a perimeter check, perhaps, or some automated function maintaining the technological shield that surrounded them. The sound was brief, barely noticeable, but it served as a gentle reminder of the world waiting beyond their intimate cocoon.

Charlie drew back slightly, his forehead resting against Bee's, eyes open and honest in the moonlight. "No matter what happens out there," he whispered, "this—what's between us—is real. Is ours."

Bee's hand curled against the nape of his neck, fingers threading through his hair in a gesture both possessive and tender. "Ours," she agreed, the simple word containing multitudes—a declaration of shared territory, of mutual claim, of deliberate choice.

The night stretched around them, hours until dawn, the luxury of time still theirs to spend as they chose. Outside, the city continued its restless dance of light and movement. Inside, wrapped in moonlight and each other, Charlie and Bee had created something new—a relationship defined not by public perception or external pressure, but by the genuine connection they'd discovered in the most unlikely of circumstances.

Together, they would write their own story.

Chapter Fourteen: The Naked Truth

❧

Sunlight clung to their skin as Charlie and Bee stumbled through the front door, trailing sand and the phantom sensation of waves across the immaculate marble floor. The scent of salt and sunscreen wrapped around them like a private atmosphere, their laughter echoing through the cavernous entryway. Charlie's fingers remained tangled with Bee's, neither willing to break the connection that had strengthened with each passing day since that night they'd defined themselves as partners—against the circus, against the world, against anything that threatened the unexpected sanctuary they'd found in each other.

"I think I have half the beach in my hair," Bee said, running her free hand through the salt-stiffened strands. Tiny crystals of sand showered onto her shoulders, catching the afternoon light. Her cheeks glowed with lingering sun, eyes bright with the particular joy that comes from hours spent in open air and warm water.

Charlie's smile deepened the lines around his eyes—the genuine ones that never appeared in carefully staged photoshoots. "You look beautiful." His gaze travelled over her beach-rumpled appearance with unguarded appreciation. "Like some kind of sea goddess washed ashore to torment us mortal men."

"A very sandy goddess," she countered, though pleasure at the compliment coloured her voice. She tugged playfully at his hand. "Come on, I need a shower before these clothes permanently fuse to my skin. Would you like to wash my back?" she said with a wink.

Charlie's response was a beaming smile as he pulled her against him, feeling her body flush up against his, he tilted her chin up so their lips met, "I think showering with you sounds like an amazing idea, just to make sure you don't slip, of course, you may have some sun stroke." He murmured against her lips.

"I definitely could have some sun stroke, I may need something firm to prop me up," she replied between kisses, running her hand down his body, letting it travel below his waistband, feeling him begin to get firm.

"We should get naked, like now." He said leading her down the hall.

They moved deeper into the house, footsteps leaving damp impressions that evaporated almost immediately in the climate-controlled air. Charlie's arm slid around Bee's waist, drawing her against his side as they walked. The casual intimacy of the gesture had become second nature over the past weeks—the invisible bubble they created whenever they touched, a private space within the vastness of his mansion.

The corridor leading to the master bedroom stretched before them, the familiar path they'd walked countless times since Bee had moved in. But today, something disrupted the familiar landscape. Charlie registered it first—the bedroom door standing slightly ajar, a thin wedge of shadow where there should have been only the seamless alignment of door and frame. He'd closed it that morning; he always closed it.

His body tensed, arm tightening around Bee's waist. She felt the change in him immediately, her own muscles responding to his sudden vigilance.

"What's wrong?" she whispered, following his gaze to the door.

"I closed that door when we left," Charlie said, his voice dropping to match hers, the playfulness of moments before vanishing completely. "Stay behind me."

He moved forward, shifting his body to place himself between Bee and whatever waited beyond that door. His shoulders squared, jaw set in a hard line as he approached. Bee followed a half-step behind, her fingers gripping the back of his damp t-shirt, her heartbeat accelerating with each step.

Charlie pushed the door open slowly, revealing his bedroom in increments. Everything seemed normal at first— the vast windows overlooking the canyon, the morning light spilling across the hardwood floor, the familiar furnishings in their proper places. Then the bed came into view, and the world tilted sideways.

A woman reclined against his pillows, naked beneath sheets that barely covered her hips. Her platinum blonde hair spread across the pillowcase where Bee's head had rested just that morning. Her clothes—expensive, carefully selected—lay scattered across the floor in what was clearly meant to appear as the aftermath of passion.

She sat up as they entered, letting the sheet fall deliberately to her waist, exposing breasts that seemed too perfect, too precisely shaped to be natural. Her lips curved into a practised smile, eyes fixing on Charlie with possessive familiarity.

"Finally home, baby," she purred, voice pitched to a sultry register. "I was getting cold waiting for you."

Bee's sharp intake of breath seemed unnaturally loud in the suspended moment that followed. Her fingers dug into the doorframe until her knuckles blanched white, body rigid with shock. The room suddenly felt overheated, airless, the scent of unfamiliar perfume overlaying the familiar clean smell of Charlie's space like a toxic mist.

Charlie's face transformed as if a mask had been ripped away, revealing something Bee had never seen before—cold, absolute fury that hardened his features into something almost unrecognisable. His jaw locked, a muscle jumping along its edge with each clenched pulse.

"Who the hell are you? And how did you get into my fucking house?" The question emerged with controlled precision each word cut from ice.

The woman's expression faltered momentarily before resettling into practised seduction. "Don't play games, Charlie. Not after everything we've shared." She stretched languidly, a movement designed to draw attention to her exposed body. "I used the code you gave me. The one you said was just for me." Her gaze shifted to Bee, dismissive and pitying. "He always does this when his little playthings are around."

Bee felt as if her lungs had forgotten how to function properly, each breath catching painfully in her throat. The woman's casual claim struck with physical force, sending cold reality crashing through the warm happiness of moments before. Her mind raced backward through the weeks since she'd moved in—had there been signs she'd missed? Late nights explained away? Texts he'd hidden? The rational part of her knew this was absurd, impossible, but doubt's cold fingers had already found purchase.

"I have never seen this woman in my life." Charlie's voice cut through the chaos of her thoughts, absolute certainty in every syllable. He hadn't moved from his protective stance, body still angled to shield Bee, but his hands had curled into fists at his sides.

The woman laughed, the sound brittle and artificial. "He's

very good at that line, isn't he?" She addressed Bee directly now, eyes glittering with something that went beyond simple malice. "Don't worry, honey. He'll call me when he's done with you—he always does. After Claire, after Jessica, after all the others. I'm the one he comes back to." She leaned forward, dropping her voice to a staged whisper. "I know how he likes to be touched, where he likes my mouth. Things he'd never tell some retail girl playing dress up in his world."

Bee's stomach lurched as if she'd been physically struck. The violation wasn't just of Charlie's home, but of their private life, their intimacy. This stranger knew details—real or imagined—that transformed their sanctuary into something exposed and contaminated.

Charlie took a step toward the bed, then stopped himself, visibly wrestling with rage that threatened to overwhelm his control. "I am calling security. You are trespassing in my home. I have never met you, never given you any access code, and never had any relationship with you."

"Such a good actor," the woman sighed, running her hand across the sheets where Charlie and Bee had lain together and made love just hours ago. "That's why you're paid the big bucks, isn't it? But we both know the truth, Madison and Charlie, forever." She smiled, the expression not reaching her eyes. "I've waited so patiently while you played with your toys."

Madison. The name hung in the air between them, poisonous in its familiarity. Bee had heard it before—in conversations with Charlie's security team, in warnings from his publicist about particularly persistent fans. Madison Vale. The woman whose letters Charlie's team intercepted, whose appearances at events had been carefully managed, whose obsession had been deemed concerning but manageable.

· · ·

Until now.

Charlie's hand moved to his pocket with deliberate control, every movement measured as if he were handling explosive material. His eyes never left Madison, watching her with the focused attention one might give a venomous snake coiled on familiar ground. "I'm calling security now," he said, voice level despite the rage visible in the rigid set of his shoulders. "This is your only warning." As he raised the phone to his ear, Madison's calculated seductiveness began to fracture, her smile twitching at the corners, her eyes darting between Charlie and Bee with increasing agitation.

"You don't need to call them," Madison said, her voice shifting from sultry to plaintive in an instant. "We don't need anyone else here. It's always been just us." She clutched the sheet to her chest now, the earlier exhibitionism replaced by something more desperate. "You promised me, Charlie. After the premiere of Darkness Falls. You said when the timing was right—"

"Security, this is Charlie," he interrupted, his back straightening as he spoke into the phone. "I have an intruder in my bedroom, female, mid-thirties, claims to have used an access code." His eyes narrowed slightly. "Yes, I need immediate removal and full system check. No, I don't want police yet. Internal handling first." He disconnected the call with a sharp tap.

Madison's face contorted, affection giving way to raw emotion. "You think they'll believe you? That I somehow broke in? I know things, Charlie. Things only someone close to you would know." She leaned forward, her movements becoming jerky, uncoordinated. "You have a scar on your left shoulder from falling off a horse when you were twelve. You hate cilantro but eat it anyway when your brother cooks because you don't want to hurt his feelings. You sleep on the right side of the bed and always set three alarms because you sleep through the first two."

Bee felt cold sweat prickling along her spine. The details were specific, unnervingly accurate. She'd traced that scar with her own fingers, had watched Charlie pick cilantro from his food when he thought no one was looking, had laughed at the multiple alarms that punctuated their mornings.

Charlie's expression didn't change, but his hand moved slightly backward seeking Bee's. She took it, grateful for the anchor as the room seemed to tilt beneath her feet.

"Your stalking is comprehensive," Charlie acknowledged, his tone flat. "Congratulations on your research, I have said all of those things during interviews. It doesn't change the fact that we've never met, never spoken, and certainly never had any kind of relationship."

Madison's eyes fixed on their joined hands, something ugly flashing across her features. "You think she's different? Special?" Her laugh emerged harsh, stripped of any pretence at seduction. "I've watched you cycle through them. The actress, the model, the artist. Now the shop girl. They never last because they never understand you like I do."

The sound of footsteps in the hallway announced security's arrival—two men in dark suits moving with efficient purpose. They paused at the threshold, taking in the scene with professional detachment.

"Mr. Benton," the taller one acknowledged. "Ma'am." He nodded toward Bee before turning his attention to Madison. "Miss, I need you to get dressed immediately. You'll be escorted from the premises."

Madison's chin lifted, a strange smile playing at her lips. "I'm not going anywhere. This is where I belong." She gestured around the room. "I picked these sheets, did you know that? I told Charlie which ones to buy because Egyptian cotton feels best against bare skin."

The security men exchanged a glance that spoke volumes about their experience with similar situations. The shorter one approached the bed, stopping a respectful distance away. "Miss, please get dressed now, or we'll have to remove you as you are."

"I'm not putting on clothes for you," Madison spat, her façade completely dissolved now, revealing something feral beneath. "Charlie, tell them who I am. Tell them about us." When Charlie remained silent, her voice rose sharply. "Tell them!"

Charlie moved closer to Bee, positioning himself firmly between her and the bed. His body radiated tension, but his movements remained controlled, deliberate. "Remove her," he directed the security team. "And find out how she got in. Every code needs to be changed, every entry point checked."

The security men moved with practiced efficiency, the taller one retrieving the top sheet from the bed with a quick, smooth motion while the shorter one blocked Madison's attempt to lunge toward Charlie. The sheet was wrapped around her struggling form despite her efforts to resist, the guards' movements firm but not rough, suggesting protocols developed specifically for such situations.

"You don't have to pretend anymore!" Madison's voice rose, brittle with desperation as they secured the sheet around her. "I understand the game, Charlie. The public girlfriend, the private truth. I've kept our secret all this time." Her eyes, wide and glittering with an unsettling intensity, found Bee's over Charlie's shoulder. "Ask him about the flowers. Red roses every Valentine's Day for five years. Ask him why he always looks for me at premieres, how his eyes find mine in the crowd."

Charlie didn't respond, his focus entirely on keeping his

body between Madison and Bee as the security team maneuvered the sheet-wrapped woman toward the door.

Madison twisted in their grip, her movements increasingly erratic, her carefully maintained appearance disintegrating with each passing moment. Her hair, previously arranged in elegant waves, now stuck to her sweat-dampened face; her makeup smeared beneath eyes that darted frantically around the room.

"This isn't how our story ends." She called, voice cracking as they guided her into the hallway. "I've kept journals of everything, Charlie. Every moment, every promise. The world deserves to know the truth about us."

One of the guards spoke quietly into a radio clipped to his lapel, his words too low to catch but his tone suggesting reinforcements or protocols being activated. The controlled way they handled Madison—firm but careful, attentive to both restraint and optics—indicated specialised training for exactly this type of situation.

"The press will hear everything," Madison continued, her threats becoming more specific as they moved her down the corridor. "How you told me to wait, to be patient while you played the Hollywood game. How you promised we'd be together once your career was established enough to withstand the scandal." Her voice rose, echoing against the high ceilings. "I have proof! Texts, gifts everything!"

Charlie remained still, his hand finding Bee's again, fingers interlacing with gentle pressure that contradicted the rigid set of his shoulders. They stood together in the doorway, watching as Madison's struggles intensified, her body writhing beneath the sheet while the guards maintained their professional composure.

"I'll tell them how you like to be touched!" Madison shouted, the words bouncing off marble and glass. "I'll tell them what you whisper when you come! Every magazine, every talk show—they'll all hear our love story!"

The security team reached the end of the corridor, Madison's voice growing more distant but no less frantic as they guided her toward the service exit. The taller guard looked back once, catching Charlie's eye with a subtle nod that communicated both reassurance and a promise of thorough follow-up.

Then they were gone, Madison's threats fading to unintelligible echoes, leaving Charlie and Bee standing in the violated space of their bedroom. The scent of unfamiliar perfume still hung in the air, a tangible reminder of the intrusion. The bed where they had slept tangled in each other's arms now seemed contaminated, sheets rumpled by an unwelcome presence, pillows bearing the imprint of a stranger's head.

Charlie's fingers tightened around Bee's his other hand coming up to brush hair from her face with a gentleness that contrasted sharply with the cold fury still evident in his expression. "Are you okay?" he asked, the first words he'd spoken directly to her since they'd entered the room.

The living room felt too bright, too exposed, with afternoon sun streaming through the wall of windows that had once seemed like a luxury but now felt like vulnerability incarnate. Charlie paced a tight circuit in front of the fireplace, phone pressed to his ear each word emerging with the controlled precision of someone containing rage so intense it threatened to consume him whole. Bee sat on the edge of the sofa, back straight, hands folded in her lap with deliberate stillness that contradicted the tremor she couldn't quite suppress in her breathing. Between them hung the invisible spectre of what had just occurred—the violation more profound than simple trespassing, the contamination that couldn't be removed with changed locks or new security codes.

"I want the entire system replaced," Charlie said into the

phone, his voice low but carrying clearly in the silent room. "Not updated, not recoded—replaced. Every panel, every sensor, every camera." He paused, listening, the muscle in his jaw jumping beneath taut skin. "I don't care what it costs or how long it takes. She got into my bedroom. This isn't a drill or a hypothetical scenario anymore."

Bee watched him move the fluid grace that characterised his normal movements now transformed into something sharper, more mechanical. She noticed details with heightened sensitivity that follows shock—the way his knuckles whitened around the phone, how his free hand opened and closed at his side, the slight hoarseness in his voice that spoke of restrained shouting.

"I want a full background check," Charlie continued, turning at the edge of the expensive rug to retrace his steps. "Everything on Madison Vale—property records, employment history, financial transactions. Especially any purchases near this address." Another pause, longer this time. "Yes, I understand privacy laws. Use the private firm, the one we used for the Claire situation."

The mention of Claire—the actress whose relationship with Charlie had ended with restraining orders and sealed court documents—sent a fresh chill through Bee's body. She had known intellectually what dating someone famous might entail: photographers, gossip, loss of anonymity. But this—a stranger in their bed, intimate knowledge of their private lives, the thinly veiled menace behind Madison's words—existed in another category entirely.

Charlie made two more calls, each more focused than the last: to his attorney about potential legal actions, to his publicist about containing any stories Madison might attempt to sell. Throughout, his pacing never ceased, his body vibrating with controlled energy that had nowhere productive to go. When he finally ended the last call, the silence that followed seemed unnaturally heavy, pregnant with all they hadn't yet said to each other.

He stood motionless for a moment, staring at the darkened screen of his phone as if it might offer solutions beyond what human voices had provided. Then, with visible effort, he crossed to the sofa and sat beside Bee—close enough to reach her, but with deliberate space between them, uncertain of his welcome.

"I'm so sorry," he said finally, the words emerging rough, as if scraped from the bottom of his throat. "I never—" He stopped, drew a breath that seemed to physically pain him. "I never wanted to drag you into this chaos."

Bee looked at her hands, noticing with detached interest that they trembled despite her efforts to keep them still. The simple gold band she wore on her right middle finger—a gift from her mother on her twenty-first birthday—caught the light as her fingers quivered.

"Is this..." She paused, trying to form the question in a way that wouldn't sound accusatory. "Is this normal for you?"

Charlie's laugh held no humour. "No." He ran a hand through his hair, the familiar gesture now sharp with tension. "I've had obsessive fans before. Letters, gifts sent to my agent, showing up at events or restaurants where I'm known to go." His eyes found hers, dark with guilt and something that looked terrifyingly like fear. "But this—getting into my home, my bedroom—no. This is different."

"She knew things," Bee said quietly, the observation slipping out before she could consider whether it would hurt him. "About you, About your habits."

"Yes." Charlie's face tightened. "Most of it could have been gathered from interviews, social media, industry gossip. Some of it—" He swallowed visibly. "Some of it suggests more extensive surveillance than we realised. The security team is checking for cameras, bugs, anything that might have been planted."

The implication hung between them—their most intimate moments potentially observed, recorded, consumed by hungry eyes that had no right to them. Bee felt suddenly cold despite the warm air flowing through the house's perfect climate control.

"This is exactly what I was afraid would happen," Charlie said, his voice dropping to just above a whisper. "Not this specifically, but something like it. The chaos of my life infecting yours. Putting you at risk."

Bee studied his face—the genuine anguish there, the fear not for himself but for her. "You think she's dangerous? Beyond the stalking, I mean."

"I don't know," Charlie admitted, the uncertainty seeming to pain him physically. "Most obsessive fans maintain a fantasy relationship that never crosses into direct confrontation. They're content with the narrative they've created." He leaned forward, elbows on his knees. "Madison crossed that line today. Dramatically. That escalation is concerning to the security team."

Bee nodded, processing this information with a calmness that felt disconnected from the trembling that had now spread from her hands to her entire body. She'd felt safe in this house, in their relationship—a fragile sense of security she'd built despite the cameras outside the gates, despite the occasional paparazzi chase when they ventured into public. That safety had dissolved the moment they'd walked into the bedroom and found a stranger in their most private space.

"The bedroom," she said suddenly, the practical concern anchoring her when emotional ones threatened to overwhelm. "We can't—I can't sleep there tonight. Not where she—"

"Of course not," Charlie agreed immediately "We'll use one of the guest suites until the bedroom can be completely refreshed. New bedding, fuck a new bed, new everything." He said, taking her hand.

She looked into his eyes, she could see that he was trying to make this right, she took a step toward him, leaving a small space between them, which he closed, pulling her against him. "How about we completely redecorate that room, instead of it being so plain, we get everything taken out, and we choose new colours, a new bed, new bedroom furniture, and we do it together, and we make it ours." He said softly, brushing her hair behind her ear.

"I think that sounds like a wonderful idea." She whispered stretching up and kissing him.

Chapter Fifteen: Damage Control

Dawn spread thin fingers of light across the mansion's marble floors, touching objects that had seemed secure and private just twenty-four hours earlier. Charlie stood at the kitchen island, shoulders rigid beneath his wrinkled t-shirt, eyes burning from a night spent staring at the ceiling of the guest bedroom rather than sleeping. The blueprints of his property lay spread before him like the anatomical diagram of a body recently discovered to be ill, each potential entry point a vulnerability he'd failed to protect.

"Yes, I understand the timeline," he said into the phone pressed against his ear, voice roughened by exhaustion. "But I need the installation completed by the end of the week, not next month."

The voice on the other end—professionally detached, carefully explaining the logistics of completely overhauling a security system for a property of this size—droned on about supply chains and technician availability. Charlie uncapped a red marker with his teeth, the sharp chemical smell briefly cutting through the lingering scent of coffee gone cold beside him.

"Double your team size. Triple it if necessary," he interrupted, circling a spot on the blueprint where the property wall dipped slightly lower than elsewhere. "Price is not an issue. Time is."

He circled another spot—a maintenance entrance rarely used but potentially accessible to someone determined enough. The marker pressed so hard it left an indentation in the paper beneath. As he worked, images from yesterday intruded with the persistence of a splinter beneath skin: Madison's body sprawled across sheets that had held Bee's scent just hours before, her calculated smile as she claimed intimacy that had never existed, the sick feeling that settled in his stomach when he realized how thoroughly she'd violated the boundaries of his life.

"The cameras need to cover every approach, not just the main entrances," Charlie continued, moving the marker to another section of the blueprint. "No blind spots. None."

The security consultant's voice shifted into a more technical register, detailing specifications for motion sensors with overlapping coverage zones, camera resolutions sufficient for facial recognition at fifty yards, thermal imaging capabilities for nighttime surveillance. Charlie nodded as if the man could see him, marking each recommendation on the blueprint with tight, controlled strokes of the red marker.

"And the guard rotation?" he asked, moving to the next page showing the interior layout.

"Minimum of two personnel on the grounds at all times, with shift changes arranged to avoid predictable patterns," came the response. "We recommend our highest clearance team members, all with military or law enforcement backgrounds."

"Done," Charlie said without hesitation. "I want their files on my desk today."

He glanced toward the hallway leading to the guest suite where Bee had finally fallen into restless sleep just before dawn. She'd been quiet after the incident, her usual directness muted by shock and something deeper that Charlie recognized as the first real understanding of what loving him might actually entail. The violation wasn't just of his privacy but of hers—her safety, her sense of security, her right to exist in this home without becoming collateral damage in a stranger's obsession.

After ending the call, Charlie moved with deliberate purpose toward the master bedroom, stopping at a workbench in the adjoining hallway where a new door lock lay waiting beside screwdrivers and mounting hardware. He'd ordered it delivered at midnight, the earliest the specialty locksmith could arrange. Picking up the solid brass mechanism, he weighed it in his palm—heavier than the decorative original, designed for security rather than aesthetics.

His hands trembled slightly as he positioned the drill against the door, the high whine of metal boring through wood setting his teeth on edge. Madison's voice echoed in his memory: *I know how he likes to be touched, where he likes my mouth. * The drill bit caught, jerking in his grip. Charlie steadied himself, muscles tightening against the memory.

The physical work of installing the lock—measuring, drilling, fitting the components together—provided a focus that kept worse thoughts at bay. Each turn of the screwdriver felt like securing something beyond the door itself, as if he could physically bar intrusive memories from their space.

His phone buzzed on the nearby table, Toby's name appearing on the screen. Charlie wiped sweat from his forehead with his forearm before reading the message:

*Worked through the night with the team. Two tabloids

approached with "exclusive Madison Vale relationship story." Both shut down with cease-and-desist letters and evidence of her previous restraining orders from other celebrities. Security footage of her removal from your property helps our case. Call me when you're up. *

Charlie set the phone down, relief mingling with renewed anger. Madison had tried exactly what she'd threatened— selling her delusional narrative to anyone who would listen. The fact that Toby had contained it this time provided little comfort; the woman had demonstrated both determination and resourcefulness that suggested this wouldn't be her last attempt.

After finishing the lock installation, Charlie retrieved his tablet from the kitchen and pulled up the newly installed security app. Live footage from multiple cameras showed uniformed guards walking the perimeter of his property, testing entry points, communicating via headsets. One guard knelt beside the gate mechanism, installing what appeared to be an additional biometric scanner. Another checked the integrity of the property wall, making notes on a handheld device.

Charlie adjusted the view to focus on the guest wing where he and Bee had spent the night. The bedroom they'd relocated to had been beautiful but foreign, the sheets clean but lacking the familiar impression of their bodies. They'd lain side by side in the darkness, physically close but separated by the silent processing of what had happened. When Bee had finally fallen asleep, Charlie had slipped out to begin the work of fortifying their violated sanctuary.

His phone buzzed again—this time with a text from John, his brother.

*Toby filled me in. You ok? Need me to come over? I can be there in 3 hours. *

Charlie started to type a reassurance but stopped, deleted it, and wrote something more honest:

*Not ok. But handling it. Security upgrade underway. Bee's still asleep. Call you later. *

He set the phone down and moved toward the glass doors leading to the deck, the view of Los Angeles spread below now seeming less like a privilege and more like exposure. The city that had given him everything he'd worked for had also created this—the pathological entitlement of strangers to his life, his space, his relationship. The same fame that paid for these walls had attracted those determined to breach them.

The tablet in his hand displayed another angle of his property, another guard testing another security feature. Charlie watched the footage with hollow satisfaction, knowing that no matter how many cameras he installed or guards he hired, the damage had already been done. Madison had infected their space with her presence, had transformed their private sanctuary into a place where they now moved with caution, where shadows held potential threats, where intimacy itself felt observed.

He returned to the kitchen as full daylight established itself across the mansion's clean lines. The blueprints still lay spread across the island, now marked with red circles and notations—a battle plan for a war already partially lost. Charlie carefully rolled them up and secured them with a rubber band, his movements precise and controlled despite the exhaustion pulling at his limbs.

The house would be secure again. The locks would be changed, the cameras installed, the guards vigilant. But the true violation—the psychological boundary-crossing that had left them both feeling exposed and vulnerable—couldn't be fixed with hardware or personnel. That wound would heal more slowly, if at all.

Luxe Boutique gleamed with understated opulence—

polished hardwood floors reflecting soft lighting, glass display cases holding accessories that cost more than a month's rent at Bee's apartment. She smoothed her hands down the crisp black dress she'd chosen for her trial shift, a flutter of optimism rising in her chest despite the events of yesterday. Here was something familiar, something she understood. Retail had its challenges, but they were predictable ones: demanding customers, long hours on her feet, the steady rhythm of folding, arranging, selling. Normal problems. Manageable problems.

"Bianca? I'm Elise." A woman in her forties approached, her silver-streaked hair pulled into a sleek chignon, her handshake firm and professional. "Welcome to Luxe. Let me show you around before we open."

Bee followed Elise through the boutique, absorbing details with practised eyes: the careful spacing between clothing racks, the strategic lighting that highlighted texture and colour, the subtle absence of visible price tags on most items—the universal retail code for "if you have to ask, you can't afford it."

"Our clientele expects discretion and expertise," Elise explained, leading Bee toward a back corner where silk scarves lay arranged in a precise gradient of colour. "They come to us not just for the merchandise but for the experience. We're selling a feeling as much as a product."

"I understand," Bee nodded, thinking of Harrington's, where Victoria had cultivated a similar atmosphere of exclusivity, though with less tasteful execution.

"This will be your section today," Elise gestured toward the scarves and the adjacent display of fine leather gloves. "Let's see what you can do with it before the doors open."

Left alone with the merchandise, Bee felt her shoulders relax slightly. This part she knew—the subtle art of arrangement, creating visual stories that drew customers from browsing to purchasing. Her fingers moved with practised precision, adjusting a blue-grey scarf to better complement the teal beside it, repositioning a pair of gloves to create a more inviting negative space. The familiar tasks grounded her, momentarily pushing away thoughts of Madison in Charlie's bed, of security upgrades, of the unsettling vulnerability that had followed her from the mansion to her car to this pristine retail space.

The first customers arrived precisely at ten, the discreet chime of the door announcing their entry. Two women in their thirties, carrying matching designer handbags, their conversation suspended mid-sentence as they scanned the boutique. Bee offered the professional smile she'd perfected over years in retail—warm enough to be welcoming, reserved enough to avoid presumption.

"Good morning," she greeted them from her position by the scarf display. "Please let me know if I can assist you with anything."

The women returned polite nods before turning toward a rack of dresses, their heads tilting together as they resumed their conversation in lowered voices. Bee returned to adjusting her display, hyperaware of their presence in the otherwise empty store. A movement caught her eye—one woman had pulled out her phone, the screen angled toward her companion. Something about the gesture—furtive, conspiratorial— sent a small chill across Bee's skin.

"That's definitely her," one whispered, not quite softly enough.

"I thought she worked at that other place—Harrington's?" the second replied.

"She quit. It was in the article with the photos."

Bee kept her eyes fixed on the scarves, fingers mechanically smoothing non-existent wrinkles from silk that already lay perfect. The women's glances burned against her skin like physical contact. She'd expected this, had prepared herself for it, yet the reality still scraped against her composure like sandpaper.

The morning continued in similar fashion. Customers entered, browsed, occasionally purchased—all while casting curious glances toward Bee. Some were more subtle than others. A woman in her fifties stared openly before approaching with a question about scarf quality that sounded like a test rather than genuine interest. A younger customer asked for her opinion on a dress with such studied casualness that the real question—*are you really Charlie Benton's girlfriend? *—hung unspoken between them.

By noon, Bee's professional smile had become a mask frozen to her face, her shoulders aching from the effort of maintaining perfect posture under the weight of constant observation. When Elise appeared to inform her it was time for her lunch break, relief flooded through her with almost dizzying intensity.

The staff break room occupied a small space at the rear of the building—utilitarian compared to the boutique's luxurious front, with a refrigerator, microwave, and rectangular table surrounded by metal chairs. Two employees already sat eating when Bee entered, their conversation cutting off abruptly as the door swung closed behind her.

"Hi," Bee offered, moving toward the refrigerator to retrieve the lunch she'd packed that morning. "I'm Bianca—it's my trial shift today."

"We know," said one—a tall woman with immaculate braids coiled at the nape of her neck. The words weren't unfriendly, exactly, but they carried weight beyond their simple syllables.

Bee nodded, unsure how to respond, and took a seat at the opposite end of the table. The silence stretched uncomfortably as she unwrapped her sandwich. The other employees exchanged glances laden with unspoken communication.

"So," the second employee finally said, leaning forward slightly, "what's he like? In real life, I mean."

The question hung in the air, simultaneously innocent and intrusive. Bee took a careful bite of her sandwich, chewing slowly to buy time. How to answer? With the truth—that Charlie was kind, funny, vulnerable in ways his public image never showed? Or with the deflection she'd been practising since their relationship became public?

"He's private," she said finally, the diplomatic response feeling hollow even to her own ears. "Just trying to live his life like anyone else."

The employees exchanged another glance, disappointment evident in their expressions. The break room door swung open, admitting another staff member who stopped short upon seeing Bee, eyes widening in recognition before darting away. The newcomer settled beside the others, their conversation resuming in hushed tones that might as well have been shouts for how clearly their subject was telegraphed.

Bee finished her lunch with mechanical movements, barely tasting the food. As she rose to return to the sales floor, she caught a fragment of whispered conversation: "—wonder how long before he trades up."

The afternoon brought more of the same, with increasing boldness from customers who had apparently heard about her presence through social media or text messages from friends. Two college-aged women entered specifically to browse in her section, giggling behind their hands and taking surreptitious photos, they thought she didn't notice. An older man with expensive cufflinks asked if she could help his wife select a scarf, his eyes lingering too long on her body as he mentioned how his daughter loved Charlie's latest film.

"That's her—Charlie Benton's girlfriend," came a whisper from behind a display of handbags, the words carrying clearly in the store's perfect acoustics. "The retail girl he's slumming with."

Another voice, equally carrying: "How long do you give it? These celebrity-civilian things never last."

"Six months, tops. His ex was a literal supermodel. This one's cute, but..."

Bee's fingers trembled slightly as she refolded a cashmere wrap, the luxurious fabric suddenly abrasive against her sensitised skin. Each whisper, each curious glance, each poorly disguised photograph chipped away at the professional demeanour she'd maintained throughout her retail career. Here, in this pristine boutique with its carefully curated atmosphere, she wasn't Bianca Anderson, experienced retail manager with an eye for design. She was an oddity, a curiosity, a temporary diversion in a celebrity's life.

A woman approached with a genuine question about the weight of a particular silk for all-season wear. Bee answered automatically, her knowledge of fabrics and construction surfacing through the haze of discomfort that had settled over her. This, at least, she could do without thinking—the actual work that had once given her satisfaction.

"Thank you," the woman said, seeming surprised by the depth of Bee's answer. "You really know your products."

"Yes," Bee replied, a small, sad smile touching her lips. "I do."

But knowledge and skill meant little, she was learning, when overshadowed by association. As the afternoon wore on and the whispers continued, that knowledge solidified into certainty: her professional identity had been subsumed by her relationship. Whatever value she brought to this role had been rendered invisible by the far more interesting fact of whom she loved.

The decision had already formed in her mind, clear and

inescapable as the reflection of her strained expression in the boutique's many mirrors.

The midday lull had just settled over Luxe Boutique when the doors swung open with theatrical force, admitting a gust of cool air and the unmistakable presence of Victoria Harrington. Her camel hair coat hung open to reveal a silk blouse that probably cost more than most people's monthly salary, her golden highlights catching the store's perfect lighting as if they'd been designed specifically for this environment. Bee's fingers froze on the silk scarf she'd been arranging, a cold weight settling in her stomach as Victoria's gaze swept the store and landed on her with predatory precision.

For one suspended moment, Bee hoped against logic that Victoria might not recognise her—that the black dress and sleek ponytail required by Luxe might render her temporarily anonymous. That hope evaporated as Victoria's lips curved into a smile that held all the warmth of a snake sunning itself on concrete.

Victoria made no immediate approach. Instead, she moved with deliberate leisure toward a display of handbags positioned just close enough to Bee's station to make her presence unavoidable. Her designer heels tapped a measured rhythm against the hardwood floor, each step a countdown to inevitable confrontation.

"Exquisite craftsmanship," Victoria murmured, loud enough to carry, as she examined a leather clutch with theatrical attention. She turned it over, inspecting the stitching with the exaggerated care of someone performing expertise rather than actually possessing it. "Though perhaps not quite up to Harrington's standards."

Bee continued arranging scarves, her movements mechanical, fingers slightly stiff with tension. Victoria's presence expanded to fill the space between them, drawing the attention of the few customers browsing nearby. A woman who had been examining gloves glanced up, her eyes darting between Victoria and Bee with quickening interest.

"May I help you find something specific?" Bee finally asked, professionalism compelling her toward the inevitable encounter. Her voice emerged steadier than she felt, the practised retail tone perfected over years of customer service.

Victoria turned slowly, as if surprised to find Bee addressing her. "Bianca, isn't it? I almost didn't recognise you in this..." Her gaze travelled the length of Bee's body, lingering on the simple black dress with pointed distaste. "...uniform."

"We specialise in luxury accessories," Bee continued, ignoring the bait. "Is there something particular you're looking for today?"

Victoria's smile sharpened, her teeth appearing briefly between glossed lips. "I suppose you don't need to worry about prices anymore, do you? Not with your... situation." The pause before the final word stretched with deliberate significance, her eyes never leaving Bee's face, cataloguing each minute reaction.

Heat crawled up Bee's neck, a flush she could feel spreading toward her cheeks despite her effort to maintain composure. Around them, the ambient sounds of the boutique seemed to dim as customers stilled, attention drawn to the tension unfolding between the two women.

"Our accessories are investment pieces," Bee responded, her voice slightly tighter. "Quality that justifies the price point."

"Oh, I know all about investments." Victoria moved closer, her perfume—something expensive and aggressively floral—invading Bee's space. "Though I've always wondered what it would take to land someone like Charlie Benton." Her voice dropped to a theatrical whisper that carried perfectly to nearby customers. "Now I know."

Bee's hands stilled on the scarf she'd been adjusting, the

silk suddenly slippery beneath fingers that trembled slightly despite her effort to control them. She was painfully aware of their audience—the customers who had stopped pretending to shop, the staff member hovering nearby with poorly disguised interest.

"Is there something specific you're interested in purchasing today?" Bee asked, each word careful, measured, a tightrope walk over the pit Victoria had opened beneath her.

"Just browsing." Victoria lifted a delicate cashmere scarf, examining it with exaggerated care. "You know, I've always found retail work so... grounding. It must be such a comfort to have something to fall back on." Her gaze flicked up to meet Bee's, sharp with calculated cruelty. "When the relationship ends, I mean. As these things inevitably do."

The scarf in Bee's hands wrinkled slightly as her fingers clenched involuntarily. She forced herself to release the delicate fabric, smoothing it with deliberate motions that gave her something to focus on besides the flush spreading across her face.

"We have some excellent new arrivals in the ready-to-wear section," Bee offered, her voice hollow even to her own ears. "Perhaps you'd like to—"

"I saw the photos, of course," Victoria continued as if Bee hadn't spoken. "Everyone has. You and Charlie at that little farmers market, playing at being a normal couple." She adjusted her designer handbag higher on her arm, the motion practised and precise. "How quaint. How... temporary."

A customer nearby had abandoned all pretence of shopping, her phone half-raised as if contemplating whether to record the exchange. Another woman whispered something to her companion, their eyes fixed on Bee with the avid interest of audiences at public executions.

"If you're not interested in making a purchase, perhaps I could help another customer," Bee said, attempting to step around Victoria toward a woman who actually appeared to be shopping.

Victoria shifted slightly, blocking her path with casual effectiveness. "You know what they say about men like him," she continued, her voice rising just enough to ensure maximum audience. "They cycle through girls like you rather quickly. I hope you've negotiated a good settlement package." Her eyes glittered with malice thinly veiled as concern. "Not that you could possibly hope to maintain the lifestyle he's temporarily afforded you."

Something cold and hard settled in Bee's chest, displacing the humiliation with an anger so focused it felt almost like calm. She met Victoria's gaze directly, keeping her voice low enough to maintain the fiction of privacy.

"I appreciate your concern for my financial well-being," she said evenly. "Though I'm curious why you're shopping here instead of your own boutique. Inventory issues? Or just checking out the competition since your best employee quit?"

Victoria's carefully maintained expression flickered, a momentary crack in her composure quickly plastered over with renewed disdain. "Simply conducting market research. One must keep abreast of what the second-tier establishments are offering."

"Of course," Bee nodded, her smile professional and empty. "Is there anything else I can help you with today?"

The question—standard retail courtesy—carried unmistakable dismissal. For a moment, Victoria seemed ready to escalate further, her body tensing like a cat preparing to pounce. Then, with visible effort, she recalibrated, her features arranging themselves into practised superiority.

"I think I've seen everything worth noting," she said, adjusting her coat with a sharp tug. "Do give my regards to Charlie. And my condolences on that unfortunate incident with his... fan. Madison, wasn't it? Such a passionate admirer."

The reference to Madison—a detail Victoria could only know through industry gossip or tabloid sources—struck Bee with physical force. Her carefully maintained facade cracked, a small inhalation betraying her shock before she could suppress it.

Victoria's smile widened at the reaction, satisfaction gleaming in her eyes. "Tread carefully, Bianca. Men like Charlie attract all sorts of... intense attention. Not everyone has the constitution for it." With a final pointed glance at the customers still openly watching their exchange, she turned and swept toward the exit, the scent of her perfume lingering like a toxic cloud.

Bee stood frozen, aware of the weight of stares pressing against her skin, the whispers already beginning around her. With careful, measured movements, she gathered the scattered scarves she'd been arranging and turned toward the stockroom door.

"Excuse me," she murmured to no one in particular, her voice scarcely audible over the pounding of blood in her ears.

The stockroom's fluorescent lighting cast harsh shadows across boxes of inventory stacked in neat rows. Bee closed the door behind her and leaned against metal shelving, her knees suddenly weak, her breath coming in shallow pulls that didn't seem to deliver enough oxygen to her lungs. The cool metal against her palms anchored her as her mind raced in chaotic circles.

Victoria's visit had been no coincidence. She'd deliberately sought Bee out, armed with information about Madison that could only have come from industry sources—a calculated attack designed to publicly humiliate her while simultaneously reminding her of yesterday's violation. The precision of it, the targeted cruelty, spoke of effort beyond simple spite.

Bee pressed her forehead against a shelf, the metal cool against her flushed skin. Outside this temporary sanctuary, customers would still be whispering, perhaps googling the Madison reference, connecting it to Charlie, to her. Whatever professional credibility she might have established during her trial shift had been systematically dismantled in the space of a five-minute encounter.

The realisation settled over her with cold clarity: she couldn't do this. No retail position, no matter how prestigious or well-paying, would allow her to escape the shadow of her relationship with Charlie. Her professional identity had been subsumed by personal association, transforming her from skilled employee to curiosity, gossip fodder, target.

Bee straightened, pulling her shoulders back as she drew a deep breath. The decision, once formed, brought a strange calm. She would finish her shift with whatever dignity she could muster, then quietly withdraw from consideration for the position. It wasn't surrender, she told herself. It was a strategic retreat—a recognition that the battlefield had changed beyond recognition.

The fluorescent lighting in the manager's office cast everything in stark relief—the sleek metal desk, the fashion magazines arranged in perfect alignment along its edge, Elise's carefully neutral expression as Bee closed the door behind her. The day's final hour of business hummed beyond the frosted glass, customers making last-minute purchases while staff began the subtle preparations for closing. Bee's trial shift was technically complete; she had proven her product knowledge, her customer service skills, her ability to maintain composure under pressure. By any normal retail standard, she had succeeded. But normal standards no longer applied to her life.

"Elise," Bee began, her voice steadier than she felt. "I wanted to speak with you before I leave today."

Elise gestured toward the chair opposite her desk, her silver-streaked chignon still perfectly intact despite the long day. "Of course. I was just about to prepare your feedback.

Overall, I think you've demonstrated excellent product knowledge and customer service aptitude."

Bee settled into the chair, spine straight, hands folded in her lap with deliberate calm. The posture of composure she'd perfected over years in retail served her now as armour against the more vulnerable truth: that she was admitting defeat, retreating from a battlefield where the rules had changed without warning.

"I appreciate that," she said carefully. "But I don't think this is going to work out. The attention I'm bringing isn't fair to the store."

Elise's expression shifted from professional assessment to something more personal, her practised retail mask slipping to reveal genuine curiosity. "You're referring to your... connection to Charlie Benton?"

"Yes." Bee met her gaze directly, refusing to show embarrassment for a relationship that brought her joy despite its complications. "As you've seen today, it creates a disruption. Customers come in to gawk rather than shop. Staff are distracted. It affects the atmosphere you've worked to create here."

Through the frosted glass of the office door, shadowy figures moved across the sales floor—customers still whispering, still casting glances toward the office where they knew Bee had disappeared. Victoria's surgical strike had been merely the most pointed example of what would become a daily reality.

"I had hoped," Elise said after a moment's consideration, "that the initial curiosity would fade. That customers would eventually see past your relationship to your actual skills." She tapped manicured fingernails against the desk's surface, a thoughtful rhythm. "But after today's... incident with Ms. Harrington, I can understand your concern."

So Elise had witnessed Victoria's performance or at least heard about it from staff or customers. Bee felt a flash of gratitude that she didn't have to explain the humiliating encounter in detail.

"It won't fade," Bee said with quiet certainty. "Not while the relationship is new and interesting to people. And incidents like today's will continue. There are those who find it... entertaining to remind me of my place."

"Your place?" Elise's eyebrow arched slightly.

"As an outsider. Someone who doesn't belong in Charlie's world." Bee's fingers tightened briefly against each other before deliberately relaxing. "I don't agree with that assessment, but it doesn't stop people from making it—loudly and publicly."

Elise studied her for a long moment, professional assessment shifting to something more personal. "For what it's worth, I think you're making the right decision for the wrong reasons." At Bee's questioning look, she continued: "The right decision because yes, the disruption is real. The wrong reasons because you're accepting their narrative that you don't belong."

Something in Elise's tone—a genuine empathy beneath the professional exterior—touched Bee unexpectedly. She reached for the temporary name badge pinned to her dress, unfastening it with careful fingers.

"I'm not accepting their narrative," she said, placing the badge on the desk with precise movements. "I'm recognising that I can't fight it while standing on a sales floor. Not effectively." The small plastic rectangle with her name printed in sans-serif font looked incongruously ordinary against the desk's polished surface—a mundane object representing a complex surrender.

"I appreciate the opportunity," Bee added, rising from her chair with the straight-backed dignity that had carried her through the day. "But I think I need to step back from public-facing work for a while."

Elise stood as well, extending her hand across the desk. "If circumstances change, or if you're interested in behind-the-scenes roles—buying, merchandising, inventory management—please let me know. Your skills are evident, regardless of who you're dating."

The validation, small but sincere, eased something tight in Bee's chest. She shook Elise's hand, grateful for the simple professional courtesy that acknowledged her as something more than "Charlie Benton's girlfriend."

"Thank you," she said simply, turning toward the door.

The sales floor had emptied of customers, though staff members still moved through closing routines, their glances following Bee as she walked toward the exit. She kept her gaze forward, chin lifted, refusing to shrink beneath their curiosity. This was not the triumphant exit she'd made from Harrington's, hurling truth at Victoria like a weapon. It was quieter, sadder, but no less necessary—a recognition that sometimes retreating preserved more dignity than standing ground on a battlefield designed for your defeat.

The mall beyond Luxe Boutique bustled with early evening activity, shoppers moving between stores with bags dangling from their arms, teenagers clustered around the food court, cleaning staff beginning to polish floors in less trafficked areas. Bee kept her head down as she navigated the crowd, hyperaware of potential recognition. Her phone buzzed in her purse—a text from Charlie, the third since lunch:

Hope your shift is going well. Security upgrade proceeding on schedule. Missing you. Call when you're done?

The simple message, evidence of his concern and connection despite the chaos unfolding in his own life, brought a tightness to her throat. She paused near a fountain to type a quick response:

Shift over. Heading to car now. Will call when I get there.

She didn't mention her decision to withdraw from the

position. That conversation deserved more than a hasty text between mall corridors. It required the nuance of voice, the reassurance that this retreat didn't represent regret about their relationship—only a realistic assessment of its current impact on her professional options.

As Bee pushed through the mall's main doors into the parking lot beyond, afternoon sunlight struck her face with unexpected warmth. She inhaled deeply, the fresh air a welcome change from the recycled atmosphere inside. For a moment, she simply stood there, face tilted toward the sun, allowing herself to feel the relief of being outside, away from watchful eyes and whispered comments.

The moment shattered at the distinctive click of a camera shutter.

"Bee! Over here! How was your first day back at work?"

A man with a professional camera had emerged from between parked cars, his lens already raised and focused on her face. Bee turned sharply away, quickening her pace toward where her car waited in the far corner of the lot. The photographer followed, his footsteps audible on the asphalt behind her.

"Is it true you quit your last job because of Charlie? Has he asked you to move in permanently? Any comment on the Madison Vale situation?"

Madison. Again that name, wielded like a weapon by strangers who had no right to the intimate violation she and Charlie had experienced. Bee's keys dug into her palm as she clutched them tighter, the physical discomfort a welcome distraction from the panic rising in her chest. She reached her car and fumbled with the lock, hands shaking slightly as the photographer drew closer.

"Just one comment for the fans, Bee!"

The car door opened, and she slid inside, pulling it shut with more force than necessary. The sound of the automatic locks engaging sent a wave of relief through her body so intense it left her lightheaded. Through the window, she could see the photographer still taking pictures—of her sitting in her car, of her hands gripping the steering wheel, of her face as she struggled to maintain composure.

Bee didn't start the engine immediately. Instead, she leaned forward until her forehead rested against the steering wheel, eyes closed, breathing deliberately slow and deep. The parking lot, her car, this moment—everything had transformed in the wake of loving Charlie. Nothing remained simple or private or ordinary.

Was she strong enough for this? The question circled in her mind, persistent and unavoidable. Strong enough to withstand the constant scrutiny, the loss of anonymity, the transformation of her identity from individual to appendage? Strong enough to face more Victorias, more photographers, more whispered judgments about her worthiness to occupy space in Charlie's world?

The answer didn't come in a single clarifying moment of certainty. Instead, it assembled itself from smaller truths: that she loved Charlie with an intensity that surprised her. That she valued her independence with equal passion. That retreating from one battlefield didn't mean surrendering the war. That finding balance between these competing needs would require creativity and courage she wasn't sure she possessed—but was determined to find.

Bee straightened, wiping at her eyes with the back of her hand. The photographer had retreated to a respectful distance, though his camera remained pointed in her direction. She started the engine, its gentle vibration grounding her in the physical reality of this moment: she was here, she was whole, she was making choices rather than simply reacting to circumstances beyond her control.

The decision to withdraw from Luxe wasn't defeat—it

was strategic recalibration. The path forward wouldn't look like she'd originally imagined, but it would be hers to determine. Hers and Charlie's together, navigating the strange new territory their relationship had created.

As she backed out of the parking space, phone buzzing with another text from Charlie, Bee felt something solid and certain settle in her chest—not answers to all her questions, but the quiet determination to find them, one difficult step at a time.

Chapter Sixteen: Breaking Point

Bee entered Charlie's mansion like a storm gathering force, her footsteps echoing against marble floors that caught the last rays of afternoon sun and transformed them into cold, pristine light. The door closed behind her with more force than she'd intended, the sound reverberating through the cavernous entryway. She stood motionless for a moment, feeling the weight of the day's humiliation pressing against her skin, the careful composure she'd maintained throughout her drive home beginning to fracture along invisible fault lines.

She moved forward, heels striking against stone with rhythmic precision that belied the chaos churning inside her. The mansion spread before her—immaculate, vast, beautiful in its expensive perfection. Today, its grandeur felt less like luxury and more like isolation, each open space another reminder of the distance between her former life and this strange new reality she inhabited.

A subtle red light blinded from the corner where ceiling met wall—one of the new security cameras installed after Madison's intrusion. Its mechanical eye tracked her movement with silent vigilance, the same technology that had once represented safety now feeling uncomfortably like surveillance. Bee looked away, focusing instead on reaching the kitchen, where she could at least pretend normalcy existed.

Charlie appeared in the doorway of his study as she passed, his expression shifting instantly from concentration to concern. He wore the faded t-shirt and jeans that signalled a day spent working from home, his hair slightly rumpled from running his hands through it while reading scripts.

"Bee?" His voice carried that particular note of careful neutrality that meant he'd already sensed something was wrong. "You're home early."

She didn't answer immediately, continuing her trajectory toward the kitchen, her body language closed and tight as a fist. Charlie followed, maintaining a careful distance that respected her evident distress while making his presence available when she was ready.

In the kitchen, Bee dropped her purse onto the marble island with enough force to send her keys skittering across the polished surface. She paced the perimeter of the room, running her fingers through hair already dishevelled from the same nervous gesture repeated throughout the day. The refrigerator hummed quietly, its expensive minimalism a stark contrast to the emotional chaos she couldn't contain.

"What happened?" Charlie asked finally, positioning himself on the opposite side of the island, giving her space while making retreat impossible.

Bee's laugh emerged sharp and brittle. "Victoria Harrington happened." She yanked open a cabinet, removed a glass, closed it with unnecessary force. "She showed up at Luxe specifically to humiliate me in front of customers and staff."

Charlie's posture stiffened, the muscle in his jaw tightening visibly. "Victoria came to your new job? How did she even know—"

"How does anyone know anything about us?" Bee interrupted, gesturing sharply toward the windows where, miles away but perpetually present, photographers still gathered at the property gates. "It's all public knowledge now. Where I work, what I wear, who I talk to." Water splashed over the rim of her glass as she filled it with trembling hands. "My entire existence has become content for other people's consumption."

She described Victoria's calculated performance—the theatrical browsing, the deliberately carrying voice, the practised concern masking malicious intent. Each word Victoria had uttered remained acid-etched in Bee's memory: *I hope you've negotiated a good settlement package. Not that you could possibly hope to maintain the lifestyle he's temporarily afforded you. *

"She made sure everyone heard," Bee continued, setting the glass down without drinking. "All the customers who were already watching me like some exotic zoo exhibit got a front-row seat to my humiliation."

Charlie's hand curled into a fist on the counter, knuckles whitening. "I'll have Toby speak to her. There are way to apply pressure—"

"That's not the point," Bee cut him off, resuming her restless circuit of the kitchen. "Victoria was just the most direct attack. The entire day was a series of smaller wounds."

She described the whispering customers, the staff who knew her name before introductions, the surreptitious photos taken between clothing racks. "I wasn't hired for my skills or experience. I was hired as Charlie Benton's girlfriend—the curiosity, the temporary diversion, the retail girl he's slumming with."

The last phrase—a direct quote overheard from gossiping customers—landed between them like shattered glass. Charlie flinched visibly, pain flashing across his features before he could mask it.

"I quit," Bee said flatly, the words hanging in the climate-controlled air. "I thanked Elise for the opportunity and walked away."

"You quit?" Charlie's voice softened with evident concern. "Bee, I'm so sorry. I know how much you wanted—"

"What choice did I have?" She gestured around the immaculate kitchen with its restaurant-grade appliances and custom cabinetry. "I can't be effective at my job when customers come in to gawk rather than shop. I can't build a professional reputation when all anyone sees is who I'm sleeping with."

The security system emitted a soft electronic tone—another perimeter check completed, another verification that their fortress remained secure against physical intrusion. But walls and cameras couldn't protect against the psychological invasion already underway.

Bee moved to the window, resting her forehead against the cool glass. The reinforced panes—designed to resist both breakage and long-range photography—felt suddenly symbolic of their entire situation: transparency that offered no actual freedom, clear barriers that separated them from the world beyond.

"I used to have a life that made sense," she said, her voice dropping to just above a whisper. "Work I was good at. A future I was building on my own terms. Now I'm just..." she trailed off, unable to articulate the strange limbo she inhabited—neither fully part of Charlie's world nor connected to her own pervious existence.

Charlie approached carefully, his reflection appearing beside hers in the window glass. "This is temporary," he offered, though uncertainty threaded through his voice. "The interest will fade. People will move on to the next story."

Bee turned to face him, arms wrapped around herself as if for protection. "Will they? Or will I always be defined by my relationship to you?" The red eye of a security camera blinked from the ceiling corner, its mechanical vigilance a constant reminder of their altered reality. "I feel like I'm disappearing piece by piece, replaced by some two-dimensional character in a tabloid narrative."

Charlie reached for her hand, his fingers warm against her chilled skin. "You're still you." He said softly. "Still Bee Anderson, still the woman who called Victoria Harrington on her bullshit and walked away from Harrington's with her head held high."

The words should have comforted her. Instead, they highlighted the disconnect between who she had been and who she was becoming—a person who retreated from confrontation rather than facing it head-on, who slipped away quietly rather than standing her ground. Even her victory over Victoria felt hollow now, tainted by the knowledge that the woman had tracked her to her new workplace, determined to reestablish dominance.

"Am I?" Bee asked the question, emerging smaller than she'd intended. "Because I don't feel like her anymore."

The security system hummed its constant electronic vigilance, a sound she'd stopped consciously registering days ago but now seemed deafeningly loud in the silence that followed her admission. Outside, twilight settled over Los Angeles, transforming the mansion's windows from transparent barriers to mirrors reflecting their own isolation.

The living room glowed with carefully designed ambiance —recessed lighting softening the angles of expensive furniture, a gas fireplace casting dancing shadows across walls adorned with museum-quality art. Charlie adjusted the flames higher as evening settled outside, darkness gathering against windows that transformed from transparent to reflective. Bee curled into the corner of a sofa, a throw pillow clutched unconsciously to her chest like armour. The room was meant to be the heart of the home, a space designed for comfort rather than display, yet tonight it felt like another stage set where they performed versions of themselves neither quite recognised.

"You could start your own business," Charlie suggested, pacing the perimeter of the hand-knotted rug with the restless energy of someone desperate to solve a problem. He wanted more than anything to tell her she could take off as much time as was needed and didn't have to worry about money, but he knew that even with the practicality of the offer, it would go against every part of who she is. "A boutique consultancy. Or an online store focusing on sustainable fashion—you've talked about that before."

His voice carried the particular cadence of someone accustomed to fixing situations, to leveraging resources and connections until obstacles disappeared. In his world, problems were opportunities wrapped in temporary setbacks. Bee watched him move, his familiar. Features drawn with concern that was both touching and somehow infuriating in its simplicity.

"Or if you wanted to stay in retail management, I know the owner of Seraphine—the high-end place on Melrose. One call, and—"

"Charlie," Bee interrupted, her fingers digging into the velvet pillow until she felt the resistance of its stuffing. "This isn't about finding another job."

He stopped his pacing, turning toward her with focused attention. "Then what? What do you need? Whatever it is—"

"That's just it," she said, her voice tightening. "You can't fix this by throwing money or connections at it. This isn't a problem with a solution. It's..." She trailed off, struggling again to articulate the nameless dread that had been building inside her since the moment they'd found Madison in their bedroom, since the whispers had followed her through Luxe, since her identity had begun dissolving into an appendage of Charlie's celebrity.

Outside, beyond the manicured grounds and reinforced walls, the faint sounds of activity at the gate filtered through—car doors closing, voices calling questions no one would answer, the distant mechanical clicks of cameras documenting nothing of substance. The security system chimed softly from a panel near the door, another alert from the property's perimeter where strangers gathered to capture fragments of their lives.

"Tell me," Charlie said, settling onto the sofa beside her, though he left careful space between them. "Help me understand."

Bee stared into the fireplace, the controlled flames licking at artificial logs with perfect, predictable patterns. Even the fire in this house was designed rather than natural, managed rather than wild. Her hands trembled visibly now, fingers white-knuckled against the pillow's fabric.

"I don't even recognise myself anymore," she confessed, the words emerging in a voice that cracked under the weight of admission. The tears she'd been suppressing since her encounter with Victoria spilled over, tracking hot paths down her cheeks. "I used to be Bee Anderson—independent, sarcastic, my own person. Now I'm just Charlie Benton's ordinary girlfriend."

Her shoulders hunched inward as she spoke, body collapsing around the wound of her words as if trying to protect it. The pillow crushed against her chest no longer provided comfort, merely something to anchor herself against as she finally voiced the fear that had been growing within her since the photographers had first spotted them at the farmers market.

"I've spent years building my life exactly how I wanted it. Making my own decisions, facing my own consequences." Her voice dropped to just above a whisper. "And in a flash, it's all just disappeared, I'm defined entirely by my relationship to you."

Charlie reached for her, his hand extending across the distance between them. "Bee, that's not—"

She pulled away from his touch, curling tighter into herself. The rejection wasn't deliberate cruelty but self-preservation, a desperate attempt to maintain what boundaries remained. "The photographers followed me to the boutique today. They knew my name, knew about Madison. They were waiting when I left, like they had a right to me." Fresh tears spilled, her breath hitching. "And I realised—this is forever now. There's no going back to being anonymous, to being just me. I will always be Charlie Benton's girlfriend, or the girl Charlie slummed it with."

The fireplace crackled, a log shifting to send a shower of sparks against the protective glass. In the corner of the room, a security monitor displayed rotating camera feeds of the property's perimeter gates where photographers still gathered, walls designed to keep intruders out, a fortress that increasingly felt like confinement rather than protection.

"I know we haven't said this to each other, but I love you, I know it's fast and I don't expect you to say it back, but I love you more than anything." Bee continued, her voice stripped raw with honesty, each word extracted as if at physical cost. "But I don't know if I can handle this—the loss of privacy, the constant judgment, the feeling that I'm losing myself piece by piece."

She pressed her fingers against her lips, trying to contain the sob building in her chest. The metallic taste of fear coated her tongue, bitter and persistent. "Every day, another piece of me disappears. The part that could walk into a store without being recognised. The part that could define herself through her work. The part that had friends who saw her, not Charlie Benton's girlfriend."

Charlie remained still, his face a study in devastation held rigidly in check. The muscles in his jaw worked silently, his breathing carefully controlled. When he spoke, his voice emerged rough with emotion he couldn't fully contain.

"I never wanted this for you." The simple admission hung between them, weighted with guilt and helplessness. "I love you too, Bee, you are the most amazing person I have ever met, I wanted to share my life with you, not erase yours."

"I know," Bee acknowledged, wiping tears with the back of her hand, the gesture childlike in its vulnerability. "That's what makes this so impossible. You didn't do anything wrong. Neither did I. We just..." She struggled for words, hands lifting in a helpless gesture before falling back to the pillow. "We fell in love. And now I'm disappearing."

This morning, I looked in the mirror and didn't recognise myself," Bee admitted, the confession barely audible above the fireplace's gentle crackle. "Not physically—though God knows I've never spent so much time on my appearance before dating you." She attempted a smile that collapsed immediately. "But inside. The person looking back wasn't the Bee who would have told Victoria Harrington exactly where to shove her comments. She was someone who slipped away quietly, who retreated rather than stood her ground."

Charlie's hand closed into a fist against his thigh, the only visible sign of the emotion roiling beneath his composed exterior. "You're still that person, Bee. Strong. Independent. Fierce."

"Am I?" She looked up at him through tears, her face stripped of pretence, rawly vulnerable in a way that made his chest ache. "Because right now, I feel like a shadow. Like everything solid about me is being worn away by the constant pressure of living in your world."

She pressed her palms against her eyes, shoulders shaking with silent sobs. When she lowered her hands, her face was blotched with emotion, eyeliner smudged beneath lashes spiked with tears—all pretence of composure abandoned.

"I don't want to lose you," she whispered, the words emerging broken and desperate. "But I'm terrified of losing myself. And I don't know if I can have both—you and me, intact, together."

Outside, the distant mechanical clicks continued, documenting the exterior of a life they couldn't see or understand. Inside, the carefully controlled fire cast warm light that failed to touch the cold fear spreading through Bee's chest—the terror of erasure, of becoming nothing more than an accessory to someone else's narrative, of loving so completely that nothing of herself remained.

Charlie sat frozen on the couch, each of Bee's tear-soaked words striking him with physical force. The careful composure he maintained through public scrutiny, through invasive photographers, through Madison's violation of their home, it fractured completely in the face of Bee's pain. His body remained rigidly still, but inside, devastation spread like ice through his veins, a cold horror at what his love had inadvertently done to the woman he cherished above all else. His hands curled into helpless fists against his thighs, nails cutting half-moons into his palms as he struggled to find words that wouldn't sound hollow against the raw truth she'd laid bare.

His mind raced through possible solutions, each more desperate than the last. They could hire additional security, create a buffer between Bee and the world. He could speak to Toby about a more aggressive PR strategy, perhaps and an exclusive interview that humanised Bee beyond "Charlie's girlfriend." They could retreat to his property in Montana—remote, private, a temporary escape until the media frenzy subsided.

But each solution crumbled as quickly as it formed. More security meant more isolation. PR strategies meant more public exposure, not less. Montana was a retreat, not an answer—the photographers would simply wait for their return. There was no fixing a system designed to consume everything it touched, to transform real people into commodities for public consumption.

The security system emitted a soft electronic tone, followed by the disembodied voice of the head security officer through the intercom: "Mr. Benton, we have additional photographers gathering at the north gate. Appears to be related to a new online article about Ms. Anderson's employment situation. Do you want us to issue a statement?"

Something in Charlie snapped, a fault line finally giving way beneath too much pressure. He stood abruptly, crossing to the window with three sharp strides. His palm pressed against the cold glass as he stared out at the L.A lights spreading below their hillside perch—thousands of twinkling points marking lives untouched by the particular prison fame had constructed around them. Lives where people walked into stores without being recognised, where relationships developed without public documentation, where identity remained self-determined rather than externally imposed.

"What if I quit?" The words emerged barely audible, his breath fogging the glass where his lips nearly touched it.

Behind him, Bee's quiet sniffling paused. "What?"

Charlie turned from the window, his expression transformed by desperate resolve. "I could walk away from all of it —the movie, the fame, everything." His voice gained strength as the idea crystallised. "We could move somewhere quiet, start over where no one knows us. Maine. Vermont. Abroad, even."

"Charlie," Bee's voice held confused disbelief, her tear-streaked face lifting toward him. "What are you talking about?"

"Acting isn't the only thing I know how to do," he continued, words spilling out with increasing urgency. "I studied literature before drama. I could teach. Write. Do voice work without the public recognition." His hands gestured expansively, as if physically grasping at these alternate realities. "We could live normally. Just us, building something that belongs to both of us equally."

Bee's eyes widened as understanding dawned—he wasn't speaking hypothetically. The tears that had been flowing steadily slowed as shock replaced despair. "You can't be serious. Acting is your life. Your passion. You've worked for decades to build your career."

"It's a job," Charlie countered, though the slight tremor in his voice betrayed the oversimplification. "A job I love, yes. But still just a job." He moved back toward her, dropping to his knees before the sofa where she remained curled around her pain. "What good is success if it destroys the person I love most? What value does any of this hand—" he gestured around the expensively appointed room, "—if it means watching you disappear piece by piece?"

Bee stared at him, conflict written across her features in transparent succession—disbelief, temptation, fear, guilt. Her hands unclenched from the pillow she'd been clutching, reaching halfway toward him before stopping. "I can't let you do that," she whispered. "Not for me. You'd resent me eventually, even if you tried not to."

"It wouldn't be for you, it would be for me, I want you, all of you, as you are, I wouldn't resent you," Charlie insisted, catching her hands in his, holding them with gentle pressure that belied the desperation in his voice. "I've spent fifteen years in the spotlight. I know what it gives and what it takes. And nothing—" his voice cracked, raw emotion breaking through, "—nothing it gives is worth what it's taking from you, from us."

He could see the temptation flickering in her eyes—the seductive pull of his suggestion. A normal life. Anonymity. The simple freedom to exist without documentation or commentary. For a moment, he thought she might accept, might agree to this dramatic solution born of desperation and love.

Instead, she disentangled one hand from his and reached toward his face, fingers tracing the line of his jaw with a tenderness that contracted his throat. "You love acting," she said simply. "Not the fame or the money—the actual work. The inhabiting of other lives, the storytelling. I've seen your face when you talk about a role that matters to you. I can't be responsible for taking that away."

"I love you more," Charlie said, the words emerging with such naked honesty that they hung in the air between them, vibrating with truth that couldn't be denied or diminished. His hands tightened around hers, his body leaning closer as if physical proximity could bridge the gap between their separate pains. "Nothing—not my career, not the money, none of it—means anything if I lose you."

The firelight played across Bee's tear-stained face, illuminating the conflict still evident there—the war between wanting to accept his sacrifice and knowing what it would truly cost him. Her breathing had steadied somewhat, though occasional shudders still moved through her, aftershocks of emotion not yet fully processed.

"I don't want to lose you either," she admitted, her voice steadying. "But I don't want you to lose yourself trying to save me."

The parallelism of their fears—each terrified of the other's erasure—hung between them, a shared understanding that needed no articulation. Charlie rose from his knees, settling beside her on the sofa, close enough now that their thighs pressed together, the contact grounding them both.

"Then we figure this out together," he said, his hand finding hers again, fingers intertwining. "Not you adjusting to my world or me abandoning it, but something new that works for both of us."

Bee leaned toward him, her forehead coming to rest against his shoulder. The simple contact, her choosing to close the distance she'd maintained throughout their conversation, sent relief coursing through Charlie's body. Not resolution, not a solution, but connection. A willingness to continue facing the problem together rather than surrendering to it separately.

"I'm so tired of fighting." She whispered against his shirt, her body softening against his. "Tired of being strong, of constantly defending my right to exist in your world."

Charlie's arm curved around her shoulders, drawing her closer. "Then don't fight tonight," he murmured into her hair. "Just be here. With me."

She lifted her face toward his, eyes still shimmering with tears but holding something else now —a hunger that matched the desperate need rising in his own chest. Her lips parted slightly, an invitation he accepted without hesitation, his mouth finding hers with gentle pressure that rapidly trans-formed into something more urgent.

The kiss deepened, their bodies turning toward each other with a primal, instinctive hunger. Bee's hands slid up Charlie's chest, her touch both anchoring and igniting him. His fingers threaded through her hair, gripping her with a careful pressure that contrasted with the aggressive demand of his mouth on hers.

Their grief and fear morphed into a carnal need, bodies communicating what words couldn't. Bee moved suddenly, straddling Charlie's lap in a fluid motion that drew a groan from deep in his throat. Her hands framed his face, her kiss turning fierce and possessive. The tears on her cheeks mixed with their joined breath, salt and warmth and the unique taste that was all Bee.

Charlie's hands found her hips, fingers digging into her soft flesh through the fabric of her dress. Their usual tenderness gave way to something feral, desperate—each touch a claim of ownership. *You're mine. Right here, right now*.

Bee attacked his shirt buttons with an urgency that made her hands shake. Fabric tore beneath her grip, exposing skin that burned under her touch. Charlie matched her intensity, his hands sliding up her thighs, pushing her dress up to her waist. His fingers traced the edge of her lace thong, making her gasp and grind against his hardening cock.

"Fuck, Bee," Charlie growled, his voice low and hungry. "What you do to me."

She leaned in, nibbling his earlobe before whispering, "Exactly what you do to me."

His fingers slipped inside her thong, stroking her slickness, making her moan and buck against his hand. He circled her clit with a light touch, teasing her. She leaned into him, "I want you."

Charlie groaned at her words, two fingers plunging into her tightness. She moaned loudly as he curled his fingers inside of her, mouth still working magic on hers, catching every gasp and moan he finger fucked out of her. His thumb rubbed circles around her clit while he moved in and out of her dripping pussy faster, turning them into two creatures of primal lust and need. Outside, L.A continued its restless existence, oblivious to the heat generating inside Charlie's mansion.

Clothes were torn away as they fucked around in a mess of lips, teeth, groans, squeezes, slaps, moans, bites, licks, grunts, nibbles, sucks, whispering praises into each other's ears, pinching, pulling, squeezing. Her nails raked down Charlie's back as she wound up tighter than a drum with every stroke inside of her. The expensive sofa creaked beneath them as they moved together in feral abandonment...His teeth sank into the soft flesh of Bee's neck, eliciting a long moan from them both as she covered his fingers in more slickness. He knew what would happen next as he felt the change in Bee's body language. Bee came hard on Charlie's fingers, clutching him closer as he stroked every involuntary spasm from Bee's orgasm until she went limp in his arms. "You are fucking amazing." He whispered noticing the faraway look in Bee's eyes as she revelled in bliss...He kissed Bee's lips softly before withdrawing from inside of her, drawing another long moan from deep within Bee's soul...On his knees before her, watching her sit there trying to catch her breath, legs still shaking from orgasm, Charlie tugged at her thong until it snapped off her body, tossing it aside. He lifted her left foot, putting it over his shoulder, then did the same with the right foot. Now Charlie was staring at Bee's glistening juices running down onto the couch between them both. He grabbed her hips pulling himself forward burying his face between her legs, hungrily lapping up every drop he could find driving her wild again.

Bee's fingers tangled in Charlie's hair, guiding him deeper into her core, his tongue tracing a fiery path from her ass to her clit. He paused just long enough to suck each spot into his hot mouth, releasing it with a loud, wet, pop. Praises tumbled from Charlie's cheek, her eyes locked onto his with a loving, lustful gaze. Her fingers trailed down to his belt, unfastening it quickly, yanking it loose from its loops. She wrapped one end around her fist, a smirk playing on her lips.

A mischievous grin danced across Charlie's lips as he unfastened his pants, releasing his throbbing cock, standing at full attention, anticipating what was to come next. He stood up, pushing Bee's legs apart, handling them roughly, drawing a deep gasp from within her. Lifting her ass off the couch, he slid one arm under each of her knees, bringing them up until they rested on either side of his head. He guided his cock directly towards Bee's wet entrance, his eyes piercing into her soul. "Is this what you want?" he growled, his voice a low, hungry rumble.

"YEEEEEESSSSS!!!" She screamed, unable to control herself any longer. With one hard thrust, he buried himself to the hilt deep inside of her. They both froze, savouring the moment, lost within each other, letting everything else fall away until nothing else mattered except right here, right now.

Slowly, they began moving against each other, building momentum quickly, becoming feverish, lost within lustful passion. They were grinding, fucking, whimpering, moaning, grunting, fucking harder, faster, deeper, soaring higher, erupting, exploding, releasing tension in wave after wave, undone.

When they finally lay spent and tangled together, the firelight painting their skin with flickering gold, Charlie pressed his lips to Bee's temple, tasting the salt of dried tears and sweat of passion. Their situation remained unresolved, the larger questions still awaiting answers neither of them possessed. But in this moment, bodies connected, breaths synchronising, hearts beating against each other through the thin barrier of skin and bone, they had found if not a solution, then at least a reminder of what made the struggle worthwhile.

"We'll figure it out," Charlie whispered against her hair, the promise both commitment and prayer.

Bee's fingers traced patterns on his chest, her head nestled in the hollow of his shoulder. "I know we will," the statement carrying both determination and lingering uncertainty.

Outside, the world waited to resume its intrusion. But for now, in the warm circle of their embrace, they had reclaimed something essentially their own—a connection no camera could capture, no headline could diminish, no stranger could truly comprehend.

Chapter Seventeen: Crossroads

The cabin materialised through layers of mist, a structure of dark wood and stone tucked among towering pines like a secret the forest had agreed to keep. Charlie guided the car along the narrow dirt road, windshield wipers pushing aside the first hesitant drops of rain, while Bee gazed out her window in silence. They had barely spoken during the three-hour drive north, each lost in private landscapes of thought, the space between them in the luxury SUV expanding despite the physical proximity of their bodies.

Charlie parked beside the cabin and cut the engine. The sudden absence of mechanical sound amplified the natural symphony around them—wind sifting through pine needles, the distant murmur or moving water, the soft percussion of intensifying rain against the roof. For a moment neither moved. The interior light gradually faded, leaving them in a grey twilight that matched the clouded sky.

"We're here," Charlie said, the unnecessary observation filling the vacuum between them.

Bee nodded, unbuckling her seatbelt with careful deliberation. "It looks peaceful."

The word hung between them—peace being precisely what they'd fled Los Angeles to find, what had become increasingly elusive in the mansion with its cameras and security guards and the lingering ghost of Madison's intrusion. Charlie's hands remained on the steering wheel for a moment longer, as if reluctant to transition from the limbo of travel to the reality of arrival and whatever waited for them here.

"Let me get the bags," he said finally, his voice rough from hours of disuse.

The air outside carried the electric charge of the approaching storm and the clean scent of pine. Charlie moved to the trunk with efficient motions, extracting their weekend bags and the box of groceries they'd packed before leaving. Bee stood by the passenger door, face tilted upward to feel the cool touch of rain against her skin. Her hair curled slightly in the dampness, framing features drawn with exhaustion and something deeper, more persistent—a weariness that sleep alone wouldn't cure.

"Should be unlocked," Charlie nodded toward the cabin's wooden door, rain beading on his shoulders and darkening his hair to black. "Key's under the mat if not."

Bee climbed the three wooden steps to the small porch, floorboards creaking beneath her weight with comfortable familiarity, as if greeting her. The door opened at her touch— no electronic security system, no cameras tracking her movement, just a simple wooden structure sheltering them from the elements. She stepped inside, eyes adjusting to the dim interior.

The cabin revealed itself in gradual details: rough-hewn beams crossing the ceiling, a stone fireplace dominating one wall, furniture that prioritised comfort over design, windows framing views of encircling forest. It was beautiful in its simplicity—honest architecture that existed to serve purpose rather than impress observers. Bee moved through the space with tentative steps, her fingers trailing along the back of a worn leather sofa, her eyes cataloguing details with habitual thoroughness.

Charlie entered behind her, water glistening on his jacket, bags hanging from his shoulders. He deposited them near the door and moved immediately toward the fireplace, his body vibrating with the need for action, for tasks to complete. The nervous energy he'd contained during their drive now found release in deliberate movements—stacking logs, arranging kindling, striking matches with precise motions that revealed the slight tremor in his fingers.

"The bedroom's through there," he said without looking up from his work, gesturing toward a partially open door. "Bathroom's attached. Kitchen is basic but functional. Owner stocks the pantry but I brought extra."

His words tumbled out with uncharacteristic haste, fragments of practical information offered in place of the deeper conversation they had both fled to this isolated spot to have. The kindling caught, flames licking upward with tentative hunger. Charlie's face glowed in the nascent firelight, shadows gathering in the hollows beneath his cheekbones, accentuating the tension visible in his jaw.

Bee drifted toward the window, drawn to the glass that now reflected her image superimposed over the darkening forest beyond. Rain streaked the panes in crooked rivulets, distorting the view into impressionistic smears of green and grey. The sound of it—steady, rhythmic, insistent—filled the cabin with gentle white noise, creating a cocoon of isolation around their temporary refuge.

"Can you hear that?" she asked quietly, her first unprompted words since their arrival.

Charlie looked up from the growing fire, confusion momentarily replacing the careful neutrality he'd maintained throughout their journey. "The rain?"

"No. The creek." Bee pressed her ear closer to the glass. "It's louder now with the rainfall. The sound...it's alive somehow."

Charlie paused, his head tilting slightly as he listened. The distant rush of water moving over stone filtered through the cabin walls, a constant murmur beneath the sharper patter of rain. His expression softened fractionally. "The property line extends to the creek's edge. We can walk down tomorrow if the rain lets up."

The simple future plan—we can walk—carried weight beyond its mundane suggestion. A small bridge extended across the uncertain terrain between them, offering connection when so much threatened to push them apart. Bee nodded, a ghost of a smile touching her lips before fading.

Charlie returned to his self-assigned tasks, moving to the kitchen area where he began unpacking their groceries. Bee watched his reflection in the window—the careful precision of his movements, the focused attention he gave to arranging items in the refrigerator, the way his shoulders remained tense despite his attempt at casual domesticity. He was beautiful even in his distress, his profile sharp against the warm light of the cabin, his hands moving with the grace that made him so compelling on screen.

Bee turned from the window, allowing herself to properly absorb the cabin's interior. A bookshelf stood against one wall, filled with the weathered paperbacks left by the owner or previous guests—dog-eared mysteries, classics with broken spines, field guides to local flora and fauna. The furniture invited relaxation with its deep cushions and absence of pretension. Handmade quilts were folded over the backs of chairs, their patterns speaking of patient craftsmanship rather than designer labels.

A floorboard creaked beneath her foot as she moved toward the stone fireplace where the fire had caught properly now, flames dancing with hypnotic rhythm. The sound of the wood—that particular organic complaint of weight against age—triggered something in her chest, a loosening of the rigid control she'd maintained since their departure from L.A.

In the kitchen, Charlie closed a cabinet with careful restraint, the soft thud resonating through the open-plan space. He moved to the refrigerator, arranging items with unnecessary precision, his back to the room. Bee recognised the familiar pattern—his retreat into practical tasks when emotions threatened to overwhelm him, the way he created physical order to compensate for internal chaos.

She moved around the perimeter of the room, maintaining distance while studying the space that would contain their reckoning. Her fingertips brushed against the rough stone of the fireplace, feeling its solidity, its patient presence. The cabin smelled of pine and woodsmoke, of rain-dampened earth and the faint sweetness of cedar. It was a good place for truth-telling—honest materials bearing witness to honest words.

The rain intensified outside, drumming against the roof with increased urgency. Charlie finished in the kitchen and stood uncertainly, hands hanging at his sides as if he'd run out of tasks to occupy them. His eyes found Bee's across the room, a brief connection before both glanced away, afraid of what might be revealed in prolonged eye contact.

"Are you hungry?" he asked, voice carefully neutral. "I could make something."

Bee shook her head, arms wrapping around herself in unconscious self-protection. "Not yet."

The unspoken hung between them, heavy as the moisture in the air. Not yet for food. Not yet for the conversation they'd come here to have. Not yet for decisions that couldn't be unmade.

Charlie nodded, accepting her answer on multiple levels.

He moved to the sofa and sat, his body angled toward the fire rather than toward her, giving her space she hadn't explicitly requested but clearly needed. The firelight played across his features, highlighting the shadows beneath his eyes, evidence of nights spent staring at security monitors rather than sleeping.

Bee remained by the window, watching rain transform the forest into liquid movement, each drop catching the last light of day before darkness claimed the woods completely. Inside, the fire provided the only significant illumination, creating a circle of amber warmth that didn't quite reach where she stood. The distance between them—physical, emotional, philosophical—felt simultaneously vast and paper-thin, a contradiction that defined the strange limbo their relationship had entered.

Thunder rumbled in the distance, a bass note beneath the percussion of rainfall. Bee turned from the window finally, moving to sit in an armchair positioned near enough to the fire for warmth but separate from the sofa where Charlie waited. The choreography of their movements—careful, considered, conscious of the other's space—spoke volumes about the fragile equilibrium they maintained.

The rain continued its relentless rhythm, surrounding the cabin with a curtain of water that isolated them more completely than any security system ever could. Here, miles from paparazzi lenses and Madison's obsession, they had found temporary sanctuary. But as they sat in firelit silence, stealing glances when the other wasn't looking, both understood that the hardest journey still lay before them—the path through their fears toward whatever future waited on the other side of this trip away.

Hunger eventually pulled them from their respective corners—a basic human need that transcended emotional complexity. Charlie rose first, stretching limbs stiff from too long held in careful stillness. The fire had settled into steady flames, casting the cabin in amber light that softened the edges of their silence. "We should eat something," he said, the practical suggestion carrying no expectation, just simple necessity.

Bee nodded, uncurling from the armchair where she'd been watching raindrops race down the windowpane. "I'll help," she offered, the first voluntary movement toward shared space since their arrival.

They migrated to the kitchen area—a modest arrangement of pine cabinets and butcher block counters that occupied one corner of the cabin's open living space. Unlike the sleek, chef-grade kitchen in Charlie's mansion, this one spoke of practicality and simplicity: a four-burner gas stove with knobs worn smooth from use, open shelving displaying mismatched plates and mugs, a small refrigerator that hummed with gentle persistence. The space required proximity, their bodies negotiating the confined area with careful awareness.

Charlie pulled ingredients from the refrigerator—fresh tomatoes, a bulb of garlic, a wedge of parmesan cheese still wrapped in paper from the specialty market they'd stopped at during their drive. His hands moved with practised confidence, the kitchen being one domain where celebrity offered no advantage over simple experience.

"Pasta?" he suggested, already reaching for a pot. "Something simple?"

Bee nodded, retrieving a cutting board from beneath the counter, her movements mirroring his in unconscious synchronicity. They had cooked together countless times in Charlie's kitchen, developing the wordless choreography of people who had learned each other's patterns. Here, in this unfamiliar space, that dance continued despite the emotional distance between them—muscle memory outlasting conscious hesitation.

The sound of Bee's knife against the cutting board created

a steady rhythm—chop, chop, pause, gather, repeat—as she transformed tomatoes into uneven chunks that glistened under the kitchen's warm light. Beside her, Charlie crushed garlic with the flat of his blade, the sharp aroma releasing into the air between them. Their elbows occasionally brushed as they worked side by side, each contact sending a current of awareness through both bodies, neither acknowledging the brief connections.

Steam rose from the pot as Charlie lowered pasta into boiling water, his face momentarily obscured in the translucent cloud. Bee added olive oil to a pan, the liquid shimmering as it heated, then sliding garlic into the hot surface. The sizzle and pop created a barrier of sound that filled the space where conversation might have been, allowing them to work in a silence that felt purposeful rather than strained.

"Red or white?" Charlie asked, reaching for wine glasses that hung from a small rack above the sink.

"Red," Bee replied, stirring the garlic to prevent burning. "It's that kind of night."

The small exchange—normal, domestic—loosened something in both their postures. Charlie's shoulders dropped slightly from their tense position as he uncorked a bottle they'd brought from his collection. The rich scent of the wine mingled with garlic and tomato, creating an atmosphere of ordinary comfort that stood in stark contrast to the extraordinary circumstances that had brought them here.

Their hands met briefly as Charlie passed Bee a glass, fingers touching around the stem. Neither pulled away immediately, the contact lingering a heartbeat longer than necessary. When they separated, something had shifted subtly in the air between them—not resolution yet, but perhaps the possibility of it, a crack in the careful distance they'd maintained since leaving Los Angeles.

The sauce came together as the pasta cooked—tomatoes

breaking down in the pan, releasing their juice to mingle with the olive oil and garlic. Charlie added a splash of wine from his glass, the alcohol hitting the hot surface with a hiss before incorporating into the thickening liquid. Bee grated cheese in fine strands that clung to her fingers, the sharp smell of parmesan adding another layer to the aromatic cloud surrounding them.

When they finally carried their plates to the small wooden table positioned near the fireplace, the domestic ritual had worked a temporary magic. The careful formality that had characterised their arrival had softened slightly, replaced by the familiar comfort of a shared meal. The table's surface bore the marks of previous diners—rings from wet glasses, small nicks from knives, the patina of use and time that spoke of humans gathering, eating, continuing despite whatever troubles pressed upon them.

Charlie poured more wine into their glasses, the ruby liquid catching firelight as it swirled. His fingers tapped an anxious rhythm against the stemware—a tell he'd never managed to eliminate despite years of media training. Bee tucked a strand of hair behind her ear, the repetitive gesture betraying her own unease beneath the calm exterior she presented.

"This is good," she said after her first bite, the simple compliment opening a path for conversation.

"Your sauce," Charlie replied, twirling pasta around his fork with careful precision. "I just handled the pasta."

"Teamwork," Bee said, the word carrying weight beyond its immediate application.

A comfortable silence settled as they ate, broken only by the soft click of cutlery against ceramic and the persistent percussion of rain against the cabin's roof. Through the window, darkness had claimed the forest completely, trans-forming the glass into a mirror that reflected their firelit figures seated across from each other, two people negotiating the geography of shared space and separate pain.

"My brother used to bring me here," Charlie said eventually, his voice pitched low beneath the rain's steady drumbeat. "After I first started getting recognised everywhere. Said I needed somewhere to remember what trees sounded like."

Bee looked up from her plate, catching the nostalgic softness that had transformed his features. "It's his place?"

"Friend of his, technically. John arranges for me to use it when..." Charlie trailed off, fork suspended above his plate.

"When you need to escape," Bee finished for him, understanding filling the gaps in his explanation.

Charlie nodded, resuming his meal with deliberate focus. "I've never brought anyone else here."

The admission hung between them, simple yet profound. This place represented Charlie's final retreat, his last bastion of privacy in a life increasingly devoid of it—and he had brought her into this sanctuary, had shared it without reservation.

"Thank you," Bee said softly, the words carrying recognition of the gift he'd offered. "For bringing me."

Their eyes met across the table, a moment of connection that transcended the careful dance they'd been performing since their arrival. In that look passed acknowledgment of what lay beneath their current struggle—the love that had survived Madison's intrusion, Victoria's cruelty, the relentless pressure of public scrutiny.

But as the moment extended, uncertainty crept back in. Charlie looked away first, his fingers resuming their nervous tapping against his wine glass. Bee returned to her meal, the food now tasteless despite its objective quality. The brief connection had illuminated what they stood to lose, making the potential cost of failure suddenly, painfully tangible.

The meal concluded in renewed silence, plates gradually emptying, wine glasses draining. Outside, the rain intensified, drumming against the roof with growing insistence. Inside, the fire crackled in counterpoint, occasional pops and hisses punctuating the heavy quiet that had descended once more.

Charlie gathered their empty plates, carrying them to the small sink where he began rinsing them with mechanical movements. Bee remained at the table, fingers wrapped around her wine glass, watching his back as he performed this ordinary task with extraordinary care, as if the proper cleaning of dishes might somehow restore order to their fractured world.

When he returned to the table, the plates cleaned and set to dry on a rack beside the sink, Charlie didn't immediately sit. Instead, he stood with his hands pressed against the back of his chair, knuckles white with pressure, his face etched with the effort of finding words adequate to the moment.

"I don't know how to fix this," he said finally, the admission emerging raw and unfiltered, stripped of the careful articulation that characterised his public speech.

Bee looked up at him, her face softened by firelight yet sharpened by the truth of their situation. Her eyes held his without flinching, her response equally unvarnished. "I'm not sure it can be fixed."

The simple exchange—honest in its uncertainty, devoid of false reassurance—hung in the air between them, neither comforting nor destructive. Just truth, unadorned and necessary, the first step toward whatever waited on the other side of this night.

Charlie nodded once, accepting her words without argument. His hands released their grip on the chair, the white-knuckled tension easing from his fingers. "Then we figure out how to live with it. Together."

He extended his hand across the table, an invitation rather than a demand. After a moment's hesitation, Bee placed her palm against his, their fingers intertwining with familiar ease despite the complicated tangle of emotions surrounding the simple contact.

Outside, the storm continued its assault, rain lashing against windows and roof with redoubled force. Inside, in the warm circle of firelight, Charlie and Bee held on to each other across a wooden table marked by time and use—two people finding temporary anchorage in the midst of a storm they had yet to navigate.

The fire needed tending. Charlie rose from the table first, drawn to the practical task that offered momentary purpose. Bee followed after a pause, carrying their wine glasses, the last of the red liquid catching firelight as she moved. The storm had settled into a steady downpour, rain drumming against the cabin roof with hypnotic persistence. Inside, the fire's warmth created a pocket of golden heat that drew them both toward its centre like moths to a welcoming flame.

Charlie knelt before the hearth, arranging another log with careful precision. His silhouette—outlined in amber light, shoulders slightly hunched—struck Bee as unexpectedly vulnerable. This man who commanded multimillion-dollar film sets, whose face launched global marketing campaigns, whose name appeared in lights tall as buildings, now reduced to his essential humanity: hands that could shake, a heart that could break, a soul that could be wounded.

Bee settled onto the worn rug facing the fireplace, legs curled beneath her, wine glass cradled in her palms. The heat from the flames warmed her face while her back remained cool, creating a physical metaphor for their situation—one side bathed in warmth, the other exposed to chill uncertainty.

The log Charlie had added caught sparks spiralling upward before disappearing into the chimney's darkness. He remained crouched before the fire, gaze fixed on the dancing flames, the light transforming his familiar features into a study of gold and shadow.

"Before you," he began, voice barely audible above the fire's gentle crackle, "my life was hollow." His fingers gripped the iron poker, knuckles whitening with pressure. "I didn't realise to what extent until I met you."

Bee didn't respond, recognising the fragility of this moment—his willingness to speak without the careful filters he'd developed over years of public scrutiny. Charlie rarely spoke about the emotional cost of his fame, maintaining a cheerful gratitude in interviews, expressing nothing but appreciation for his extraordinary life. The raw admission represented a departure from his practised narrative, a trust that both honoured and terrified her.

"The mansion echoes," he continued, still watching the fire rather than meeting her eyes. "Did you notice that? All that space, all those perfect rooms, and sound just...dissipates." His hand moved from the poker to the stone edge of the hearth, fingers tracing rough texture with absent attention. "Before you moved in, I'd sometimes stand in the entryway and say something out loud, just to hear how quickly the sound disappeared."

His voice caught slightly on the final word, a nearly imperceptible hitch that revealed the emotion underlying his measured delivery. "Everyone wants something—access, opportunities, association. Even the people I consider friends have agendas sometimes." A bark of laughter escaped him, sharp and self-deprecating. "God, that sounds paranoid, doesn't it?"

"It sounds lonely," Bee said softly

Charlie nodded, his profile etched against the firelight. "It is. Was." His hands moved to the fire tools again, adjusting logs that needed no adjustment, the restless motion betraying his discomfort with stillness, with vulnerability. "Then you texted the wrong number, and suddenly there was someone who didn't know who I was. Who called me on my bullshit. Who saw me—actually saw me—instead of the idea of me."

He finally turned toward her, his expression open in a way that made her chest ache. "Do you know how rare that is? To be truly seen?"

The question hung between them, rhetorical yet demanding answer. Bee's fingers tightened around her wine glass, the coolness of the glass grounding her against the tide of emotion rising in her throat.

"I think I do," she said carefully. "It's why this has been so hard—losing that sense of being seen for myself. Becoming an accessory to someone else's story."

Charlie's face contracted with pain, his eyes dropping back to the fire. "I never wanted that for you."

"I know." Bee set her glass aside, wrapping her arms around her knees, pulling her sweater tighter around her body as if against physical cold rather than emotional exposure. "That's what makes this so impossible. No one did anything wrong. We just...exist in different worlds."

Her fingers moved to the worn texture of the wooden floor, tracing random patterns across the grain. "I've always defined myself by my independence," she admitted, the words emerging rough-edged with suppressed emotion. "Maybe too much. After my dad left when I was twelve, I watched my mum struggle to redefine herself as something other than someone's wife. She'd lost herself so completely in his identity that when he was gone, she didn't know who she was anymore."

Her shoulders hunched inward, physical protection against emotional vulnerability. "I promised myself I'd never do that—never build my identity around someone else. And now..."

"Now you're being defined by your relationship to me,"

Charlie finished, understanding darkening his features. "By strangers who know nothing about you except that you're with me."

Bee nodded, her throat too tight for words. The fire popped suddenly, sending a shower of sparks against the protective screen. Outside, thunder rolled across the sky, a low rumble that vibrated through the cabin's wooden bones.

"I'm terrified," she confessed, the admission barely audible above the storm's symphony. "Not of the paparazzi or the loss of privacy—though those things are hard enough. I'm terrified of waking up one days and not recognising myself. Of becoming a shadow of the person I was, existing only in relation to your light." Her eyes lifted to his, raw with honesty. "And I'm equally terrified of losing you because I can't adapt to your world."

Charlie moved from his position by the fire to sit beside her on the floor, close enough for conversation but maintaining a small distance that acknowledged her need for space. His hands trembled visibly as he rested them on his knees, no longer attempting to hide his vulnerability.

"When I was twenty-three," he said, gaze fixed on the middle distance, "I got my first major role. Suddenly people knew my name, wanted my autograph, analysed my every word and movement. I remember standing in a bathroom at some industry party, staring in the mirror, and thinking, who am I supposed to be now?" His voice quieted further, forcing Bee to lean slightly closer to hear him over the rain. "Sometimes I'm still asking that question."

The admission—this successful, seemingly confident man confessing to his own identity crisis—created a bridge between their separate fears. Bee's hand moved across the small space between them, fingers hesitantly covering his. The simple contact carried more meaning than any grand gesture could have, an acknowledgment of shared understanding despite their different perspectives.

"I'm scared I'll drown in your world," she whispered. "And I am scared you'll resent me for not swimming well enough."

Charlie turned his hand beneath hers, their palms pressing together, fingers intertwining with practised familiarity. "I'm scared I'll lose you to the undertow my life creates," he admitted. "That one day you'll decide the price of loving me is too high." His thumb traced circles against her skin, the gentle motion at odds with the pain evident in his expression. "And I'd understand. I would."

The fire crackled softly, wooden bones surrendering to transformation. Rain continued its steady percussion against the roof, creating a symphony of natural sounds around their quiet confessions. In this simple cabin, miles from the complications that had driven them here, truth emerged unvarnished and essential—not solutions, but acknowledgments. Not answers, but honest questions.

"I don't want anyone but you," Charlie said, the words emerging with quiet certainty. "I've had relationships built on mutual convenience, on shared status, on compatible career trajectories. None of them touched what we have. I honestly don't think I had been in love before now." His fingers tightened around hers. "But I won't watch you disappear because of me. I can't."

Bee leaned her head against his shoulder, the physical connection bridging emotional distance. "I don't want anyone but you either," she whispered against the soft fabric of his shirt. "I just need to find a way to keep myself while loving you."

They sat in silence as the fire gradually died down, embers glowing beneath partially consumed logs. The storm outside softened from driving rain to gentle patter, the change in rhythm subtle but noticeable in the quiet room. When Charlie finally rose to check the fire one last time, his movements carried the weight of emotional exhaustion.

"We should try to sleep," he suggested, adding a final log to sustain the fire through the night. "Things might seem clearer in the morning."

Bee nodded, gathering their wine glasses while he turned down the lamps, the cabin gradually transforming from golden warmth to cool shadow. In the bedroom, a queen-sized bed waited, its handmade quilt turned down invitingly. They move around each other with careful awareness, preparing for sleep with the practiced motions of a couple accustomed to sharing space. Teeth were brushed, faces washed, clothes shed down to underwear—all in a silence that felt less strained than it had hours before, though still laden with unresolved questions.

When they finally lay side by side in darkness, the only light a faint glow from embers visible through the bedroom doorway, Bee felt Charlie's hand seeking hers beneath the covers. Their fingers intertwined, a physical connection maintained despite the emotional complexities still spiralling between them.

"We'll figure this out," he murmured, the words holding equal parts determination and uncertainty.

Bee squeezed his hand in response, unable to promise but unwilling to surrender. Above them rain continued its gentle pattern against the roof, a natural lullaby that surrounded their temporary sanctuary. Neither slept immediately, both lying awake in the darkness, conscious of the warmth where their bodies touched, the sound of each other's breathing, the enormity of what they stood to lose and the uncertain path toward preserving what mattered most.

Bee rolled toward Charlie, resting her head on his chest, one hand placed gently above his heart. Charlie held her close, as if she might slip away if he didn't, he leaned down and pressed his lips to her forehead. "I love you so much," he whispered, tenderly tucking a loose strand of hair behind her ear. Bee raised her head to meet his gaze. "I love you too," she smiled, pushing herself up slightly to brush her lips against his. The kiss was soft, tender, a testament to the depth of their feelings. Charlie cupped her face, deepening the kiss, and Bee ran her fingers along his chest, welcoming the growing intimacy.

"Bee," Charlie whispered against her lips, a soft plea. "I need you," she whispered back. Charlie moved closer, his hand tracing down her body, exploring her naked breasts, pausing at the waistband of her underwear. "These must be uncomfortable to sleep in," he murmured, a hint of amusement in his voice. Bee hooked her fingers in his boxers, "Let me help you get comfortable too," she murmured against his lips.

With their clothes discarded and their bodies pressed together, their desire was clear. Bee climbed on top of Charlie, straddling his lap. She positioned him at her entrance and, in a slow, exquisite movement, lowered herself onto him. They moaned in unison, a shared expression of pleasure. Bee stilled for a moment, then began to rock gently, Charlie's hands exploring her body, massaging her breasts, and circling her nipples with his thumbs. This was more than physical; it was an emotional connection, a true act of making love.

Bee supported herself with her hands on Charlie's chest, his hands gripping her hips as she rode him, grinding against him. He found the bundle of nerves between her legs, circling slowly, almost painfully so. Bee threw her head back, sensation overwhelming her as she felt the muscles deep within her begin to clench. As she found her release, Charlie joined her, his body tensing as they cried out in pleasure together.

Bee collapsed onto Charlie's chest, both of them breathing heavily, silently acknowledging the profound change that had just occurred. Bee moved to his side, remaining snuggled into his chest, Charlie's arms wrapped around her. They had no need for words; their bodies had said it all. Slowly, they drifted off to sleep together.

Outside, the forest stood as a silent witness, ancient trees weathering yet another storm, offering a mute testimony to survival. Inside, two people who had found unexpected love in a world that sought to commodify even the most genuine emotions lay together in the darkness, facing truths that couldn't be resolved in a single night, but must be lived through, one breath, one heartbeat, one shared moment at a time.

Chapter Eighteen: Charlie's Choice

Dawn crept through the windows of Charlie's home office, casting long shadows across the hardwood floor. He sat motionless at his desk, phone clutched in one hand, the other pressed against his temple where a headache had taken up residence hours ago. Sleep had proven elusive these past two nights, his mind churning through the same circular thoughts since his raw, honest conversation with Bee. The decision had crystallised somewhere in those sleepless hours—clear, terrifying, and somehow inevitable.

Charlie glanced at his reflection in the darkened computer screen—stubbled jaw, hair standing at odd angles, eyes rimmed with exhaustion. Two nights ago, sitting with Bee in the cabin, words had spilled from him in an unplanned confession: how hollow success had become, how suffocating the constant scrutiny felt, how desperately he wanted something more authentic than what his career currently offered. She had listened without interruption, her fingers intertwined with his, and when he finally fell silent, she'd asked one simple question that had haunted him since: "What would make you truly happy, Charlie?"

The question had unravelled something inside him. Now, as morning light strengthened across the room, Charlie knew the answer with unexpected clarity.

He stared at the phone in his hand, Toby's name displayed on the screen, his thumb hovering over the call button. The clock on his desk read 6:18 AM—early, but Toby would be awake. His agent operated on a perpetual state of industry alertness, as iff the possibility of a missed call might translate directly to missed opportunity.

Charlie pressed the button before he could reconsider, bringing the phone to his ear. Three rings, then the click of connection.

"Charlie." Toby's voice emerged crisp and alert, betraying no hint that the call had come at dawn. Papers rustled in the background—already at his desk, then. "Just reviewing the scripted questions for your Morgan Walsh interview. The metrics are excellent. We've got three new script inquiries since yesterday, and Elena Vasquez's people are pushing for a meeting next—"

"Toby," Charlie interrupted, his voice rough from lack of sleep. "I need to tell you something."

A brief pause. "What's wrong? Is it the Madison situation again? I can have security—"

"I'm thinking about taking a break from acting." The words emerged with surprising steadiness. "Indefinite. Starting now."

The silence that followed stretched so long that Charlie checked his screen to ensure the call hadn't dropped. Finally, Toby's voice returned, stripped of its efficient polish.

"What exactly do you mean by indefinite?"

Charlie leaned back in his chair, eyes fixing on the ceiling. "I mean I'm stepping away. No new projects. No development deals. No press commitments beyond what's absolutely required for current contractual obligations."

"Because of what happened with Madison?" Toby's tone sharpened with concern. "Charlie, that's exactly why we upgraded security. We can add more measure if you're feeling unsafe—"

"It's not about Madison," Charlie said, though the invasion had certainly contributed to his current state of mind. "This is about what I need. What I want my life to be."

Toby's breathing changed, quickening slightly—the sound of a man rapidly calculating implications. "The Vasquez project is practically greenlit. The Invisible Line adaptation is gaining serious momentum. Your interview is to remind everyone why you're valuable. This timing is..." He hesitated, searching for diplomatic phrasing. "Puzzling."

"I understand the professional implications," Charlie said, his free hand curling into a loose fit on the desk. "I'm not asking for your permission, Toby. I'm telling you what's happening."

Another stretch of silence, heavier than the first. When Toby spoke again, his voice had softened from business efficiency to something more personal. "Is this about Bee?"

Charlie closed his eyes, considering the complexity of the question. "It's about me. About the life I want versus the one I have. Bee is part of that, yes, but this isn't some ultimatum she's given me." He exhaled slowly. "It's a choice I'm making, she doesn't actually know the decision I came to yet."

"You've worked fifteen years to build this career," Toby said, his tone careful but pointed. "Fifteen years of sacrifices, strategic choices, relationships managed for optimal career trajectory. And now you're willing to risk it all for—"

"For what?" Charlie challenged, a flicker of irritation breaking through his exhaustion. "For happiness? For something real? Yes, absolutely."

Papers shuffled again on Toby's end of the call—the sound of a man falling back on routine when confronted with the unexpected. "Stepping away doesn't have to mean burning bridges," he said finally, his voice taking on the measured tone of someone beginning to negotiate. "We could frame it as a sabbatical. Creative recharging. Six months, maybe a year."

Charlie recognised the offer for what it was—Toby beginning to shift from resistance to management. "Maybe," he conceded. "But I'm not putting an arbitrary timeline on this. When and if I come back, it will be on different terms."

"Terms which would be...?"

"Mine," Charlie said simply. "Projects I believe in. Limited press. Privacy as a non-negotiable condition."

Toby's sigh carried through the phone, resignation mingling with reluctant respect. "This is going to create waves, Charlie. Big ones. The industry doesn't respond well to actors who step away at their peak."

"I know."

"Your leverage will decrease with every month you're absent."

"I know that too."

Another pause, shorter this time. "Are you absolutely certain about this?"

Charlie's gaze drifted to the wall opposite his desk, where framed posters from his most successful films hung in carefully arranged chronology. His face stared back at him in various guises—the action hero, the romantic lead, the tortured villain. Personas he'd inhabited with professional skill but increasingly felt disconnected from the man he wanted to be.

"Yes," he said. "I am."

"Then I'll handle it," Toby replied, his voice settling into the determined tone that had navigated countless professional challenges over their years together. "But I need you to understand the potential consequences. Projects will vanish. Opportunities will go to other actors. The industry has a short memory for those who step away."

"I understand," Charlie said. "But wait on taking any action until after I talk to Bee. I don't want her finding out through industry channels or the press. I'll call you when I'm ready for you to move forward."

"Of course," Toby agreed, his tone softening further. "For what it's worth, Charlie, I hope this gives you what you're looking for."

After ending the call, Charlie set the phone down on his desk with deliberate care. He pushed himself to his feet, moving to stand before the wall of framed posters that chronicled his rise through Hollywood. His fingers traced the edge of the earliest frame—his first leading role at twenty-six, eyes bright with ambition and possibility.

He ran his hands through his dishevelled hair, the physical sensation grounding him in the reality of what he'd just set in motion. The feeling that washed over him was complex— terror at stepping away from the identity that had defined him for fifteen years, but beneath it, something else. Relief. Liberation. The strange lightness of setting down a weight carried for so long it had become part of him.

Now he just needed to tell Bee.

The morning sun had climbed higher by the time Charlie found Bee on the terrace, its warmth at odds with the blanket she'd wrapped tightly around her shoulders. She sat in one of the Adirondack chairs, knees pulled to her chest, gaze fixed on the ocean spreading endlessly before them. Something in her posture—the slight curve of her spine, the way her body seemed to fold inward—made her appear unexpectedly small against the vast horizon, as if the expansive view had somehow diminished her rather than the reverse.

Charlie paused in the doorway, watching her profile

against the backdrop of blue. The wind lifted strands of her dark hair, carrying them across her face before she absently tucked them behind her ear. The gesture was achingly familiar, yet something about this moment felt precariously balanced, as if he stood at the edge of a before and after in their lives.

He crossed the flagstone terrace with deliberate steps, making enough noise that she would hear his approach without being startled. Bee turned slightly as he neared, offering a smile that didn't quite reach her eyes.

"Hey," she said simply, her voice nearly lost in the constant whisper of waves against the cliffs below.

"Hey," he echoed, lowering himself into the chair beside hers. Their shoulders almost touched, separated by mere inches that somehow felt like miles. "You're wearing a blanket. Are you cold?"

She shrugged, fingers tightening on the fabric's edge. "Not really. It just felt... I don't know. Comforting, I guess."

Charlie nodded, understanding more than he could articulate. The weight of his decision pressed against his chest, words crowding his throat without finding proper formation. He cleared his throat once, then again, the sound harsh against the rhythmic backdrop of ocean waves.

"Beautiful morning," he offered finally, immediately cringing at the banality.

"Charlie." Bee turned to face him fully now, her eyes searching his with the directness he'd always admired, even when it made him uncomfortable. "What's going on? You look like you haven't slept in days."

His hand moved to his watch, fingers automatically adjusting the band that needed no adjustment. The familiar nervous habit betrayed him, as did the shadows beneath his eyes.

"I haven't. Not really." He exhaled slowly, gaze dropping to his hands. "I've been thinking about our conversation. From the other night."

"About feeling trapped?" Bee supplied, her perception cutting through his hesitation. "About the walls closing in?"

Charlie nodded, grateful for her ability to navigate directly to the heart of things. "Yes. And about what would make me happy. What would make us happy."

He shifted in his chair, angling his body toward hers though his eyes remained fixed on his hands. His thumb traced the edge of his watch, circling its face with restless energy.

"I called Toby this morning," he said, voice dropping lower, as if sharing a secret with the wind and waves as much as with her. "I told him I'm taking a break from acting. Indefinite. Starting now."

Bee's sharp intake of breath was audible even above the ocean's constant murmur. Charlie forced himself to meet her eyes, finding them wide with surprise, questions forming but not yet voiced.

"I know it's sudden," he continued, words coming faster now that he'd begun. "Or maybe it's not sudden at all. Maybe it's been building for years, and I just couldn't admit it until recently. Until you."

His hand moved from his watch to his hair, fingers raking through the strands with nervous energy. "The Madison thing, the constant invasion of privacy, the scrutiny—they're all symptoms, not the disease. The real problem is that somewhere along the way, I lost myself in this career. I became what everyone expected rather than who I wanted to be."

Bee remained silent, her eyes never leaving his face, absorbing each word with the intensity that made conversation with her so different from the superficial exchanges that filled his professional life.

"Before you," Charlie said, his voice breaking slightly on the words, "I had everything and nothing at the same time.

The house, the career, the acclaim—all of it hollow because none of it was real connection. None of it was genuine." He leaned forward, emotion making his movements more emphatic. "I won't go back to that emptiness. I can't."

His gaze fell to the blanket wrapped around her shoulders, the physical barrier that seemed to mirror something internal. "I know this affects you too. That's why I wanted to tell you immediately, before Toby takes any action. This isn't just my life anymore; it's ours. Or at least, I hope it is."

Charlie finally reached across the space between them, his hand finding the edge of the blanket, fingers brushing against the fabric without quite touching her. "I promise to do whatever it takes to create a life where we can both be happy. Where neither of us has to shrink ourselves to fit into the other's world."

Bee's hands emerged from beneath the blanket, trembling slightly as they came to rest in her lap. Her eyes had taken on a liquid quality, sunlight catching on unshed tears that made the blue more vivid.

"Whatever it takes?" she repeated, her voice steady despite the emotion visible in her expression. "Charlie, that's your entire career. Fifteen years of work. Your identity."

"It's a job," he corrected gently. "A job I've loved, yes. A job I might return to someday, but only on different terms. Only if it can coexist with what matters more." He reached for her hands, covering them with his own, feeling the slight tremor that ran through them. "You've shown me what real life can be, Bee. Not the performance of living that I've been doing for years, but actual connection. Actual joy."

Charlie's voice broke on the last word, the emotion he'd been containing throughout his early morning call with Toby finally finding release. "I don't know exactly what comes next. I don't have a five-year plan or a strategy. I just know that whatever it is, I want to face it with you."

His grip on her hands tightened, his eyes searching hers with naked vulnerability. "Will you stay with me through whatever comes next? Even if it's messy and uncertain and completely unscripted?"

Tears spilled onto Bee's cheeks now, leaving silvery trails in the morning light. For one terrible moment, Charlie thought they were tears of sadness or regret. Then her lips curved into a smile that transformed her entire face, brightness breaking through like sun after storm.

"Yes," she whispered, the single word carrying more certainty than any elaborate declaration could have. "Of course yes."

She moved forward in a single fluid motion, the blanket falling from her shoulders as she closed the distance between them. Her arms encircled his neck, her forehead pressing against his, their breath mingling in the narrow space between their lips.

"I'm not with you because of your career," she said, each word distinct and deliberate. "I'm with you because of who you are beneath all that. Because of how you look at me in the morning before you're fully awake. Because of the way you argue about film endings and make coffee with ridiculous precision and care about things with your whole heart."

Charlie felt something tight in his chest finally release, tension uncoiling as her words washed over him. He pulled her closer, one hand cradling the back of her head, fingers threading through her hair.

"I love you," he whispered against her temple. "Not just some of you, not just the convenient parts. All of you."

They held each other as the ocean crashed against the cliffs below, the sound a perfect accompaniment to the moment—powerful, unpredictable, beautiful in its wild certainty. The waves would continue their relentless approach regardless of human concerns, just as time would carry them forward into whatever came next. But now they would face it together, no longer separated by the artificial boundaries of fame or the walls built for protection that had instead created distance.

Charlie closed his eyes, breathing in the scent of her hair, feeling the solid reality of her in his arms. For the first time in longer than he could remember, the future held more promise than fear.

Chapter Nineteen: Bee's Brave Stand

They moved from the terrace to the living room as morning stretched into day, the intensity of their conversation following them like a third presence. Sunlight filtered through the expensive curtains, casting elongated shadows across the hardwood floor and highlighting the tension in their postures. Charlie settled into the corner of the sofa, his body angled toward Bee as if physically unable to face any other direction, while she perched on the edge of the cushion beside him, her earlier tears dried but their tracks still visible on her flushed cheeks.

"I've been thinking about specifics," Charlie said, leaning forward, his hands gesturing with renewed energy. "We could travel—not the promotional kind with schedules and handlers and contractual appearances—but actual travel. Places I've filmed but never really seen." His eyes brightened with possibilities that seemed to unfold before him. "We could spend a month in that coastal town in Spain where I shot 'Midnight Tides.' The locals barely recognized me by the end of production. Or New Zealand—there's this cabin on the South Island overlooking a lake so clear you can see straight to the bottom."

Bee watched his face as he spoke, the animation in his features both beautiful and troubling. His hands moved through the air, mapping invisible geographies, building worlds with words and hope. She recognized this version of Charlie—the one who approached challenges with the same focused intensity he brought to his roles, committing fully to whatever path he chose. It was the quality that had made him exceptional on screen. It was also what made this moment so dangerous.

"We wouldn't have to worry about paparazzi or schedules or image management," he continued, his words accelerating with enthusiasm. "Just us, exploring, living." He paused, drawing a breath that seemed to centre him. "I have investments, savings—more than enough for us to live comfortably without work for... well, indefinitely if we wanted. Though I'd probably find something eventually—directing maybe, or producing. Something behind the camera."

The sunlight shifted, catching on the crystal water glasses on the coffee table, sending fractured light dancing across the ceiling in patterns that reminded Bee of underwater reflections. She watched them as Charlie continued outlining his vision of their future—a future constructed around escape rather than engagement, retreat rather than resolution.

"I've already told Toby to cancel the Vasquez project meetings," he said, his voice dropping to a more practical register. "And I've asked him to pause development on 'The Invisible Line.' There's a clause in my contract that allows for personal emergencies, which—"

Bee reached for his hands, stilling them mid-gesture. Her fingers closed around his with gentle pressure that belied the trembling she felt inside. The contact interrupted his flow of words, bringing his focus fully to her face, to the conflict she could no longer conceal.

"Charlie," she said, her voice thick with emotion. "I love

you for being willing to give up everything for me." She swallowed, struggling to articulate feelings that swirled like currents beneath the surface of her composure. "But I would never forgive myself if you resented me later."

His brow furrowed, the familiar crease appearing between his eyes that signalled confusion or concern. "I won't resent you," he said, turning his hands to clasp hers more firmly. "This is my choice. My decision."

"A decision you're making because of me," Bee countered, her thumb absently tracing the line of his knuckles. "Because of what happened with Madison, because of the photographers, because of everything that's made me feel unsafe or exposed."

"Not just because of that," Charlie insisted, leaning closer. "Because I want something real. Something true. I've spent fifteen years pretending to be other people. I want to just be me now. With you."

Bee felt tears threatening again and blinked them back with determined control. The sunlight caught in Charlie's hair, illuminating strands of gold and copper among the brown. She focused on this detail, anchoring herself against the tide of emotion that threatened to sweep away her resolve.

"I believe you mean that now," she said carefully. "But what about a year from now? Five years? Acting isn't just your job, Charlie. It's part of who you are. I've seen how you light up discussing a character, how you notice details about people that most miss, how you process emotions through stories." Her voice softened. "It's one of the things I love about you."

Charlie started to speak, but Bee pressed her fingers gently against his lips, stopping him. "Please, let me finish." When he nodded, she continued, her voice steadier. "I didn't fall in love with some alternate version of you that exists outside your career. I fell in love with you—all of you, including the parts shaped by your work."

The curtains stirred with a subtle current from the central air, sending the light patterns skittering across the ceiling in new configurations. Charlie watched her face with the intensity she'd grown to recognise—the focus he typically reserved for understanding a character's motivations now directed entirely at comprehending her.

"I'm not saying never make changes," Bee clarified, her hands still holding his. "I'm saying don't make them as a reaction. Don't make them because you think it's what I need."

"But the stress it causes you—"

"Is something I need to learn to handle," she interrupted, her voice firming with conviction. "This isn't just about you protecting me anymore. It's about me being brave enough to stand by you, fame and all."

Charlie's expression shifted, surprise replacing concern. "You've always been brave, Bee."

She smiled, the expression tinged with sadness. "Not about this. I've been running away—quitting my job, hiding in your house, avoiding facing what a relationship with you really means." Her fingers tightened around his. "I've been using my independence as an excuse when really, I've been afraid."

The confession hung between them, weighted with implications neither had fully articulated until now. Charlie's thumbs traced circles against her palms, the small motion conveying comfort while he processed her words.

"I don't want you to sacrifice your dream for me," Bee continued. "And I don't want to be the reason you walk away from something that's fundamentally part of who you are." She looked directly into his eyes, her gaze unflinching despite the vulnerability of the moment. "What I want is for us to figure out how to build a life that includes your career and my sanity. There has to be a middle ground between you giving up everything and me hiding forever."

Charlie's body seemed to release a tension he'd been carrying, his shoulders dropping slightly as he exhaled. "You really believe we can find that balance?"

"I don't know," Bee admitted, her honesty characteristically direct. "But I think we owe it to ourselves—to what we've built together—to try before you throw away fifteen years of work."

The sunlight had strengthened, the shadows on the floor shortening as morning advanced. Outside, the distant sound of waves against the cliff face provided a steady rhythm beneath their conversation, constant, persistent, a natural force that neither retreated nor overwhelmed.

"I just want you to be happy," Charlie said finally, his voice quiet. "To feel safe. To have the life you deserve."

"I want the same for you," Bee replied. "Which is why I can't let you make this sacrifice without being absolutely certain it's what you truly want—for yourself, not just for us." She reached up to touch his face, fingers tracing the stubble along his jaw. "And I'm not convinced you are. Not yet."

Their gazes held, a current of understanding passing between them that transcended words. The challenge before them had shifted—no longer about escape but about engagement, not about walls but about boundaries. Not about sacrifice but about building something sustainable together.

Bee rose from the sofa, the need to move suddenly overwhelming. Her body often expressed what her words were still forming—a habit from childhood that no amount of adult self-discipline had managed to break. She paced toward the floor-to-ceiling windows, then back again, her fingers working against each other in unconscious motion. Charlie watched her without interruption, giving her the space to find her way through whatever she needed to say next, his eyes tracking her movement with patient attention.

"I've always prided myself on my independence," she said finally, stopping to turn toward him, her hands now gesturing in emphasis. "Being self-sufficient, handling my own problems, never needing rescue." A hollow laugh escaped her. "When Victoria tried to humiliate me at Harrington's, I walked out with my head high. When customers treated me like furniture instead of a person, I maintained my dignity. I've always believed I could handle whatever came my way."

She resumed pacing, her steps quicker now, energy building with her words. "But this—the constant scrutiny, the cameras, the speculation, the invasion—it's been terrifying in ways I wasn't prepared for." Her hands lifted, palms up, as if trying to hold the weight of invisible evidence. "And instead of admitting that, I've been using my independence as a shield. Telling myself I just needed space, time, distance, when really..."

She stopped abruptly, turning to look directly at Charlie. "I've been afraid. Not just uncomfortable or annoyed or overwhelmed—truly afraid. And admitting that feels like failing somehow."

Outside, the first soft patter of rain began to touch the windows, gentle at first but steadily intensifying. The sound created a subtle backdrop to her confession, nature providing percussion to her emotional rhythm.

Charlie rose from the sofa and moved to her, taking her restless hands in his. The simple contact seemed to ground her, her fingers curling around his with grateful pressure. "Being afraid doesn't make you any less independent," he said softly. "It makes you human."

"I know that intellectually," Bee acknowledged, her eyes dropping to their joined hands. "But emotionally? It feels like weakness." The rain strengthened outside, drops streaking the vast windows in chaotic patterns. "Remember when we found Madison in our bed?"

Charlie's fingers tightened slightly around hers at the memory. "Of course."

"I told you I was fine afterwards. That I was just practical —we needed new sheets, a different room." Bee's voice dropped lower, as if sharing a secret she'd kept even from herself. "But I wasn't fine. For weeks, I checked every closet when we came home. I listened for noises in the night. I'd wake up sometimes and just stare at the door, imagining it opening." Her breathing quickened with the admission. "She didn't just invade our house; she invaded my sense of safety. The one place I should have felt secure became another source of anxiety."

The rain drummed steadily now, creating a cocoon of sound around their conversation. Charlie guided her back to the sofa, sitting close enough that their knees touched, his hands still holding hers.

"Why didn't you tell me?" he asked, his voice gentle rather than accusatory.

"Because you were already blaming yourself. Already installing security systems and changing locks, and hiring guards." She met his eyes. "And because I thought if I just pretended to be okay, eventually I would be."

Charlie nodded, understanding in his expression. "What would have helped? Not what I thought would help—what would you have needed?"

The question surprised her, evident in the slight widening of her eyes. She considered it, the rhythm of the rain filling the silence between them. "Acknowledgment, maybe. Permission to be not okay without you trying to fix it immediately. Time to process without feeling like I was adding to your guilt." She squeezed his hands. "And maybe a therapist who specialises in privacy violations. I think I underestimated the psychological impact."

"We can arrange that," Charlie said, nodding thoughtfully. "Starting today, if you want."

"And then there was Luxe Boutique," Bee continued, her

voice stronger now that the first admission had broken through her defences. "The customers taking photos, the whispers, Victoria's ambush—all of it made me feel like I'd lost my professional identity overnight. Like I wasn't Bianca Anderson, retail manager with skills and experience, but just 'Charlie Benton's girlfriend' who people either wanted to use or gawk at."

"That's on them, not you," Charlie said, a flash of anger crossing his features before he controlled it.

"Yes, but it's still my reality to deal with." Bee shifted, tucking one leg beneath her as she turned more fully toward him. "I need to figure out what kind of work I can do that uses my skills but doesn't expose me to that kind of treatment." Her fingers tapped against his palm, ideas already forming. "Maybe something less public-facing. Or with a company large enough to have security protocols for high-profile clients— they might understand how to handle staff privacy too."

Charlie nodded, his expression opening with interest rather than protectiveness. "That makes sense. What kind of roles are you thinking about?"

"Buying, maybe. Or merchandising, visual design." A small smile touched her lips. "I've always had a good eye for how things should look together, what creates harmony in a space." She gestured vaguely toward the tastefully appointed living room around them. "It's actually what I wanted to study before financial realities pushed me toward management faster."

The rain had settled into a steady rhythm, drops no longer racing down the windows but creating a constant veil of water that softened the view beyond. The sound filled the room with white noise that felt protective, intimate, as if they were conversing inside a bubble separate from the outside world.

"And then there's the paparazzi," Bee said, her voice tightening. "The constant feeling of being watched, photographed, speculated about. The guy who followed me to my car after Luxe, the ones who wait outside restaurants we visit, the comments online about what I'm wearing or how I look standing next to you." Her free hand moved in a frustrated gesture. "I hate how it makes me second-guess everything—my clothes, my expressions, whether I should hold your hand in public or if that will trigger another round of headlines."

Charlie leaned forward slightly. "That's the part I don't know if we can ever fully solve," he admitted, his honesty matching hers. "We can minimise it with strategy, but as long as I'm recognised, there will be some level of interest in us."

"I know," Bee said, surprising him with the certainty in her tone. "And I'm not asking for it to disappear completely. I'm asking for us to find ways to manage it together—to create enough protected space that the public interest becomes something we deal with rather than something that defines us."

The rain had transformed the quality of light in the room, softening the earlier harsh sunlight into something diffused and gentle. It caught on the planes of Charlie's face as his expression shifted from concern to something that looked remarkably like hope.

"We could establish clearer boundaries," he suggested, his voice gaining enthusiasm. "Certain places or times that are just for us, off-limits to work and public obligations. Places where we go that we never post about or mention publicly."

"And I could have more control over which events I attend with you," Bee added, building on his thought. "Not hiding that we're together, but being selective about where I'm willing to be photographed. Quality over quantity."

Charlie's face had transformed as they spoke, the worried tension giving way to something lighter, more open. His eyes traced her features with a mixture of relief and admiration that made her breath catch.

"You're really not giving up on us," he said, the statement carrying a hint of wonder.

"Of course not," Bee replied, her directness returning as she found firmer emotional ground. "I'm just refusing to let fear make our decisions—yours or mine." She gestured toward the window where rain continued to fall in steady sheets. "The world out there is still going to be complicated. But I'd rather face it with you than hide from it without you."

The rain wrapped around them like a blanket of sound, creating a temporary sanctuary where truth could be spoken without fear of judgment or exposure. In this sheltered moment, with admission came possibility—not of perfect solutions, but of a path forward they would navigate together.

Charlie's home office held none of the intimidating glamour of a Hollywood executive suite, despite the awards discreetly displayed on floating shelves and the framed film posters lining one wall. Instead, the space felt genuinely lived-in—notebooks with dog-eared pages stacked beside screen-plays marked with his handwritten notes, a well-worn leather chair bearing the imprint of his body after countless hours of reading. Bee settled into the chair beside his at the wide mahogany desk, their shoulders nearly touching as Charlie pulled a leather portfolio from a drawer and extracted several sheets of heavy cream stationery embossed with a subtle monogram.

"I always think better when I write things down," he explained, uncapping an expensive fountain pen that felt both pretentious and perfectly suited to him. "Old habit from when I was first learning lines."

Bee nodded, appreciating this glimpse into his process—the small rituals that anchored his work and thinking. She reached for a pen from the holder between them, testing its weight in her hand. "So we're making actual lists? Concrete plans?"

"Exactly." Charlie drew a line down the centre of the first page, creating two columns. "Problems and solutions," he said, labelling each side with his surprisingly elegant handwriting. "Let's start with what we know works, then move to what we want to try."

The intimacy of sitting beside him, bent over the same page, brought a different quality to their planning than the emotional conversation in the living room. This felt like a partnership in its most tangible form—literally creating something together, word by word, idea by idea.

"First," Charlie said, writing as he spoke, "you mentioned feeling overwhelmed by the attention and logistics when we're in public together." His pen paused, hovering above the solution column. "What if you had your own personal assistant? Someone whose sole job is to manage the parts of public life that stress you most—arranging secure transportation, screening incoming requests, coordinating with my team for events you choose to attend."

Bee's initial reaction was resistance—another layer of insulation between herself and the world, another adjustment to accommodate Charlie's celebrity rather than addressing it directly. But she considered the practical benefits before responding, trying to separate her pride from her actual needs.

"I don't want someone hovering constantly," she said finally. "That would make me feel like I've lost even more normalcy. But having dedicated support for public appearances..." She tapped her pen against the paper, considering. "Someone who knows the venues in advance can coordinate with security, maybe handles the details so we can focus on each other—that could work."

Charlie nodded, writing down the refined idea. "They'd work for you, not me," he emphasised. "Your priorities, your boundaries."

"I like that distinction," Bee acknowledged, warming to

the concept. "And it would help with another issue—which events I attend versus which ones you handle alone." She leaned forward, adding a note in her own handwriting beneath his. "I don't need to be at every premiere or industry event," she said pragmatically. "But I want to be there for the ones that matter to you."

"How do we determine which those are?" Charlie asked, genuinely curious rather than challenging.

Bee considered the question, appreciating that he was asking rather than assuming. "The projects you're most passionate about. The directors or castmates who've become actual friends. Milestones rather than obligations." She smiled slightly. "Basically, if you'd want to share the experience with me even if the cameras weren't there, that's when I should be there."

Charlie's expression softened, his hand briefly covering hers on the desk. "That's a better metric than anything my publicist has ever suggested."

The rain had lessened outside, its rhythm against the windows more sporadic now. Occasionally, a stronger gust of wind would drive a sudden shower against the glass before subsiding again, nature's rhythm syncing with their conversation's ebb and flow.

"What about your career?" Charlie asked, turning to a fresh sheet of paper. "You mentioned buying, merchandising, visual design..."

"I've been thinking about that," Bee said, leaning back slightly in her chair. "Retail management gave me skills in operations, personnel, and understanding consumer behaviour. But what I really love is creating environments—arranging elements to evoke specific feelings or experiences." Her fingers traced invisible patterns on the desk as she spoke. "I've always had a knack for spatial relationships, for seeing how things could fit together in ways others might miss."

Charlie watched her with undisguised admiration. "You transformed your apartment with practically no budget. I remember thinking it felt more like a home than this place ever has, despite costing a fraction as much."

"That's what I mean," Bee nodded, energy building in her voice. "It's not about expensive pieces; it's about understanding flow, balance, the conversation between objects and space." She hesitated, then added more quietly, "I've considered interior design, but going back to school at my age..."

"Why not?" Charlie challenged gently. "You have the eye, the instinct, the practical experience managing projects and people. The degree would just formalize what you already know."

"And the tuition? The time without income?" Bee countered, old habits of financial practicality asserting themselves.

Charlie started to speak, then stopped, visibly reconsidering his approach. Instead of immediately offering financial support—which Bee knew would trigger her independence reflex—he asked, "If money weren't an issue, would you want to pursue that path?"

"Yes," she admitted without hesitation. "But money is always an issue."

"It doesn't have to be," Charlie said carefully. "Not because I'm solving your problems, but because we're partners. If I were going back to school, wouldn't you support me however you could?"

The question disarmed her practised defences. "Of course I would."

"Then let me do the same for you," he said simply. "Not as charity or dependency, but as investment in our shared future. In what makes you happy."

Bee felt something shift inside her—a reorganisation of priorities and principles that made room for this new understanding of partnership. Independence didn't have to mean doing everything alone; it could mean choosing interdependence with open eyes and mutual respect.

"We should talk to Toby," she said, redirecting the conversation slightly while she processed this realisation. "About releasing a statement regarding our relationship. Something that establishes boundaries without seeming defensive."

Charlie nodded, pulling another sheet of stationery toward them. "What do you think it should include?"

"Honesty about our relationship," Bee said immediately. "No hiding that we're serious, that we're building a life together. But clarity about our expectations of privacy." Her pen moved across the paper, jotting key points as she spoke. "We're not hiding, but we're not performing for them either."

Charlie watched her write, his expression thoughtful. "You know, when I told Toby I was quitting acting, his first instinct was to negotiate—to frame it as a sabbatical, to find a middle ground that preserved my career options while giving me what I needed." He smiled slightly. "Sounds familiar now."

"He was right," Bee said, looking up from her notes. "Not about the specifics, maybe, but about the approach. Extremes rarely solve complex problems."

Outside, the rain had stopped entirely. Sunlight broke through the clouds, sending a shaft of golden light through the office windows that illuminated their hands on the desk— his tanned and manicured from years of camera-readiness, hers strong and capable with the practical elegance of someone who worked with her hands. Different, but complementary. Like them.

"So I'll call Toby," Charlie said, "tell him I'm not quitting but renegotiating my relationship with the industry. Fewer projects, more carefully chosen. No press that isn't directly related to the work. Clear boundaries around our personal life."

"And more importantly," Bee added, "boundaries that we

enforce together, consistently." She tapped the statement they'd begun drafting. "This isn't just words on paper. It's how we actually live—choosing where to be visible, where to maintain privacy, which battles are worth fighting."

Charlie looked down at the pages they'd covered with notes, plans, strategies—the physical manifestation of their commitment to finding a middle path. "This feels right," he said quietly. "Not running away, not surrendering, but engaging on our terms."

Bee squeezed his hand, the simple gesture containing layers of meaning they'd spent the morning excavating together. "We're not hiding," she repeated, the phrase becoming something of a mantra. "But we're not performing either."

The sunlight strengthened as clouds continued to part, illuminating dust motes dancing in the air between them—small particles made visible only because of how they interacted with light. Bee thought there was a metaphor in that, something about how relationships revealed aspects of yourself that remained invisible otherwise.

"I should call Toby soon," Charlie said, gathering their notes into the leather portfolio. "Let him know the sabbatical is off, but the boundaries are non-negotiable."

"And I'll research design programs," Bee added, allowing herself to embrace possibility rather than defaulting to practicality. "Maybe start with night classes while I explore behind-the-scenes retail roles."

They stood together, the physical action marking a transition from planning to implementation. The lists they'd made weren't perfect solutions—no strategy could completely eliminate the challenges they faced—but they represented a shared approach to navigating them. Not Charlie protecting Bee through sacrifice, not Bee hiding from difficult realities, but both of them choosing engagement over avoidance, boundaries over walls.

As they left the office, Bee paused in the doorway, looking back at the desk where they'd sketched the outlines of their path forward. Sunlight now flooded the room, transforming the space with the simple magic of natural light finding its way through clouds. The metaphor wasn't lost on her—clarity after confusion, warmth after cold, direction after uncertainty.

They would face challenges still. The world beyond these walls remained complicated, intrusive, occasionally hostile to the private happiness they were building together. But for the first time since Madison had shattered their sense of security, since Victoria had weaponized their relationship, since photographers had turned their connection into content, Bee felt something unexpected: not just determination or courage, but genuine optimism. They had found their approach—not retreat but engagement, not surrender but strategy, not isolation but carefully guarded connection.

Charlie's hand found hers as they walked away from the office, their fingers interlacing with the easy familiarity of bodies that had learned each other's contours. Not a dramatic gesture, not a passionate declaration, but the quiet, consistent choice to move forward together—the most powerful statement they could make.

Chapter Twenty: United Front

The lamplight cast a warm glow over the scattered newspapers and glossy magazine pages spread across Charlie's desk, their bold headlines announcing relationships, speculating on futures, and dissecting pasts with equal conviction. Bee sat cross-legged in one of the study's leather armchairs, a tablet balanced on her knee as she scrolled through yet another online article about them, while Charlie leaned against the edge of his desk, his eyes moving between the physical clippings and Bee's face, gauging her reactions more carefully than the words before them. Outside, the security cameras swept their vigilant paths, occasionally casting moving shadows through the windows like phantom reminders of why they sat surrounded by the printed evidence of their public dissection.

"Charlie Benton's New Flame: Retail Romance or Calculated Career Move?" Bee read aloud, her tone deliberately flat as she quoted the headline. "That's creative. I particularly enjoy how they managed to question both your motives and my existence in a single line."

Charlie's jaw tightened, the muscle visibly flexing beneath

his stubbled skin. "They've been recycling the same five headlines for decades. Just change the names and run it again."

The security system hummed quietly in the background, a constant white noise that had become the sountrack to their evenings. Once, Bee had found it intrusive; now, it registered as a strange comfort—evidence of protection in a world increasingly determined to breach their privacy.

"This one's my favorite," Charlie said, plucking a tabloid from the pile and holding it up. "Apparently, we met through a high-end escort service where you were moonlighting between retail shifts."

Bee snorted. "If I were moonlighting as an escort, I wouldn't have needed the retail job." She tossed her tablet onto the cushion beside her and stretched her arms overhead, the soft cotton of her oversized sweater riding up to reveal a sliver of skin. "Also, I'm clearly not charging enough if this is the best accommodation I've secured."

Charlie's laugh was genuine despite the circumstances, the sound warming the book-lined sanctuary he'd created in this corner of his sprawling home. He pushed off from the desk and moved to the small bar cart nestled between two bookshelves, pouring amber liquid into crystal tumblers.

"The key," he said, handing one glass to Bee, "is managing what they can capture." He settled into the chair opposite hers, the leather creaking softly beneath his weight. "I've learned a few tricks over the years."

The scent of his cologne—sandalwood with undertones of something citrusy—mingled with the smell of old books and the whiskey they sipped. Bee breathed it in, finding herself anchored by the sensory details of this moment even as they discussed the disorienting experience of becoming public property.

"Decoy cars are essential," Charlie continued, swirling the liquid in his glass. "I have three identical SUVs with tinted windows. One leaves from the front gate making a show of it, while we slip out the service entrance in another." He leaned forward, elbows on his knees, warming to his subject. "Timing matters too. Photographers change shifts around meal times—most clear out around noon, so that's the sweet spot for leaving unnoticed."

Bee watched him, fascinated by this glimpse into the machinery of celebrity—the counter-measures developed to preserve some semblance of normalcy in the face of relentless pursuit.

"Then there's clothing," he added. "Certain fabrics reflect flash photography, creating a bloom effect that ruins their shots." His fingers traced patterns in the condensation on his glass. "I have jackets specifically designed with reflective threading that looks normal to the naked eye but turns their photos worthless."

"You've put a lot of thought into this," Bee observed, not quite sure whether to be impressed or concerned by the elaborate strategies.

Charlie's shoulders lifted in a small shrug. "It becomes second nature after a while. Part of the job description no one tells you about when you're starting out."

His gaze dropped to a magazine lying open between them, its pages displaying a series of unflattering shots of Bee leaving Luxe Boutique. In one, her face was caught mid-expression, features contorted in what appeared to be disgust but had actually been a sneeze. The caption read: "Trouble in Paradise? Charlie's New Girlfriend Appears Distraught After Failed Job Interview."

Bee's fingers reached out, tracing the outline of her distorted image. The paper felt cool and slick beneath her touch, the reality of her captured form simultaneously foreign and uncomfortably familiar. Charlie watched her, his expression darkening as he noticed her discomfort.

"We could issue cease and desist letters for some of these," he offered, voice tightening. "There are legal remedies—"

"And give them more to write about?" Bee shook her head. "Besides, I do look like I just ate something that disagreed with me."

Charlie set his glass down with more force than necessary, the crystal connecting with wood in a sharp sound that punctuated his frustration. "This is exactly why we need systems in place. Multiple exits, scheduled movements, clothing strategies—"

"We can't live like fugitives, Charlie." Bee's voice was gentle but firm. "I understand the need for precautions, but some of this feels... extreme."

"It's not extreme, it's necessary," he insisted, rising to pace the length of the study. Security camera shadows tracked his movement, ghostly reminders of their perpetual observation. "You saw what happened at Luxe. The way they treated you. The way Victoria used our relationship as a weapon."

Bee watched him move, recognizing the protective instinct driving his agitation. "We need to set boundaries, not build walls," she said softly. "The difference matters."

Charlie stopped his pacing, turning to face her with an expression torn between frustration and vulnerability. "Boundaries can be crossed. Walls are safer."

"Safer, yes. But walls work both ways—they keep things out and they keep you in." Bee set her glass beside his and stood, moving to where he stood framed by bookshelves laden with volumes that had shaped him. "I don't want to live in a fortress, even one as beautiful as this."

The tension in his shoulders softened slightly as she approached. His hand lifted to brush a strand of hair from her face, his touch feather-light against her skin. "I just want to protect you from all this," he said, gesturing toward the scattered evidence of their public dissection.

"I know." Bee leaned into his touch, her eyes meeting his with unflinching directness. "But I need a partner, not a security detail. We figure this out together."

Charlie's thumb traced the curve of her cheekbone, his eyes following the movement as if memorizing the terrain of her face. The protectiveness remained in his expression, but it had softened into something more vulnerable—concern mingled with a deeper emotion that made her breath catch.

"Together," he echoed, the single word carrying the weight of promise.

Bee lifted her head, rising slightly on her toes to press her lips against his. What began as comfort deepened almost instantly, the accumulated tension of their discussions finding release in the contact. Charlie's arms encircled her waist, drawing her against him with a need that matched her own rising desire.

"I need you tonight," she whispered against his mouth. "Just you. Not the strategies or the security measures or the public versions of ourselves. Just us, forgetting everything else. Help me forget."

Charlie immediately responded with action rather than words, his mouth pressing against hers his hands cupping her face with growing urgency as he walked her backward until her legs hit the edge of his desk. Papers fluttered beneath her as he lifted her onto the surface, magazines and clippings sliding to the floor in a waterfall of distractions dismissed by the immediate reality of their bodies pressing together.

Charlie stood firmly between her knee's, he pulled his top off over his head, while Bee ran her hands down his chest, taking her hands below his waist band, he bent for a moment lowering his pants and boxers, as he stood back up he ran his hands up Bee's legs lifting her skirt and tugging at her underwear, she shuffled slightly so they could be discarded, with underwear removed he ran his fingers between her folds, causing her to throw her head back at the sensation, kneeling before her he kissed her sweet spots while removing her skirt also, he stood up admiring her nakedness. "You are so fucking gorgeous." he breathed as he stood firmly between her legs again.

Bee's legs wrapped around his waist, pulling him closer as she sat on the desk. Charlie's hands gripped her breasts, his thumbs circling her nipples as he thrust into her. Bee leaned back, her eyes fluttering closed as she gave herself over to the sensation. Their movements quickened, their breaths coming in ragged gasps. Bee's fingers dug into his shoulders as his thrusts became more forceful, he gripped her hips tightly pulling her onto him with each thrust.

They cried out each other's names as they reached their climax, the emotional release as powerful as the physical.

Afterward, they moved to the sofa, pulling a blanket over themselves. Bee curled up against Charlie's chest, their heartbeats gradually returning to normal. The scattered articles lay forgotten on the floor, their bold headlines and speculative captions rendered temporarily powerless by the reality of what existed between them.

Sleep found them there, still intertwined, the security cameras continuing their silent patrol outside while inside, protected by walls both literal and metaphorical, Charlie and Bee found temporary sanctuary in each other's arms.

Morning light poured through the kitchen's east-facing windows, turning ordinary objects into studies in gold—the copper-bottomed pans hanging above the island, the amber bottle of maple syrup beside the stove, the honey-colored strands in Bee's dark hair as she moved between refrigerator and counter with casual familiarity. Charlie watched her from his position at the espresso machine, his hands moving through the practiced ritual of morning coffee while his mind lingered on the previous night—their bodies tangled together in his study, momentarily free from the scrutiny that had driven them there in the first place.

"I've been thinking," Bee said, cracking eggs into a bowl with precise movements. "Your stealth tactics are impressive, but they're reactive. What if we tried something more proactive?"

Charlie raised an eyebrow, tamping coffee grounds with the pressure that had become second nature after years of morning routines. "I'm listening."

"Boundaries," Bee said, whisking the eggs with deliberate strokes. "Not walls, like we talked about. Actual, practical techniques for handling people who push too far." She glanced up, meeting his eyes across the kitchen island. "I spent years managing difficult customers in retail. Different context, same skills."

Charlie placed a cappuccino beside her, the foam decorated with an abstract leaf pattern that spoke of countless mornings spent perfecting the technique. "You want to teach me retail skills?"

"I want to teach you how to say no without being a jerk," Bee clarified, her lips curving into a smile that softened the bluntness of her words. "How to maintain your space without hiding behind security or tinted windows." She poured the eggs into a heated pan, the soft sizzle providing percussion to their conversation. "Let's role-play some scenarios."

"I can think of a few things we could role-play," he said with a smile then sipping his coffee. Bee exaggeratedly rolled her eyes, then paused, her expression said deep in thought. "We can touch back on that later." she said giving him a playful wink.

Charlie's initial skepticism gave way to curiosity. He leaned against the counter, cradling his own coffee cup. "Alright, Professor Anderson. The classroom is yours."

Bee nodded, her expression shifting subtly as she

adopted a character—shoulders hunching slightly, eyes widening with artificial excitement, voice climbing to a higher pitch. "Oh my god, you're Charlie Benton! I can't believe it! Can you sign my arm? No, my chest! I want to get it tattooed! Can I take a selfie? My friends will never believe this!"

She advanced toward him, invading his personal space with the practiced precision of someone who understood exactly where the line of comfort lay—and deliberately crossed it. Charlie found himself instinctively backing up until the edge of the counter pressed against his lower back.

"Uh, sure, I can sign something for you," he offered, reaching for an imaginary pen.

Bee broke character, shaking her head. "Too accommodating. You're reinforcing that this level of intrusion is acceptable." She stirred the eggs with one hand while gesturing with the other. "Try again. This time, acknowledge the enthusiasm but establish a clear boundary."

Charlie straightened, considering her feedback. When Bee resumed her performance—this time adding an imaginary phone thrust toward his face—he responded differently.

"I appreciate your support," he said, his voice warm but firm as he raised a hand in the universal 'stop' gesture, maintaining a clear foot of space between them. "I'm happy to sign something for you, but I prefer not to do photos while I'm having a private meal."

Bee's face lit with approval as she returned to the stove. "Much better. Direct but kind. Now let's try the hugger."

For the next scenario, she approached with arms wide open, making grabbing gestures. "Charlie! I feel like I know you so well! Come here, give me a hug! We're practically family!"

This time, Charlie was ready. He extended his hand for a handshake instead, creating a barrier with his arm while maintaining a pleasant expression. "Nice to meet you. A handshake works better for me, if that's alright."

"Perfect," Bee nodded, breaking character again. "You're giving an alternative that allows connection without crossing your boundary." She transferred the eggs to two plates, adding toast and sliced avocado. "The key is consistency. If you make exceptions, people learn that your boundaries are negotiable."

They settled at the kitchen island with their breakfast, the domestic simplicity of the moment contrasting with the unusual nature of their conversation. Outside, the carefully manicured grounds of Charlie's property stretched toward distant security fencing, the barrier between their sanctuary and the world beyond visible even from here.

"Let's try something harder," Bee suggested between bites. "The stealth photographer—someone pretending to be a normal fan but actually angling for content they can sell."

She stood, wiping her hands on a napkin before assuming a new character—this one more subtle, less obviously intrusive. Her posture became casual, her expression merely friendly rather than overexcited.

"Excuse me, Charlie? Sorry to bother you. I'm such a fan of your work." She approached with respectful distance, nothing in her demeanor raising immediate alarm bells. "My nephew is in the hospital and he loves your films. Would you mind if I got a quick video saying hello to him? It would mean the world."

Charlie hesitated, compassion warring with caution. The scenario Bee had created was deliberately designed to target his decency, to make refusal feel cruel. He could see the trap, yet still felt the pull to accommodate.

"That's really tough," he said finally. "I hope your nephew feels better soon. I don't do videos, but I'd be happy to sign something for him, or if you have a piece of paper, I could write him a quick note."

Bee's smile was genuine as she dropped the act. "Excellent. You acknowledged the emotional appeal without letting it override your boundary. You offered an alternative that's still kind but protects your privacy."

Charlie reached for his coffee, considering how much thought Bee had clearly given to these interactions—scenarios he'd encountered countless times but had never approached with such deliberate strategy.

"How did you get so good at this?" he asked, watching as she cleared their plates with efficient movements.

"Eight years in retail," Bee replied, stacking dishes in the sink. "Customers believe the slogan that they're always right, which means frontline workers need strategies to say no without saying no." She glanced over her shoulder at him, a strand of dark hair falling across her cheek. "The difference is that I had a manager to back me up. You're on your own in these encounters."

"Not anymore," Charlie said quietly, the simple statement carrying layers of meaning beyond its syllables.

Bee turned, leaning against the sink as she studied him. "No, not anymore," she agreed. "But you still need the skills. You can't always have a security detail or—"

"Or you," Charlie finished for her, understanding dawning. "You're teaching me to fish rather than just giving me fish."

"Something like that," Bee acknowledged with a small smile. "You don't have to be rude to be firm. That's the key most people miss. Rudeness actually undermines boundaries because it makes you look defensive. Calm clarity is much more effective."

Charlie moved to help with the dishes, the simple domestic task grounding their theoretical discussion in physical reality. "It's strange," he admitted, "having to learn this now. You'd think after years in the public eye, I'd have figured it out already."

"Most celebrities never do," Bee observed, passing him a plate to dry. "They swing between excessive accommodation and complete isolation, with security handling the messy middle. Neither approach builds actual skills."

The conversation paused as Charlie's phone vibrated against the counter, Toby's name appearing on the screen. Charlie dried his hands and answered, putting the call on speaker.

"Morning, Toby. You're on speaker with Bee."

Toby's voice emerged from the device, his characteristic dry tone immediately recognizable. "Good morning, lovebirds. Hope I'm not interrupting anything scandalous."

"Just breakfast," Charlie replied, exchanging a smile with Bee. "What's up?"

"Another tabloid story brewing," Toby said, his voice shifting to a more professional register. "This one's claiming Bee left her job at Luxe because you're controlling her career moves. They've got quotes from 'anonymous sources' saying you're isolating her professionally to keep her dependent on you."

Bee's expression tightened, her hands stilling on the plate she'd been rinsing. Charlie watched her face, gauging her reaction with the attentiveness that had become second nature.

"That's creative," Bee said after a moment, her voice steady despite the muscle that jumped along her jaw. "Considering I haven't told anyone except Elise why I withdrew my application."

"Which means either Elise is talking, or they're fabricating completely," Toby concluded. "I'm inclined to believe the latter, but worth knowing either way. I can make some calls—"

"No," Charlie interrupted, his eyes still on Bee. "No more reactive firefighting. We need a proactive approach." His hand moved across the island toward Bee's, their fingers finding each other with instinctive certainty. "A statement. On our terms."

"A boundary, not a wall," Bee added, her fingers tightening around his.

There was a brief silence from Toby's end of the call. "Sounds like you two have been strategizing," he said finally, a note of approval in his voice. "Send me what you come up with. And Charlie—that interview we discussed? Might be time to reconsider."

"We'll talk about it," Charlie promised, his thumb brushing across Bee's knuckles. "Later, Toby."

As the call ended, Charlie and Bee remained connected across the kitchen island, their joined hands a physical manifestation of the partnership they'd been discussing all morning. Outside, the security cameras continued their vigilant sweep, but inside, something had shifted—a subtle rebalancing of their approach to the world beyond their sanctuary.

"Together, then," Charlie said, the words both question and statement.

"Together," Bee confirmed, her direct gaze meeting his without hesitation. "Setting boundaries, not building walls."

The morning light had shifted, no longer painting everything in gold but illuminating the kitchen with clear, uncompromising brightness. It felt appropriate somehow—a visual reminder that the strategies they were developing required clarity rather than the soft edges of accommodation or the harsh shadows of isolation.

The dining room table, designed to host elaborate dinner parties for Hollywood elites, had transformed into a war room of sorts—laptops open at opposite ends, papers scattered across its polished surface, coffee mugs leaving rings on drafts discarded hours ago. Night had fallen outside, the darkness making the windows reflect their concentration back at them like mirrors. Charlie sat with fingers poised above his keyboard, deleting and retyping the same sentence for the fourth time, while Bee highlighted passages on a printed draft, her lower lip caught between her teeth in the expression Charlie had come to recognize as her problem-solving face.

"This isn't working," Charlie said, pushing back from the table with a frustrated sigh. "Listen to this: 'We categorically reject the baseless allegations regarding the nature of our relationship and respectfully demand the immediate cessation of intrusive speculation into our private affairs.'" He looked up at Bee. "It sounds like a legal document, not a personal statement."

"It sounds like a celebrity statement," Bee agreed, setting down her highlighter. "Written by committee and vetted by three layers of management."

Charlie ran a hand through his hair, the strands standing up in testament to how many times he'd repeated the gesture over the past two hours. "That's the point, isn't it? To sound authoritative? These tabloids won't back off unless we're forceful."

Bee shook her head, rising to refill their coffee mugs from the carafe a housekeeper had silently delivered an hour earlier. "Forceful isn't the same as authentic. People can sense the difference." She placed his refreshed mug beside his laptop, her fingers briefly resting on his shoulder. "The more it sounds like a celebrity statement, the more it reinforces the distance between you and your audience."

"So what's your approach?" Charlie asked, reaching up to cover her hand with his own, the momentary connection grounding them both in the midst of their strategic discussion.

Bee returned to her seat, pulling her laptop closer. "We need to sound like real people, not celebrities issuing a manifesto." She turned the screen toward him, revealing a draft with significantly less formal language. "People connect with humanity, not authority."

Charlie leaned forward to read her version, brow furrowing slightly as he absorbed the more conversational tone, the personal touches, the absence of the legal-sounding phrases his publicists had always insisted upon. "It's vulnerable," he observed, not entirely comfortable with the concept.

"Exactly," Bee nodded, watching his reaction carefully. "Vulnerable without being weak. Honest without oversharing. It's the difference between a boundary and a wall."

Charlie glanced between the two versions, the contrast stark even in their formatting—his in rigid paragraphs with precise spacing, hers in a more natural flow that mimicked actual speech patterns. It represented their differing approaches not just to this statement, but to the entire situation they found themselves navigating.

"I don't know if I can do vulnerable in public," he admitted, the confession itself a private vulnerability he would have concealed from almost anyone else. "I've spent my entire career maintaining a certain image, a certain distance."

"And how's that working out?" Bee asked, not unkindly, her directness tempered by the genuine concern in her eyes. "The walls you've built haven't actually protected your privacy —they've just made invasion more valuable because it's rarer."

Charlie stared at his version of the statement, seeing it suddenly through her eyes—stilted, artificial, the practiced words of someone more concerned with perception than connection. "So we meet in the middle," he suggested, moving his chair around the table to sit beside her rather than across from her. "Your humanity, my boundaries."

They bent over her laptop together, the previous distance —both physical and philosophical—collapsing as they worked side by side, debating word choices, sentence structures, the subtle nuances that would convey both authenticity and firmness.

"Not 'request privacy'—too passive," Charlie argued, pointing at the screen. "But 'demand privacy' sounds entitled."

"'Ask for privacy'?" Bee suggested. "Simple, direct, human."

Charlie nodded slowly, watching as she made the change. "And here—where you've written about 'our relationship'— we should be more specific. Not just about dating, but about building something meaningful together."

Bee's fingers paused over the keyboard, her eyes meeting his with a question she didn't need to voice aloud. Charlie nodded again, answering her unspoken concern about revealing too much of what existed between them.

"You're right," he said softly. "Humanity, not just authority."

As they continued crafting and refining, their approaches gradually harmonized—Charlie learning to soften his defensive edges, Bee incorporating the clear boundaries he needed while maintaining the authentic voice she valued. The statement evolved through multiple revisions, each one bringing them closer to language that felt true to both their needs.

"I think we've got it," Bee said finally, leaning back in her chair to stretch arms that had stiffened from hours hunched over the laptop. "Want to read it aloud? Sometimes hearing it makes a difference."

Charlie pulled the laptop toward him, clearing his throat before beginning to read:

"We're writing this together because we want to address something important to us both. Recently, there has been increasing speculation about our relationship, some of it intrusive and much of it untrue. We understand public interest, but we're asking for privacy as we build our lives together.

Bee has made her own decisions about her career path based on her goals and experiences, just as she's made her own choice to be in this relationship. We're committed to each other and to creating a life that balances public and private in a way that works for us both. We won't be addressing further rumors or responding to speculation. Thank you for respecting that this is our life, not entertainment."

As he read, Bee watched his face, noticing something fascinating and telling—the subtle shift in his expression, his posture, even his vocal patterns as he moved through the text. The Charlie who began reading was the public figure, the carefully controlled celebrity with perfect diction and measured tones. But somewhere in the middle, he transformed, becoming simply Charlie—the man who laughed with her in the kitchen, who let his guard down in the darkness of his bedroom, who had fallen asleep in her arms in his study. The distinction was subtle but unmistakable, a dropping of masks that felt more significant than the actual words being spoken.

When he finished, a brief silence filled the space between them, heavy with the weight of what they'd created—not just a statement, but a declaration of their partnership, their shared approach to the challenges facing them.

The security system broke the moment with a soft electronic tone, alerting them to movement at the front gate. Charlie glanced at his phone, checking the security app that had become a constant presence in their lives.

"Just the evening delivery," he said, showing her the screen where a courier's truck was visible at the gate. "Probably those books you ordered."

The interruption served as a pointed reminder of why their statement mattered—of the constant monitoring, both electronic and human, that surrounded their lives. The security lights along the driveway cast a protective glow that was simultaneously comforting and isolating, marking the boundaries between their sanctuary and the world beyond.

"Do we need to change anything?" Charlie asked, returning his attention to the statement on the screen.

Bee shook her head, a small smile playing at the corners of her mouth. "No. It's us. Both of us." She reached across the small distance between them, her fingers finding his on the keyboard. "It says what we need it to say, without building walls or abandoning boundaries."

Charlie nodded, his expression softening as he looked at their joined hands against the backdrop of the words they'd crafted together. With a few keystrokes, he attached the document to an email addressed to Toby, adding only a brief note: "Our statement. Release as is, no edits."

The decisive click of the send button echoed slightly in the spacious dining room, a small sound with potentially significant consequences. Charlie closed the laptop, pushing it aside as if physically setting aside the task they'd completed.

"Whatever happens next," he said, turning to face Bee fully, their knees touching beneath the table, "we face it together."

Bee nodded, her fingers still intertwined with his, the simple physical connection reinforcing the deeper one they'd been building through each challenge, each negotiation, each compromise. "Together."

Outside, the security lights illuminated the carefully maintained perimeter of Charlie's property, casting their protective glow over the grounds. Inside, in the warm pool of light above the dining table, Charlie and Bee had crafted something else entirely—not walls of isolation or forced exposure, but boundaries they'd defined together, lines drawn with mutual understanding rather than fear or entitlement.

The statement would be released tomorrow, their words

carried to thousands of screens, dissected by commentators, analyzed by fans. But tonight, in the quiet aftermath of its creation, what mattered most was what it represented: a shared vision, a collaborative approach, a partnership strong enough to face whatever came next—together.

Chapter Twenty-One: The Interview

The television studio air felt artificially cool against Charlie's skin as he followed a production assistant through a labyrinth of cables and equipment. Overhead, grid-mounted lights burned with merciless clarity, designed to eliminate shadows and expose every pore, every micro-expression, every moment of uncertainty. Charlie adjusted his cuffs—a gesture more about centering himself than fixing his appearance—and drew a deep breath that carried the scent of electronics warming, makeup setting powder, and the faint chemical sweetness of someone's perfume. The interview with Morgan Walsh had been his idea —part of the proactive strategy he and Bee had discussed— but standing here, surrounded by the mechanical eyes of cameras and the attentive gazes of the production team, he felt the weight of vulnerability they'd consciously chosen.

"We're set up in Studio Three, Mr. Benton," the assistant said, gesturing toward a set of double doors. "Ms. Walsh is already inside."

. . .

Charlie nodded, pausing just outside the entrance. He closed his eyes briefly, centering himself as he recalled Bee's voice from that morning: "Remember, boundaries not walls. You don't have to answer everything she asks. Redirect when necessary. Most importantly, stay authentic—that's what they can't manipulate."

The memory of her standing in their kitchen, hands cupped around a coffee mug as she dispensed advice with the calm authority of someone who'd faced down entitled customers for years, steadied him. This interview wasn't about performing; it was about establishing control over his own narrative. Their narrative.

Studio Three opened before him like the interior of an elaborate machine—sleek, modern, purpose-built. Three cameras on fluid mounts stood at different angles, operators making minute adjustments to their positions. A sound technician moved between two leather chairs arranged on a slightly raised platform, attaching nearly invisible microphones to their undersides. The backdrop featured a tasteful gradient of blue tones, institutional yet intimate, designed to frame conversation rather than distract from it.

Morgan Walsh sat in one of the chairs, head bent over a tablet, scrolling with the practiced efficiency of someone reviewing notes they already knew by heart. Her dark hair fell in a perfect bob that swung forward to partially obscure her face, a physical barrier she could deploy or retract at will. Without looking up, she raised one finger in acknowledgment of Charlie's arrival—a gesture that managed to be both dismissive and commanding.

"Charlie," she said finally, setting the tablet aside and rising. Her handshake was firm, professional, her smile not reaching the analytical sharpness of her eyes. "Thank you for making time. It's been, what, three years since our last sit-down?"

"The 'Darkness Falls' press tour," Charlie confirmed, settling into the chair opposite hers. The leather felt cool against his back, slightly too firm to allow complete relaxation—by design, he suspected. "Good to see you again, Morgan."

A makeup artist appeared at his side, dabbing powder across his forehead with gentle precision. Charlie submitted to the routine with practiced patience, continuing his conversation with Morgan as if they weren't being prepared for display.

"Your statement caused quite a stir," Morgan observed, her voice neutral but her eyes tracking his reaction with predatory focus. "Bold move to address the speculation head-on."

"It felt like the right approach," Charlie replied, careful to maintain the casual tone of pre-interview conversation while remaining aware that everything—every word, every gesture—was being evaluated. The makeup artist retreated, and a sound technician approached to clip a microphone to his tie.

. . .

"Five minutes," called the director from behind the central camera.

Morgan leaned forward slightly, lowering her voice to create an illusion of privacy in a room designed to broadcast every syllable. "Just so you know, I'll be asking about the relationship, of course. The Madison Vale incident. The impact on Bianca's career." She paused, watching him. "Standard fare."

Charlie nodded, recognizing the tactic—framing invasive questions as "standard" to pre-emptively invalidate any objections. "Of course," he said, his tone pleasant but noncommittal.

"Sixty seconds," announced the director. The studio's ambient noise reduced as crew members settled into position, cameras locked on their marks, monitors glowing with anticipation.

Charlie took another centering breath, focusing on the physical sensations that grounded him—the pressure of the chair against his back, the cool weight of his watch against his wrist, the memory of Bee's hands cupping his face that morning. "Remember why you're doing this," she'd said. "Not for them. For us."

"And we're live in three, two..." The director pointed silently as the red lights on the cameras illuminated.

. . .

Morgan's transformation was immediate and complete—her posture shifting, smile widening, eyes warming with practiced sincerity. "Good evening and welcome to 'Industry Insider.' I'm Morgan Walsh, and tonight I'm joined by one of Hollywood's most enigmatic leading men, Charlie Benton." She turned toward him, her body language open yet commanding. "Charlie, thank you for being here."

"Thank you for having me," Charlie replied, matching her professional warmth with his own carefully calibrated presence—engaged but not eager, relaxed but not casual.

"Let's start with your career trajectory," Morgan began, settling into the rhythm of the interview. "Your last three films have shown a distinct shift toward more complex, morally ambiguous characters. Is this a conscious choice?"

The question was a softball—exactly what Charlie had expected her to lead with. The familiar territory of discussing his work allowed him to establish comfort before the inevitable shift toward more personal matters. He responded with thoughtful analysis of his recent roles, the directors he'd chosen to work with, the themes that attracted him at this stage of his career.

Morgan nodded along, asking intelligent follow-up questions that demonstrated her research and industry knowledge. But Charlie could feel the underlying current beneath the professional exchange—the measured pacing of a predator circling before striking. In her slight shifts of position, the subtle changes in her tone, he recognized preparation for the pivot.

"Your latest project, 'The Invisible Line,' deals with themes of public perception versus private reality," Morgan said, transitioning smoothly. "Given recent events in your personal life, I wonder if that resonated with you on a more personal level?"

There it was—the first probe toward the territory she truly wanted to explore. Charlie maintained his expression, neither leaning away from the question nor eagerly embracing it.

"Art often reflects life in unexpected ways," he acknowledged, his fingers pressing slightly into the leather armrests—a small outlet for the tension he refused to show in his face. "Though the script was written long before my current relationship began, I think we all understand the gap between how we're seen and who we are."

Morgan's eyes narrowed slightly—the minute tell of a journalist recognizing a response that acknowledged her question without providing the emotional content she sought. She recalibrated, leaning forward with practiced intimacy.

"Speaking of your current relationship," she continued, "fans were surprised by your choice of partner. Bianca Anderson seems quite... different from your previous relationships with industry insiders." The pause before 'different' carried deliberate weight. "So tell me, Charlie, what exactly drew you to someone so... ordinary?"

The question hung in the air, its condescension thinly veiled as curiosity. Charlie felt his jaw tighten, a flash of heat rising at the base of his neck. The studio lights suddenly seemed brighter, hotter against his skin. In his peripheral vision, he saw a camera operator shift slightly, sensing potential drama in his reaction.

Charlie inhaled slowly through his nose, his fingers pressing more firmly into the armrests as he anchored himself against the instinct to react defensively. The measured breathing techniques he'd practiced with Bee regulated the flash of anger, transforming it into something more controlled, more deliberate.

"What an interesting framing," he said, his voice level but carrying a new undertone of steel. His eyes met Morgan's directly, neither aggressive nor retreating. "I'd challenge the premise of your question, Morgan. There's nothing ordinary about Bee's intelligence, her wit, her perspective." He smiled slightly, genuine warmth breaking through his professional veneer. "What drew me to her was her authenticity—something extraordinarily rare in my experience. She sees the world with remarkable clarity."

Morgan's expression flickered—a microsecond of recalculation visible before her professional mask reengaged. The exchange had shifted slightly off her planned script, the control she'd expected to maintain through provocative questioning encountering unexpected resistance.

"Authenticity is certainly valuable," she conceded, regrouping. "But surely the cultural differences must create challenges? You move in elite circles; she worked retail. You attend premieres; she shopped at discount stores. How do you bridge such different worlds?"

Charlie recognized the trap—the invitation to either acknowledge problems in their relationship or to sound condescending about Bee's background. He maintained his measured breathing, the controlled rhythm keeping his expression open while his mind worked through the boundary techniques Bee had taught him.

"You know, Morgan," he said, leaning forward slightly to match her posture, creating a sense of engagement rather than defensiveness, "one of the many things I've learned from Bee is that those 'different worlds' are largely artificial constructs. The human experiences that matter—connection, understanding, trust—transcend those superficial boundaries." He paused, allowing his genuine feelings to show through his carefully maintained composure. "If anything, her perspective has enriched my life immeasurably."

The red lights of the cameras stared unblinkingly, recording every word, every micro-expression. Behind them, Charlie could sense the crew's attention sharpening, recognizing that this interview was veering from the expected script into something more authentic—and potentially more compelling. Morgan's eyes narrowed slightly, the predatory focus intensifying as she prepared her next approach.

Morgan reached for her water glass, the brief pause a calculated moment to reset before pressing harder. Her smile tightened into something more predatory as she set the glass down with deliberate precision. "Let's talk about the Madison Vale incident," she said, her voice dropping to convey confidentiality while the microphones captured every syllable. "Sources close to the situation suggest this wasn't the first time an obsessed fan has breached your security. Some industry insiders wonder if your relationship with Bianca might be putting her at unnecessary risk." She leaned forward, the movement slight but significant. "Have you considered that someone from your world might be safer than exposing a civilian to these dangers?"

Charlie felt the trap closing—Morgan's question packaged concern for Bee's welfare inside an implication that their relationship was fundamentally mismatched. He measured his response, refusing to be rushed despite the cameras recording his every moment of hesitation.

"Security is something I take extremely seriously," he acknowledged, his voice level. "Not just for myself, but for anyone close to me. The Madison incident was disturbing, but it's been addressed comprehensively." He met Morgan's gaze directly. "As for who belongs in 'my world,' as you put it—I think Bee and I are quite capable of determining that for ourselves."

Morgan nodded, seemingly appreciative of his answer while already formulating her next approach. "Of course. Though sources close to you suggest this relationship is more publicity stunt than romance." Her tone sharpened, the pretense of casual inquiry falling away. "Care to comment?"

The accusation hung in the air between them. Charlie registered a slight movement from one of the camera operators —an adjustment to capture his reaction more precisely. He maintained his composure through another measured breath, though his fingers pressed more firmly into the armrests, the pressure grounding him against rising indignation.

"I'm curious about these 'sources close to me,'" he said, his tone conversational but underlaid with steel. "Because the people who actually know me understand that publicity is the last thing I seek in my personal life." He leaned back slightly in his chair, a subtle reclaiming of space. "I've never used relationships as career strategy, and I certainly wouldn't start now."

"And yet," Morgan countered, "the timing is interesting. Your last film underperformed. Trade publications speculated about your next contract. Then suddenly, there's this charming narrative about a wrong number text leading to unexpected romance." Her smile didn't reach her eyes. "It's like something from one of your romantic comedies."

. . .

Charlie felt heat rising at the base of his neck, a flush of anger he controlled through deliberate focus on his physical responses. "Life is full of unexpected connections," he replied, his smile matching hers in its professional restraint. "Sometimes reality is more surprising than fiction."

Morgan shifted strategies again, reaching for the tablet beside her chair. "I've been looking into Bianca's background," she said, glancing at the screen as if consulting notes, though Charlie suspected it was merely theatrical. "Retail management at mid-range boutiques. No college degree. No family connections in the industry." She looked up, her expression a perfect blend of confusion and condescension. "What I'm struggling to understand is what sustains your interest in someone with such an... unremarkable background."

The words landed like a physical blow, not for their criticism of him but for their dismissal of Bee—her intelligence, her strength, her fundamental worth reduced to credentials and connections. Something shifted inside Charlie, a tectonic movement beneath the carefully maintained surface of his public persona. His posture changed, body leaning forward, eyes focusing with an intensity that made Morgan blink.

"What you call unremarkable, I call refreshing, and it shows that even you can have moments of not doing your job thoroughly, Bee actually has a finance degree, and it was high end boutiques that she managed." he said, his voice dropping to a passionate intensity that commanded attention. "Bee sees me —not the celebrity, not the bank account—just me." The words emerged without calculation, without the filtering process that had governed his public statements for years. "Do you have any idea how rare that is?"

The studio fell silent, the ambient sounds of equipment and breathing seeming to fade beneath the unexpected authenticity of his response. From the corner of his eye, Charlie noticed crew members exchanging glances, sensing the shift in energy that transformed a routine celebrity interview into something more compelling.

"In an industry built on illusion," Charlie continued, "Bee stands firmly in reality. She calls me on my nonsense. She asks questions no one else would dare to ask. She makes me laugh —not the polite chuckle you offer at industry parties, but real laughter that comes from somewhere genuine." His hands had relaxed their grip on the armrests, now moving with natural emphasis as he spoke. "She's rebuilt a life multiple times through her own determination. She's faced down people who tried to make her feel small and emerged stronger."

Morgan's expression had shifted, the predatory focus giving way to something more attentive, more present. She had come seeking vulnerability to exploit, but found instead a passion that demanded respect.

"Before Bee," Charlie said, the words flowing now without the careful editing that had characterized his public speech for so long, "I measured success by industry metrics—box office returns, critical reception, the square footage of my home. She's helped me rediscover what actually matters." A smile touched his lips, genuine and unguarded. "Last week, we spent an entire day hiking a remote trail with no cameras, no recognition, just experiencing something beautiful together. That day is worth more to me than any premiere or award."

The red lights of the cameras continued their unblinking observation, but Charlie no longer felt their pressure. He was speaking not for their mechanical eyes but directly to anyone who might question the authenticity of what he and Bee had built together.

"She's taught me to value moments over appearances," he continued, the conviction in his voice resonating through the studio. "To find joy in ordinary things—a shared meal we cooked together, a debate about film endings that lasts until midnight, the simple pleasure of walking through a farmers market without an entourage." He paused, gathering thoughts that felt too important to express carelessly. "Bee doesn't care about the trappings of celebrity. She cares about substance—in herself, in me, in the life we're building."

Morgan's tablet lay forgotten beside her chair, her attention fully captured by the transformation occurring before her. The calculated interview she had planned had evolved into something she couldn't control but recognized as potentially more valuable—authentic emotion from a man known for his careful public image.

· · ·

"You speak about her with remarkable... conviction," Morgan observed, her tone lacking the sharp edge that had characterized her earlier questions.

"Because what we have is remarkable," Charlie replied simply. "Not in the way tabloids define it—not because of status or appearance or industry relevance. It's remarkable because it's real. Because we chose each other with open eyes, fully aware of the complications, and decided those complications were worth navigating together."

Charlie could feel the atmosphere in the studio had altered— the crew's attention shifted from professional observation to genuine engagement. A sound technician had leaned forward slightly, caught in the pull of unexpected sincerity. The camera operator directly to his left had softened her stance, the rigid professionalism giving way to human interest.

"When I'm with Bee," Charlie said, his voice quieter but no less intense, "I'm not performing. I'm not calculating how my words might be interpreted or how my actions might be perceived. I'm just living. Do you know how extraordinary that is for someone who's been in the public eye since their tweens?" He shook his head slightly, a gesture of wonder rather than denial. "She doesn't love Charlie Benton, movie star. She loves me—my flaws, my fears, my terrible taste in certain films, my tendency to overthink everything. She loves the person behind the carefully managed image."

· · ·

Morgan was silent for a moment, recalibrating her approach in real time. The predatory gleam had faded from her eyes, replaced by something more thoughtful, more measured. When she spoke again, her voice carried a different quality—less performance, more genuine curiosity.

"You've never spoken this way about previous relationships," she observed, the statement neither accusation nor praise, simply acknowledgment.

"No," Charlie agreed, a small smile touching his lips. "I haven't."

The simple confirmation hung in the air between them, more revealing than any elaborate explanation could have been. Morgan's expression shifted again, professional assessment recognizing that the interview had veered into territory more valuable than her planned provocations—authentic emotion from a celebrity known for careful control.

"We'll take a short break," she said, addressing the camera with practiced smoothness while her eyes remained on Charlie, recalculating, reassessing. "When we return, more of my conversation with Charlie Benton."

The red lights on the cameras dimmed, signaling the transition to commercial. Charlie exhaled slowly, becoming aware of the energy he'd expended in his passionate defense. The studio remained unusually quiet, the normal bustle of a commercial break subdued by the lingering impact of what had just transpired.

The director's countdown signaled their return from commercial, the studio lights seeming less harsh now, the atmosphere altered by what had transpired before the break. Charlie settled back in his chair, no longer feeling the stiffness of the leather as a deliberate discomfort but simply as a physical reality to be acknowledged and accepted. Morgan had used the brief pause to reapply lipstick and reset her professional demeanor, though something had changed in her approach—a subtle recalibration visible only to those practiced in reading the minute tells of calculated personas. The predatory edge had been replaced by something more measured, more journalistically sound. The red lights blinked on, and they were live again, Morgan turning toward the camera with practiced precision.

"Welcome back to Industry Insider. I'm Morgan Walsh, continuing my conversation with Charlie Benton." She shifted toward him, her posture professional but less aggressive than before. "Charlie, let's talk about your upcoming projects. There are rumors about a potential collaboration with director Elena Vasquez, who's known for her unflinching exploration of moral ambiguity. Can you confirm those discussions?"

The pivot was transparent—a retreat to safer professional territory after the unexpected emotional depth of their previous exchange. Charlie recognized the strategy, the attempt to reestablish control by returning to scripted questions with predictable answers.

"Elena is a remarkable filmmaker," he confirmed, his response measured but engaged. "We've had preliminary conversations about a project that explores themes of perception and reality—how we construct narratives about ourselves and others." He paused, noting the parallel to their current situation. "It's still in early development, but her vision is compelling."

Morgan nodded, seemingly relieved to return to the familiar rhythm of industry discussion. "Your production company has also optioned the rights to Richard Mercer's novel 'The Invisible Line.' What drew you to that material?"

"The central question it poses," Charlie replied, maintaining eye contact with a directness that had been absent in his earlier, more guarded responses. "How do we maintain authentic connections in a world that commodifies personal experience? That feels particularly relevant to me right now."

A subtle shift occurred in his posture—not disengagement, but gentle redirection. Charlie leaned forward slightly, reclaiming agency in the conversation's flow. "If you don't mind, Morgan, I'd like to address something important."

Morgan's eyebrow arched slightly—surprise at his assumption

of control tempered by journalistic interest in where he might take the conversation. "Of course."

"We've discussed my relationship with Bee, and I appreciate your questions, even the challenging ones." Charlie's voice carried the same authentic quality that had emerged during his passionate defense, but now tempered with deliberate calm. "I understand the public's fascination. When you've spent years watching someone on screen, it's natural to feel invested in their personal life."

He paused, choosing his words with care. The studio remained unusually quiet, crew members watching with undisguised interest—no longer simply recording but actively engaged in the unfolding moment.

"What I hope people can understand is that what Bee and I have built together is real and private," Charlie continued. "Not private in the sense of secretive or hidden, but private in the sense of personally meaningful—something that exists for us rather than for public consumption."

Morgan studied him, professional assessment recognizing the shift in dynamic—the interview subject gently but firmly establishing parameters. "Yet you chose a public life," she observed, the statement not accusatory but probing.

"I chose a public career," Charlie corrected with a small smile that held no antagonism. "There's a distinction worth making.

My work belongs to audiences—they can critique it, analyze it, love it or hate it. That's the contract I willingly entered." His fingers interlaced loosely in his lap, body language open rather than defensive. "But my relationship isn't a performance or a product. It's my life."

The subtle correction hung between them, not confrontational but clear in its boundary-setting. Morgan nodded slightly, acknowledging the distinction with unexpected respect.

"You mentioned the Madison Vale incident earlier," Charlie added, addressing directly what Morgan had attempted to use as a wedge. "That was deeply disturbing—an invasion of our home, our safety, our most private space. What made it worse was seeing it weaponized in the press, treated as entertainment rather than what it was: a violation that affected real people with real feelings."

Morgan's expression shifted, something almost like contrition crossing her features before her professional mask reasserted itself. "The line between news and entertainment has certainly blurred," she acknowledged, neither fully accepting responsibility nor entirely deflecting it.

"It has," Charlie agreed. "And I understand the ecosystem we all operate within. But I hope we can find a balance that acknowledges my gratitude for public support without treating my personal relationships as content to be consumed."

· · ·

The statement carried no accusation but established a clear position—respectful yet firm, grateful yet bounded. Morgan recognized the shift, professional instinct sensing a powerful closing moment rather than an adversarial stance.

"What would you say," she asked, leaning forward slightly, "to fans who feel entitled to details about your personal life? Who believe their support of your career grants them access to your private world?"

It was a complex question, layered with potential pitfalls—the risk of seeming ungrateful, entitled, or disconnected from the fan base that supported his career. Charlie took a moment, the pause not hesitation but thoughtful consideration.

"I would say thank you," he began, sincerity evident in his voice. "Thank you for caring enough to be interested, for connecting with my work, for supporting projects that matter to me." His expression warmed with genuine appreciation. "That connection is meaningful, and I don't take it for granted."

He shifted slightly in his chair, maintaining eye contact not just with Morgan but seeming to address the camera directly. "I'm grateful for my fans, truly. But my relationship isn't enter-tainment—it's my life. The same way their relationships with their partners, their families, their loved ones are their lives." The simplicity of the statement carried unexpected power. "I hope they can extend to Bee and me the same respect they would want for their own meaningful connections."

. . .

Morgan nodded, recognizing that they had arrived at a natural conclusion—not through her careful steering but through Charlie's authentic engagement. "Charlie Benton, thank you for joining us tonight. This has been... illuminating."

"Thank you for having me," he replied, the standard response carrying unexpected warmth.

The red lights on the cameras faded, signaling they were off air. The studio's atmosphere shifted immediately, the tension of live broadcast giving way to the relative privacy of production wrap-up. Crew members moved with renewed purpose, beginning the process of dismantling equipment and resetting the space.

Morgan remained seated, her professional persona slipping slightly as she regarded Charlie with newfound curiosity. "That was unexpectedly genuine," she admitted, extending her hand. "Not the interview I prepared for."

Charlie shook her hand, feeling the subtle equalization in their interaction—no longer interviewer and subject but two professionals acknowledging a shared experience. "Not the interview I expected to give," he replied with a small smile.

"Your PR team will be pleased," Morgan observed, gathering

her notes with practiced efficiency. "Though I suspect that wasn't your primary concern."

"It wasn't," Charlie acknowledged, rising from his chair as a technician approached to remove his microphone. "Though I hope I represented Bee and myself... accurately."

Morgan nodded, a hint of professional respect evident in her expression. "You did. For what it's worth, I think I understand now." She paused, considering her words with uncharacteristic care. "What you see in her. Why she matters."

The simple acknowledgment carried unexpected weight—recognition from someone who had begun the interview with dismissive condescension. Charlie nodded, accepting the statement for the concession it represented.

As the technician finished removing his microphone, Charlie reached for his phone, checking it for the first time since the interview began. Three messages from Bee appeared on his screen, the most recent sent just minutes ago:

Just watched the interview live. You were incredible. Boundaries, not walls. So proud of you. Coming home with celebratory takeout from that Thai place you love. I have dessert handled. x

· · ·

The simple message—supportive, practical, infused with her characteristic directness—made him smile despite the exhaustion settling into his muscles after the intensity of the past hour. He slipped the phone into his pocket, the weight of it against his hip a tangible connection to her even in her physical absence.

"Thank you again, Morgan," he said, extending his hand for a final farewell. "It was... unexpectedly valuable."

She accepted his hand, her grip firm and professional. "Next time you have something to say, my show is always open." A hint of her journalistic instinct resurfaced. "Especially if it's as compelling as today."

Charlie nodded, recognizing the professional respect in her offer. As he followed a production assistant toward the exit, he felt the subtle but significant shift in his relationship with the media machine that had both elevated and constrained him for years. Not a complete transformation, but a recalibration—boundaries established not through walls of silence or calculated performance, but through authentic engagement on his own terms.

Outside, the California afternoon sun felt warm against his face after the artificial cool of the studio—a physical reminder of the world beyond cameras and calculated questions. Charlie loosened his tie slightly, drawing a deep breath of unfiltered air as he reached for his phone again. He reread Bee's message, then typed a simple response:

. . .

Heading home now. Save me some pad thai. Can't wait to see you. Or what you have planned for dessert. x

The unaffected simplicity of the exchange—ordinary words between two people who had chosen each other despite extraordinary circumstances—felt like the most honest interview answer he could have possibly given.

Chapter Twenty-Two: A New Chapter

Morning light spilled through the wall of windows in Charlie's home office, fracturing into dust-moted beams as it filtered through the surrounding pines. The mountains rose beyond the glass in weathered blue waves, their ancient shoulders draped in fog that would burn away by mid-morning. Charlie adjusted his reading glasses, pushing them higher on the bridge of his nose as he turned another page of the script. His coffee—the third cup of the morning—had gone cold beside his right hand, forgotten in the absorption of his work. Outside, a mourning dove called to its mate, the sound piercing the comfortable silence that blanketed their secluded home.

Charlie sighed, reaching for the red pen he kept precisely aligned with his notebook. He made a single mark in the margin—a stark X that condemned the entire page—before flipping back to the script's cover. "The Arrangement," read the title page, followed by a logline promising a romantic comedy about a celebrity who hires a fake girlfriend to boost his image. Charlie set it atop the growing stack of rejected screenplays, a wry smile tugging at his lips. Once, he might have considered it—the box-office potential, the easy chemistry with whatever up-and-coming actress the studio paired him with, the comfortable familiarity of a genre that had built much of his early career.

Now it seemed hollow, almost offensive in its formulaic approach to something he had lived in far more complex dimensions.

He removed his glasses, pinching the bridge of his nose where they had left faint indentations in his skin. The morning had yielded four rejections and not a single prospect worth pursuing. His new criteria eliminated most of what his agent sent: no superficial treatments of relationships, no roles that glorified emotional unavailability, no characters whose development was sacrificed for plot convenience. The standards had cut his potential projects by two-thirds, but the ones that remained held substance that mattered.

Charlie reached for the coffee mug, grimacing slightly at the temperature before drinking it anyway. The ceramic was cool against his palm, a hand-thrown piece Bee had brought home from a local artisan's market. Its glaze reminded him of the ocean they'd left behind—blues and greens swirling into patterns that never repeated. Like so many things in their home, it carried meaning beyond its function, a tactile reminder of choices made together.

The next script in his diminishing pile bore a title embossed in silver foil: "The Unseen." Charlie opened to the first page, fountain pen poised to make his usual notations. Within three pages, his hand had stilled, the pen resting forgotten beside his notebook as he leaned forward, drawn into the narrative with an intensity he hadn't felt in months. The story unfolded with subtle complexity—a man rebuilding his life after losing everything, finding unexpected connection with a woman who saw beyond his carefully constructed facade. Not a romantic comedy, not an action thriller, but something that defied easy categorization.

Charlie's hand moved to his notebook, jotting observations in his precise handwriting. The protagonist's journey echoed elements of his own transformation without mimicking it directly. The dialogue carried authenticity rarely found in early drafts. Most importantly, the female lead existed as a fully realized character rather than a device for the male protagonist's growth.

He was fifty pages in when a movement across the hall caught his peripheral vision. Charlie glanced up, his focus shifting from fictional characters to the very real woman visible through his open door. Bee stood at her workbench, head bent in concentration, dark hair gathered in a loose knot at the nape of her neck. Sunlight caught the curve of her cheek, illuminating the slight furrow of concentration between her brows. Her hands moved with practiced precision over her work, fingers nimble as they folded tissue paper around something he couldn't quite see.

Charlie set the script aside, allowing himself a moment simply to watch her. After months together in their new house and their mountain sanctuary, the sight of her still caused a peculiar tightening in his chest—not the desperate intensity of their early days, but something deeper, more rooted. She wore faded jeans and one of his old sweatshirts, the sleeves pushed up to her elbows to keep them clear of her work. No makeup, no performative elements, just Bee in her natural state, focused and present.

The home around them held the comfortable silence of shared space—not the absence of sound but the presence of peace. Wind whispered through pine needles outside, creating a gentle susurration that formed the baseline of their mountain soundtrack. The old house creaked occasionally, settling into itself with sounds they'd learned to interpret like a familiar language. From Bee's workspace came the soft rustle of tissue paper, the snip of scissors, the barely audible hum of a melody she might not even realize she was voicing.

Charlie inhaled deeply, letting the scents of their home fill his lungs—pine and cedar from the forests surrounding them, coffee lingering from breakfast, the faint trace of the lavender sachets Bee tucked into dresser drawers, and underneath it all, the clean mountain air that had been their first requirement when searching for this property. No smog, no exhaust fumes, nothing manufactured or artificial.

Nine months had passed since Madison Vale's intrusion into their bedroom, since the security breach that had catalyzed their decision to create something new together. The mountain property, three hours from Los Angeles and deliberately omitted from any paperwork connected to Charlie's name, had become their true home while his coastal mansion transformed into an occasional workplace—a location for necessary meetings and a decoy for persistent paparazzi.

Here, among the pines and silence, they had built something neither had fully believed possible: ordinary life, extraordinary love, the balance of privacy and connection they'd struggled to find in the fishbowl of celebrity. No photographers hiding in bushes, no drones circling overhead (after the security team had dealt with the first few attempts), no Madison Vales breaching their sanctuary.

Across the hall, Bee looked up suddenly, as if sensing his attention. Their eyes met through the two doorways, and her expression softened, lips curving into the smile she reserved only for him—the one that created a dimple in her left cheek and crinkled the corners of her eyes. She didn't wave or speak, just held his gaze for a long moment of wordless communication, an entire conversation contained in the simple acknowledgment of each other's presence.

Charlie smiled back, the gesture as natural as breathing,

before she returned to her work and he to his. The script beckoned, but he allowed himself another moment to absorb the quiet perfection of this ordinary Tuesday morning—the mountain light, the comfortable silence, the woman across the hall who had transformed his definition of home.

Bee smoothed the tissue paper with practiced fingers, creating crisp corners before folding it around the hand-dyed silk scarf. The shimmering fabric—an interplay of indigo and cerulean that she'd designed specifically for winter collections—disappeared beneath the delicate wrapping. She secured it with a length of midnight-blue ribbon, tying it with the precise bow that had become her signature packaging style. The simple logo stamped on the cream-colored tag read "Nectar & Hive"—the name she'd chosen for her boutique business, a playful nod to her nickname that only those closest to her would recognize.

The converted sunroom that served as her studio captured the best light in the house, with windows on three sides framing the surrounding forest like living artwork. Pine boughs swayed gently outside, casting shifting shadows across her workbench—a solid oak slab Charlie had found at an estate sale and refinished himself, his hands sanding away decades of neglect to reveal the honey-colored grain beneath. Bee's workspace reflected the meticulous organization she'd developed through years in retail management: shipping supplies arranged in clear acrylic containers, inventory tracked in a leather-bound ledger, her design sketches pinned to a cork board above her sewing machine.

She reached for the next order from her carefully arranged queue—a cashmere-blend wrap in muted sage that complemented the customer's previous purchases. Bee knew most of her clients by name now, though they knew her only as the anonymous artisan behind Nectar & Hive. She had cultivated a dedicated following who appreciated both her aesthetic and her philosophy of timeless, versatile pieces that transcended seasonal trends.

"This is for Elaine in Chicago," she murmured to herself, consulting the handwritten note she included with each order. "Her daughter's medical school graduation." Bee smiled, remembering the detailed message Elaine had included with her order—how the wrap would be a surprise for a daughter who had studied through bitter Midwestern winters, how the sage green matched her eyes. These personal connections, these glimpses into strangers' lives and celebrations, had become an unexpected joy of her new venture.

The transition from retail manager to independent business owner hadn't been straightforward. After withdrawing from consideration at Luxe Boutique, Bee had spent weeks questioning her path forward, caught between her love for Charlie and her need for professional identity. The solution had emerged organically during their search for a new home— a place away from paparazzi and invasive fans.

"I need something that's mine," she had told Charlie one evening, curled against him on the sofa of his coastal mansion while security cameras swept the perimeter outside. "Something that uses my skills but doesn't put me on display."

They had brainstormed together, her retail expertise meeting his understanding of navigating public life while preserving private space. Bee's eye for quality accessories, her connections with artisans and suppliers, and her talent for identifying gaps in the market had coalesced into Nectar & Hive—a boutique online business specializing in limited-edition accessories designed by Bee and produced in collaboration with carefully selected craftspeople.

Now, eight months later, her business operated entirely on her terms. No physical storefront meant no curious customers hoping to glimpse Charlie Benton's girlfriend. No staff meant no workplace gossip. Her name appeared nowhere on the website or packaging, allowing her work to stand on its own merits rather than riding the coattails of Charlie's fame. The separation had been deliberate and absolute—a boundary, not a wall, between her professional identity and her personal life.

Bee hummed softly as she completed the packaging, adding a handwritten thank-you note before placing the wrapped parcel in a branded box. The melody—something from the playlist Charlie had created for her workshop—flowed unconsciously from her lips as she moved through the familiar rhythm of her process. Each package received the same careful attention, each note personalized with details that transformed a transaction into a connection.

Her eyes drifted to the wall beside her desk, where dozens of customer thank-you notes created a patchwork of appreciation. Unlike the glossy magazine clippings that had once documented her relationship with Charlie, these represented genuine connection without the distortion of public scrutiny. A teacher in Maine who wore Bee's scarf to receive a state award. A grandmother in Texas who had ordered matching wraps for herself and her granddaughters. A cancer survivor in Oregon who wrote that wearing beautiful things helped her reclaim her sense of self.

These stories, these connections formed through craft rather than celebrity, had become Bee's private constellation of meaning—points of light that illuminated the path she'd chosen. Charlie understood this in ways she never had to explain. He recognized her need for purpose beyond being "Charlie Benton's girlfriend," just as she understood his need for roles that reflected his evolving sense of self.

The business had grown steadily through word-of-mouth and carefully targeted online marketing, reaching a sustainable level that allowed Bee to maintain quality and personal connection without becoming overwhelming. She had declined several offers to expand into department stores, choosing instead to preserve the direct-to-customer relationship that kept her work meaningful.

Bee glanced up from sealing another package, her eyes finding Charlie through the doorway of his office. He sat with his reading glasses perched on his nose, completely absorbed in a script that seemed to have captured his attention. The slight furrow between his brows signaled deep concentration—a good sign after weeks of rejecting projects that failed to meet his increasingly selective standards. She watched his hand move to make a note in the margin, the gesture deliberate and thoughtful.

As if sensing her gaze, Charlie looked up, their eyes meeting across the hallway that separated their workspaces. The smile that spread across his face—slow and genuine, crinkling the corners of his eyes in the way that never appeared in his professional photographs—sent a familiar warmth through Bee's chest. Six months of waking beside him in their mountain retreat had done nothing to diminish the simple joy of these exchanged glances, these moments of wordless connection amid their separate pursuits.

Charlie lifted his coffee mug slightly in question. Bee nodded, touching her own empty tea mug in acknowledgment. Without speaking, he rose and disappeared toward the kitchen, the familiar pattern of their days unfolding with comfortable predictability. They had developed a language of small gestures and shared routines, a dance of independence and togetherness that required no audience.

Bee returned to her packaging, fingers moving with practiced efficiency as she prepared the day's shipments. Through the open windows, the scent of pine mingled with the approaching promise of rain—a perfect afternoon for working indoors while mountain weather painted shifting patterns across the forest. The life they had built here contained none of the glamour that tabloids associated with Charlie Benton, none of the public performance that had characterized their early relationship. Instead, it offered something far more precious: authenticity, privacy, the freedom to be fully themselves both together and apart.

She tied another perfect bow, smoothed another handwritten note, and savored the quiet satisfaction of work that was entirely her own—connected to her past expertise but unburdened by the complications that had followed her relationship with Charlie. Nectar & Hive existed in a space outside public scrutiny, a creation that honored both her need for independence and her desire for meaningful work. Like their mountain home, it represented a boundary thoughtfully maintained rather than a wall hastily erected—a distinction that had become central to their shared philosophy.

A flash of movement caught Charlie's eye—something mechanical and deliberate hovering just beyond the line of pines that marked their property boundary. He set the script aside, reaching for the binoculars he kept in his desk drawer for birdwatching. Through the magnified lenses, the object came into focus: a drone, its camera lens glinting in the midday sun as it hovered with unnatural stillness, pointed directly at their home. Charlie lowered the binoculars, his expression shifting not to alarm but to resigned familiarity. They had prepared for this eventuality—it wasn't a question of if but when.

"Bee," he called, his voice measured and calm. "Protocol three."

Across the hall, Bee's hands stilled on her packaging. She didn't ask questions or rush to the window. Instead, she reached beneath her workbench and pressed a small button— the silent alarm that would alert their security team stationed in the guesthouse a quarter-mile down the private road.

"Location?" she asked, already moving toward the tablet mounted on her studio wall.

"Northwest boundary, about fifty yards beyond the creek bend." Charlie rose from his desk, moving with deliberate calm rather than hurried panic. "Looks commercial-grade. Not the neighbor's kid this time."

They moved in parallel, a choreography developed through multiple rehearsals and occasional real implementations. Charlie proceeded methodically through the house, closing blinds in a specific sequence designed to thwart any attempt to piece together the home's floor plan from fragmented footage. The custom blinds—a specialty material that appeared ordinary but prevented thermal imaging—descended with quiet efficiency, transforming sun-filled rooms into private spaces within seconds.

Bee accessed the security system through the tablet, her fingers moving across the screen with practiced precision. The property's defensive measures activated in sequential order: perimeter sensors heightened to maximum sensitivity, cameras disguised as landscape lighting pivoted to track the intruder, and a decoy signal initiated from their communications hub to confuse any attempt at electronic eavesdropping.

"Sending statement alpha to Toby," she said, tapping a final command that dispatched their pre-written response to intrusions—a brief, legally vetted paragraph that their publicist could release if the drone footage appeared online. After several such incidents at Charlie's coastal property, they had developed a library of prepared statements, each calibrated to different types of privacy violations.

Charlie completed his circuit of the house, the last set of blinds closing with a soft click. The home's atmosphere transformed, shifting from sun-dappled openness to a dimmer, more contained environment. He rejoined Bee in the central hallway, their movements converging with the practiced timing of dance partners.

"Security confirms visual," Bee reported, glancing at her

phone where a text had appeared. "They're deploying the counter-measure."

Charlie nodded, his hand finding the small of her back in a gesture both protective and grounding. "How are you doing?"

The question—simple but weighted with shared history—acknowledged what these moments still cost them. Despite their preparations, despite the systems they had developed to handle intrusions, each breach carried echoes of Madison Vale standing in their bedroom, of photographers shouting questions at Bee outside Luxe Boutique, of private moments transformed into public consumption.

"I'm good," Bee answered, leaning slightly into his touch. "Better than last time." Her voice carried no tremor, her eyes meeting his with clear determination rather than anxiety. "You?"

"Annoyed, not rattled," he confirmed, the distinction important to them both.

Their security measures had evolved with each violation, growing more sophisticated as they learned the patterns of intrusion. The property itself had been selected with privacy as the primary consideration—twenty acres of forested mountain land with a single access road and natural boundaries that complicated aerial surveillance. The house sat in a small clearing surrounded by old-growth pines, their dense canopy providing overhead coverage that drones had to descend below to capture usable footage.

The security system represented the culmination of bitter experience transformed into proactive protection. After Madison's breach of their coastal home, Charlie had worked with specialists to develop a comprehensive approach that balanced their desire for natural living with their need for privacy. Cameras disguised as landscape features monitored the property's perimeter without creating the fortress-like appearance they had both rejected. Motion sensors differentiated between wildlife and human intruders. The windows—specially designed with a film that appeared transparent from inside but prevented clear visibility from outside—allowed them to maintain their connection to the surrounding forest.

Most importantly, they had developed protocols—numbered responses to different types of intrusions that eliminated the need for panicked reactions or extended discussions in the moment. Protocol three: drone sighting, minimal visible response, no acknowledgment of awareness. The goal was not to provide reaction footage that would make the intrusion more valuable to whoever had sent the drone.

"Counter-measure deployed," came the text update on Bee's phone.

Charlie glanced at the security tablet, where a split-screen display showed the drone's position and the response: their own security drone, launching from a concealed position to intercept the intruder. The security drone carried no weapons, no dramatic technological interventions—just a programmed flight path that would position it between the intruder and the house, blocking camera angles and escorting the unwelcome visitor back beyond property lines.

"Should be over in about five minutes," Charlie noted, watching the two mechanical objects on the screen. "Want some tea while we wait?"

The deliberate normality of the question reflected their shared philosophy: acknowledgment without surrender. They would take necessary precautions, implement their security protocols, and then continue their day rather than allowing the intrusion to claim more time and emotional energy than it deserved.

Bee nodded, following him to the kitchen where the electric kettle waited. The house remained dim with the blinds drawn, but the space felt secure rather than confining—a temporary adjustment rather than a permanent retreat. As

Charlie filled the kettle, Bee leaned against the counter beside him, their shoulders touching in casual intimacy.

"I think it's been almost three months since the last one," she observed, reaching for mugs from the cabinet. "Longer than before."

"They're getting less frequent," Charlie agreed, selecting tea bags from the wooden box on the counter. "The new property registration seems to be working."

The paperwork for their mountain home existed under layers of LLCs and blind trusts, disconnected from either of their names. The strategy—developed with attorneys after repeated breaches at the coastal property—had proven more effective than they'd initially hoped. Combined with their minimal trips to Los Angeles and careful management of Charlie's public appearances, it had created genuine privacy that only occasional intrusions interrupted.

The heavy bolt on their front door—installed the day they moved in—gleamed in the dimmed light of the kitchen, a tangible symbol of the boundaries they maintained. Unlike the elaborate electronic security at Charlie's coastal mansion, this home's protections blended into its rustic character— reinforced windows disguised as traditional wooden frames, security cameras weathered to match the exterior lighting, bolt locks that appeared decorative but could withstand significant force.

"Do you ever regret it?" Charlie asked suddenly, the question emerging in the intimate space between them as the kettle began to heat. "Choosing this life? All the precautions, the protocols?"

Bee turned to face him fully, her expression softening as she reached up to brush a strand of hair from his forehead. "Not for a second," she said, the simplicity of her answer carrying the weight of absolute certainty. "This is our life, not entertainment—remember? We decided that together."

Charlie smiled, recognizing his own words from the statement they had crafted in his dining room months ago. He leaned forward, pressing his forehead gently against hers in a gesture more intimate than a kiss—a moment of connection that no drone could capture, no tabloid could commodify.

"Security confirms intruder has retreated," came the update on Bee's phone. "All clear."

They remained still for a moment longer, sharing breath in the quiet kitchen before separating to finish making tea. Outside, beyond the drawn blinds, their security team would be conducting a thorough perimeter check, ensuring the drone had truly departed rather than repositioned. Inside, Charlie and Bee moved with the comfortable synchronicity of partners who had faced worse intrusions and emerged stronger for them.

The blinds would open again soon. The sunlight would return to their spaces. The protocols had served their purpose, allowing them to respond without reacting, to protect without retreating. The intrusion had created a moment of tension but failed to disrupt the foundation of the life they had built together—solid ground beneath the occasional tremors of unwanted attention.

The delivery truck's departure left behind a cardboard box that sat accusingly on their kitchen island, its contents exposed to reveal the damage. Specialty paper—hand-marbled sheets in blues and golds that Bee used for wrapping her most premium items—had been crushed beneath a broken bottle of olive oil from their grocery delivery. The liquid had seeped through the packaging, transforming the delicate papers into soggy, stained masses. Bee stood with her hands on her hips, surveying the mess with a measured breath that would have been a frustrated sigh in their earlier days together.

"That's the last of my winter packaging," she said, carefully lifting a sheet that disintegrated between her fingers. "I have eight orders promised for delivery by Friday, all using this paper." Her voice remained steady, analytical rather than panicked. "And the artisan who makes it is away at a craft fair in Vermont until next week."

The evening light had begun its slow retreat, casting long shadows through the kitchen windows recently reopened after the drone incident hours earlier. Charlie abandoned the recipe he'd been reviewing for dinner, moving to stand beside Bee at the island. His shoulder brushed against hers as he assessed the damage, their bodies aligning with the comfortable familiarity of frequent contact.

"How many sheets do you need to fulfill the current orders?" he asked, already reaching for a notepad on the counter.

"Sixteen at minimum," Bee replied, methodically separating the ruined papers from the few salvageable pieces. "But I like to have extras in case of mistakes."

Charlie nodded, making notes in his precise handwriting. "And the ribbons?" he asked, gesturing toward the spools of hand-dyed silk that had partially escaped the oil's destruction.

"Three spools completely ruined," Bee confirmed, her fingers stained as she unwound a length of midnight-blue silk to check for damage. "I need at least two colors for the outstanding orders."

Without discussion, Charlie shifted into problem-solving mode, clearing space on the island to spread out Bee's order book and shipping calendar. This was not the first logistical challenge they had faced together, nor would it be the last. What had changed was their approach—the calm assessment that had replaced anxious reaction, the immediate partnership that required no negotiation.

"Show me which orders are affected," Charlie said, standing close enough that his arm pressed against hers as they bent over the leather-bound book. The physical contact—

casual, constant, unconscious—reflected the evolution of their relationship from the careful distance of early days to the comfortable intimacy of shared space.

Bee flipped through her order book, indicating eight entries with her finger. "These are all high-end pieces—the cashmere wraps and hand-painted silk scarves. They're the ones I promised the special winter packaging for."

Charlie studied the list, his reading glasses perched on his nose in a gesture Bee found endearing despite the circumstances. "What if we created an alternative packaging concept?" he suggested. "Something equally special but different. We could present it as a limited edition rather than a compromise."

His use of "we" came naturally now, the boundaries between her business and their shared life comfortably blurred without either losing its distinct identity. Charlie respected Nectar & Hive as Bee's creation while offering support that never crossed into management or control.

"I have those sheets of handmade paper from the Japanese artisan we met at the arts festival," Bee said, her mind already recalibrating around the possibility. "They're cream rather than blue, but the texture is extraordinary."

"And what about using dried lavender stems instead of ribbon?" Charlie added, gesturing toward the garden visible through the kitchen window. "We have plenty from your fall harvest, and it would add a sensory element to the unboxing experience."

Bee nodded, already reaching for a fresh sheet in her notebook to sketch the new concept. Charlie moved around the island to the refrigerator, returning with two glasses of the local pinot noir they'd discovered on a weekend exploration of nearby vineyards. He set one beside her, his fingers lingering briefly against hers in a touch that communicated support without interrupting her creative process.

"What about the messaging to customers?" he asked, leaning against the counter as she worked. "We should frame it positively."

Bee's pen moved across the page, outlining a new design that incorporated elements they already had on hand. "I'll explain that I've created a special winter solstice packaging available only to select customers," she said, the solution taking shape beneath her hands. "I can emphasize the connection to our mountain home—the lavender we grew, the paper made by the artist who works just over the ridge."

Charlie smiled, watching her transform potential disappointment into opportunity. "They'll probably request it specifically next time," he observed, taking a sip of his drink.

They worked side by side at the kitchen island, Bee sketching packaging concepts while Charlie organized the available materials. The mess of oil-soaked paper was cleared away, replaced by fresh possibilities spread across the wooden surface. Charlie's hands moved alongside Bee's, sometimes passing materials, sometimes briefly covering hers in moments of connection that punctuated their work.

"Remember when this would have sent us both spiraling?" Bee asked, looking up from her design to find Charlie's eyes on her, warm with appreciation. "Me panicking about customer expectations, you worrying that I was unhappy?"

Charlie laughed, the sound soft and genuine. "I would have immediately offered to charter a private plane to Vermont to track down your paper artisan," he admitted, "completely missing the point that you didn't need a grand gesture, just practical support."

Bee leaned into him slightly, her shoulder pressing against his chest in a moment of affectionate contact. "And I would have insisted I could handle it alone because I was so determined to prove my independence."

"We've come a long way," Charlie acknowledged, his arm slipping naturally around her waist.

The statement held layers of meaning beyond the simple words—acknowledgment of the journey from their first tentative connections through public scrutiny, security breaches, and the carefully constructed peace they now shared. They had learned to navigate challenges as partners rather than as individuals merely occupying adjacent space.

"That's why we're better at solving things together," Bee said, echoing his earlier thought as she reached for her wine glass. "We've figured out the balance."

Outside, the mountain dusk had settled into deeper blues, the forest transitioning toward evening stillness. Charlie glanced at the clock, then back to the supplies they had organized on the counter. "Do you want to keep working, or shall I start dinner? We could eat on the deck if you're up for it."

The question contained no pressure, only options. Another evolution in their relationship—the understanding that sometimes work took precedence, that flexibility served them better than rigid expectations. Bee surveyed the materials they had assembled, the sketch of her new packaging concept nearly complete.

"I can finish the prototype tomorrow," she decided, closing her notebook. "Dinner on the deck sounds perfect."

They moved together through the familiar ritual of meal preparation, Charlie handling the main course while Bee assembled a salad from greens they had grown in their kitchen garden. Their movements around each other had the fluid choreography of long practice—anticipating needs, sharing space, brief touches exchanged like punctuation in their physical conversation.

An hour later, they sat across from each other at the small table on their deck, candles flickering between them as twilight deepened around the mountains. The day's challenges—the drone intrusion, the damaged supplies—had been addressed and set aside, neither dismissed nor allowed to dominate their evening. Charlie raised his glass slightly, the candlelight catching in the ruby depths of the wine.

"To creative solutions," he offered, his eyes holding hers across the small distance.

"And to partners who make them possible," Bee completed, touching her glass to his with a delicate chime that carried across the quiet deck.

Above them, stars emerged in the darkening sky, pinpricks of light unclouded by city glow. Around them, the forest settled into nocturnal rhythms—owl calls, the rustle of night creatures, the gentle whisper of wind through pine needles. Their mountain sanctuary, hard-won and carefully protected, held them in its peaceful embrace as they shared the meal they had prepared together, their conversation flowing with the comfortable intimacy of two people who had found their way through chaos to something solid and enduring.

The candles burned lower, casting golden light across their faces as evening deepened into night. Tomorrow would bring new packages to prepare, scripts to review, perhaps another boundary to defend. But tonight, in the quiet space they had created together, Charlie and Bee simply existed in the present moment—connected, content, and completely themselves.

Chapter Twenty-Three:
The Surprise Party

The mountain road wound higher as Charlie guided his least conspicuous vehicle—a dark blue SUV with no connection to his public image—around curves that revealed then concealed vistas of forested valleys. Beside him, Bee hummed along to the radio, her fingers tapping a rhythm against the window frame as the late afternoon sun caught in her hair. The invitation to dinner at John's new mountain retreat had been a welcome break from their careful routine, a chance to share their sanctuary with someone who understood its value.

"John mentioned something about a local pinot he discovered," Charlie said, downshifting as they approached another switchback. "Said it puts ours to shame."

"Fighting words," Bee replied, smiling as she tucked a strand of hair behind her ear. "Think this place is as remote as ours?"

Charlie nodded, appreciating her practical question that acknowledged their shared priority: privacy. "John gets it. He used an LLC structure similar to ours for the purchase. And he's even deeper into the mountains—another twenty minutes past the nearest town."

The road narrowed, trees pressing closer on either side as they climbed. Their mountain home had taught them to appreciate these natural barriers—dense forest and winding roads discouraged casual visitors, created buffer zones that security systems alone couldn't provide. John's invitation had specified directions rather than an address, another layer of protection they both recognized and valued.

"That must be it," Bee said, pointing toward a wooden sign nearly hidden among pine branches, the name "Highpoint" carved in simple letters. Charlie turned onto a gravel drive that curved up through a stand of aspens, their leaves trembling silver-green in the early evening light.

"That's... a lot of cars," he observed, tension immediately tightening his shoulders as they emerged into a clearing where several vehicles were parked in a neat row. He slowed, eyes scanning the surroundings with the habitual wariness that had become second nature. "John didn't mention other guests."

Bee's hand came to rest on his forearm, warm and grounding. "They look like rental SUVs, not media vans," she noted, her retail-trained eye for detail shifting to their new context. "And no cameras that I can see."

Charlie nodded, forcing his fingers to relax on the steering wheel as he pulled alongside the other vehicles. They had developed a shared language for assessing situations, reading potential threats, distinguishing between normal variation and actual concern. This fell into uncertain territory—unexpected but not immediately alarming.

They followed a stone path from the parking area, rounding the side of a timber-framed house that echoed the rustic elegance of their own retreat. The sound of voices carried on the evening air—conversation, laughter, the clink of glasses—along with the gentle notes of acoustic guitar. Charlie's pace slowed, his body unconsciously positioning itself slightly in front of Bee's, a protective habit formed through months of navigating public spaces together.

The path opened onto a terraced garden that stepped down the mountainside in elegant tiers. String lights hung in graceful arcs overhead, their soft glow complemented by paper lanterns that swayed gently in the mountain breeze. Flowering vines climbed trellises, their blooms pale against the deepening blue of twilight. And throughout the space, scattered at tables draped in simple linen, were people—not strangers with hungry cameras and probing questions, but familiar faces turning toward them with genuine warmth.

Charlie's parents rose from a nearby table, his mother's hands clasped in delight. His father, rarely demonstrative, stood with uncharacteristic eagerness. Bee's closest friend from college waved from across the garden, seated beside Charlie's long-time agent Toby. Even Victoria, the hotel concierge who had first connected them, stood near a small bar, raising a glass in their direction.

Before either could process the scene, John appeared between two lantern-lit trees, arms spread wide in theatrical welcome, his familiar grin both mischievous and affectionate.

"The guests of honour arrive!" he announced, voice carrying across the gathering without need for microphones or amplification. "Just in time!"

Champagne corks popped somewhere in the background, the sound startling in its festivity. Charlie's arm instinctively encircled Bee's waist, drawing her closer as confusion replaced his initial tension.

"John," he began, his voice lowered as his brother approached. "What is this?"

John's grin widened as he embraced Charlie, then Bee, with exuberant affection. "Your engagement party, of course!"

he declared, just loudly enough for nearby guests to hear and smile in response.

Bee's body tensed against Charlie's side, her confusion evident in the slight furrow between her brows. "But we're not —" she began, keeping her voice to a whisper.

"Not officially engaged yet, I know," John interrupted, his voice dropping to match their hushed tones while his expression remained jubilantly proud for any watching eyes. "But I needed a good reason to get everyone here without raising suspicions. 'Casual dinner' wouldn't have brought Mom and Dad up from Arizona, would it?"

Charlie stared at his brother, comprehension dawning. "You... manufactured an engagement party? For us?"

"I orchestrated a gathering of people who love you, in a secure location, with no press, no publicists beyond Toby— who's family anyway—and no agenda beyond celebration." John's expression softened, the teasing giving way to sincerity. "When was the last time you had that, Charlie?"

The question hung between them, its simple truth disarming Charlie's instinctive objection. He glanced around the garden again, seeing not intrusion but invitation, not exposure but sanctuary. Every face belonged to someone who had earned their trust, who had protected rather than exploited their privacy, who had valued them as people rather than assets or entertainment.

"But..." Bee hesitated, her practical nature asserting itself even as her expression softened. "Won't this create expectations? Questions?"

John shook his head, gesturing toward the gathered guests now engaged in their own conversations, giving the three of them space for private discussion. "Everyone here understands discretion. I made that abundantly clear in the invitations. This is a bubble, Bee—a few precious hours where you two can just... be. With people who care about you."

Charlie felt something tight within his chest begin to loosen, a knot of habitual caution slowly unwinding. His gaze met Bee's, finding in her eyes the same cautious hope that rose within him—the possibility of normalcy, of celebration uncomplicated by the machinery of celebrity.

"Besides," John added, his grin returning as he pulled two flutes of champagne from a passing tray and handed them over, "I've already told everyone this is just a 'pre-engagement' celebration—my way of encouraging my commitment-phobic brother to make an honest woman of you, Bee."

Before either could respond, John turned toward the gathering, raising his own glass high. "Everyone! A toast to my brother Charlie, who has finally—miraculously—found someone willing to tolerate his terrible taste in action movies, his obsessive organization of the spice rack, and his inability to tell a joke without explaining the punchline!"

Laughter rippled through the garden, warm and genuine. Glasses rose in response, faces turned toward them with affection rather than the hungry curiosity they had grown accustomed to deflecting.

"To Charlie and Bee," John continued, his teasing tone softening into something more sincere. "Who remind us that real connection isn't about status or spotlight, but about seeing each other—truly seeing—and choosing each other anyway."

"To Charlie and Bee," echoed the gathered voices, the simple phrase carrying none of the artificial polish of industry functions or the invasive entitlement of public attention.

Beneath the table where they had been guided to sit, Bee's hand found Charlie's, her fingers intertwining with his in a gesture that had become their private language. He squeezed gently, meeting her eyes over the rim of his champagne flute. No words passed between them, none were needed—just the shared recognition of this rare gift: a moment of celebration that asked nothing of them beyond their presence, that required no performance, no carefully maintained boundaries.

For one evening, they could simply be Charlie and Bee, surrounded by love that sought nothing beyond their happiness.

The party flowed around them like water finding its natural course, conversations forming and reforming in organic patterns as guests moved between tables with the easy familiarity of people connected by genuine bonds rather than industry obligations. Charlie found himself accepting congratulations with a strange blend of awkwardness and gratitude—awkward because the engagement wasn't yet real, grateful because the warm wishes came without cameras documenting every reaction, without journalists dissecting every word for hidden meaning.

"Your secret mountain hideaway suits you," Toby said, clinking glasses with Charlie as they stood near a stone fire pit where flames cast dancing shadows across the flagstone terrace. "You look... unburdened."

Charlie smiled, appreciating his agent's characteristic directness. "Funny how not being stalked by drones improves one's complexion."

"And Bee?" Toby asked, his gaze shifting toward where she stood across the garden.

"Thriving," Charlie answered, his own eyes following the same path. "Her business is growing exactly how she wanted—slowly, authentically. No shortcuts, no leveraging my name."

They fell silent, watching as Bee gestured animatedly while speaking to Charlie's parents. His mother leaned forward, completely engaged, while his father—a man who had built his accounting practice on careful reserve—threw his head back in unexpected laughter. The sound carried across the garden, startling in its rarity.

"I've never seen your father laugh like that at industry functions," Toby observed.

"He doesn't," Charlie confirmed, something warm unfurling in his chest as he watched the interaction. "Dad keeps his professional face on for those. This is... different."

Charlie excused himself from Toby, drifting closer to catch fragments of Bee's story—something about a customer who had ordered a custom scarf with very specific requirements, only to return it because the package didn't smell "expensive enough." Bee's delivery was pitch-perfect, her timing drawing another round of laughter from his parents.

"So I started infusing the tissue paper with this essential oil blend that costs practically nothing," she concluded, "and now I get emails about how 'luxuriously aromatic' my packaging is."

"Perception is everything," his father nodded, his expression holding none of the careful assessment he typically reserved for Charlie's career decisions. "Smart business adaptation."

"That's our Bee," his mother added, reaching to pat Bee's hand with easy affection. "Always seeing the practical solution while the rest of us overthink."

Our Bee. The simple phrase echoed in Charlie's mind, settling somewhere deep and permanent. He watched as his mother—who had weathered decades of scrutiny as the parent of a child star turned A-list actor—treated Bee not as his latest relationship but as family. There was no performance in her affection, no careful calculation of how this connection might affect her son's public image or career trajectory.

The realization that had been forming for months crystallized in that moment: Bee wasn't just the woman he loved; she was the future he wanted. Not someday, not when the timing was perfect, but now—in this garden surrounded by the only people who truly saw them.

The music shifted as twilight deepened into evening, acoustic guitars giving way to string quartets playing slower melodies that drifted through the garden like another layer of scent alongside the jasmine and roses. Lanterns glowed more prominently against the darkening sky, their light catching in the crystal glasses and creating pools of gold on the wooden tables. Conversations quieted slightly, becoming more intimate as the space transformed around them.

Charlie's gaze swept across the gathered faces—each one representing a piece of his or Bee's life untainted by the machinery of fame. These were the people who called when security breaches made the news to check on their wellbeing rather than for exclusive details. The ones who respected their boundaries instead of probing for weaknesses. The ones who loved them for reasons that had nothing to do with red carpets or magazine covers.

Across the garden, Charlie caught John's eye. His brother had been moving between guests with the practiced ease of a natural host, ensuring glasses remained filled and conversations flowing. Now he stood still, watching Charlie with an expression that shifted from inquiry to understanding. Something passed between them—a silent communication honed through decades of shared experiences and private language.

John nodded once, decisively, before excusing himself from his conversation. Charlie watched as his brother disappeared into the house, returning moments later with purposeful strides. As John approached, his hand slipped into his jacket pocket with casual precision.

"Walk with me a minute?" John suggested, guiding Charlie toward a quieter corner of the garden where a stone bench sat beneath an arbor heavy with night-blooming vines. "I have something for you."

Charlie followed, curious and suddenly nervous without

fully understanding why. The bench was cool beneath them as they sat, the party continuing at a comfortable distance.

"I had a feeling," John began, his typical teasing absent for once, "watching you two these past months. The way you look at her when you think no one's paying attention."

"Is it that obvious?" Charlie asked, his voice lower than the music that provided gentle cover for their conversation.

John smiled, the expression softening his features in the lantern light. "Only to someone who's known you your entire life." He reached into his pocket, withdrawing a small velvet box that caught the light as it passed between them. "This was Grandma's. Mum gave it to me last year to hold until... well, until you found the right person."

Charlie's fingers closed around the box, its weight insignificant compared to what it represented. His palm felt suddenly damp, heart accelerating as the abstract notion of "someday" collapsed into the immediate present.

"I've been thinking about it," he admitted, not opening the box yet, feeling its contours against his skin. "Kept telling myself to wait for the perfect moment, which is another way of saying I was overthinking it. Again."

"You? Overthinking?" John's teasing tone returned, though gentler than his usual ribbing. "Shocking development."

Charlie smiled despite the nervous energy coursing through him. "I didn't have a ring yet. Wasn't sure how to buy one without the purchase becoming public knowledge before I could even ask her."

"Grandma's ring has no digital footprint," John pointed out. "No sales record, no insurance adjustment, no trail for anyone to follow." He glanced toward where Bee still sat with their parents, now joined by her college friend. "It's also a classic design that suits her—elegant without being flashy."

Charlie finally opened the box, revealing a platinum band

supporting a cushion-cut diamond flanked by smaller sapphires. The setting was vintage without appearing dated, the stones catching and refracting the garden lights in brilliant prisms.

"It's perfect," he breathed, closing the box carefully and slipping it into his own pocket, where it seemed to radiate warmth against his thigh. "But tonight? Is that too... convenient? Following your fake engagement party with a real proposal?"

John considered this, his expression thoughtful. "I arranged this gathering because I saw you were ready but stalling. The party is just context—the decision is yours." He stood, clapping Charlie on the shoulder. "Though I wouldn't mind being upgraded from host of a 'pre-engagement celebration' to the brother who facilitated the real thing."

As John returned to his hosting duties, Charlie remained on the bench, his hand occasionally pressing against his pocket to confirm the box's presence. Across the garden, Bee had moved to help a server arrange a dessert display, her practical nature making her an automatic participant rather than a passive guest. She laughed at something the young woman said, her head tilting back slightly, throat exposed in a moment of unguarded joy.

The garden had transformed fully into its evening enchantment, string lights reflecting in wine glasses and casting gentle illumination across faces relaxed by good food and better company. The music wrapped around conversations like silk, binding disparate moments into a cohesive whole. Charlie watched as Bee moved through this magical setting, her simple navy dress catching the light as she turned, the woman he loved utterly herself among people who recognized her value independent of her connection to him.

His fingers closed around the velvet box in his pocket once more, decision crystallizing into certainty. The perfect moment wasn't about location or timing or elaborate arrangements. It was about honesty—the same quality that had drawn him to Bee from their first unexpected connection. The ring felt right against his palm, its presence a promise waiting to be spoken aloud.

Charlie found Bee near the dessert table, her fingers arranging a fallen rose back into a centerpiece with the same care she applied to her packaging designs. The velvet box in his pocket seemed to have developed its own gravity, pulling his awareness to its presence with each step. She looked up as he approached, her smile softening into something quieter, more intimate—the expression she reserved for him alone in their private moments away from the world.

"There you are," she said, reaching for his hand with natural ease. "Your mum was just telling me about your first school play. Apparently you refused to go on unless they let you rewrite your lines."

"Creative differences with the director," Charlie replied, his voice steadier than the quickened rhythm of his heart. "Even at eight, I was insufferable."

Bee laughed, the sound blending with the music that floated around them. "I would say particular, not insufferable. A quality I've come to appreciate."

Her fingers were warm against his, familiar and grounding even as anticipation coursed through him. Charlie glanced across the garden, catching the distant figures of guests engaged in conversation, the party having evolved into smaller, more intimate groupings as the evening deepened.

"Can I show you something?" he asked, a slight roughness in his voice that made her tilt her head in curiosity. "John mentioned a spot on the property I think you'd love."

Bee nodded, allowing him to guide her away from the center of the gathering. They moved along the edge of the terrace where stone steps descended to a lower level of the garden. A path of flat rocks emerged, each one illuminated by small lanterns that created pools of golden light against the surrounding darkness. Charlie felt Bee's dress brush against his leg as they walked, the silk catching momentarily on the rough fabric of his pants before sliding free.

"This is beautiful," Bee murmured as they followed the lantern path. Night had fully claimed the mountain, transforming the garden into an island of warm light surrounded by velvet darkness. Above them, stars emerged in brilliant clarity, the absence of city glow revealing constellations often hidden from view. "John has a good eye for property."

"Family trait," Charlie replied, his free hand brushing the box in his pocket as if to reassure himself of its presence. "Though I think my mountain has better sunrise views."

"Our mountain," Bee corrected gently, the simple amendment carrying years of meaning—their shared sanctuary, their deliberate choice to build a life together away from scrutiny.

The path curved around a stand of aspens, their leaves whispering in the gentle night breeze, before revealing its destination: a wooden gazebo perched at the very edge of the property, its open sides framing views of the valley below and mountains beyond. More lanterns hung from its rafters, casting warm light across the weathered boards of its floor and illuminating delicate vines that climbed its support posts. Beyond its sheltering roof, mountains cut dark silhouettes against the star-filled sky, their ancient presence a reminder of perspective—of troubles that seemed momentous reduced to insignificance against geological time.

Charlie guided Bee up the three wooden steps into the gazebo's embrace. Her dress rustled softly against the planks, the sound mingling with the rhythmic chirping of crickets from the surrounding meadow and the distant, gentle cadence of music from the party. Night-blooming jasmine wove through the gazebo's latticework, releasing its sweet perfume into the cool mountain air.

"I had no idea this was here," Bee said, moving toward the railing to gaze out at the valley below, where scattered lights from distant homes created earthbound constellations. "It's like something from a dream."

Charlie watched her profile in the lantern light, the soft glow highlighting the curve of her cheek, the line of her neck, the dark waves of her hair. His fingers trembled slightly as he joined her at the railing, close enough that their shoulders touched.

"Do you remember," he began, his voice lower than the cricket song surrounding them, "when you first texted me by accident? That wrong number that somehow went right?"

Bee turned toward him, her expression curious at this unexpected direction. "Of course. My scathing review of my dating experience and Tinder's lack of review feature, accidentally sent to a Hollywood star." Her lips curved in a small smile. "Not my most collected moment."

"It was the first honest interaction I'd had in months," Charlie said, turning to face her fully. "No agenda, no performative flattery, just... authenticity. Even when you realized who I was, you didn't change—didn't suddenly treat me differently."

A slight breeze stirred the lantern flames, casting shifting patterns of light across the wooden floor. In the distance, laughter rose briefly from the party before subsiding back into the general murmur of conversation.

"Before you," Charlie continued, taking both her hands in his, "I lived inside carefully constructed boundaries. Protection that became isolation. Privacy that became loneliness." His thumbs traced circles against her palms, a tactile connection to anchor the words that rose from somewhere deeper than practiced speech. "You walked through all that with such... ease. Not forcing your way past my defenses but simply making them unnecessary."

Bee's eyes softened, her fingers tightening around his as she listened without interruption, giving him the space to find words for feelings that had been building for months.

"You see me," Charlie said, his voice catching slightly on the simple phrase that contained multitudes. "Not Charlie Benton the actor, not the public image or the bank account or the industry asset. Just me—the man who organizes his spice rack alphabetically, who falls asleep during the movies he claims to love, who still gets nervous before every scene."

A smile touched Bee's lips at these familiar details, these private truths they had discovered together in the sanctuary of their mountain home. Charlie felt something shift within his chest, fear giving way to certainty, hesitation to clarity.

"With you, I don't have to perform or calculate or edit myself," he continued, the words flowing more freely now. "I can just... be. That gift—that freedom—is something I never expected to find."

Charlie released one of her hands, reaching into his pocket where the velvet box waited. Bee's eyes widened slightly as he withdrew it, comprehension dawning in her expression. The cricket song seemed to intensify around them, the night holding its breath as he lowered himself to one knee on the wooden planks of the gazebo floor.

"I know this might seem sudden," he said, looking up at her face illuminated by lantern light and stars, "or maybe long overdue. I've been overthinking it, waiting for some perfect moment that doesn't exist." His fingers trembled slightly as he opened the box, revealing the ring that had passed through generations of his family—platinum and diamonds catching the light in brilliant facets. "The truth is, every moment with you feels right in ways I never knew to hope for."

Bee's free hand rose to cover her mouth, her eyes bright with emotion in the golden light.

"Bianca Anderson," Charlie said, her full name carrying the weight of formal declaration even as his voice softened with intimate tenderness, "will you marry me?"

The question hung in the space between them, simple words carrying the promise of a shared future. Bee's eyes filled with tears that caught the lantern light as they spilled onto her cheeks. She nodded, the movement small at first, then more emphatic as she found her voice.

"Yes," she whispered, the single syllable carrying absolute certainty. Then louder, with a small laugh that contained both joy and released tension: "Yes, of course I will."

Charlie rose to his feet, his hands not quite steady as he removed the ring from its velvet nest and slipped it onto her finger. It settled there as if designed for her, the vintage setting complementing her hand with perfect symmetry. Before he could speak again, Bee pulled him toward her, her arms encircling his neck as she drew him into a kiss that contained all the words that language couldn't adequately express.

Charlie's arms wrapped around her waist, lifting her slightly as the kiss deepened. Against his chest, he could feel the rapid beating of her heart echoing his own, their pulses syncopating in shared excitement. When they finally separated, foreheads still touching, breath mingling in the cool night air, Bee's smile held the particular radiance of joy untouched by performance or calculation.

"John's going to be insufferably pleased with himself," she murmured, her fingers threading through the hair at the nape of Charlie's neck.

"He can have this one," Charlie replied, his hands settling at her waist, keeping her close within the circle of his arms. "Small price to pay for stealing his engagement party thunder."

Bee laughed, the sound pure and unrestrained, carrying

across the quiet night. Above them, stars witnessed their private joy; below in the valley, distant lights marked other lives unfolding in parallel; and behind them, the soft sounds of celebration continued, unaware that its premise had just transformed from fiction to truth.

Time seemed suspended in the lantern-lit gazebo, the world beyond its wooden railings fading into pleasant irrelevance as Charlie and Bee remained wrapped in each other's arms. The ring caught fragments of light as Bee's hand rested against his shoulder, tiny prisms dancing across the weathered boards beneath their feet. Charlie pressed his lips to her temple, breathing in the familiar scent of her hair, the reality of the moment settling into something solid and permanent within his chest.

"I've been carrying this decision for months," he murmured against her skin. "Not whether to ask you, but how. When. Where." His fingers traced the curve of her spine through the silk of her dress. "I kept waiting for the perfect circumstance, the ideal setting, I was also worried about the purchase getting leaked."

Bee leaned back slightly to meet his eyes, her smile both teasing and tender. "And it turns out to be at your brother's fake engagement party for us."

"Life has a certain poetry," Charlie agreed, his thumb brushing across her cheek. "Though I suspect John's timing wasn't entirely accidental, the ring that you are wearing was our grandmother's, our mother gave it to John to hold until the time was right."

As if summoned by the mention of his name, a familiar voice called from the path below the gazebo. "Are you two still up there? The chocolate soufflés won't wait forever, you know."

John's footsteps sounded on the wooden stairs, his arrival heralded by the creak of aging boards. Charlie and Bee separated slightly but remained connected, his arm around her waist, her hand still resting on his chest. The interruption wasn't unwelcome—John's timing had always possessed its own peculiar perfection, even when it appeared inconvenient on the surface.

"So?" John asked as he reached the gazebo's entrance, his figure silhouetted against the lantern-lined path behind him. "Did he finally ask, or do I have to rename this an 'almost engagement party'?" His tone carried the familiar teasing lilt that masked genuine affection, a language of brotherhood developed over decades of shared history.

Charlie and Bee turned toward him, still wrapped in each other's arms, their faces illuminated by the gentle glow of the hanging lanterns. The matching smiles they wore needed no verbal explanation, but Bee provided one anyway, lifting her left hand where the ring caught the light in brilliant facets.

John's reaction transformed his features, the practiced nonchalance giving way to genuine delight. He whooped—a startlingly joyful sound that echoed across the quiet garden—before bounding up the remaining steps to embrace them both in a sudden, enthusiastic hug that nearly unbalanced the three of them.

"About damn time," he declared, clapping Charlie on the back with enough force to make him wince. "I was starting to think I'd have to propose to her for you."

"I'd have turned you down," Bee retorted with a laugh, her arm still wrapped around Charlie's waist. "No offense, but I prefer the brother who doesn't interrupt private moments."

"Interrupt? I enhanced," John corrected, his grin widening as he stepped back to admire the ring on Bee's finger. "Grandma's looks perfect on you. Like it was waiting all these years." The sincerity in his voice momentarily replaced his usual playful deflection, revealing the depth of emotion beneath the teasing surface.

Before either could respond, John turned toward the path and cupped his hands around his mouth. "They did it!" he called, his voice carrying through the night air toward the distant glow of the main garden. "Champagne! The real celebration starts now!"

Charlie felt Bee's body tense slightly against his, her eyes meeting his with a question—were they ready to share this moment, to expand their intimate circle to include the gathered guests? He squeezed her hand gently in reassurance, understanding her hesitation. For so long, their relationship had existed under scrutiny, their private moments at risk of becoming public property. This instinctive caution had become part of their shared language.

"It's just family," he reminded her softly. "Our people. No cameras, no strangers."

Bee relaxed against him, nodding as her smile returned. "Our people," she echoed, the simple phrase carrying layers of meaning developed through months of navigating the complicated intersection of public and private.

Down the lantern-lit path, figures appeared—first as shadows moving through pools of light, then resolving into the familiar faces of their closest connections. Charlie's parents led the procession, his mother already wiping at her eyes, his father's usual reserve softened into visible emotion. Bee's college friend followed, accompanied by Toby and Victoria, all three carrying champagne flutes that caught the light as they moved.

The contrast between this approaching crowd and the faceless masses that had once surrounded them at industry events struck Charlie with unexpected force. These were people who had earned their trust, who had protected rather than exploited their privacy, who celebrated their connection rather than dissecting it for public consumption. The approaching footsteps carried no threat, only genuine joy.

"You two," his mother said as she reached the gazebo, her voice catching slightly. "My beautiful boy and the woman who brought him back to us." She embraced Bee first, then Charlie, her arms conveying what words couldn't adequately express.

His father followed, the handshake he offered Charlie transforming mid-gesture into an embrace that communicated decades of restrained but unwavering support. "Well done," he said simply, the two words containing volumes.

The gazebo filled with their closest circle, the intimate space expanding to accommodate this shared joy without losing its essential character. Someone had brought a bottle of champagne, its cork releasing with a festive pop that echoed against the wooden rafters. Crystal flutes appeared, passed hand to hand until everyone held a portion of effervescent gold.

"A toast," John declared, raising his glass as he assumed the role of master of ceremonies with characteristic ease. "To Charlie and Bee—who found each other through a wrong number and proved that sometimes the best connections come from the most unexpected beginnings."

"To finding what's real in a world of illusion," added Toby, his industry cynicism momentarily replaced by genuine sentiment.

"To boundaries, not walls," Bee's friend offered, referencing a phrase that had become central to their approach to living under public scrutiny.

The glasses rose in unison, the simple ritual binding them together in celebration. Charlie kept Bee close against his side, her warmth a constant anchor as congratulations flowed around them. The champagne tasted sweeter somehow, enhanced by the context of genuine connection.

More guests arrived from the main garden, drawn by John's announcement, but the gathering maintained its intimate character—conversations overlapping in a gentle harmony of voices, laughter rising and falling in natural rhythms, the collective joy creating a bubble of warmth that pushed back against the cool mountain night.

Throughout it all, Charlie found himself repeatedly drawn to the simple sensation of Bee's fingers intertwined with his—the physical connection that had become their silent language of support through public scrutiny, security breaches, and the careful construction of their shared life. Now that same gesture carried new meaning: promise, commitment, future.

"Happy?" he asked quietly during a momentary lull, his lips close to her ear to create privacy within the celebration.

Bee turned toward him, her expression holding the particular radiance that belonged to her alone—not the manufactured glow of red carpet appearances or the careful composure of public scrutiny, but the genuine warmth that emerged when she felt truly safe.

"Completely," she answered, her free hand rising to rest against his cheek. "Though I'm already planning our escape back to our mountain." The teasing in her voice carried understanding of their shared preference for quiet intimacy over extended social engagement, even with beloved companions.

"First thing tomorrow," Charlie promised, turning his head slightly to press a kiss against her palm. "But tonight..." He glanced around at their gathered loved ones, at the genuine joy unmarred by hidden cameras or ulterior motives. "Tonight we can just be here. Present."

Bee nodded, her smile deepening as she leaned into him. "Together."

The celebration continued around them, champagne bottles opening, toasts multiplying, plans for the wedding already being enthusiastically debated among their closest supporters. The gazebo lanterns swayed gently in the mountain breeze, casting shifting patterns across faces alight with genuine happiness. Beyond its wooden railings, stars continued their ancient patterns across the velvet sky, unchanging witnesses to this moment of human connection.

Charlie's arm remained around Bee's waist, her head occasionally resting against his shoulder as they moved through conversations with easy synchronicity. The ring on her finger caught the light as she gestured, its presence already seeming natural, as if it had always belonged there. For this rare evening, they existed without the weight of public performance or careful privacy—simply Charlie and Bee, surrounded by love that asked nothing beyond their happiness, celebrating a connection that had flourished despite every complication the world had placed in its path.

Chapter Twenty-Four:
Red Carpet Revelations

The stylist's fingers worked with butterfly delicacy along the seam of Bee's gown, making one final adjustment to the midnight-blue silk that cascaded from her shoulders to pool elegantly at her feet. In the mirror's reflection, Bee watched the woman's concentrated expression, the tiny silver pins held between pursed lips, the precise movements that transformed fabric into armor for the evening ahead. Her own fingers found her wedding ring, twisting it in a nervous gesture that had become habit over the past year, the platinum band cool and solid against her skin—a tangible reminder of the promise that anchored her when everything else felt untethered.

"Stop fidgeting or I'll stick you," the stylist murmured through her fence of pins, though her tone held no real admonishment. "Almost done."

Bee exhaled slowly, forcing her hands to still at her sides. The suite's air felt thick with the mingled scents of hair products, perfume samples, and the subtle hint of the roses Charlie had arranged to have waiting when they checked in—a tradition he'd maintained since their honeymoon. Outside the window, Los Angeles sprawled in a glittering expanse, the early evening sky deepening to indigo above a city that had once seemed determined to consume them both.

Two years since a wrong-number text had altered the trajectory of her life with the force and precision of a celestial event. Now here she stood in a couture gown worth more than her first car, preparing to step back into the spotlight that had once burned so harshly against their privacy.

"Nervous?" asked the makeup artist, returning to add a final touch to Bee's lips—a shade carefully selected to complement but not compete with the gown.

"Realistic," Bee replied, meeting the woman's eyes in the mirror. "Red carpets aren't exactly designed for comfort."

Her reflection stared back at her—familiar yet transformed. The stylist had worked subtle magic with her dark hair, arranging it in an elegant sweep that emphasized the clean lines of her neck and shoulders. The dress—selected after weeks of careful consideration—managed to be both dramatic and understated, its deep blue recalling the mountain twilight of their sanctuary home. Nectar & Hive, her business, had flourished in the relative quiet of their first year of marriage, allowing her to maintain her independence while supporting Charlie's cautious return to selected projects.

Her fingers found the ring again, its weight familiar yet still somehow surprising each time she noticed it. Not the vintage piece from the proposal—that she had already grown accustomed to—but the matching bands they had exchanged in a ceremony attended by only twenty people, the location kept secret until the morning of the wedding itself. No photographers, no press release, just an intimate gathering of those who had earned their trust.

The stylist stepped back finally, satisfaction evident in her nod. "Perfect. Not a thread out of place."

As the styling team gathered their supplies, Bee remained

before the mirror, practicing the smile she would need to maintain for hours—genuine enough to avoid appearing cold, reserved enough to maintain the boundary between public persona and private self. Charlie had taught her the technique during those first chaotic months together, before they had retreated to create their mountain sanctuary. Now it came naturally, another tool in their arsenal of privacy protection.

In the adjoining room of the suite, separated by a door left partially ajar, Charlie adjusted his bow tie for the third time, fingers working with practiced precision against the starched collar of his shirt. The tuxedo fit impeccably—it should, given the number of fittings—but he felt the familiar tightness across his shoulders that had nothing to do with tailoring and everything to do with the evening ahead. He inhaled deeply through his nose, held the breath for a count of four, then released it slowly through parted lips, just as the meditation instructor at their mountain retreat had taught them.

In the mirror, he studied his reflection with the critical eye of someone accustomed to being assessed by millions. The stylist had applied just enough product to keep his hair in place without making it appear unnatural. The faint lines at the corners of his eyes—deeper now at thirty-seven than when he had first met Bee—remained unobscured, part of their mutual agreement to present themselves authentically rather than artificially preserved. His publicist had argued against this decision, but Charlie had remained firm. The boundary was clear: he would return to public life, but on terms that honoured what he and Bee had built together.

This film marked his return after a deliberate eighteen-month absence—a period devoted to their marriage, their mountain home, and reevaluating his relationship with an industry that had simultaneously elevated and constrained him. The script had been among those he had set aside the morning of his proposal,

"The Unseen" now transformed into the film premiering tonight. The story had resonated with him then, even more so now—a man rebuilding his life, finding unexpected connection, learning to be seen for who he truly was rather than the image he projected.

A soft knock at the adjoining door interrupted his thoughts.

"Come in," he called, turning from the mirror as the door opened fully to reveal Bee.

The sight of her—elegant in midnight silk, her eyes finding his with the directness that had first captured him—caused his breath to catch slightly. Not from surprise at her beauty, though that remained undimmed, but from the realization that she was his wife, that they had crafted a life together despite every complication the world had placed in their path.

"Hi," she said, the simple greeting carrying layers of private meaning as she crossed the threshold into his space. "Ready for this?"

Charlie closed the distance between them, his hands finding her waist with instinctive certainty. "With you? Always."

His lips brushed against hers—careful not to disturb her makeup while still conveying the depth of his feeling. Her hands rose to rest against his chest, fingers smoothing an imaginary wrinkle from his lapel in a gesture that had become part of their shared language.

"They're going to ask about the mountain house," Bee said, her voice lowered though they were alone in the suite. "And the wedding."

"We stick to the script," Charlie replied, his thumb tracing small circles against the silk covering her waist. "Acknowledge without details. Friendly but vague."

Bee nodded, her eyes meeting his with the clear focus that

had guided them through far more challenging situations. "Boundaries, not walls."

The phrase—their mantra through the turbulent early months, through security breaches and tabloid intrusions, through the careful construction of their life together—settled between them like a shared breath. Charlie's arm circled her waist, drawing her closer against him, feeling the solid reality of her presence against the abstract anxiety of the evening ahead.

A discreet knock at the outer door signaled their car had arrived. The protective bubble of the suite would soon give way to the exposure of the premiere, to cameras and questions and the careful performance of public life. Charlie's arm remained around Bee's waist as they gathered their final items —her clutch, his watch, the matching silver wedding bands that caught the light as they moved.

The elevator descended in silence, Charlie's hand finding Bee's, their fingers intertwining in the automatic gesture that had sustained them through countless public appearances. The hotel's back entrance provided minimal protection—a short walk to the waiting car, a brief respite before the main event. Bee's dress whispered against the pavement as Charlie helped her into the vehicle, the driver closing the door behind them with practiced discretion.

As the car pulled away from the curb, the city lights streamed past the tinted windows in rivers of gold and white. Bee's hand remained in Charlie's, her warmth a constant against the artificial cool of the vehicle's interior. Neither spoke, the silence comfortable rather than strained—a moment of collected calm before the chaos to come.

The car slowed as they approached the theater, the congestion of vehicles signaling their proximity to the premiere. Through the windshield, Bee could see the strobing flashes of cameras, the red carpet stretching like a crimson river toward the building's entrance, the crowd held back by velvet ropes and security personnel. Her fingers tightened slightly around Charlie's, an unconscious response to the sensory assault visible even through the car's tinted windows.

"Together," Charlie said, the single word carrying the weight of all they had built, all they had protected, all they had chosen to share on their own terms.

Bee nodded, her wedding ring catching the light as she turned toward him. "Together."

The car stopped, and the door opened to reveal the full force of the premiere—camera flashes creating artificial daylight against the darkening sky, the heat of spotlights cutting through the evening cool, the wall of sound that rose from hundreds of gathered observers. Bee's hand found Charlie's arm as they prepared to step from the vehicle's shelter into the clamor of public attention. Their eyes met for one final private moment, a silent exchange of strength and support, before they turned together to face the red carpet's demands with the united front they had carefully constructed and fiercely protected.

The heat hit them first—a physical wave generated by lights, bodies, equipment. Then the sound—overlapping shouts of Charlie's name from photographers positioned along the carpet, the higher pitch of fans behind barricades, the constant mechanical clicks of cameras capturing every movement. The scent of excitement hung in the air, mingled with perfume, hair products, the faint metallic tang of equipment warming under lights. Bee's fingers pressed slightly into Charlie's arm as they took their first steps together, their practiced smiles appearing with synchronized precision as they moved into the sensory storm of the premiere.

Charlie's hand settled at the small of Bee's back as they took their first deliberate steps along the crimson path. Their movements had the fluid synchronicity of dancers who had rehearsed extensively—each pause precisely timed, each smile deployed with strategic intent. To observers, they appeared simply as a striking couple enjoying their moment; only those closest to them would recognize the subtle signals they exchanged, the gentle pressure of fingers indicating when to stop, when to continue, when to engage. The boundary between public performance and private connection blurred in these small touches, creating a language only they fully understood.

"Charlie! This way!" The photographers' voices blended into a single demanding entity, punctuated by the mechanical staccato of camera shutters. "Bee! Over here!"

They paused at the first designated photo spot, turning toward the press line with practiced precision. Charlie's arm curved around Bee's waist, his touch light yet anchoring. Her body angled slightly toward his, creating a composition that photographers had come to recognize as their signature pose—intimate without being overtly demonstrative, connected without appearing dependent. Bee's hand rested briefly against Charlie's chest, her wedding ring catching the lights in brilliant flares that would appear in tomorrow's coverage.

"Beautiful! Give us another!" called a photographer they recognized from previous events—one of the few who respected boundaries, who never shouted personal questions during photo opportunities.

Charlie's smile deepened slightly in acknowledgment. They shifted position with subtle grace, his hand never leaving the silk-covered curve of her waist, her body maintaining its slight inclination toward his. These weren't the practiced poses of his previous red carpet appearances—arms stiffly positioned, smiles fixed and distant. The difference was evident to anyone who had followed his career: this was Charlie Benton genuinely comfortable, genuinely present despite the chaos surrounding them.

They moved forward after thirty seconds—long enough to provide quality images, brief enough to maintain control of their experience. The strategy had been developed during their first public appearances as a married couple: engage selectively, remain moving, never linger long enough for the initial professional courtesy to degrade into invasive questions.

Halfway down the carpet, a small commotion drew their attention. A young girl, perhaps twelve, had somehow secured a position along the barricade. She held a homemade sign above her head, the glitter-decorated cardboard trembling slightly in her grip: "BEE & CHARLIE: REAL LOVE IS WORTH FIGHTING FOR."

Bee's steps faltered, her eyes meeting Charlie's in a brief moment of genuine surprise. The girl's sign quoted Charlie's words from the Morgan Walsh interview that had marked a turning point in their public narrative—words that had been repurposed in countless fan edits and social media posts celebrating their relationship.

Without speaking, Bee made a decision. She squeezed Charlie's hand once—their signal for a deviation from the planned progression—and moved toward the barricade. The security guard stepped forward automatically, then paused at Charlie's subtle headshake.

Bee knelt carefully, the midnight silk of her gown pooling around her like spilled ink against the red carpet. The position would horrify her stylist, but the expression on the young girl's face—wide-eyed disbelief transforming into tremulous joy— made such concerns irrelevant.

"Hi there," Bee said, her voice pitched to carry to the girl but not much farther, creating an island of relative privacy amid the clamor. "That's a beautiful sign you made."

"I—I've been following your story since the beginning," the girl stammered, her voice cracking with emotion. "You guys showed me that real relationships aren't like in movies. They're better."

Charlie crouched beside Bee, his hand settling on her shoulder as he extended his other toward the girl's sign. "May I?"

The girl nodded, her hands shaking as she passed the glitter-covered creation across the barricade. Charlie produced a pen from his inner pocket—another part of their red carpet strategy, always prepared for such moments—and signed his name along the bottom edge before passing it to Bee, who added her own.

"What's your name?" Bee asked, her genuine smile replacing the public version she had maintained for the cameras.

"Emma," the girl replied, fingers clutching the barricade so tightly her knuckles whitened.

"Thank you for being here tonight, Emma," Charlie said, returning the sign with careful hands. "It means more than you know."

As they rose and continued down the carpet, Bee's fingers found Charlie's, squeezing briefly in shared acknowledgment of the moment's unexpected poignancy. The photographers had captured it all, of course—her kneeling despite the gown, Charlie's protective stance beside her, their signatures added to the girl's handmade creation. Tomorrow these images would circulate alongside the polished portraits from earlier, showing both versions of their public presence.

The media pit loomed ahead—the section of carpet where reporters clustered with microphones and recording devices, their questions overlapping in a competitive cacophony. Charlie felt Bee's stride shorten almost imperceptibly, a subtle indication of the apprehension they both felt. This was the gauntlet that could not be avoided at a premiere of this significance—the obligatory sound bites that would be dissected across entertainment networks by morning.

They approached the first position, microphones extending toward them like probing fingers. The reporter—a woman with aggressively highlighted hair and a smile that never reached her eyes—leaned forward with practiced eagerness.

"Charlie, Bee! Congratulations on your first red carpet as a married couple. Bee, you're looking absolutely stunning tonight. I have to ask—did you feel pressure to match the typical celebrity spouse type after marrying someone of Charlie's stature?"

The question landed with deliberate weight, its phrasing a thin disguise for the implied criticism. Charlie felt Bee's body shift beside him, her spine straightening almost imperceptibly. Her smile remained in place, though it cooled several degrees.

"I think we've established I'm not typical at anything," Bee replied, her tone light yet firm. "Including my approach to red carpets. The only pressure I feel is making sure I don't trip over this gorgeous dress."

Charlie laughed, the sound genuine despite the context. His hand at her waist tightened slightly in silent appreciation of her deft deflection.

"Charlie," the reporter pressed on, "your latest film marks your return to the spotlight after taking time away. Was that decision influenced by your relationship?"

They stood slightly angled toward each other, a position they had refined through multiple public appearances—not quite facing the reporter, not quite turned away, their bodies creating a subtle barrier against intrusion while remaining engaged.

"My break was about reassessing priorities," Charlie replied, his gaze briefly meeting Bee's before returning to the reporter. "When you find what matters, you make decisions differently. This project spoke to me because it explores authentic connection in a world that often values appearance over substance."

As if choreographed, Bee seamlessly picked up the thread. "The script is extraordinary. I cried reading it, and I'm not easily moved by fictional stories."

The hand-off appeared natural, unrehearsed, though they had developed this technique through careful practice—never allowing one of them to bear the full weight of questioning, never separating into solo interviews that could be edited to create artificial distance between them.

They moved through the remaining media positions with the same coordinated approach, their responses varying slightly but their physical connection remaining constant. Charlie's hand never left the small of Bee's back; her body maintained its subtle inclination toward his. When questions veered toward their private life—their mountain home, their wedding, their future plans—they redirected with practiced ease, acknowledging without revealing, engaging without exposing.

To observers, they presented a united front without appearing defensive, accessible without being vulnerable. The boundaries they had fought so hard to establish were maintained not through walls of silence or curt dismissals, but through this careful dance of presence and privacy, engagement and protection.

As they approached the final stretch of carpet, Charlie's fingers pressed gently against Bee's silk-covered back—their signal that the gauntlet was nearly complete. Her hand rose to rest briefly against his chest in response, a gesture too subtle for cameras to capture meaningfully but clear in its communication: I'm here. We're doing this together.

The theater entrance beckoned ahead, promising relative sanctuary from the relentless attention. Bee's steps aligned perfectly with Charlie's as they moved forward, their bodies maintaining the physical synchronicity that had characterized their entire progression along the crimson path. The flashing lights continued their strobing assault, but the worst was behind them—the boundary maintained, the connection preserved, the public performance executed without sacrificing their private truth.

The final interview station stood beneath a branded backdrop, camera equipment arranged in a semicircle to capture every angle of their approach. Unlike the hurried exchanges of the media pit, this represented the evening's single substantive conversation—the interview that would be featured in tomorrow's entertainment coverage, excerpted across social media, analyzed for nuance and subtext. The reporter, Eliza Chang, had built her reputation on conversations that balanced respect with insight, earning her the rare distinction of being someone both publicists and celebrities could trust. Charlie recognized the strategic wisdom in Toby's arrangement—if they had to provide one meaningful interview, better with someone who wouldn't weaponize vulnerability.

Eliza stepped forward as they approached, her handshake firm and professional, her smile genuine rather than performed. "Charlie, Bee—thank you for making time tonight." She gestured toward two director-style chairs positioned beside her own. "Just a few minutes before you head inside?"

Charlie nodded, his hand finding the familiar curve of Bee's waist as they settled into the arranged seats. The positioning had been negotiated in advance—no high stools that would make Bee's gown management difficult, no awkward angles that might be interpreted as distance between them. The camera's red light blinked on, transforming their conversation from private exchange to public record.

"It's been quite a year for you both," Eliza began, her voice pitched perfectly for the microphones without seeming artificially modulated. "Your first anniversary recently passed, I believe? Congratulations."

"Thank you," Bee replied, her smile warming at the mention of their milestone. "It somehow feels both longer and shorter than a year."

"Time compresses and expands," Charlie added, his fingers lightly brushing against Bee's hand where it rested between their chairs. "The quiet moments stretch beautifully, while the chaos blurs together."

Eliza nodded, her eyes reflecting genuine interest rather than the hunger for exploitable content that characterized many interviewers. "You've managed to create a life that balances privacy with your public roles—something many consider impossible in today's media environment. Looking back at the scrutiny you faced early in your relationship, how did you navigate through that to where you are now?"

The question acknowledged their journey without demanding specific details—another reason Charlie respected Eliza's approach. He exchanged a brief glance with Bee, a silent confirmation of who would take the lead on this response.

"Trial and error, honestly," Charlie admitted, his expression thoughtful. "In the beginning, I approached privacy like a fortress—walls up, drawbridge raised, everyone kept at a distance." His hand moved to cover Bee's more fully, their wedding bands briefly aligned. "Bee helped me understand that isolation isn't the same as protection. That boundaries can be maintained without disconnection."

Bee's fingers turned beneath his, interlacing in a gesture that had become their silent language of support. "We learned to differentiate between private and secret," she added. "Our relationship isn't hidden—it's just not packaged for consumption."

Eliza leaned forward slightly, recognizing the substantive

nature of their response. "That distinction seems crucial. There were particularly challenging moments—the security breach at your home, the speculation about your career choices, Bee. How did you maintain your connection when it seemed the world was determined to insert itself between you?"

The reference to Madison Vale's intrusion hung briefly in the air—a moment they never discussed in interviews, though its impact had shaped their approach to security and privacy. Charlie felt Bee's hand tighten slightly around his, a momentary tension that passed between them like an electrical current.

"What we have is worth fighting for," Charlie said, his voice dropping to a register that carried unexpected emotional weight. The words emerged without the careful calculation that had once governed his public statements—direct, unfiltered, genuine. "Bee taught me that privacy isn't about building walls, it's about setting boundaries. About deciding what parts of our lives belong to us alone, and what we're willing to share."

He paused, drawing a breath that seemed to center him. The ambient sounds of the premiere—the continued camera clicks, the murmur of conversations, the distant calls of photographers—seemed to fade as he continued.

"There were moments when it would have been easier to retreat completely," he acknowledged, his eyes meeting Eliza's with unusual directness. "To disappear into our mountain home and never emerge. But that would have been surrender, not solution."

Bee's free hand lifted, almost unconsciously, to briefly touch his cheek—a gesture so intimate and unplanned that several nearby onlookers exchanged glances. The camera operator adjusted his position slightly, capturing the moment with unobtrusive precision.

"We decided to engage on our terms," Bee continued, her hand returning to her lap though her eyes remained on Charlie's profile. "To be present without being exposed. It's a constant balance, but one worth maintaining."

Eliza nodded, allowing a brief silence to acknowledge the weight of their words before shifting direction. "Charlie, this film marks your selective return to acting after a deliberate step back. What drew you to this particular project after declining so many others?"

The question invited professional rather than personal reflection, a courtesy Charlie appreciated. He straightened slightly in his chair, his expression shifting as he considered his response.

"The script spoke to themes I've been exploring in my own life," he explained, his passion for the project evident in his animation. "Questions of authenticity, of being seen versus being known. The character's journey from protective isolation to vulnerable connection resonated deeply."

Before he could continue, Bee interjected with quiet certainty. "He's always been brilliant at what he does. Now he just chooses projects that matter." Her tone carried no performative support, just simple conviction. "The difference in his approach now is that he evaluates roles based on what they contribute rather than what they require."

Charlie turned toward her, momentarily forgetting the cameras, the microphones, the gathered observers. Something passed between them—a private acknowledgment visible to others but comprehensible only to them.

Around them, the crowd had grown unusually quiet, conversation stilling as onlookers strained to catch their words. The typical red carpet cacophony had diminished to a murmur, attention focusing on the unexpected authenticity emerging from what should have been a routine interview. Several industry veterans exchanged impressed glances, recognizing the rarity of genuine emotion in a setting designed for calculated presentation.

"That's beautifully put," Eliza acknowledged, her professional detachment softening visibly. "One final question before you head inside—what would you say has been the most significant change in your life since finding each other?"

The question could have invited platitudes, the kind of generic response that filled entertainment segments without revealing anything meaningful. Instead, Charlie's answer emerged with the clarity of something long considered but never before articulated publicly.

"She reminds me every day what's real and what matters," he said, his voice steady but layered with emotion that reached beyond the camera's frame to touch those listening. "In an industry built on illusion, that's a gift beyond measure."

Eliza thanked them, recognizing the gift of their candor with a simple nod that acknowledged the boundary between professional courtesy and personal intrusion. As the camera's red light blinked off, Charlie rose first, extending his hand to help Bee from her chair. The midnight silk of her gown cascaded around her as she stood, catching the premiere lights in subtle waves of reflection.

They moved away from the interview setup with matching strides, hands naturally finding each other as they approached the theater entrance. Behind them, the red carpet continued its frantic energy—photographers capturing the arrival of other celebrities, reporters seeking sound bites, fans calling names through the evening air. But as Charlie and Bee passed through the entrance doors, that chaos receded, the sounds diminishing as they moved deeper into the venue's relative sanctuary.

The theater lobby enveloped them in comparative quiet, the plush carpeting absorbing sound, the lighting more subdued than the harsh illumination outside. Charlie's arm slipped around Bee's waist once more, the gesture no longer performative but simply natural—the unconscious gravitation of two people accustomed to finding anchor in each other's presence.

As they followed an usher toward their reserved seats, the red carpet's demands fell away behind them like a tide retreating from shore. What remained was the essential truth they had fought to protect through security breaches and public scrutiny, through tabloid speculation and industry pressure: not the carefully managed image of Charlie Benton and his wife, but simply Charlie and Bee—connected, committed, choosing each other with each step forward into the evening, and beyond.

Chapter Twenty-Five: Home Is Where the Heart Is

The fireplace cast dancing shadows across their living room, its flames catching in the copper accents that Bee had carefully selected for their mountain sanctuary. Outside, a gentle snowfall had begun, white flakes drifting past windows designed to give them perfect views of the forest while preventing any unwanted gazes from peering in. Charlie's reading glasses perched on the bridge of his nose as he flipped through another script, his sixth of the evening, while Bee's legs stretched comfortably across his lap, her back supported by a nest of pillows against the sofa's arm. The stack of rejected screenplays on the floor had grown steadily taller as the night progressed, victims of their increasingly refined standards.

"Listen to this dialogue," Charlie said, his voice carrying the particular blend of amusement and exasperation that Bee had come to recognize as his response to particularly egregious writing. He cleared his throat, adopting the exaggerated tone he reserved for readings that deserved mockery. "'I've never felt this way before—it's like you've unlocked a part of me that I didn't know existed.' Who talks like that?"

Bee's lips curved into a smile as she set aside her mug of chamomile tea on the reclaimed wood coffee table they'd discovered at an artisan's workshop three valleys over. "People who've never had an actual conversation, apparently, although we reached almost the same level of corny."

Charlie's hand rested on her ankle, his thumb absently tracing circles against her skin as he flipped the page with his free hand. The casual contact between them had become so natural that neither acknowledged it consciously anymore—a constant, comforting connection maintained even as they focused on other tasks. The expensive cashmere throw that draped across Bee's legs had been a wedding gift from Charlie's mother, its soft weight a shield against the mountain chill that crept in despite the fire's steady warmth.

"The premise isn't terrible," Charlie continued, sliding his glasses higher on his nose with a practiced gesture. "Man discovers his childhood imaginary friend was actually real and now needs his help... There's something there, but the execution..." He trailed off, shaking his head.

"Add it to the 'potential but problematic' pile?" Bee suggested, reaching for the script to examine the pages that had drawn his attention. Their hands brushed in the exchange, a momentary increase in the constant physical dialogue that flowed between them.

The living room around them reflected their shared aesthetic—neither the sterile sophistication of Charlie's former coastal mansion nor the purely practical approach Bee had once applied to her apartments. Leather-bound books shared shelves with handcrafted pottery. A vintage camera Charlie had collected sat beside one of Bee's first fabric experiments for Nectar & Hive. The furniture—substantial without being ostentatious—had been selected for comfort rather than appearance, though the two qualities had proven not to be mutually exclusive.

Charlie shifted slightly, adjusting his position to better support Bee's legs across his lap while reaching for another script from the dwindling "to read" pile. His fingers traced the embossed title—"Threshold"—before opening to the first page. They had developed a system over the months: he would read first, setting aside anything with obvious issues, then pass the promising ones to Bee for her unfiltered assessment. Her perspective, unburdened by industry politics or career calculations, had proven invaluable in identifying projects with substance beneath their surface.

"What happened with the historical drama? The one about the lighthouse keeper?" Bee asked, her eyes still scanning the script in her hands.

"Scheduling conflict," Charlie replied, his attention already caught by the opening scene of the new screenplay. "They need to shoot this summer, and we agreed..." He glanced up, meeting her eyes with a smile that softened his features in the firelight. "No major projects during our second year."

The commitment had been made after careful consideration of their priorities—not a reaction to external pressure but a deliberate choice to preserve the foundation they had built together. The industry had adjusted to Charlie's selective approach, his market value increasing with his scarcity rather than diminishing as some had predicted. One carefully chosen role each year had proven sufficient to maintain his career while allowing him to prioritize their life together.

Beyond the windows, the snowfall intensified, transforming the forest into a ghostly landscape of white-dusted pines. The security lights—disguised as rustic path markers— cast a subtle glow that extended precisely to their property line before fading into darkness. Charlie had insisted on state-of-the-art systems after the Madison Vale incident, but Bee had equally insisted these measures blend seamlessly into their mountain aesthetic. The result was protection that remained invisible unless you knew exactly what to look for.

"Oh, this one's interesting," Charlie murmured, his body tensing slightly with the engagement that signaled a promising find. He'd read twenty pages without interruption, a clear indicator of quality given his increasingly discriminating standards.

Bee's hand moved to his shoulder, fingers sliding beneath the collar of his henley to connect with skin. The touch asked a question that didn't need voicing: Worth sharing?

Charlie nodded, continuing to read but leaning slightly into her touch. "It's unusual—genre-bending. Starts as a psychological thriller but evolves into something more... existential." His voice carried the quiet excitement that emerged only when material resonated beyond technical appreciation. "The protagonist's arc is complex without being contrived."

"Save it for me," Bee replied, setting aside the script she'd been reviewing to reach for her tea again. The liquid had cooled, but she sipped it anyway, enjoying the subtle blend of chamomile and lavender from their garden. Her eyes drifted to the wall of windows, tracking the snow's graceful descent through darkness. The simple pleasure of watching weather from a secure sanctuary still hadn't diminished, even after months in their mountain home.

Charlie's arm slipped more fully around her legs, pulling them slightly higher onto his lap as he continued reading. The adjustment brought her closer, the distance between their bodies diminishing without conscious intent. This gravitational pull between them—the unconscious seeking of proximity—had been present from their early days together, but had deepened into something more fundamental after marriage, a physical harmony that required no thought or effort to maintain.

Outside, the wind picked up, its low moan audible

through the insulated windows. The sound made their shelter feel even more precious—a warm haven against the wilderness beyond. The security panel beside the front door glowed with reassuring green indicators, its modern technology incongruous against the rustic wood wall but non-negotiable in their balanced approach to privacy and protection.

Bee watched Charlie's face as he read, noting the subtle shifts in his expression that told her more about the script's quality than any verbal assessment could. The slight furrow between his brows indicated concentration rather than skepticism. The occasional upward tick at the corner of his mouth suggested lines that resonated. His glasses had slipped again, but he was too absorbed to notice or adjust them.

The domesticity of the moment—its ordinary perfection—struck her suddenly. This quiet evening reviewing scripts was the antithesis of red carpets and flashing cameras, yet contained a richness that no premiere could match. The privacy they had fought for, the sanctuary they had built together, allowed for these unguarded moments of simple connection—Charlie's hand warm against her ankle, her body relaxed against his, the steady rhythm of their breathing unconsciously synchronized in the firelit room.

"Mark this one," Charlie said finally, reluctantly closing the script after reaching its midpoint. "I want to finish it, but I think you should start from the beginning. There's something here."

He placed the screenplay on the small "promising" stack—notably shorter than its rejected counterpart—and stretched his arms above his head, his spine arching slightly with the release of tension. As his arms came down, they settled naturally around Bee, drawing her closer against him, her head finding the familiar hollow of his shoulder as if guided by memory rather than conscious direction.

The fire crackled, sending a fresh wave of warmth across

the room as snowflakes continued their silent descent beyond the windows. Tomorrow would bring fresh considerations, more scripts to evaluate, perhaps decisions to make. But for now, in the quiet sanctuary they had created together, Charlie and Bee simply existed in perfect, ordinary communion—connected, protected, and completely themselves.

They fell into a comfortable silence as Charlie reached for another script from the "promising" pile, this one bound in pale blue with silver lettering across its cover. Bee shifted against him, her body making slight adjustments to maintain their connection as she reached toward the coffee table for her own selection. The movement caused the cashmere throw to slip slightly from her legs, and Charlie automatically pulled it back into place with an absent-minded tenderness that required no thought. The fire had settled into steady amber coals, casting a warmer, more subdued light across the room as the evening deepened around them.

Bee angled her body slightly, creating a small space between them while maintaining the contact of her legs across his lap. Charlie noticed the adjustment but thought nothing of it, his attention already captured by the opening pages of the new screenplay. The quiet between them felt like another form of conversation—a shared contentment that required no verbal affirmation.

"This character description is remarkably specific," Charlie murmured, more to himself than to Bee as he turned a page. "Usually they're so generic you could cast anyone, but this writer has a clear vision."

Bee made a soft sound of acknowledgment, but her attention remained fixed on the script in her own hands. Her fingers traced a particular passage, lingering there as if weighing something in her mind. Charlie continued reading, unaware of the deliberate pause in her movements, the slight shift in her breathing pattern that might have alerted him to the significance of the moment.

"Charlie," she said finally, her voice carrying an unfamiliar note that caused him to look up from his pages. "Listen to this passage."

He adjusted his reading glasses, giving her his full attention as she began to read aloud. Her voice took on a quality he hadn't heard before—carefully measured, as if each word carried additional weight beyond its surface meaning.

"'Sarah places her hand on her abdomen, the gesture protective though nothing shows yet,'" Bee read, her eyes remaining on the page rather than meeting his. "'The knowledge of new life grows within her even as she struggles to find the words to share it. How do you tell someone their world is about to change completely? That everything they thought they knew about their future has suddenly expanded to include possibilities never before considered?'"

Charlie's brow furrowed slightly, his mind processing the words purely as narrative while missing their application. He couldn't place the script she was reading from—the pile they'd been working through contained mostly action thrillers and psychological dramas, nothing with this domestic intimacy.

"Which one is that?" he asked, leaning slightly to glimpse the cover. "I don't remember seeing anything with that kind of scene."

Bee continued as if she hadn't heard his question, her voice growing softer but more deliberate with each word. "'The secret fills her completely, altering her perception from the inside out. The world looks different when you're carrying its future within you.'"

A vague dissonance began to form in Charlie's mind—something about the passage felt unusually specific, almost targeted in its relevance. He reached for the script in her hands, confusion deepening as he caught a glimpse of its cover.

"Wait, that's 'Threshold'—I was just reading that. There's no pregnancy scene in the first fifty pages." His voice carried genuine perplexity as he tried to reconcile the discrepancy. "Are we looking at different drafts?"

Bee finally lowered the script, revealing that the pages were open to an entirely different section than the one she had been reciting. Her eyes met his directly, holding a depth of emotion that stopped his questions mid-formation. The firelight caught the slight dampness gathering at the corners of her eyes, transforming them into something luminous and profound.

"There isn't any pregnancy scene in this script, Charlie," she said quietly.

The words hung between them, simple yet immense in their implication. Charlie stared at her, his mind struggling to bridge the gap between what he thought he'd heard and what she was actually telling him. The script slipped from his fingers, falling forgotten to the floor with a soft thud that neither of them acknowledged.

"You're..." he began, the word trailing into silence as comprehension dawned across his features in waves. His eyes widened, lips parting slightly as he drew a sharp breath that seemed to catch in his throat. "Are you saying—"

Bee nodded, a single, deliberate movement that transformed speculation into certainty. Her hand moved to rest against her abdomen—the same protective gesture she had described moments before, though beneath the soft fabric of her sweater, nothing yet showed of the change occurring within.

"I found out three days ago," she whispered, her voice steady despite the emotion evident in her eyes. "I wanted to find the right moment to tell you."

Charlie's hand moved of its own accord, reaching toward her with fingers that trembled visibly in the firelight. He hesitated just before contact, his palm hovering inches from her stomach as if suddenly uncertain of his right to touch this new reality. Bee's hand covered his, guiding it gently to rest against her. Through the soft material of her sweater, he felt nothing different—no physical evidence of the miracle she had just revealed—yet everything had changed in an instant.

"We're having a baby," he said, the words emerging with a wondering inflection that transformed the statement into something between question and prayer.

Bee's smile broke through the suspended moment, relief and joy intermingling as she watched comprehension solidify in his expression. "We're having a baby," she confirmed, her free hand rising to cup his cheek, thumb brushing against the rough stubble along his jaw.

Charlie's face underwent a remarkable transformation—surprise giving way to wonder, wonder yielding to a joy so profound it seemed to illuminate him from within. His eyes, wide with the impact of her revelation, now filled with sudden moisture that caught the firelight as he blinked rapidly.

"A baby," he repeated, the simple word containing universes of meaning in his voice. The script that had occupied his attention moments before lay forgotten on the floor, its fictional world rendered instantly insignificant compared to the reality unfolding between them.

Time seemed suspended in their mountain sanctuary—the snowfall continuing its silent descent beyond the windows, the fire crackling softly in its stone embrace, the world outside existing in a different dimension entirely from the profound intimacy of their shared revelation. Charlie's hand remained against Bee's abdomen, a connection to something still too small to detect yet already reshaping their universe from its microscopic beginning.

"How are you feeling?" he asked finally, his voice dropping to a reverent hush as his eyes searched her face with new awareness, as if seeing her for the first time through the lens of this knowledge.

"Different," Bee answered, her honesty as natural as breathing between them. "Not physically, not yet. But I feel... expanded somehow. Like I'm suddenly aware of being more than just myself." Her fingers intertwined with his where they rested against her stomach. "Scared. Excited. Everything at once."

Charlie nodded, understanding flowing between them without need for elaborate explanation. His eyes held hers with an intensity that communicated what words couldn't adequately express—gratitude, awe, love deepened by this new dimension of their connection. The scripts surrounding them, the career considerations that had occupied their evening, all receded into temporary irrelevance as they remained locked in this suspended moment of shared wonder.

Outside, the snow continued to fall in silent benediction upon their mountain sanctuary, nature's quiet witness to the whispered revelation that had just transformed their carefully constructed world from within. The fire crackled once, sending sparks upward in a brief, celebratory dance of light, as if the universe itself acknowledged the significance of what had just passed between them.

The suspended moment shattered as Charlie surged forward, all hesitation evaporating in a rush of pure, unfiltered emotion. His arms encircled Bee with sudden urgency, lifting her from the couch in a single fluid motion that sent the cashmere throw tumbling to the floor. Her surprised laughter filled the room as he stood, cradling her against his chest with a strength born of overwhelming joy. The scripts that had occupied their evening scattered beneath his feet, their pages fluttering forgotten as he turned in a small, celebratory circle, Bee's body pressed tightly against his.

"We're having a baby," he repeated, the words emerging with newfound conviction, wonderment transformed into exultation. His voice caught on the final syllable, emotion temporarily closing his throat as he lowered his forehead to rest against hers.

Bee's arms wound around his neck, her fingers threading through the hair at his nape in the familiar gesture that had become their private shorthand for deepest intimacy. "We are," she confirmed, her own voice unsteady with emotion.

Charlie's lips found hers in a kiss that contained multitudes—gratitude, celebration, tenderness, and something new that hadn't existed minutes before. Her tears met his, salt mingling between them as the kiss deepened, neither certain whose emotion overflowed first. When they finally separated, both breathing unevenly, Charlie carefully lowered Bee back to the couch, though he remained kneeling before her, unwilling to create any distance between them in this watershed moment.

His hands framed her face with exquisite tenderness, thumbs brushing away the moisture from her cheeks even as his own eyes remained bright with unshed tears. The firelight caught in the dampness, transforming ordinary emotion into something almost sacred in its illumination.

"How long have you known?" he asked, his voice hushed as if they were in a sanctuary rather than their living room. His gaze studied her face with new awareness, searching for changes he might have missed, signs that had been present but unrecognized.

Bee leaned into his touch, her own hands rising to cover his where they cradled her face. "I suspected last week—little things that didn't add up. I took a test three days ago, then another the next morning to be sure." Her smile contained both vulnerability and strength, the particular blend that had first drawn him to her. "I wanted to tell you immediately, but it felt too important for a hurried conversation between your conference call and my supplier meeting."

Charlie nodded, understanding perfectly her desire to create space around such momentous news. "Three days of carrying this alone," he murmured, a hint of gentle reproach mingling with admiration in his tone. "That must have been..."

"Excruciating," she finished for him, laughter bubbling beneath the admission. "I almost told you a dozen times. This morning when you made breakfast, last night when we were falling asleep..." Her fingers traced the contours of his face, as if relearning features made new by this shared knowledge. "But I wanted a moment like this—just us, unrushed, where we could both fully absorb it."

Charlie settled beside her on the couch, his arm circling her shoulders as his other hand returned to rest against her stomach with reverent wonder. The physical reality remained unchanged beneath his touch—no visible evidence yet of the life beginning within—but his perception had altered completely, transforming the familiar landscape of her body into something miraculous.

"Have you seen a doctor yet?" he asked, practical concerns beginning to surface through the haze of emotional impact. "Do we know how far along? When—"

Bee placed her finger against his lips, halting the sudden rush of questions with gentle amusement. "I have an appointment next week. Based on dates, I think about seven weeks." Her expression softened as she watched the calculations forming behind his eyes. "Remember that weekend storm when we lost power? When we spent the entire day in bed because the generator only heated the bedroom?"

Charlie's eyes widened slightly as memory aligned with

mathematics. "That was—we—" His stammering gave way to a laugh of pure delight. "Of course it happened then. The universe has a certain poetry, doesn't it?"

"It does," Bee agreed, settling more comfortably against him, her head finding its natural place against his shoulder. "I've been thinking about the nursery. The room adjacent to ours gets perfect morning light."

"The one with the mountain view," Charlie nodded, his mind already racing ahead to transformations yet to come. His fingers traced idle patterns against her abdomen as he spoke, unconsciously protective of what couldn't yet be detected. "We'd need to bring the crib away from the windows, though. For temperature regulation."

Bee smiled against his shoulder, recognizing the beginning of what would undoubtedly become extensive research into optimal nursery arrangements. Charlie approached parenthood as he did everything that truly mattered to him—with thorough dedication and careful attention to detail.

"Do you think the baby will have your eyes?" she asked, her voice softening with the speculation that would occupy many conversations in the months ahead. "That particular green that changes with the light?"

"I'm hoping for your smile," Charlie countered, his fingers gently tilting her chin upward to study the feature in question. "The way one corner lifts slightly higher than the other when you're truly happy."

Their speculation continued, voices growing softer as the fire settled into embers and snow accumulated on the windowsills outside. Names were suggested tentatively, some dismissed with laughter, others set aside for further consideration. They discussed practical adjustments—whether Charlie's schedule should be modified further, how Bee might adapt her business to accommodate the baby's arrival, whether they should expand their security measures given this new vulnerability.

Beneath these practical considerations flowed a current of emotion too profound for simple articulation. The family they had built together—just the two of them against public scrutiny and invasion—was expanding from within, creating new dimensions of both joy and vulnerability. The sanctuary they had fought to establish would now shelter not just their love but its living embodiment.

As their conversation gradually quieted, replaced by comfortable silence filled only with the occasional pop from the dying fire, Charlie's hand remained protectively splayed across Bee's still-flat stomach. Her fingers intertwined with his, both physically connected to the miracle they couldn't yet see but already loved beyond measure.

"I never imagined this level of happiness was possible," Charlie murmured, his lips close to her ear, breath warm against her skin. "Every time I think we've reached the capacity of what a heart can hold, you prove me wrong."

Bee turned her face toward his, their noses almost touching in the intimate proximity that had become their natural state. "It's terrifying," she admitted, the honesty between them as essential as breathing. "To want something this much. To have this much to lose."

Charlie nodded, understanding the shadow that briefly crossed her expression. "But that's always been true for us, hasn't it? The more precious something is, the more frightening it is to risk." His free hand rose to brush a strand of hair from her forehead, tucking it gently behind her ear. "We've faced worse threats than dirty diapers and sleepless nights."

The quiet joke achieved its purpose, drawing a smile from Bee that chased away the momentary apprehension. She settled more completely against him, her body relaxing into the support of his as fatigue—perhaps the first physical sign of the changes occurring within her—began to assert itself.

"We should go to bed," Charlie suggested, noting the heaviness of her eyelids, the slight slackening of her muscles against him. "We have approximately seven months to get all the sleep we can before it becomes a scarce resource."

Bee made a soft sound of agreement but didn't move immediately, seemingly content to remain exactly where they were, suspended in this perfect moment between realization and whatever came next. Charlie understood without explanation, his arms tightening slightly around her in wordless acknowledgment of her desire to linger in this sacred space they had created together.

Against her ear, his lips formed words meant only for her —a whispered promise that made her smile and burrow deeper into his embrace. Their hands remained joined over the place where their child grew, invisible yet undeniably present, as the fire's final embers cast a gentle glow across the room. Outside, snow continued its silent accumulation, wrapping their mountain sanctuary in a protective blanket of white— nature's quiet affirmation of the shelter they had built, not just for themselves now, but for the future taking shape within their embrace.

Also by Lisa-marie Wilson

Haunted Memories of a Broken Girl

Haunted by visions of a violent crime, Kelly's melodic voice offers solace amidst the chaos of her past. Lawyer Michael Lawson is captivated by her singing, his own memories stirred by her haunting presence. When he rescues her from danger, a chilling realisation sets in - Kelly bears an uncanny resemblance to a long-lost childhood friend's deceased wife.

As their connection deepens, Kelly's fragmented past unravels. Each revelation brings them closer to a shocking reality: Kelly is Helayna Cook, the missing daughter of arms tycoon Richard Cook.

Navigating the treacherous waters of truth and deception, their unexpected romance blossoms. But sinister forces lurk in the shadows, determined to keep buried what should never see the light of day. Threats loom and loyalties are tested as Kelly and Michael find themselves ensnared in a dangerous game of obsession and vengeance.

To survive, they must confront the ghosts of their pasts and unearth the secrets shrouding Kelly's mother's untimely demise - before a malevolent force silences them forever.

You Will See Me

When the lifeless body of Louise Mansfield is found on the bustling Chicago River Walk, seasoned detective Samuel Barron is thrust into a macabre investigation that unravels a web of dark secrets and chilling connections. Louise, daughter of the influential Senator James Mansfield, had been striving to escape her turbulent past as an exotic dancer and reconcile with her powerful father before she became the target of a sadistic killer's wrath.

As Samuel delves deeper into the case, he uncovers a sinister pattern linking Louise to five other tormented women, all tied to the charismatic senator. The discovery hints at a twisted serial killer fixated on beautiful victims associated with the prominent politician.

The tension escalates when the primary suspect meets a gruesome demise in a manner mirroring the previous murders, pushing Samuel to confront a ruthless and calculating murderer with a disturbing agenda.

The investigation takes an alarming turn when someone they least expected, is driven by a volatile obsession to protect the Senator's reputation, escalating their vendetta by targeting the Mansfield family. In a heart-pounding race against time, Samuel finds himself in a deadly showdown with the killer, unearthing the depths of their malevolent rage. Their harrowing clash culminates in an intense confrontation of wits and wills, revealing a tapestry of hidden truths, envy, and intricate familial bonds.

Haunted by the specter of this chilling case and facing a new wave of brutal crimes, Samuel realizes that history has a way of resurfacing when least expected. To thwart the cycle of violence and deceit, he must confront his own demons and navigate through treacherous waters to prevent further tragedy. In this riveting tale of suspense and redemption, Samuel grapples with the enduring legacy of past sins in his relentless quest for justice amid shadows that refuse to fade.

Betrayal of Blood

In a whirlwind of betrayal, Sarsha Mitchell's once-promising future implodes when she catches her fiancé, James, entangled with her very own sister. Reeling from the heartbreak, Sarsha takes flight, leaving the shards of her shattered dreams behind. With her picture-perfect life in ruins, she seeks solace on an impromptu getaway to their abandoned honeymoon destination with her loyal confidante, Jess.

From the sun-kissed shores of Perth to the dazzling allure of the Gold Coast, Sarsha attempts to outrun her anguish amidst carefree escapades and electrifying nights out. Just as the shadows of her past threaten to engulf her present, a chance encounter at a club propels Sarsha into an unexpected charade with a mysterious stranger named Riley.

As sparks ignite between Sarsha and Riley during their fabricated romance, healing begins to seep into her wounded soul. However, upon their return to Melbourne, old wounds are ripped open anew as James refuses to relinquish his hold on her heart while envious desires stir chaos within her own family.

Supported by Riley's unwavering presence and unwavering gallantry, Sarsha finds the courage to confront the toxicity suffusing her familial bonds. Yet just as hope blossoms for a brighter tomorrow, a cruel act of revenge orchestrated by James and Megan threatens to shatter everything they hold dear.

In a race against time and treachery, Sarsha stands vigil by Riley's bedside, clinging to hope amidst the turmoil. Together, they uncover the depths of deceit woven by those she once trusted most. With Riley's love paving the way towards redemption and renewal, Sarsha severs the ties that bind her to darkness and steps boldly into a future brimming with promise

From Broken Roads to Healing Hearts

When Natalie's car breaks down on a secluded Tasmanian road, little does she know it will lead her to a ruggedly handsome stranger named Kai and his highland cow farm. Far from the city bustle, Natalie and Kai find themselves tangled in a web of past heartbreaks and hidden scars.

Amidst the picturesque countryside, they form an unexpected bond, discovering solace and passion in each other's arms under the starlit sky. But as secrets unravel and old flames flicker back to life, they must confront their demons together or risk losing everything they've found.

A Dark Descent into Chaos

Caught in the sinister grip of Sydney's underworld, at just 23, she becomes Diego's pawn, a mere facade of a girlfriend to the heartless crime lord. Imprisoned in opulence at Diego's Rose Bay mansion with no way out, Mila endures a life of torment and manipulation. Joe Sullivan is no stranger to shadows and secrets. With a steely gaze that betrays his hidden motives, he infiltrates Diego's inner circle on a covert mission for the authorities. Witnessing Diego's brutal nature firsthand, Joe risks everything to shield Mila from the savagery that lurks within their glamorous facade.

Bound by a dangerous game of deception and desire, Mila and Joe must join forces to uncover the truth amidst a battlefield of power-hungry adversaries. As their partnership deepens, forbidden attraction ignites, threatening to consume them both. With danger closing in and lives hanging in the balance, Joe is determined to protect Mila at any cost, even if it means forsaking everything he holds dear.

In a whirlwind of perilous escapades, high-stakes confrontations, Mila and Joe must navigate a treacherous path towards freedom and justice. But in a world where loyalties shift like shadows and love teeters on the edge of ruin, will they emerge unscathed from the dark empire they're entwined in?

Friend or Foe weaves a tale of passion, loyalty, and sacrifice against the backdrop of Sydney's underworld glamour and danger. In a battle where survival could mean surrendering to love's embrace, will Mila and Joe triumph over the sinister forces that seek to tear them apart?

When We Close Our Eyes

After tragedy strands Casey and Kirk in separate worlds of longing, an unlikely encounter entwines them in a slow dance toward solace. Their love, a tender construction of two battered hearts, finds a tenuous rhythm until a specter from Kirk's past tears through the fragile façade. Obsessed and ruthless, Layla—his ex-wife—emerges from shadow with a plan to reclaim what she believes is hers. As threats mount, Casey and Kirk must fight not only for their love but for their lives, finding strength in their scars and shelter in each other.

Lucky in Love and Bullets

Kitty and Peter are madly in love. Kitty, a successful hair stylist, and Peter, a partner in a prestigious law firm, celebrate a lavish wedding in Hawaii. Their perfect day turns tragic when a gunman appears. Kitty is shot in the head. She regains consciousness in the hospital with no memory of Peter, though she recalls everything else. Kitty struggles to reconnect with Peter, who moves into a separate bedroom. Suspecting he is hiding something, she returns to work and meets Fynn, a handsome new client.

Kitty and Fynn find themselves in dangerous territory with criminals as they try to uncover the truth about why she was shot on her wedding day, with each discovery they see how involved Peter was with the wrong kind of people

Twisted Obsession In the shadows of a seemingly perfect life, Anya Willows discovers that the past she thought she'd escaped is about to collide with her present in the most terrifying way imaginable. After years of uncertainty, Anya finally finds stability with a loving boyfriend, a loyal best friend, and a newfound relationship with the father she never knew. But when tragedy strikes and her world begins to crumble, Anya finds herself at the centre of a twisted web of obsession, deceit, and murder. As the body count rises and the lines between friend and foe blur, Anya must confront a darkness that has been stalking her since childhood. With each shocking revelation, she's forced to question everything and everyone she thought she knew. Who can she trust when the very foundations of her life prove to be built on lies? In this heart-pounding psychological thriller, love becomes a weapon, trust becomes a liability, and the truth becomes the most dangerous thing of all.

www.ingramcontent.com/pod-product-compliance
Lightning Source LLC
Chambersburg PA
CBHW031735180726
48283CB00005B/1518